Praise for
A Name of Her Own

"*A Name of Her Own* is without question Jane Kirkpatrick's finest work to date, and that is saying a lot. A definite winner!"
—T. DAVIS BUNN, author of *Drummer in the Dark*

"Jane Kirkpatrick writes the kind of book you can get lost inside. She is a master of the language with her surprising analogies and poetic phrases. The reader will not soon forget this fascinating, sometimes haunting tale."
—LINDA HALL, author of *Katheryn's Secret* and *Sadie's Song*

"Here is an authentic retelling of one of the great western adventures, unique as the voice of the Iowa Indian woman who lived it. Jane Kirkpatrick has turned the dry bones of historical fact into a vivid human narrative."
—JOHN C. JACKSON, historian and author of *Children of the Fur Trade*

"Through Jane Kirkpatrick's stories, I learn more about myself, my life, and my God. *A Name of Her Own* reminded me about the importance of decisions, big and small, the resilience of the human spirit, and the power of love. Jane's fiction is, as always, the best of the best."
—LISA TAWN BERGREN, author of *Christmas Every Morning*

"Jane Kirkpatrick is one of the finest historical novelists in contemporary America. Her story of Madame Marie Dorion, who accompanied her husband in William Price Hunt's Astor Expedition (1810–1812), is the true and compelling tale of a formidable Iowa Indian woman's journey through tragedy, heartache, and ultimately triumph…. Jane Kirkpatrick provides an insight to the hardships, inhospitable geography, and ordeals of that historic time, at the same time illustrating the dignity and indomitable human spirit of this historic figure."
—MARIANNE LONG and VICTOR ROUBIDOUX, Iowa Tribe historians

"Jane Kirkpatrick's *A Name of Her Own* is a prime example of the old-west traders-and-trailblazers fiction at its historical best. It's a book to savor, to read slowly, not so much concerned with how it ends, but experiencing every mile of the rugged journey."

　　—JANET CHESTER BLY, author of *Hope Lives Here*

"Through the depth of her research and her ongoing dialog with the people of the Iowa Nation, Kirkpatrick wins my trust as an interpreter of historical characters and events."

　　—DENISE WILLIAMSON, author of *The Dark Sun Rises*
　　and *When Stars Begin to Fall*

"In *A Name of Her Own* Jane Kirkpatrick brings a voice from the past to the hearts of the present. Marie Dorion's timeless struggle for recognition, approval, safety, and love, and her tenacious fight to raise her sons to be accepted and to matter in the world, are themes that beat in every woman's breast…. Jane makes this woman's life so real we ache and marvel at once…. It is a joy to open oneself to the past and find it still so relevant."

　　—KRISTEN HEITZMANN, author of the Rocky Mountain Legacy series

"From the first page of *A Name of Her Own*, I knew I was in the hands of a master storyteller. Jane Kirkpatrick took me on an adventure and let me walk into the pages of history with her characters in a way that many writers attempt but few accomplish."

　　—COLLEEN COBLE, author of *Wyoming*

"With a clear voice, Jane Kirkpatrick captures an intriguing sense of place and destiny in *A Name of Her Own*. She elevates the art of historical storytelling by weaving her threads of fact with her rich, well-informed imagination. Once you meet the enduring Marie Dorion, she will never leave your memory."

　　—ROBIN JONES GUNN, best-selling author of more than fifty books,
　　including The Glenbrooke series

A Name

of Her Own

OTHER BOOKS BY JANE KIRKPATRICK

NOVELS

Kinship and Courage Historical Series
All Together in One Place
No Eye Can See
What Once We Loved

Dreamcatcher Collection
A Sweetness to the Soul
Love to Water My Soul
A Gathering of Finches
Mystic Sweet Communion

NONFICTION

Homestead
A Simple Gift of Comfort (formerly *A Burden Shared*)

THE TENDER TIES HISTORICAL SERIES

A Name of Her Own

JANE KIRKPATRICK

AWARD-WINNING AUTHOR *of* ALL TOGETHER IN ONE PLACE

WATERBROOK
PRESS

A Name of Her Own
Published by WaterBrook Press
2375 Telstar Drive, Suite 160
Colorado Springs, Colorado 80920
A division of Random House, Inc.

Scripture quotations are taken from the *King James Version* of the Bible.

This book is a work of historical fiction based on real people and real events.
Details that cannot be historically verified are products of the author's imagination.

The floral design on the cover is reminiscent of the Iowa Nation beadwork and is
used by permission of the Museum at Warm Springs, an entity of the Confeder-
ated Tribes of Warm Springs, Warm Springs, Oregon. The design is from a beaded
bag in the permanent exhibit gallery.

ISBN 1-57856-499-9

WaterBrook and its deer design logo are registered trademarks
of WaterBrook Press, a division of Random House, Inc.

Library of Congress Cataloging-in-Publication Data
    Kirkpatrick, Jane, 1946–
        A name of her own / Jane Kirkpatrick.
            p. cm. — (Tender ties historical series ; 1)
        ISBN 1-57856-499-9
        1. Dorion, Marie, 1786–1850—Fiction. 2. Overland journeys to the
    Pacific—Fiction. 3. Northwest, Pacific—Fiction. 4. Women pioneers—
    Fiction. I. Title. II. Series.
        PS3561.I712 N36 2002
        813'.54—dc21
                                                                    2002008686

Printed in the United States of America
2002

10 9 8 7 6 5 4 3

This book is dedicated to

the People of the Iowa Indian Nation
and
Blair Fredstrom.

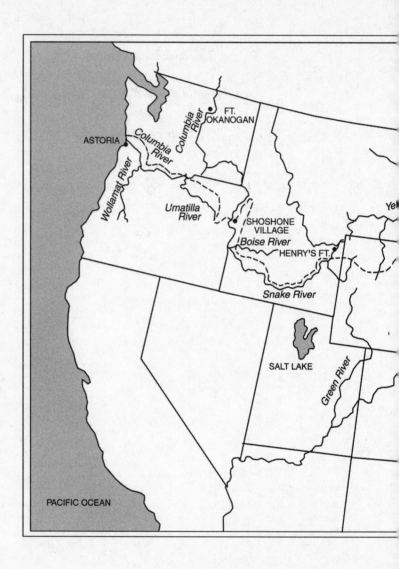

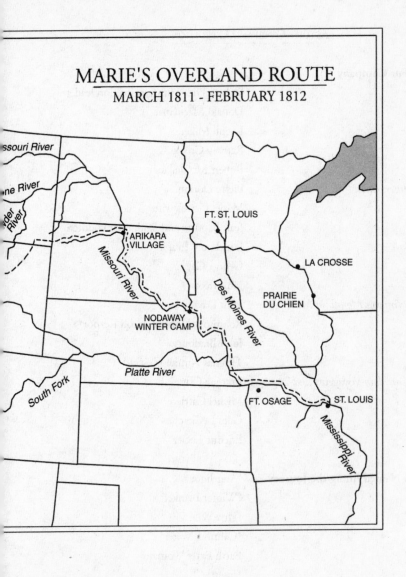

MARIE'S OVERLAND ROUTE

MARCH 1811 - FEBRUARY 1812

Cast of Characters

Yankton Sioux Village   Holy Rainbow

ASTOR'S OVERLAND EXPEDITION

Pacific Fur Company

Partners: Wilson Price Hunt, expedition leader
                                     Donald Mackenzie
                                     Joseph Miller
                                     Ramsey Crooks
                                     Robert McClellan

Hunter/Interpreters: Pierre Dorion
                                     Marie, Pierre's wife
                                     Jean Baptiste and Paul, their children

Camp Boys: Jean Louis Toupin
                                     George Gay

Clerks: John Reed

Hunters/Trappers/Mountain Men: John Day
                                     Robinson, Hoback, Jacob Reznor

Scientists: John Bradbury
                                     Thomas Nuttall *(Le Fou)*

French-Canadian Voyageurs *and* Engages: Antoine Clappine
                                     Michel Carriere
                                     Giles LeClerc
                                     Etienne Lucier

Women Named Along the Journey   *Angelique
                                     *Winter Blanket
                                     *First Wife
                                     *Calming Water
                                     Earth Eater Woman
                                     *Josette
                                     Sally

                                     *denotes fictional character

MISSOURI FUR COMPANY

Partners: Manuel Lisa

Willliam Clark

Reuben Lewis

Interpreters: Toussaint Charbonneau

Sacagawea ("Janey"), Charbonneau's wife

Eduard Rose

Scientist: Henry M. Brackenridge

ASTOR'S OCEAN EXPEDITION

Partners Arriving on The Tonquin: Duncan McDougall

David Stuart

Robert Stuart

Thomas McKay

Clerks: William Wallace

Alexander Ross

John Halsey

Ross Cox

Alfred Seton

Gabriel Franchere

Hunters: Ignace Shonowane

Sarah, Ignace's wife

two sons

Duncan McDougall's Chinook Wife: Ilchee

Sandwich Islanders: Paul Jeremie

Poi, Paul's wife

NORTH WEST COMPANY

Fur Traders and Factors: David Thompson

John George McTavish

We name ourselves by the choices we make....
To name is to love. To be Named is to be loved.
—MADELEINE L'ENGLE

There is love…within Doors and while that is the Case
many a bitter blast may be borne from without.
—GEORGE BARNSTON, FUR TRADER

The beloved of the LORD shall dwell in safety by him;
and the LORD shall cover him all the day long,
and he shall dwell between his shoulders.
—DEUTERONOMY 33:12

Prologue

1803, somewhere along the Des Moines River

The mother ran like a wounded doe, breathing hard, mouth open. She stopped once, gasping. A green cast from the north sky sent light like a flickering snake across the snow. She had to keep going. To stop long meant death for her daughters. She had to keep going, though her heart pounded and a tight slice of pain pierced her chest. Fever-weakened, she moved on, her hair hanging from the knot at the back of her neck. Behind her, in the snow-covered hut, her daughters lay wrapped in a robe, alone, their lives slipping away. She had to get help. The friars would help. She'd told the girls that the black robes would help.

The mother gulped in the cold air, pushed past the fever, her tears dried on her cheeks. She ran through willows, her face scratched by their supple branches. *Spring. It would soon be spring.* If only her daughters listened to her, obeyed her, and stayed in the safety of the robe. The death pox oozed around them, sucking life from those she'd loved. But her daughters lived, might stay living if she got help. She had to keep going. A mother kept going.

She ran on, her legs weak as wet cattails. Then like water from a spilled copper pot, she gave out. The friar's words from a psalm came to her as she fell, *"I am poured out like water."*

The mother heard a cry, her own voice? An echo? Her daughters? She turned to look, stumbled. Her fevered face hit the hard snow, cracking the bone of her cheek. *My heart is like wax; it is melted…"*

Her eyes lay open and the image of her younger daughter's face came to her, a last longing before the mother felt lifted to light.

Part 1

1

Je Viens Après Lui or I Come After Him

1811, eight years later in St. Louis, on the Missouri River

The young mother stirred the soup with the iron ladle, sending the scent of cooked meat into the cabin's close quarters. She inhaled, ready. Her husband laughed with his son, playing on the hard-packed floor, and Jean Baptiste laughed back. Good. Her elder son was a solemn soul, not a brother to joy, so this giggle was a gift to both her and his father.

Outside, horses stomped with impatience, and beyond at the wharf, she heard the thump-thump of wooden barrels being loaded in *bateaux*. She blew on the broth, tasted it, then stood to her full height. Her back ached with the weight of her youngest son nestled in a deerskin sack between her shoulder blades. The toddler, just over one year old, reached up to brush against her copper earrings. *"Non, non,"* she whispered. *"Attends un moment."* She patted Paul's small hand, wondered if he sensed her disquiet. Children could feel what their parents felt, wasn't this so?

She took a deep breath. She'd been putting it off, not wanting to be demanding on this last day, and yet the gray-snow sunset would soon arrive. The last meal of the day would be served to the expedition partners, and her husband would be asked to join them. There was much she still didn't know, much he still hadn't said.

She had to make plans, for her sons if not for herself. As soon as her husband ate, she must settle this.

"Papa, *non! Non!*" four-year-old Jean Baptiste shouted as he scampered from his father.

Pierre Dorion grinned, sat like a bear on his haunches. He leaped up toward the boy, hands formed like paws, and grabbed for his son, who squealed as though trapped. The father lunged, his mouth almost a sneer in the midst of dark beard. He captured the child, held him tight. "Baptiste!" Pierre said as the child twisted, squirmed over his father's arm. He tickled the boy. Was Baptiste laughing or crying? she wondered.

"*Non,* no, Papa!"

Her son cried. Pierre's wide fingers dug deeper. "Are you weak?" he said.

"Can't you hear? He gets frightened," she said. Her voice distracted Pierre enough that the child wiggled free and ran behind his mother's skirt. She could hear his puffing, felt his pull on her dress. Soup spilled from the ladle. "Leave him, now, Pierre. Come, eat." Her words had a lilt to them, a mix of her Ioway mother's scolding blended with soft French, the language she knew best.

"You tell me what to do, *femme? Non,*" her husband said, pushing himself to stand. He pulled up his wool socks, adjusted the leggings, tight below this knees. "This is not the way. Not on my last day." Pierre moved like a ferret across the room.

Though she stood nearly as tall as her husband, he loomed over the three of them now, and she stepped back. Paul began to cry as Pierre stretched around her, bumping the toddler cradled on her back as he grabbed for Baptiste's arm. Her elder son shouted, a sharp slice of sound in the air. She turned as Pierre's fingers twisted the leather fringes hanging from Baptiste's hide shirt, the boy's slender arm twisted too. Pierre pulled the child to him. "We are amusing ourselves, *n'est ce-pas?*"

Baptiste's breath came in quick bursts.

"Non," she said to calm the child, then to her husband said, "You go too far. He needs a rest now."

Baptiste wailed then, and Pierre shook the child, held his palm up as though to strike. "No weeping," he said. "You are too much like your mother."

"J'en ai assez!" She stepped between them. "Enough," she said, her quickness surprising and breaking the father's hold on his son.

Baptiste fled then, slipped between his parents, and pushed open the peeled-log door, leaving it wide to dusky sky.

"You make the boy weak with your interruptions," Pierre said. "I will bring him back. Teach him not to run from his father."

"Non," she told him, her small hand on his sleeve. Her eyes dropped. "You eat. Let me bring him back."

"I teach him how to be strong, nothing else. It is a father's right." He pulled away from her hand.

Paul wailed then. She reached behind to bounce him, gently lifting his bottom. He was wet. She should change him.

"It is a father's right, eh?" She nodded, agreed. "Good. You go find him." He reached for her chin, lifted it, pinched it only a little before she pulled free. His heavy black brows over narrowed eyes rose as she stared at him. "What else will you deprive me of on my last day, eh, *femme?*"

"What do you deprive me of?" she said, her jaw lifted and firm. She handed him the ladle. "Eat now."

He paused before taking the iron spoon from her. "You are mule headed, *femme.*"

"I am unbending as an oak," she said, lowering her eyes as she brushed past him. She grabbed a two-point trade blanket as she pushed through the door, her baby bouncing on her back.

A breeze floated from across the Mississippi River, arrived as March air. The young mother squinted in the distance, barely catching her four-year-old son's buckskin-clad back as he raced toward the fur-trading fort's log gate.

"Baptiste," she shouted. He often found hiding places away from his father's excesses, but he'd been told not to go inside the fort. He'd get in trouble there.

The boy sent two men carrying fusils off balance as he scurried on by. One went down on his knee in the mud, the wet turning the tanned hide of his leggings dark. "Dorion's kid'll be our death," she heard the man say as he pushed the rifle butt into the earth to help him stand. He scowled at the woman as she approached, her slender hand shadowing the setting sun from her dark eyes.

"Or his ma's," said the other, though he laughed through his snarled whiskers.

"You want I should catch the little savage up for you?" the first asked her.

She shook her head. She heard the word savage as *sauvagesse*. For her, it meant someone close to wildness, free, connected more to rivers and trees than to the presence of people spitting out words with foul meanings. Her sons were like that, free, or could be, away from this St. Louis town.

Paul bounced on her back as she moved. She didn't need a troubling child now, not when she had so much needing bargaining. Her husband had said nothing about the advance, the money he must leave her if she and her sons would be safe these two, maybe three years he'd be gone. *Nothing!* Yet she knew he'd been promised more money than any of the French Canadians, more than any interpreter could hope for. Three hundred dollars with two hundred given before the expedition departed. She had seen none of it.

She stopped, slid Paul out of the sack at her back, and held him to her chest, wrapping the blanket around them both. Her sons were usually the wings to her heart, making her soul soar with their smiles and soft touches. But today, when she had so much to make happen, they both felt heavy as bone.

In the thawing mud and snow, she could see that Baptiste's small feet had not gone inside the fort, but around it, heading toward the wharf. Perhaps he'd get halted there, attracted by the activities, what with the expedition so close to leaving. She settled Paul at the front of her and stood straighter, adjusting the knot of fine black hair at the back of her neck. Paul reached up to play with the copper coils at her ears. "No," she said, pushing his little hands back inside the blanket. He whimpered. "Not now, sweet one," she said and smiled.

Maybe she did make the boys weak.

She had to remind herself that Pierre was a good father, even if he did frighten the boys with his rough ways at times. It was not because he meant to hurt them. He always settled down in time, did the right thing. If he hadn't been drinking. He didn't know his own strength, that was all. Hadn't he said as much those times he'd left bruises on her?

Pierre Dorion, a mixed-blood man, crossed his arms over his wide chest. That woman could rile him so! He watched now as his *épouse*, his wife, moved like wind through the willows, swaying as she walked-ran after their son. She was a beauty. Strong, long legs that allowed her to jump fallen logs without effort. She rarely let Baptiste race far before she caught him. She just didn't always know her place as a wife. She'd probably sweet-talk the child into coming back when what the boy needed was a firm hand. But she'd be alone soon. She may as well do it her way, since she would when he was gone anyway.

Pierre was hungry. He pulled the latchstring and walked to the trammel where the copper pot hung on the S-shaped iron at the hearth. She'd put the flour biscuits beside it, and he ripped a chunk and dipped it into the stew. The scent made his mouth water. A delicacy. He hadn't seen buffalo meat since his Sioux village days. Clerking at this St. Louis on the Missouri these past two years kept him from hunting for their own fresh meat. She must be trying to tempt him before he headed out. He caught a dribble with his left hand, stuffed it into his mouth, then wiped his palm clean on his leather pants. She was softening him up for something, serving buffalo, making biscuits instead of lye-soaked hominy.

Maybe she thought he'd forgotten to give her the advance money and that he needed sweetening to remember.

He winced. She'd have the advance money, all right. When she found out the attachments to it, she would be furious. But he would be long gone by then. He would not have to see the fire in her dark eyes, nor cover his ears against the sharpness of her tongue, a sound that pierced him, though the worry of it never stopped him in time from acting and doing things that brought on her outrage and his later deep regret. Pierre Dorion knew his country wife well, and he knew what she would think of that Spaniard Manuel Lisa saying Pierre Dorion still owed money.

The debt had been unfairly charged, a manipulation, as only Manuel Lisa knew how to do. His *femme* would realize this, in time, when she calmed down. She'd find a way to keep the advance money. She might need to leave town, but she'd never liked St. Louis anyway. Manuel Lisa had the ear of William Clark and Reuben Lewis, brother to the former governor, Meriwether. Now, there was a man who'd taken St. Louis by storm. He had everything, that Meriwether Lewis—money, influence, fame. But he'd taken his own life the year before. Who could make sense of that?

Yes, she'd have to leave St. Louis. Pierre swallowed. These things could not be helped.

Manuel Lisa was a partner in Lewis and Clark's fur trading company. John Jacob Astor's rival, or so Manuel Lisa thought. Pierre grunted. Lisa's company would only be a rival if they still had Pierre Dorion to interpret for them, which they didn't. Astor's company would trample them all. After they reached the Pacific, Pierre Dorion's name would be remembered by more than just his sons. And his wife would then forgive him.

Lisa would charge her with the debt, no doubt, but it would be like taking a deer's leg from the mouth of a mother dog. Pierre grinned at the picture of it, his strong, firm-jawed *femme,* withstanding the likes of that dark-faced Manuel. In the end, she'd defeat him with tears and toughness. Keep the money and be the stronger for it. She'd forgive Pierre then for not telling her of it earlier. She always forgave him.

Wilson Price Hunt, the Astoria expedition's leader, had promised the cash would be delivered just before they left. He had been paying their expenses ever since Pierre signed on in February. Hunt had committed to Pierre's price—three hundred dollars—because he knew that only with Pierre Dorion serving as interpreter could the mission succeed. He'd receive two-thirds of the advance before they left. Any day now, he'd have it, though he wondered if Hunt might have heard the rumors of the Lisa debt and waited until the last moment to provide the advance, worrying perhaps that Pierre might spend the money in some bar.

Pierre chewed, opened the door again. A trillium pushed its way through the leaf-spotted mud beneath the oak trees, casting long shadows over the fort's log walls. The scent of wet earth met him. It was nearly spring. They should have left earlier to make it to the Columbia and the Pacific before autumn. Pierre had urged Hunt to hurry, as best he could. But not having the clout of a partner or clerk, at least not yet, Pierre had been ignored. Or maybe his mixed blood kept his ideas shadowed. Hunt had a way about him, his own timing. He tended to details that would've been better left to underlings. Astor had put his faith in Donald Mackenzie and Wilson Price Hunt, though the latter, at twenty-six years of age, was young to have a partnership, younger than Pierre by some five years.

Today they would load the last of the *bateaux*. Tomorrow, he'd have his money, give it to his *femme*, and the expedition would head out, hopefully before Lisa even knew they'd left. Pierre washed the bread down with cold water, wiped his beard with the back of his hand. He stood in the open doorway now, leaning against the post, the sun still warm on his face. Voices rose in song from the wharf. The French-Canadians always sang as they worked.

Yes, he would help the fur trade push west, and if Astor's plan succeeded, the Pacific Fur Company would own the Asian trade. Anyone affiliated would be rich beyond measure. This was a good thing he was doing for his *femme,* even if she didn't understand it all yet. He'd help her understand tonight. Their last night together.

He'd miss the woman though she could irritate him at times, the way a sparrow troubled a hawk, flying at its tail as it swooped and soared. But this was no trapping expedition where women and children came along, salting hides, tending their men. No, this journey of all men would establish routes through unknown areas, make a way for future trade. Women would only slow them down.

Pierre wiped his brow of the warmth of the stew and the fire. He felt sleepy, and the buffalo robe spread on the floor beckoned. He'd take a quick nap, eh? He lay down thinking still of Lisa encountering his *femme* after the expedition left. He yawned. Pierre always had a plan. Sometimes he couldn't carry his efforts to resolution, but he always knew someone else who would.

The young mother scanned the wharf, irritated that she hadn't seen this coming, hadn't prevented it. But here there were no sisters or grandmothers to help. A mother here worked alone. "Baptiste!" she shouted, trying not to sound so angry that her son would stay hidden, but not too friendly that he'd think it was a game. This mothering was a constant negotiation, as much as her husband's work interpreting between tribes. She smiled to herself. Mothers could teach those Astorian partners something about bargaining. "Baptiste! Come now!"

She thought she heard a distant shout. Should she walk the dock or head toward the boardwalk of the town? Paul whimpered in her arms. "Sh-h-h now. *Silence absolu,*" she whispered. She peeled her son's fingers from his grip on the copper earrings she wore. He struck at her with his fist, pulling on the gurrah muslin that filled the bodice of her scooped-neck dress. She should put him onto her back again, but he was easier to keep quiet when carried in front. Paul must be hungry. He pulled at the gurrah, his fingers wrapping easily inside the soft striped cloth.

"Later, Paul," she told the child. He was only fifteen months, but she talked to him as though he were an adult so Pierre would not accuse her of making him weak, like a girl.

"We must find your brother," she said, drawing dark hair from Paul's eyes. He clutched at her face again, and she held his fingers. *"Non!"* she told him. *How had she raised such a demanding child?* Her eyes scanned beyond Paul's head, seeking Baptiste.

Baptiste might have raced toward the town rather than the wharf. She stood at the edge of the fort squinting to better see to the end of the muddy street. A horse clopped into view, passed so close in front of her that she stepped back. Her eyes caught those of a woman, seated behind a man, sideways, perched on her pillion, the small pillow attached to a man's saddle for just that purpose. The woman's fingers awkwardly gripped the side of the pillow. She held her knees together, her calico dress long, her feet dangling over the side of the scruffy-looking mount while the man faced forward as though unaware a woman sat behind him.

Je viens après lui—I come after him, she thought. Women always went after their men. In these towns, they were stuck there behind their men as though on pillions, as though they were nothing more than rolled-up saddle packs. Here, a woman couldn't even mount a horse without someone else's help.

The woman's eyes stared out at her, the face solemn, judging, before turning away. *Did she know that woman?* Something seemed familiar about her.

Maybe Pierre hoped she would take the children and return to his Sioux village where things were freer; expect her to live with his mother, Holy Rainbow.

No. Mixed-blood sons belonged with their fathers. They needed their fathers. Even if Pierre gave her the money, how would two hundred dollars protect her sons from robbers and ill-spirited men for three years, protect them from those in power in a place where mixed-blood children without a benefactor lived in risk? Sacagawea had her husband *and* Captain Clark.

Who would she and her children have? No one. Pierre was not thinking. He couldn't be.

Pierre's wife stopped short. Perhaps he planned to set them all off, to disclaim that he even had a wife and sons, the way some European traders did. Perhaps he tired of her and her unbending ways. Maybe that was why he had given her no advance money. Her heart pounded. Could a wife so misjudge a husband? Maybe Pierre believed she was a poor mother and he would find another for his sons when he returned! *If* he returned. Paul cried. She loosened her hold.

She was a poor mother. She frightened her baby and had lost her elder son!

No sight of the child in the streets, she turned back toward the wharf. Was that woman judging her, the one riding behind her husband while she merely walked? Everyone judged mothers from the way their children ranged or clutched at clothing. Usually they were European eyes, fur trappers and traders, clerks and shopkeepers, who judged. Sometimes, more often than she wished, other mothers' eyes watched her, the eyes of small-waisted women. She tried not to notice, but she did, even now as she fast-walked down the wharf, calling out Baptiste's name.

Her moccasins scraped on the wooden dock where canoes and pirogues thumped against the water-splashed pilings. French and English words from the French-Canadian *voyageurs* filled the air.

"Baptiste!"

She shifted Paul to her hip. While she retightened the two-point trade blanket, Paul struck at her breast. *"Non!"* she said aloud, more to herself than to Paul. She must not let the thoughts of the mother on the horse or any others distract her from finding Baptiste, bringing him home so she had time to talk with Pierre.

I am no good at this mothering, no good!

A narrow shadow fell on the bales of supplies loaded onto Hunt's pirogues. She heard a shout; someone called her. A bustle of big-armed men wearing red knit belts around their waists hovered near the dock, no longer loading. Hat tassels folded over their dark, long hair. The camp boy—what was his name? Toupin, yes, Jean Louis Toupin. He called to her. "Madame Dorion," Toupin said. "I believe I've found what you look for."

He motioned her closer, then had her stop, put his finger to his lips as though to quiet her. He dropped down onto his stomach, leaned over the dock toward the water. He reached up under the board slats, then pulled out her son, dangling him by the arm. Still holding the boy, he rolled over and sat Baptiste on the dock. Baptist lowered his head.

"He hangs like a possum underneath," Toupin said in French. "His little fingers and toes grip up through the openings of the boards." He patted where he'd seen them. Toupin stood up. "They look like little ticks at first. Lucky I don't step on them. He must have strong fingers. He'll make a good cordeller someday, pulling the heavy boats with the ropes." The young man grinned as he pressed Baptiste's hand into hers.

The boy didn't smile, but he didn't resist, apparently not minding that gentle Toupin had found his *confidentiel* place.

"*Merci,*" she said. "*Merci, merci.*" She kissed Baptiste's head.

"It's my pleasure, Madame Dorion," Toupin said. He nodded his head once.

"*Merci,*" she said again, then to her son she made herself scowl. "You might have fallen into the river, been squashed like a bug by the boats. You see them?" She pointed to the heavy wooden canoes. "They are loaded. They will take your father away tomorrow, and we waste time here looking for you." Baptiste hung his head. "You must come when I call. I have much to do to keep you safe; more, once your father leaves."

"Best you listen to your mother," Toupin told him. "See if you can clutch as firmly to her hand as you did to the boards." Toupin's smile forced creases into red cheeks revealing just a hint of dark beard. He stood, his hands at his hips. "I leave seven brothers and sisters behind in Mackinonge, Canada," he said. "Your *garçon* will be all right, madame."

She thanked him again and it seemed to her he blushed. She turned. *Madame.* No one had ever called her that before. It was a word reserved for the wife of someone who headed a fur factory, a *bourgeois's* wife. She was far from that. At least right now she was. Someday, if Pierre chose wisely, she might have such a title. But now she could barely claim the name of mother with one son hungry at her breast and the other just found, pulling against her hand. She brushed at her eyes that wept with so little nudging.

"Woman, strong you may be but you have not wagered well this night," Pierre said.

"*Non?*" she said.

Pierre's wide hands pressed against her shoulders. His fingers sunk into the buffalo robe she laid on that just moments before had wrapped them in a warm embrace and kept them from the cold night air. "No," he said. "I have you now where I want you, eh?" She surprised him with the flick of her bare legs twisted against his. A fire burned low in the hearth; wood crackled. "Whoa, now!" he said as she slipped her legs up and pushed back against his chest with the flat of her feet.

In an instant, she had keeled him over and now straddled him, her dark hair loose from its knot at her neck falling over her shoulders. The gurrah underdress twisted at her hips. The boys squealed in laughter, cheering their parents on.

"Just this night, that's all I have left," she said. She breathed hard, tossed the hair from her eyes, and straightened the thin linen so her bare knees showed. The copper earrings tinkled. "Then you will be gone and we are left behind, *oui?*"

"*Femme,*" Pierre cooed, his voice deep. He reached up and gently rubbed the sharp bones beneath her eyes. "So beautiful," he sighed. "I would take you with me, but Astor would not permit it. Hunt would not permit it. Even Donald Mackenzie would object, eh? You would have trouble keeping those boys safe on such a long journey. See how hard it is to hold Baptiste, even here?"

"They could burrow like marmots in the *bateau*," she said. "He wants to go with you." She swallowed. "We all want to go along."

"Where do you get such ideas? From that Sacagawea who took her son on that dangerous journey?"

Sacagawea! That's who the woman was who rode behind the man on the horse. The woman who saw the Western sea and came back to speak of it.

He moistened his lips. "We have talked of this. Accept this, eh? Clark took her because she was a good tool. She knew the language farther along. You do not know the words to help an important expedition. I do. You stay behind this time. We don't trap. We take no furs with us. We go west to find a route to take pelts straight from the Columbia River to Canton, so they don't have to travel back this way. Astor's fort at the Pacific will be talked about everywhere. It will save time and money and change everything, *femme*." He ran his finger over her cheekbone, his eyes moist. She'd remember those eyes always. The color of gray snow—what her people called themselves, Bah-Khi-Je, the gray snow people. "You do as you're told," he said.

"You leave us behind for other reasons, then," she challenged. "I know. I hear." She crossed her arms over her breasts.

"*Femme.*" He smoothed the thin cloth, his hands following the contours of her hips and thighs. "How did we go from being warm and sweet together to...this, eh? It is our last night for maybe three years. But I will return. You know this." His voice was smooth as a lonely loon's. "Come. Let us not frighten our sons."

She leaned down as though to kiss him.

"This is better," he whispered. He relaxed, reached his arms around her shoulders, pulled her to him. His breath felt warm.

She bit his lip instead.

He cried out, twisted his head, pressed his mouth with his fingers. He looked to see if she'd drawn blood, then rolled her over so he laid beside her, his arm across her chest, pinning her there. He was as strong as a *voyageur* from his years of paddling and pulling upriver, though now he clerked in the fur factory, wrote numbers, and carried slender lead to make his way in the world instead.

"Our sons fear only their mother being set off," she said, "left behind by a father who does not care for them, who brings them into this world but does not keep them at his side."

"No, *femme*, no, no. It is not like this. I go for you, for them." He loosened his grip. "Believe me now. As soon as Hunt gives the advance you will have it, and you will be safe here. You're a good mother. You will be enough for them for the years I'm gone. This is something I must do. Something...my father..."

"There is talk of war," she said.

"Just talk."

She decided. "If I win this wrestle, you take us with you."

He laughed. "What kind of mother would risk *les garçons,* eh? Put her children on a knife's edge?"

"You risk by going away," she said. "You risk by setting us off, as though we were nothing to you. I hear this." She felt herself starting to cry. She pulled away from his caress, but he pushed her back onto the robe, pinned her.

"You rush to judgment," he said. He brushed her cheek with his whiskers, hard enough that it hurt. She knew she'd have red cheeks in the morning. "I don't set you off like some rich trader who wants a European wife. I don't do this. You are all the *femme* I want." He kissed her then, his mouth hard on hers.

She felt his thumbs sink into her, and she twisted away, stood. She yanked the buffalo robe, spilling him onto his side and threw it around her, intending to run out into the night. "I win this wrestle," she said. "You take us along."

He caught her ankle, jerked her back to him, and pulled her down. Quick as a lynx he straddled her, his knees pinning her arms to her sides.

"Femme," he said, his fingers pressed hard against her chin, his voice soft, the pain piercing. He leaned over her, blew out the oil lamp. "You

will stay behind as you are told. It is not your decision, *femme*. Some things you can't choose."

Her mind drifted. He had known her since her thirteenth winter, his gray ash eyes finding hers inside a pox-laden lodge. She had had a name then, had softly asked that he use it. He never had. *Femme,* he called her. When he claimed her as his wife three years later, he still had never used her given name, still called her *femme.* He was lazy, using the same name. *Femme—I come after him. Never beside him; always after.*

Just this last night, that was all they had left. Then, only memories and an uncertain future. She struggled. He held her firm. There was no use in fighting him; she didn't want to. She felt like melted wax with him. She was weak, so weak. She had to find a way to make him take them along, even if it was *je viens après lui.*

"Ah, *femme,*" he mumbled into her ear.

"You do not even know my name," she said. Her voice cracked. "I am only *femme* to you, nothing more. Even on our last night."

He leaned his head back. She could see the firelight reflected in his eyes, the profile of his straight nose, the outline of his strong jaw covered with a black, curly beard. "What should I call you?" he said. "What my mother does? 'Her to Be Baptized'? You like that better?"

"No. It says I am unfinished."

"You are my wife, my *femme,* nothing else."

"I am more than that," she said. "*Femme* means 'I come after you.'"

"You do."

She struggled. He held her quiet. She could hear his breathing, smelled smoked hide lingering on his chest.

"You are the mother of my sons, eh? I trust you to take care of them."

"Then use my mother name," she said.

"Your mother name?"

"Marie," she whispered.

He paused as though thinking.

"Have I known this name?"

"It is what I choose to call myself," she said. Tears spilled from her eyes, eased into her ears. "A mother name. But sons need a father with them."

"No more talk now." He pressed the back of her neck, pulling her to him. "Give me reasons not to forget you."

"Say I won the wrestle," she persisted.

He laughed, a deep laugh that shook his chest against her. "You win with words, *femme*. I give you that."

"I win this wrestle then." She smiled. She was Marie, a word that meant mother, and a mother always found a way.

2

Her to Be Baptized

Wilson Price Hunt took the stiff collar from its box. He would change
from his New Jersey clothes, wear the frontiersmen's leathers and leggings when they reached Nodaway, five hundred miles north on the
Missouri, where the majority of the men had wintered. They couldn't
spend so much money at that remote site. And what they wore there
didn't matter. Here, there was still something to be said for a gentleman's dress. It built confidence, something he needed right now.

He tucked the collar onto his shirt, slipped on his wool waistcoat,
pulled the ruffled sleeves down at his wrists. He adjusted the tailored
pants at the waist and stood sideways to the mirror. Acceptable. He had
bags under his eyes that he touched gently. He hadn't been sleeping
well, despite his nightly reading of his slender book of Psalms.

Light seeped into his quarters through the frosted window. With
his fingers he scraped at the glass, then breathed to create an opening to
see if men stirred at the bachelors' quarters. In the dim dawn light stood
the camp boys, Jean Louis Toupin and the English boy, George Gay,
flapping their arms around themselves as they broke the thin crust of ice
over the mud in the yard. Good. They'd help get the fires going, prepare
for a midmorning meal and perhaps tonight they would sleep at St.
Charles, the first stop upriver. He could hear the pigs grunt in their
pens. A rooster crowed. Smoke drifted up from beyond the fort's walls.
That would be Dorion's hut, the man already awake.

The thought of that half-breed made him frown. The man had driven a hard bargain demanding three hundred dollars. But he needed him with his gift of French and signs and fluency in the Sioux language. The expedition needed him. And it pleased him no dash of salt that he'd heard Manuel Lisa was distressed that he'd signed Dorion on. That in itself meant Dorion was good even if a bit unpredictable. He knew Astor worried over the Indian relationships. Captain Clark had told him all mixed-bloods were…volatile, but necessary.

"A *metis* like Dorion, half Sioux and half French-Canadian, knows the Indians," Clark had told him. "His father came well recommended. But the breeds also know how the Eastern tribes were devastated by Western expansion," Clark continued. "One has to be wary about where such…survivors will stand in a struggle. Dorion especially. He and two of his brothers nearly killed their father in a barroom brawl once. If family alliances can't keep you from harm, what will?"

That story haunted Hunt.

Still, Lisa didn't engage those who weren't worthy, and Dorion had worked for Lisa. Maybe the story of the family brawl was merely rumor. If he could find another interpreter…no. There wasn't time.

Hunt pulled the plank chair out and sat at the small table set close to the window to save as much as possible on oil light. He'd make a few notes in his journal, spend a moment thanking Providence for their good fortune and asking blessings for the journey he hoped would truly begin in earnest this very day.

His prayers drifted into worry. The recruitment had been plagued with disaster. Men had been reluctant to sign on, finally doing so only to run up bills at merchants in Montreal. A good number left his employ before arriving at St. Louis. A few more had dwindled before being sent to Nodaway, even with the Scotsman Donald Mackenzie urging them to remain. Could Lisa be behind these defections? No, the Spaniard wasn't *that* cunning, surely. Then conversations with the North West Fur Company to join their efforts had dissipated like so much fog. Worse, the trade talks between England and America faltered, threatening war.

Now there was this last Astor letter. He wasn't sure if that was an omen of evil or good. He sighed, got out the powder for his ink-and-quill pen, tapped it absently as he stared out the small window. He'd have to talk with Donald Mackenzie about it soon. Astor had named the two of them as lead partners—Mackenzie, with experience as part of the North West Company; Hunt as the American with Astor's ear. Together, they'd recruited and weathered the difficult days of putting the expedition together. Together, they'd spoken with William Clark, discussed which interpreters to hire, what maps and trails would best meet their needs.

After their last evening with Clark, on their way back in the carriage, Mackenzie cautioned him about the famous Captain: "Aye. And the man's running a rival company, Wilson. Can't be taking his every word as gospel. He's much to gain at our failure, laddie."

"He seemed fair enough to me," Hunt had said. "Even had the map copied for us." He tapped the scroll on his lap. The parchment rolled to Wilson's right, toward the heavy body of Mackenzie as they rounded a corner.

"You're believin' it's authentic then?"

Hunt bristled. "He's an American, as am I."

"He's a partner with Lisa, who is not," Mackenzie reminded him. "And you've hired away Lisa's interpreter. They may not be holding you in the highest regard, Wilson, with that little coup."

Mackenzie had said no more about it that night, though Hunt had wondered what they'd do if the expedition found itself in a dispute, needing to rely on that map of Clark's over their guide's directive.

Astor had settled part of that matter with this letter.

Perhaps their employer worried over a British citizen being part of the leadership, what with America and England's trade negotiations gone sour. All the French-Canadian partners had supposedly given up their British citizenship. He figured Mackenzie had, though he hadn't claimed so that night in the carriage. Mackenzie was a Scotsman who probably thought his Scot tradition took precedence over English or American ways.

Hunt would show Mackenzie the letter when they broke their fast, and then he'd stress the need for them to move forward. There were dozens of details he wished he could finalize, but he knew Mackenzie wanted to move, and frankly, Dorion had pushed it too. Hunt squared his shoulders, pushed against the table and stood. Only the camp boys kept their opinions to themselves, it seemed. He could be grateful for that.

As soon as the scientists Bradbury and Nuttal arrived they could leave, all of them. The scientists' commitment to join them had been the final triumph for Hunt's overland expedition. To have men of education like those two willing to come along meant others would take the expedition seriously too. Posterity would be gifted with not just the expedition leader's biased view on things. It could be said that even clerks' words were suspect since they were junior partners of sorts, hoping to gain prestige and move up in the ranks. But scientists had nothing to gain by making the journey sound rosier than it might be. Hunt wanted accuracy and authenticity. An honest appraisal. The scientists would give that.

His stomach growled. Toupin and the other *engages* wouldn't serve a meal until midmorning, but perhaps a biscuit could be had. He picked up the letter. Took a deep breath. No. He needed to finish writing. There was time to let Mackenzie know.

Marie lay on the feather-filled buckskin sleeping pad, the buffalo robe pulled up to her chin. She watched Pierre quietly as he pulled his nankeen britches up to his bare waist. A dim morning light eased into their hut, heightened by the fire in the hearth he'd poked into a low flame. His thick dark hair hung long, not yet pulled back into its queue, and he stared at his sons, asleep. He squatted then, reached out as though to touch Baptiste's face, his hand hovering like a butterfly over the boy's forehead. He pulled his palm back. His hands hung loose between his knees a moment, then he wrapped his arms around his chest as though to keep himself from reaching out. The boys slept. They needed to sleep. He must know that, though Marie could tell by the look on Pierre's face that he wished to touch them, hold them. He *did* want them along, she realized. He just couldn't say it.

She watched him stand. He turned to her, pushed at her with the toes of his foot. "Your boys will wake you soon enough, *femme,*" he said. "My mother would never let her husband rise first to build the fire. It marks a lazy woman."

"Your mother was never left behind," Marie told him.

Pierre reached for his cup, dribbled water onto Marie's face. "You will no longer be Her to Be Baptized as my mother calls you."

She sputtered, shook her head. "I am not incomplete just because I do not choose the friar's water," Marie told him.

"I made a joke," he told her. He pulled the robe back.

"That water did nothing to save my mother," Marie said. "Why should I choose it?" She stayed, her arms across her chest.

"That Snake woman, Charbonneau's wife, wouldn't let her husband leave without getting up to tell him *adieu.*"

"Was she known on the expedition as Charbonneau's *femme?*"

"You can ask her after I'm gone," Pierre said. "You always want to gossip with women. Now you can. It gives you something to do. I go to talk with Hunt now. Get the advance…which I give to you." He squatted, pinched at her pointed chin. She twisted away. He stood.

Her breasts felt full. Paul cried now from the mat beside her. The child woke often through the night to nurse. Perhaps her mother-in-law, Holy Rainbow, was right. Perhaps she was lacking.

No! She'd earned her name, and it was not Her to Be Baptized.

"While I'm gone, you will live better than even…Charbonneau's wife," Pierre told her.

"Which one?" she said. He scowled. "An Indian woman left behind by her husband in this St. Louis on the Mississippi will soon disappear," she said. "Be no more than dust in the street, no different than the dung that drops from busied horses. And if war comes, then—"

"Go to Prairie du Chien, or to your Des Moines," he spit out the words.

"They will go with the English if there is war," she said.

He shrugged. "Then go to Crawford's at little St. Louis." His voice became lighter, as though he had just thought of this splendid idea. "This would be good. Crawford knows you. He will take care of you."

"So it is true," she breathed, pulling the robe up to her throat. "You are setting me off."

Pierre blew a breath out through his nostrils. Jamming his toes into his moccasins, he tugged at the smooth leggings he wore only in this St. Louis. They made his legs look less muscled than she knew they were, made him look more American. He buckled the garter below the knee, straightened the fringe down the front. "If I do not come back, I have brothers. They will take you as a wife."

"You scrape the last of your hide with that argument," she said. "A St. Louis woman puts up with such statements. Not this l'Ayvoise woman. Do I not salt your hides well so they arrive sweet? Did I not learn to fight off wolves through the night while my father slept and my mother stripped the hide from the buffalo he shot? Do I—"

"*Oui,*" he said. He pulled on his shirt over his hair, tucked the square of the bottom into his breeches. His ash-gray eyes narrowed, even though his mouth softened into a smile.

"It is not safe for me to stay behind," she whispered.

He bent to her. "I would take you with me," he told her. "But I don't need a guard at the fire. I speak for the Americans, negotiate between the Sioux and the Arikaras and maybe keep them at peace. And the tribes beyond them. The Americans know they need smooth waters between people if they are to make money. I need to have worries only for myself with such important words exchanged, eh?"

She knew he was right, and yet the ache of it, of being left, of living without him for so long threatened to choke her, to weigh so heavy on her chest that she would die of the ice that would fill the crack in her heart.

"Let's have our marriage blessed then, before you go. To assure our sons you will return," she said. "I will find a friar."

"Now? *Non.* There is no time. It is not the right reason. No priest will baptize and bless a marriage just to satisfy a woman who doesn't want to be left behind." He stayed silent, tying the leather shirt's thongs at his neck. He pulled his hair back into a queue, tied a twist to it. "You'll be all right here, *femme.* You're strong."

"Is it this confession the priests require? You have things you hide?"

"Ah, woman…think of *les enfants* if not of me." With his chin he motioned to the boys. Baptiste, awake now, dangled a piece of rawhide string with a goose feather attached in front of Paul who laughed when his breath pushed it away. "That is the most important *raison* I go. For them. For their future. You are the mother of my sons. You stay here to take care of them." He looked around, grabbed his belt with the knife on it.

"Being a good mother is a reason to have me stay behind but not a reason to have our marriage blessed by your priests before you go?"

He crossed his arms over his chest, his legs spread, reminding her of the X marked on bales of hides destined for the old XY Company.

"You wallow like a buffalo," he said. "It is different now with Hunt. These men are different." He reached for a wool cap, fingered the colored tassel. "You always want more than I can give," he said before heading toward the post.

She blinked back tears. She did want more—if only she had the courage to live with her choice.

Pierre strode to the wharf, scanning the boats bobbing on the black water in the morning mist. If only he could make his *femme* understand. He'd never told her how he'd been stepped over by his own father when Lewis and Captain Clark had sent "Old Dorion," his father, back with the chiefs to meet with President Jefferson. His father, leaving the Corps of Discovery as Clark called it; his father, sending him, the eldest son, off, with no part of the journey west and no part of the journey back East with the chiefs, either.

And later, Meriwether Lewis had made sure his own brother Reuben Lewis's company and Manuel Lisa got the contracts to return the chiefs to their homeland, blocking out any Dorion income or honor. There might have been other journeys, but one of the Mandan chiefs had died in the company of old Dorion, and now some tribal leaders resisted traveling to meet the president as they'd told Lewis and Clark they would.

Pierre could not help make that happen. His father had told him to finish the trade with the Arikaras and head back from the Little Sioux River, portaging to the Des Moines, then further east, around La Crosse and south, toward Prairie du Chien. He had been a dutiful son and done as he was told. It was then he knew there would be no future for him in transporting chiefs or being in the government's employ. He was a mixed-blood, and they would have no part of him. He'd hang his hope on private enterprise, on this Astor expedition.

Hunt's westward trek would be the envy of all the fur companies plying for the Western trade. If he had to give up his wife and sons for a short time, so be it. The glory of their return would be worth any sacrifice. He wished his father had lived to see this.

His *femme* had always traveled with Pierre, ever since they'd said their vows early in 1806. She'd joined him as he moved up the Des Moines where she'd delivered their first child inside the small fort run by Crawford that was called St. Louis too. It bore the same name as this big Spanish-dominated city he now stood in. Two cities as different as sun and moon. So much for names.

That same Clark, who caused that rift between him and his father, now partnered in the very company of Lisa, a man who made claims on Pierre Dorion's money and reputation.

His father had wounded Pierre deeply, sending him away those years before. This expedition was his healing.

Pierre watched a clerk checking the manifest beside a *bateau*. *Engages* still unloaded a wagon with "Moorhead" stamped on the side. Sounds of wooden barrels thumped into boats were magnified in the dense morning fog. More trade goods, what they'd need in exchange for safe travel through the tribal lands.

A barge-like *bateau* appeared through the mist. Pierre frowned. Was that one of Lisa's? The fog gobbled it up before Pierre could be sure.

He'd confront Wilson Hunt about the advance straightaway. The expedition leader was accustomed to residing inside the waxed walls of Washington, conversing with men like the former president. Pierre would bask in that shadow and perhaps one day he, too, would sit across from greatness and tell the tale of westward expansion the way Reuben Lewis soaked up the prestige of his brother Meriwether's journey all the way to the Pacific.

Pierre would move from guide and interpreter and hunter to partner. Maybe even become a chief factor, a *bourgeois*, where men relied on his cunning and experience and judgment. And where his wife would be called madame.

But first he had to prove himself in dealing with men like Lisa to show himself worthy.

Pierre bent to lift the end of a coopered barrel that held trade goods such as curtain rings and papers of vermilion. He rolled it toward the *bateau*, gave an order to Gervais, one of the *engages*. He would show Hunt that he was a man who could do many things on this expedition, including help with loading. Hunt was untried in the wilds, but a man was formed by the challenges he accepted, by the risks he took, not *just* how he did with them. Didn't a dog take up the scent of a hunt, setting a whole pack in motion, stimulating the effort even when it did not know for sure where the fox hid, didn't know how many brambles he'd have to scramble through? It was the push of it, the uncertainty in part that drove men like Hunt. Men like him, too.

If Hunt succeeded, the Americans would win that vast Indian trade. And the pelts and hides and robes could be taken directly north then, to

Sitka and on to China without having to haul them east. Direct trade with the Asians, that was Astor's dream, and he, Pierre Dorion, would make that happen with his words and become wealthy in the process.

Yes, yes, the buffalo robe trade must still come overland, east. Few Asians or Europeans were interested in the warmth of the heavy hides. The fools! But the Americans knew their worth. And so the river routes to the East to accept the hides and supply the tribes were a must for the taking over of this Western country, making all of it part of the Americas.

Pierre took in a deep breath, rolled another barrel toward the boat. He felt the excitement of the coming journey. That was what he had to keep his eyes on now, not on the lonely face of his *femme* waving good-bye; not on her disappointed eyes as he refused to have the marriage blessed with the time so short; not on her angry scowl when she learned of the money he would leave but that Lisa would argue with her over just as soon as Pierre left.

Manuel Lisa grimaced as he stood at the bow of his twenty-ton barge. In and out of the fog, he watched the French-Canadians loading Hunt's boats. He heard them singing and shouting in French. He had his own crew, a good crew. They'd help send rumors along that he planned to go as far as Henry's Fort near the Yellow Stone River, to find his lost partner who had failed to return when scheduled. It was as good a reason as any to head out in spring into untouched territory. If it just happened to be around the same time as Hunt's journey west, well, that was coincidence. At least that was what he'd tell any who asked.

But he didn't yet have all the goods he needed. Clark had put in several thousand dollars, so had Reuben Lewis, and he had as well. But they needed twenty thousand more dollars to buy supplies to fill the barge. And if they hoped to leave when Hunt did, they were running behind.

Lisa signaled to bring the barge in. The fog kept him from seeing what Hunt was up to this morning—except for the presence of Dorion at the dock. The man's looming height and broad girth made him stand out, even in a dense fog.

Lisa reached for the knife in a sheath tied at his thigh, used the blade to pick at his teeth. *Dorion.* His skill with language paled in importance to the many alliances the half-breed had with the tribes. Practically every younger brother had married into one tribe or another, and they all claimed Dorions as "their traders." Lisa wasn't sure that even Clark understood how much the family's influence could affect diplomacy and policy. It was about alliances. It was all about trades. He replaced the knife, pressed both hands to push back his wavy, greased hair behind his ears, felt it gather at his neck. Nonetheless, he had a good interpreter. Eduard Rose resided already at Lisa's fort with Reuben Lewis. He could say he was merely bringing supplies to that outpost while he searched for his lost employee. Astor, the financier, understood. He could tell the New York papers that his ship sailed around the horn to build a fur factory and that Hunt headed west just to make it easier to take furs to China, but Lisa knew: Thousands of Indians were ripe for copper pots, rolled tobacco, guns, and beads. If war broke out, there'd be no English goods to trade the Indians for their furs; they'd come to the Americans then, and whoever had made contact with the Western tribes first would be remembered as "their traders."

Hunt planted seeds for Astor, for the market he planned to grow. Hunt was just like Lisa. They were two of a kind.

Marie's husband sat at the *bourgeois* table at the midmorning meal. The large, red-headed Scotsman sat next to him. *Mackenzie?* Yes. So many of the partners had names that sounded like sneezes: Mackenzie, McClellan, the Stuarts and Crooks. Wilson Price Hunt with his hawk nose had not appeared yet, which struck Marie as odd.

The partners had their meals cooked separately and served first; a slow pace that whetted the women's and *engages'* appetites. Lye-soaked hulls of corn and boiled river water served to the lesser ones often failed to satisfy. It was the way at the posts, even the American posts, whose factors said "equality" marked them as separate from the British. Marie had trouble seeing the differences.

"Oh yes, it is two hundred dollars or more. I hear this," Angelique told Marie, taking her attention from Pierre. The woman sitting beside her came from back East. Iroquois. Her top teeth jutted out over her bottom lip. Probably from holding the hides in her mouth, to keep them secure while she worked, a practice Marie rejected even though it took her longer to scrape the hides Pierre brought in.

Marie continued to eat the cornhusks, folding it into her mouth with her fingers, wishing instead for the soup made from the insides of bison bones and their heated blood, delicacies here; staples years past near her home on the Des Moines. Here the women and lesser beings at the post had no fresh buffalo hump and very little dried. She'd saved dried meat from an earlier time to serve Pierre yesterday, for all the good it had done her.

No trout or goose either, though her husband ate his share at Hunt's table. Once, her preparation of buffalo and berries ground into fat had brought favor to her husband as he traded the bags to trappers for their long winter's journey. In this St. Louis place, she merely raised the skin-filled bags that weighed more than Baptiste, bags prepared by other women, raised them to hang from the smoke-stained rafters.

She could go back to making pemmican, would need to if what Angelique said was true. She may well get the advance, but it would take every bit of skill she had to keep it, according to Angelique. That woman had a downriver route into information. Marie supposed that being the wife of a *voyageur* got her inside the expedition's news, though usually such women got merely scraps and not the first cuts. Maybe it was only a rumor.

Paul stirred in his baby board beside her, smacking his lips. She'd brought the child with her to the post. Baptiste sat chewing his hard biscuit, eyeing his father for the first sign that he could approach the men's table. Paul's eyes remained closed in sleep. Marie pretended to pay no attention to Angelique. Pierre didn't like it when she talked with the traders' or *voyageurs'* wives. He said they filled her head with trouble. "You eat fast, then tend the babies," Pierre always said. "You have time to listen, you listen to me."

When Mackenzie and others filled the room, he wouldn't notice how long she lingered at the table with another woman, she hoped.

"Lisa says your husband drank all the whiskey at Fort Mandan so the Spaniard had none left for trade." Angelique continued, not needing evidence of Marie's interest. "Two winters past. Lisa hangs on to the whine of that debt. Your husband swallows the profits of the trip." Angelique nodded as though knowing all. "He owes Lisa two hundred dollars." Angelique paused. "You could come to Montreal with me. When my husband pushes the *bateau* out into the water, we go back home. My family would take you in. I have many brothers." She slapped at her own son's seven-year-old hand that had just reached for a scrap of biscuit. The boy howled.

Marie looked up to see her husband staring at her from across the room, a scowl on his face. He raised his chin toward Angelique. She knew he meant she shouldn't listen, should leave this woman's presence. Could he hear what Angelique said? He pushed his stool back.

A weight lay on her chest. It paralyzed, kept her from moving.

"I cannot believe he does not tell you this." Angelique clucked her tongue.

"He tells me," Marie lied. "Pierre tells me everything, even when he doesn't want to."

Angelique wiped her fingers on her stained dress. Marie wondered if she had chalk enough to wipe out the stains or if she simply did not care.

"Is my bundle ready?" Pierre said as he grabbed Marie's elbow, pulled her away from the woman.

"The one you owe Lisa?" she charged. Paul startled in his sleep, awoke.

"I carry him, Mama," Baptiste said, rushing to pick up the cradle-board. Paul's eyes were alert now, watching. Baptiste frowned as Pierre talked. Her son had his own set ways, his little bow legs making him walk like an old man sitting astride his horse too long, his round face marked by a downturned half-moon of mouth.

"Just a big one to be still in his board, sleeping," one of the *engages* commented. He wagged his finger at Baptiste. "Should be out towing barge lines." The *engage* laughed. Baptiste didn't. "Just looks a little peaked, *n'est ce-pas?*"

Marie swallowed hard, looked to see if her husband listened to this chatter or just seethed with her ignoring him.

The *engage* insisted. "Needs vinegar, *n'est ce-pas?*"

Paul didn't suckle with heartiness, but he didn't seem ill either. He was perhaps ready to move from her breast. She had kept him there, close to her, needing her. For a moment she wondered if she kept Paul longer in his board because he did look sickly and she had not acknowl-edged this before. She squinted at Paul. No, he was merely small, not like Baptiste who already stood nearly as tall as the trader's slab counter.

Paul had an…affliction, Holy Rainbow had said. She remembered that her mother-in-law had whispered this on the day Paul was born. Pierre shook his head at the infant's birth, stared at her, then the infant. Shook his head again, said, "*Non.* We will live with the affliction."

Marie had run her fingers over the child's small face, his eyes pinched closed from the assault of leaving water and warmth to discover the cold world. He had all his feet, his toes, his fingers. His mouth formed a large O of thin lips. His eyebrows were perfectly arched, though long, almost joining at the center. He already had a head full of hair. What did they see in Paul that she could not?

She had not argued with the name Paul, the name Holy Rainbow gave the child. It was a name easily said, though it drifted off the tongue quickly like the last puff of smoke from a fading fire.

"*Femme.* Give me a hand here," Pierre said, bringing her back to the moment. He moved her away from Angelique, loaded stocks of lead balls from the back shelving. He motioned with his head toward a coopered barrel. "Lift the lid," he ordered.

She slid her hands underneath the wooden circle. For all her height and size, she was often surprised by how small her hands were. They were strong though. She gripped her short fingers against the barrel. She thought but did not say that the lead should go into a tin-lined box, not into a barrel with cooper's rings around it to keep it whole. But it would not be wise to correct him in public.

"Best put those into tin, Dorion," the partner named Mackenzie said.

"*Oui,*" her husband agreed. "I told you to open that other barrel," Pierre said, motioning to her with his chin.

"You've someone else now, who will take over the post here?" Mackenzie asked Pierre. "And your advance, it is handled to tend to your family?" He spoke with a brogue, rolled the *r*'s.

The Scotsman was a huge man, who would enter the door sideways and still his belly would rub against the posts. Once inside, he moved constantly as though his flesh pushed him here and there even if his bones stopped.

"*Oui,*" Pierre said, "she will be well tended, once I meet with Hunt." He did not look at Marie as she rolled the empty barrel to him, giving it an extra shove. He sucked in a breath, pulled the cover off to show the tin.

Mackenzie said. "It's about opening markets for later traders." *About.* He said the word as though speaking of a boot, what some white men wore on their feet. "That's what you must convey to the Indians we meet up with."

Hunt entered then, puffing and pulling on his collar. He wore a pinched face, his cheeks splotched with red. He looked as though he barely had more summers than Marie's own twenty. She wondered when he would adopt the more practical dress of breeches and buckskins, what a man wore heading away from fine tables. *Maybe they aren't leaving today.*

"This is our day then, gentlemen," Hunt said, rubbing his hands together as though cold. The pinched look might be an adjustment to the smoky room. Above her, peeled pine with pitch bubbled into amber balls. The scent of smoked hides, the pungent smell of beaver pelts, of otters, pushed out from the storage room.

Hunt nodded to her. The acknowledgment surprised her.

"Dorion was just saying all is arranged. His wife is positioned as soon as the advance is paid out," Mackenzie told Hunt. "There's not much left for us now but to leave."

It was now or never.

"*Payer un prix excessif,*" Marie said, touching her finger to her nose.

"What?" Mackenzie said, turning to her. "You owe what through the nose?"

"My husband has a bill to pay yet. To Manuel Lisa. It is why he must have so much for an advance." Her words rushed like wind. "He has no money to leave for his sons if he pays the bill." She swallowed, ignored her husband's glare. She could nearly hear his heart beating from where he stood across the room. "It is not fair, but there is a way around this." He took long steps toward her. She flinched with the speed of it.

"Dorion? What's this about?" Hunt said. "Astor will want no—"

"He charged ten dollars a quart," Pierre nearly shouted, his face red. "Lisa's a thief. You know this. It was not a fair charge!"

"McClellan would agree with you," Mackenzie said. "He detests that little Spaniard. Still…"

"Is this true?" Hunt asked. "You owe this?"

"You didn't hear the rumors, Wilson? I'm surprised," Mackenzie said. "We heard them as far north as Nodaway."

"St. Louis is riddled with rumors," Hunt said. "Like the pox."

Mackenzie pulled at the reddish hairs at the side of his face. He paced while he talked, his bulk rattling tins on the shelves.

"When he pays," Marie persisted, her heart pounding, "my husband has no money to leave for his children. This Astor, he would not want this kind of trade, *non?*"

"It is none of Astor's affair," Pierre said. "It is a husband's affair. I will tend to it as a husband must."

A powder pouch she'd made of mallard wings hung behind the slab counter, the deep blues and greens and grays shimmering in a single shaft of light from the scraped-hide window. She would claim that pouch. Perhaps she'd need it to trade for food for her babies. Trades. Always trades.

"You're not planning to put her off, surely, Dorion?" Mackenzie said, turning toward Pierre.

"I—"

"No," Marie said. She took a deep breath, felt the weight on her chest lifting. "He will pay Lisa. And he will take us along."

Behind her she heard Angelique gasp at her boldness. Mackenzie snorted. He looked like an irritated buffalo, raising his chin and shifting his head to the side, both wary and wise.

"Not possible," Mackenzie said. "A woman? Children—"

"It will not be the first time a woman has made her way to that westering water place. Charbonneau took his Snake wife and child along," Marie said.

Pierre jerked his head toward her.

"But we've no time to prepare for additional people, for what a mother would need. And children…" Mackenzie said. "No. Besides—"

Hunt cleared his throat. "Ah, Donald. Actually, Mister Astor says I'm to decide such things now. If there's a dispute…"

"Since when?"

Hunt cleared his throat again, reached into his blouse, and withdrew a letter. "It arrived early this week. I…I've been meaning to discuss it with you. So much happening…"

Mackenzie lifted the red wax seal with his fingernail. He read, his puffy face flushed. Marie smiled at an *engage* now bouncing Paul at his knee. She dared not look at Pierre.

"Well then," Mackenzie said. "The decision is yours, Wilson." The blotches in his face faded. He handed the letter back.

Pierre's face, too, had returned to its natural color of walnut, though his eyes still narrowed and he spoke through clenched jaws. "I should have managed my affairs better."

"Indeed," Hunt told him. "But what to do?" He flapped the letter against his palm as he chewed on his cheek.

Pierre sighed heavily. Marie recognized the tone, warning of a change. "I will have to stay here and work for Lisa, for the debt owed. It is what he wishes, *n'est ce-pas?* To keep me here, so you will not succeed. If I pay the debt and leave with you, what will my wife do?" He raised his hands as though without choice. "Though it is not true, what Lisa claims, I have no money to argue with that Spaniard. I believed even Lisa might take pity on a woman and two children, which is why I said nothing earlier. I hoped that if he took the matter to court, a judge would see through him, protect the children. But if paying the debt is the honorable thing that your Astor would want, then I'll be forced to remain in Lisa's employ or my family has nothing."

"You could pay the debt, Wilson," Mackenzie said. "Then the woman would have means to survive here on the advance."

"I've already put out twice what I should have for his services." Hunt chewed on his lip, continued snapping Astor's letter in his palm.

"The Snake woman—" Marie began.

"What? Speak up," Hunt said.

Marie started again. "The Snake woman, Sacagawea, did more than speak Shoshone words. She and her son signaled peace by their presence. Astor sends so many men. The tribes may fear that you bring guns to trade to their enemies," Marie said. "A woman and children in your midst says different."

Hunt frowned, looked to Pierre.

Had she said this poorly? It troubled her to say the things she felt inside using English. In this St. Louis place, where English was spoken with as many twists and pitches as the Missouri in spring, she felt as though she lived inside a cave. And in the dark spaces of hesitation where the firefly flew without light, she could stumble. A mother always risked stumbling.

"She's right," Pierre said. "My *femme* is right. We can't know what the tribes will assume by the size of the expedition. They'll want to exchange furs—which we're not accepting, eh? So they'll wonder what we are doing in their country."

"America's country," Hunt said.

Pierre shrugged. "They may not agree, eh?"

"It'll be your job to convince them," Mackenzie said.

"We must depart today," Hunt said. "And with you." He pointed at Pierre with the letter. "All the more reason, because Lisa is doing whatever he can to prevent it. I've no intention of paying more for your services, Dorion. We are overextended now." He lifted his hands. "Providence, pray help me!" he said.

A log crackled and pitched out into the room from the fireplace. Marie grabbed the twist of iron and pushed it back, sweeping the hot ashes in with the side of her foot.

"She's quick, my *femme*."

"We will be of no trouble," Marie said.

Mackenzie snorted. One of his scent hounds bounded in through the door then, followed by the camp boy, Toupin. Mackenzie patted the dog's cream-colored head as it stood panting, jumping lightly, front paws on the big man's chest. A Porcelaine breed, it yowled now with a kind of musical bark. The *engage* held its leather strap loose in his hand.

"My *femme* is kept in line with a firm hand," Pierre said, nodding toward the leash.

"Is she?" Hunt stared, then said, "I guess if we can put up with dogs, we can put up with women and children." He stuffed the letter back into his blouse, clapped his hands in decision. "So be it, then," he said. "A woman and children tell the tribes we come in peace, they keep Lisa off our tail. And they keep my interpreter happy. You pay what's owed, Dorion. Providence has provided a way through a difficult place."

Marie glanced at her husband. She'd made a trade and incurred a debt she knew she would pay for later.

3

Setting Off

At sixteen years of age, Jean Louis Toupin liked to call himself a French *voyageur* rather than an *engage*, though he was barely older than the English camp boy, George Gay. Yes, *voyageur* had a finer sound, Toupin thought, and hadn't Hunt treated them as though they were more than mere camp cooks? They'd been allowed to winter in St. Louis, and just now he'd been a party to negotiations, right here before his eyes while a dog jumped about singing a tune with its bark! Wait until he told George that not only were dogs coming with them but a woman and children, too! His eyes scanned the crowded room.

He liked her, that Madame Dorion. Not just because she was pretty—which she was—or because she spoke a soft French. Life in Montreal, away from his village, had exposed him to English and French as well as a smattering of German, and he'd even picked up some Iroquois words when he'd been on a short trapping expedition into that tribe's waters. Languages came easily to him, the way playing a musical instrument did to George Gay. But he wasn't one to wave his red *L'Assomption* sash the way some did to bring attention to it.

He found himself a little tongue-tied around Madame Dorion most of all because she worried over her boys so, just as his own mother worried over him. It made him miss his mother all the more.

She had let him go on this expedition because of the money. He knew that. He'd put his advance on an account at the trading post so she could buy food and shirts and red yarn for the little ones. She understood that a young man needed to step out on his own, and a camp cook was a good place to begin. But it was Mister Astor himself who had inspired Toupin to leave his familiar Montreal for such a long journey as Hunt was leading. He'd committed to three years, leaving his mother and so many younger brothers and sisters behind.

The talk two years earlier had been of little else in Montreal than Astor's recruitment. The man had both the money and political clout to send out two expeditions at the same time: one by sea around the horn on the ship *Tonquin;* and one overland, led by Hunt. Both were designed to capture the Asian trade away from the British and Canadians and any other Americans with even a hint of that ambition. All that, while rumors of war between England and America floated around like cottonwood fluff in spring. Americans were risky adventurers, Jean Toupin thought. Now he was one of them too.

Hunt called him by the American name, John, but he thought of himself as Jean, a French-Canadian. He'd wanted a role as the ship's boy, but the sixteen-year-old brother of the *Tonquin*'s captain had won that berth.

It was just as well. In the months since, Toupin had joined that English lad George Gay and others heading from New York to this frontier post of St. Louis. Toupin had grown to like the hustle and bustle of the town, but he was ready to get on with the adventure of discovery. He'd heard of Shining Mountains said to be rugged and covered with snow year-round; of places where beaver and otter ran thick enough to cross a stream on yet never get your feet wet, and of fierce yellow bears and deserts so vast and windswept that one could go days without seeing grass or finding water.

He'd also heard of the dozens of tribes who spoke different languages with clicks and hums off their tongues and words like dances motioned with their hands.

But his real interest was the mighty river, the Columbia, and a chance to see the Western sea. He wasn't sure what pulled him there. It was almost…mystical. He told his mother and brothers and sisters he wanted to be part of the expedition that opened up the Columbia for trade. He wanted to listen to the words of new people and discover their meanings. It would be something to tell his children about. When he had children. He thought of his little sisters' dark curls and his younger brothers wrestling like pups on the feather tick. He felt an ache in his side he'd try to soothe later with a quick letter scribbled for home. It would be his last letter for a long time once they set off for the wilderness.

He'd tell them about Mackenzie's dogs and of the little boy he'd rescued yesterday and of the woman joining them. And he'd share what he'd seen at the wharf that morning after the fog lifted. He'd watched a blue heron rise up from a shallow edge upriver, its slender legs dragging against the air almost as though they didn't belong to the huge wings gaining height. It was how he thought of the expedition: a huge effort drawn from such a wide expanse of wing, from one nation to another, one coast to another, miles and miles apart, while the slender boats they'd be cordelling upriver were like the heron's legs dragging against the current, across a continent, taking them to unknown places safely, able to do necessary work once they arrived. He smiled to himself. His mother would probably tell him he'd just described her task as a widow, raising eight sons and daughters into responsible adults. Responsible *voyageurs,* just as he hoped he'd become.

Baptiste pulled on the dog's leash and Toupin stood. *"Non,"* the French-Canadian said.

"Non. Non. Everyone says *non,"* Baptiste said, his face in a scowl.

Marie's eyes met Jean Toupin's gaze. She reached for her son, and they both turned as two slender men dressed in waistcoats and wearing top hats ducked through the narrow door. The men's bodies and the dogs' scented the small space.

"Nuttall," Hunt said, clearly delighted. "I see you've brought Bradbury. Excellent, excellent. We've but a few details and then, we're off, gentlemen, doing honor for Mister Astor. We'll have your fine commentary and specimens and something a little extra: Dorion here has convinced us the value of bringing a woman and children along."

"I say," Nuttall said. "Is that wise?"

"Lewis and Clark found it useful," Mackenzie noted, and Marie thought she saw a look of appreciation for Mackenzie cross Hunt's eyes.

Nuttall adjusted his glasses, looked around. "This is the little man?" He put his hand out to Baptiste. The boy stared at him, sober as a priest. Marie touched his shoulder, urging him forward. The boy leaned back. "Ah, I see he's learned. It isn't proper to chat with strangers," Nuttall said. "Quite right. I take no offense."

"Your boy can help young Toupin look after my dogs." Mackenzie's jowls wiggled even after he stopped talking. He said to Marie then, in French, "Would you like that? What's the boy's name?"

"Jean Baptiste," Marie told him. "We call him Baptiste."

"Baptiste. Yes. They're costly now, these dogs. Bred so a walking man can keep up with them, as they're working the prey. I don't take their keeping lightly."

"*Gentil,*" Toupin showed Baptiste as he stroked the lean dog's smooth body, pulled gently on the white ears speckled with ginger-colored spots. Marie thought the dog had soft, gentle eyes that looked straight into Baptiste's. Her son looked away, not wanting to challenge. Toupin nodded to her, smiled.

This is going to work! They were all going West!

"Dorion, you go pay Lisa," Hunt directed. "Quickly. Leave no indication that we're ready to set out. Just tell the man…that you've had a change of heart and want to…be debt free."

"He charged overmuch," Pierre said. "Same as robbery that he—"

"A run-in with Manuel Lisa?" Bradbury whistled low.

Hunt turned to him, frowned, then raised his finger. "Ah, I remember. You rode out with him last year by stage, didn't you, Bradbury?"

"He's quite passionate about trade," Bradbury told him.

"No matter," Hunt added. To Dorion, raising his hand to stop further discussion he ordered, "Pay the debt."

"We'll set off yet today?" Nuttall asked. When Hunt nodded, he said, "We'd hoped to receive one more post before leaving. One's expected tomorrow. How would it be if we stayed back a day, picked up the mail, and then rode to join you? We'd surely catch you in a day or two."

"Fine, fine," Hunt said.

"Are we at last prepared then?" Mackenzie said. "We can be departing, get some benefit from all those men at Nodaway spending Mister Astor's funds?"

Hunt nodded. "Join us by St. Charles. And we'll pick up whatever additional things we need at Morrison's supply. He's promised us two hundred gallons of whiskey. Will that be enough do you think, Dorion?"

Pierre's face deepened to the color of a mallard's breast feathers. "Ask my *femme*," he said. "She seems to know what's needed."

Marie could feel the growing excitement of the *voyageurs,* the partners, even her husband. Her own heart soared. She was setting off, not being set off as Angelique implied. She was taking her sons to be with their father, as a mother should. If it improved their status, her husband's, or even her own, well that was maple-cone sugar shaved to sweeten the dish.

Marie noted the supplies being loaded still. Nine hundred eighty pounds of biscuits, fifty bushels of corn, six barrels of flour. They'd all arrived from the supplier named Moorhead. The *engages* loaded rifles and muskets and bayonets and lead canisters of powder meant for trade and howitzers for influence. Even ointments and axes, lanterns and oils found their way on the manifest. Pierre had clerked and knew how to keep records, so Marie recognized the papers that kept track of what was loaded. She did not need to read them. She counted them in her mind and kept them in her memory. Surely there was enough to care for her children on this journey.

Hunt had ordered opium for pain and mercury ointment for the diseases white men said came from the Indian women. They always blamed the women for the consequences of their own lapses.

All of St. Louis and neighboring St. Genevieve and St. Charles would be sad to see the Astorians leave. The seamstresses that provided flannel shirts or the little stores where the *engages* bought their socks and thread, tea and sugar, would all find empty places in their coin purses once they set the keelboats west.

Marie had known some of the St. Louis traders even before she and Pierre arrived in the city. The Scotsman Aird from Prairie du Chien now traded in St. Louis and befriended the Astorian group. Many a night Aird had talked with Hunt and Ramsey Crooks, another partner, while Marie listened to the side, unnoticed like a spider on the wall. They spoke of following Lewis and Clark's trail west but had heard a rumor that a shorter route existed, south, one that Aird said would take them more quickly over the mountains to the Columbia. Even the red-haired Clark, he said, suggested there might be an overland route.

Marie was pleased she'd listened, hadn't realized that knowing of their plans would matter to her as it did now. She could be of assistance as Sacagawea had—she'd remembered the details of discussion of routes. She'd made no idle boast.

But she must keep her wits about her though, remember well, and know when to say what she knew. Never stumble. And someday, maybe someday, her husband would move through the ranks and take her with him as a *bourgeois's* wife. Whatever glory came to Hunt would fall on her husband's shoulders and then to their sons. It was all about doing right for her sons.

She sat now in the *canot du nord,* a flat-bottom canoe that carried six paddlers, a steersman, her children, herself, and several thousand pounds of goods wrapped into greased canvas bales or buried into fine coopered barrels. Paul nestled into a woven board that she would eventually strap with leather thongs to her shoulders. Awake now, the baby gazed and watched her face, looked around, temporarily entertained by the new sounds and smells. *Voyageurs* wore colored plumes in their hats today; carried paddles painted red and blue and yellow, probably handed down from fathers to sons.

Baptiste crawled over her. He actually laughed, something she rarely heard him do. He spoke in French to young Toupin, who already had sweat on his brow. "Careful," she told her older son. "Be careful of your brother."

"The little one is excited," Toupin said. The *engage* stood at the front of the boat, the *devant* position, and Marie wondered if Toupin worked as a steersman as well as a camp boy. "I have a little brother his age. Francoise. He is named for my father. I leave him in Canada."

"With his mother?" Marie asked.

Toupin nodded. He had eyes the color of acorn shells, darker than Pierre's. He looked with kindness at her sons. "Your husband is successful to make a bargain that brings his family along."

"He is a negotiator," Marie said.

Toupin nodded. He stood slightly shorter than Pierre, stocky and strong, but he was merely a boy. A good boy, Marie thought. "I like to hear *les garçons* chatter like geese as we work," Toupin said. He spoke in French, but when someone shouted to him in English he turned and waved. "We are ready then. Yes." When he twisted back, he adjusted his scarf at his waist. It was a finely stitched sash done in heavy wool using reds and blues, not like the familiar trade pieces. The brisk breeze flattened even his heavy corduroy pants.

"My mother's work," he said, fingering the fringe. "To remind me of her until I return on board ship."

"You won't come back overland?" Marie asked.

He shook his head. "It'll be safer to go home by ship, not so dangerous as crossing the mountains." He bent to move some piece of cargo at his feet, then stood, a startled expression on his face. "But you will be safe," he assured her. "Your husband, he will keep you and *les enfants* safe. Monsieur Hunt, he is a good man, we believe. And none of us would want to distress Monsieur Dorion." He grinned. "Such a man who could convince the partners to bring his wife and little ones along, such a man could bring the fires of Hades down upon someone who brings harm to his family." His voice cracked, carried a chuckle in it, even when he spoke of something serious as he did now. "Most of us will be warm enough pulling a *bateau* without the likes of Hades fire upon our backs."

A large, mustached man stepped into the boat. "Off you go now, Toupin. I've got the pole. You go out there and pull when we shout. I give you the chance to learn a man's work, yes?" He winked at Marie, and his mustache, draped on either side of his chin, wiggled as he spoke. Baptiste reached out as though to touch the mustache, and the *engagé* laughed and started to sing.

Marie thought to pull Baptiste back, but he turned at the sound of his father's approach, pulled his fingers back quickly. Pierre nodded to Toupin as he stepped near the canoe, dropped a bag at Marie's knees, causing her to wince with the weight. He made no apology.

"You are fortunate, Monsieur DeRoin," Toupin said, his cap in his hand, "to have your family with you." He spoke the name differently than Americans did.

"When the brats're bawling in the night you might not be envying me."

Pierre said the words lightly, and Marie wondered if her husband hadn't noticed being called with the title of "Monsieur." He was not a chief factor, not a *bourgeois* yet, but surely the title pleased. Perhaps he would overlook her pressing Hunt, shaming Pierre in public as she had. This *voyageur* recognized Pierre as someone special, someone with promise, wrapped up inside potential. A monsieur. She would remind him of this later, when he'd had time between the morning events and their departure.

When they camped that night, she'd tell Pierre that Jean Toupin, this boy with acorn eyes, saw his negotiating as what had won Hunt over. Pierre would like that. And he had pronounced their name "DeRoin" as the French did, to rhyme with the river Des Moines. How names were pronounced meant little to the Americans; but this French-Canadian boy understood as did her people. Pierre would see that no one thought he'd lost face by her speaking out on behalf of their sons.

"*Soyez tranquille!*" Pierre shouted from behind her. Baptiste dropped like a turtle, neck pulled into his shoulders.

Marie swallowed. She patted Baptiste's arm. Pierre was just edgy from meeting with Lisa to pay the debt, she reasoned. It couldn't have been a pleasant task.

The boats shoved out. Marie noted that the water ran high and full which would make the journey easier. They might even be able to use sails to move them upstream. But it would still mean pushing against the current. At least they weren't towing the huge Schenectady barge Hunt had ordered. That had been taken to Nodaway last fall.

Baptiste waved at Angelique and others standing at the wharf in front of the post. Most of St. Louis had come out to watch and wave at the four-*bateau* brigade. The wind lifted Baptiste's dark hair at his forehead. He turned and bumped, barely missing Paul, his moccasin-covered feet stepping onto her thigh, then slipping off into the boat. She grunted, tried to turn him around. "Wait until I put your brother onto my back," she told him.

"*Soyez tranquille!*" Pierre shouted again from the birch bark canoe behind them.

Baptiste turned and twisted onto her lap, his legs straddling her knee. "Mama," he said. "*Nous voilà!*"

"*Oui,*" she told him. "We are on our way."

The *engage* behind her helped put the willow frame with Paul in it onto her back. Then she curled her arms around Baptiste so that he faced away from her. "But you must try to still yourself as your father tells you. He is not happy with…so much to think of. We must pretend to be like fireflies in daylight. So no one knows we are here."

Baptiste pulled his head into her neck as though they shared a secret. She smelled the smoke in his hair and felt the firmness of his shoulders pressed into her breast. A breeze pushed against the copper twists in her ears.

She had done the right thing for her children, for herself and her husband. She couldn't contain the joy she felt at going along, at not being left to wait for someone she loved to return.

Returning by ship would be less dangerous, Toupin had said. She'd not considered any danger. She made herself think of other things.

Did she have everything necessary? She'd had little time to gather items from their now abandoned hut, to wrap them into the leather parfleche. She'd scurried out as soon as her husband's form had darkened the doorway, not wanting to be alone with him.

"You go pay Lisa." She'd pushed past him toward the canoes, pretended lightness, anticipation, as she heard her leggings swish in her fast-walk toward the post's storehouse.

Pierre'd followed her, still scowling, grabbing at Baptiste, pulling on the boy's arm, the child's feet barely touching the ground. She'd clutched her son, almost hissed at Pierre to go tend to his business. Then she'd rushed her sons inside the post. She didn't take the mallard pouch. Instead, she looked for dried food she could pack into the leather bag. She would bring nothing frivolous, nothing he could complain about.

Now here they were moving from the Mississippi to the Missouri River. The breeze moved across her face. A light spray rose as the boat hit a ripple. Canadians trudged along the shore, ropes over their shoulders, slopping down into the water then back out, holding the towlines that pulled the boats when the current proved too much for paddlers. They sang as they worked, their voices drowned out by the flocks of waterfowl migrating north. Hunt grinned as he turned to wave at Mackenzie in the canoe behind Marie.

Marie, too, felt light as a feather. Why should such a journey be kept only to men? She would make Pierre glad they were along. She would work hard so the journey proved easier for him, so he could concentrate on his duties. She would tell him this when they stopped for the night at St. Charles. It would be all right when he saw how easily they fit in, even with so little time of preparation, how she kept the boys from being a bother. She must keep the children calm, keep them from troubling their father, keep them from being noticed by the partners.

There were sixteen in this party. Once they reached Nodaway, another forty or so men would join the expedition. What trouble would two children and a woman be with all that activity?

Now, in her mind, she went through the list of items she'd packed. Folding tin candlesticks, for easier packing; her clover leather punch, an extra ladle and priming horn. Reed, the clerk handling the storehouse for the expedition, would have a hank of tow, the flax fibers used for cleaning Pierre's rifle. She felt the back of her neck, pressed her hand at the knot there. She had the ivory comb, the only real present Pierre had ever given her. There'd be no need for a bee box. She'd have to make another once they arrived at the salt sea—if honeybees lived there. She wondered. Maybe they didn't. So much she just didn't know.

Her sewing kit! She hadn't taken it. Needles, threads, and sinew along with bags of tiny beads she'd left behind. She'd have to trade something for those items when needed, so she could make repairs on shirts and leggings. Or maybe Hunt would let her put it on their account.

She felt for the knife at her waist. Yes. The stiletto fit her small hands. As long as she had that, she could solve most problems. She had remembered to bring what she must for her husband's comfort—except for the sewing kit—and for the children. Her own inconveniences could be set aside. A small price to pay for pushing to get her own way. No, she pushed for her sons.

When they arrived at St. Charles, Marie set the sleeping hut close to the rest of the party, quickly pitching their rolls of birch bark, settling them over arcs of branches. "We will want privacy," Pierre told her. He directed her to move the hut. "From now on, I will say where we put the tent. You do not decide things on this journey, *femme*," he said the word as though she was foul. "Keep this in mind."

She nodded, grateful he'd struck her only with sharp words. She moved to where he directed her, under the branches of a red willow. Farther from the river, the site still offered up rushing sounds, a mallard fluttering as it set its wings and landed on the water. She had to redo most of her work, but she didn't complain. Not wise to complain.

The wintering partners, those who had control over the daily details of this expedition, waited while the *engages* set their tents up, rolled the mats out for the food. This meal would be dried pork, dried beans with cold water carried in basket-covered jugs. These were followed by whiskey.

As was the custom on an expedition, after eating, the partners handed out short doses of the liquor, even to Pierre who jerked his head back and swallowed. He wiped his mouth with his wrist and motioned for more. Hunt hesitated but complied. Before long Pierre had stumbled to their tent and promptly fallen asleep.

In the night, while an owl hooted in the distance, Pierre had pulled her to him beneath their buffalo robe. He said nothing, but she felt his breath on the back of her neck, a caress on her shoulder, the heaviness of his wide hand as it lay on her hip. "My *femme*," he said, his words a whisper. "Ah, my *femme*."

He would forgive her boldness. Forgiveness took time, wasn't that what Holy Rainbow once told her? Old habits broke less easily than horses to a bit. Marie felt sure. He would be pleased to have her there to share his bed at night. She would make this so, and did.

Near dawn Marie awoke to the sound of horses and voices. English words with an English accent. She peered out through the tent opening and recognized Nuttall and Bradbury, the scientists who were to join them at St. Charles. They must have gotten in early. She stretched in the warmth of the robe.

But they spoke quickly. The horses they rode on stomped, and she heard the clanking of a chewed bit. Was it time to get underway? Moonlight filtered through the willows. Men held candles in the distance. She'd thought they'd preserve candles until truly needed.

She sighed. Maybe it was time to get up. She'd slept well and so had the boys. She rolled over to reach for her husband.

He wasn't there.

Now Nuttal and Bradbury's voices grew louder. Was that Hunt's voice, too? She couldn't make out what they discussed, but she heard her husband's name, then the distinct rhythm of his voice. She squinted to see him. Her heart started to pound.

It was early morning. Beneath the yet-to-bud-out branches of cottonwood and willows, Marie lay alone under the heavy robe. Both boys slept quietly, Baptiste making snoring sounds. Marie peered through the tent opening, shifted so she could see someone moving beyond Nuttall. *Pierre.*

Her husband stood, his shoulders hunched over, listening closely to Bradbury, their breaths coming as clouds in the cool morning air. Hunt stood there too, his calves bare of leggings. He looked as though he'd been roused from his sleep. Mackenzie, the big man, approached too, now, the dogs panting and sniffing at the end of long leashes.

Mackenzie lifted his pinkish face to stare toward Marie and Pierre's tent, the candlelight casting dark shadows on his stern face. He shook his head, turned back. Marie's heart pounded loud in her ears. She swallowed. Should she move closer to hear?

Pierre's voice raised then, and she saw her husband stomp away and stride back, his arms in motion as though flailing at a dog with a whip. Hunt seemed to wince, lean away from Pierre. Nuttall put a hand out. To calm Pierre? He jerked free.

Mackenzie's dogs barked now and when he turned, Marie saw that

Pierre's face looked dark. He shouted something, then turned and fast-walked toward their tent.

A hot sun of high noon beat down on Pierre, Marie, and the boys as they made their way overland. Pierre rode Nutall's horse with the baby's willow board attached by thongs to the front rigging ring. Inside, Paul hung, his head still, his eyes shifting from side to side, alert. Marie stumbled beside with Baptiste's hand sweaty inside hers. She brushed at bugs that flew close to his face. It was early for gnats but here they were just the same.

When Baptiste threatened to whimper she bent down to him. *"Non!"* she said, jerking his arm harder than she intended. "We must be still now. Walk. Just walk."

Willow branches with new buds slapped against her face, but she held her hand out so that they didn't snap at her son. When he tired, she picked him up and carried him on her hip, his head rested on her shoulder.

"How far do we go?" she asked Pierre, the first words she dared speak in the hours since he'd entered the tent, told her to get up and keep quiet.

"Not far enough," he said.

It was not until they were several miles up from St. Charles that Pierre pulled the horse up, tied it to a tree, and jerked a hastily wrapped pack from its back. The tent pieces of birch bark unrolled, and he pointed to where he wanted her to set it up. Marie scurried, bending branches over a pile of darkened wet leaves. "We will wait here," he said.

"But why?" Baptiste whined. "Where are the dogs?"

"Because your mother has begun a terrible thing," Pierre said. "She has made her way on this journey, and now because I leave without paying a debt not owed—"

"You didn't pay—"

"No! I didn't owe the debt, woman. Lisa charged more than ten times the value of that whiskey, just to hold me to his employment. He had a warrant issued for my arrest!" He pointed at his chest, his elbows bent and his chest out. "Your father." He shouted to Baptiste. "When I do nothing. I owe nothing."

"Hunt tells you to pay the—"

"Now all believe I ran out on a true debt. Why else would a man leave with his wife and children, take them along on such a dangerous trip? I must be running from some bad thing, *n'est ce-pas?* Hunt's face turned purple with a warrant that if served means I must go back. That stalls his expedition once again!" He shook his head. "Bradbury and Nuttall, they overhear this plan while they waited for their mail. They rode without their posts, because of you, *femme.*" He pushed at her as she knelt and she fell back, sharp branches jabbing at her palms. "Rode all night long. Because of you."

"It is not my shame," she said.

He struck her across the mouth then, the sting both familiar and surprising. "Oh yes. You are a part of this. They come to warn me so I can make my escape." He pushed the air with his hands. "But we must all escape or they would know I traveled with Hunt. Because you are along. Lisa tries to find me, to take me back." He stood over her, scowling.

"How long will we stay, Papa?" Baptiste asked, his voice deep for one so young.

Pierre stared at the boy as though seeing him for the first time. "What?"

"How long do we stay?"

"They will pick us up in the morning. So we go hungry this night. No time for food," he said. He glared at Marie. "All this rushing you cause."

Pierre stopped rocking suddenly, like a deer hearing a sound in the trees. Marie knew the motion, knew what it signaled by the prickles of fear racing across her shoulder. He sneered at her, raised a fist to her face. "Well, I have one thing to help a man deal with such troubles as his wife brings to him."

She turned her head from him, her hand pressed against the sting at her mouth, fearful he would strike her again, but he stepped away from her. Instead, he pulled a small bag from around his back, hidden beneath his buckskin shirt. Marie felt her stomach pinch as Pierre removed the cork from the willow-covered jar and took a drink. "Whiskey," he said, holding the flask up close to her eyes. "And not just a finger full as that Hunt serves out, eh?"

"Come, Baptiste," she whispered. "Leave your father. He is restless."

She stood, lifted the board from the horse, unwrapped Paul. She walked a short distance from where she'd unrolled the birch pieces of their tent and sat Paul down on the buffalo robe. He wobbled, adjusting to the hours of riding wrapped in buckskin. "I have dried meat," she whispered to Baptiste. She lifted her dress, grateful she'd tied a small skin bag of meat and berries taken from the storehouse rafter just before they left St. Louis. Baptiste broke a chunk of the pemmican off, and Marie lifted Paul to her breast. She turned, putting her back between Pierre and her sons. He would shout when he wanted her. That was his way.

"Femme," she heard Pierre say after a few minutes, so close behind her she smelled whiskey. Her eyes scanned for Baptiste. He chewed on the pemmican, safe. She pulled Paul closer to her breast, bent over him in protection, braced herself for what she knew she couldn't stop.

Toupin sang out with the rest of them as they moved upriver. Today they had breeze enough to set a small sail. That made everyone cheer. Too bad the Dorions weren't there to see it. Had they turned around? Decided against going west?

Not that it mattered, except that the children gave him…cheer. He guessed that was the word. He liked carrying the older one on his shoulders, and even the baby had been entertained as they made the cooking fire last evening.

Sometimes, Hunt told him, he and George Gay would be sent on ahead, making their way along the shoreline until they found a suitable campsite. It was a mark of trust that Hunt permitted mere camp boys to locate such places. At St. Charles they camped at a place many others had stayed at first, the grass beaten down into mud. But once in the wilds, as Hunt called it, they would have to use their judgment, not just settle where others had before them, to find suitable places for nearly seventy men—and one woman and two children.

Then this morning they'd loaded up without the Dorions anywhere in sight. Even their tent was gone. But the scientists had made it in earlier than expected. Already the *engagés* called Nuttall *Le Fou*—The Fool—as he made them wait until he lifted a tiny bud from a leggy branch or stepped into a mud flat to recover an egg that turned out to be a rock. Bradbury still rode his horse along the sparse trail paralleling the river. *Le Fou* often walked beside him. Toupin didn't know what they'd done with the other horse. He guessed Hunt had made a change. Maybe sent the Dorions back to St. Louis on it. Who would be the interpreter now? he wondered. Perhaps he could help.

No need for Hunt to explain it to the likes of him, that was sure. Still, he wondered. He would have liked to tell the boys good-bye and nod his hat to their pretty mother.

Pierre could hear them coming up the river, singing their French songs. He recognized Michel Carriere's booming voice joined by that English camp boy's fiddle as he stood near the bow. The sounds aggravated his thumping head. They were signaling him. All must be well despite the craziness of Lisa's last-minute effort to hold him from this journey. Lisa's agents must not have reached them. They'd had too much of a head start.

It was a good sign. He must remind himself. His skills were so valued that Hunt agreed to take his entire family with him, even at the last moment. He was even willing to skid around the law in order to keep him as an Astorian and not lose him to Clark and Manuel Lisa's company.

Oh, he knew that Hunt didn't want Manuel Lisa's fingers clutching at this expedition's throat. But that, too, was good. It helped Pierre to know this. Information meant influence. It was what he did to interpret and guide, use information to acquire what was needed—for others and himself.

Now he'd find out just how important Hunt saw his wife and children.

Pierre walked to the water's edge, staying back inside the brush enough to be sure it was Carriere and the others paddling the pirogue and not some trick of Lisa's meant to get Pierre to show himself. He was a man of many tricks, that Spaniard.

Pierre's eyes hurt in the morning sun. His knuckles were swollen and red.

When he saw it was Michel, Pierre stepped out of the brush, waved. He put his hands down, watched as the steersmen motioned back, turned to say something to one of the *milieu*, middle oarsmen. The head boat turned toward the sand bar just downstream from where he stood. The men prepared to beach it.

What came next would be the difficult part. He knew that. It would tell the tale at how well he used words to convince and deceive, both necessary at times.

He forced a smile and walked toward the line of boats. He would act calm, as though nothing was amiss. He hoped only the lead canoe would come in, that the rest would pass on by, keep going on to Nodaway. But it seemed several were beaching, giving a time for the men to stretch, allowing the *engages* to rest.

There would be more explaining now when they did not see his *femme* and the children. Maybe they wouldn't notice his family was missing. But some Americans and even some of the North West Company men, as Mackenzie had been, paid attention to the doings of women, more than they should. He hoped it wasn't so this time. It would mean more words to ease the wonderings of more people. He did not relish this, but such was the dilemma his *femme* had put him in.

Pierre pulled on his beard. He waved. Hunt waved back. *"Bienvenue,"* he said. "It is good you have arrived for me. I am free of Lisa at last," he said, "thanks to your efforts."

"Where are *les enfants?*" the *voyageur* Toupin asked. He gazed behind Pierre, searching.

"My *femme* has a strong will. This you know, or she would not be with us. She wishes to walk a ways. Will meet us closer to Nodaway."

"Nodaway? That's a far ways, mate," George Gay offered, still holding the fiddle.

"Indeed," Hunt said. He had that scowl again. "Several days' walking—she's just going to follow the river?"

"Weeks of walking." Pierre shrugged his shoulders, lifted his palms to the air. "Who can know the ways of a woman?"

4

Paddle-Minded

Manuel Lisa paced. The high heels of his hand-cobbled boots clicked on the wood floor of the solicitor's office, all the louder to mark his fury.

"Maybe there's a way to turn this into something good, Manuel," his solicitor said. He tapped a quill pen at the edge of his mahogany desk.

"Listen. The man's gone. Everyone knows where he went! He even took his family with him."

"Calm yourself, Manuel."

"It is not my way," he said. "So. You tell me I have to pursue the man to get my money?"

"I'm afraid so. If you're certain he left with Hunt. It may not be worth the expense, señor. And who knows how far out the law reaches," his lawyer told him.

"Listen. I spare no expense to recover a debt," Lisa said. "No one uses Manuel Lisa."

"You might send someone after him, as you did some years back for, what was his name? No matter. You got that debtor back."

"Dead," Lisa said.

"Yes. And Lewis and Clark's half-breed Drouillard paid the price for that, if I remember. And you got your money."

"An occupational hazard for a mixed-blood," his voice lightened as he recalled that success.

"It does suggest that people may have good reason not to want to be in your employ, Manuel. Why not give yourself a few days to consider your options. It's only two hundred dollars, and the charge was a tad…excessive, even at factory prices. The man had just had a son born. Celebratory whiskey, a judge might say."

"He signed the note."

"Even a drunk has rights, Manuel."

"I have rights too," Lisa said. He lifted heavy brows. "It is my right to collect."

"Whatever suits you," his lawyer said. "I often wonder why you seek my advice. You so rarely follow it."

Lisa turned on his heel, letting the door slam shut behind him, then nearly running down the wooden steps. Dorion had played right into his hands! Who could fault him for pursuing the man? He was owed a debt. If the idiot had paid it, Lisa would have had no end of jawing with Clark about heading as far as necessary into the West. Now he was chasing a fugitive! Even Clark couldn't question that.

First, he had to find twenty beastly strong *engages* to move his barge. And he had to get the boat filled with goods. He could risk his own money, but twenty thousand dollars for all the trade supplies? If the Crow or Blackfeet got wind of it, they could easily wipe him out, take the goods and blankets and not leave a beaver hide in their place. The irony was that he needed the protection of numbers, numbers such as Hunt had. At the same time, he had to catch then pass up Hunt, to start to bargain before Astor's men could. Delicate, very delicate.

But worth the gamble. His old Spanish contact had told him that his former employee, Henry, might have held back on him. The man had cached nearly fifty packs of pelts in 1808. At today's prices they were worth $25,000. Somewhere near the river Lewis named for himself, a fortune lay buried. It just happened to be on Hunt's route. And now Dorion had given him reason to pursue, so no one would suspect a thing. First things first. Money for stock. Quickly. Then load and leave. Supplies could be a problem what with Hunt having cleaned out so many St. Louis merchants. Could he even fill his barge? It would be a phenomenal task to take so large a craft, loaded, up the Missouri and still catch Hunt. But once he caught up with Hunt's expedition, he'd find a way to piggyback through Sioux Territory, find safety in numbers. One of the partners, McClellan, didn't like him much, but Hunt at least respected Lisa. He might be able to negotiate a joint journey upriver. Then in the night, he'd pass Hunt, lure Dorion with drink to go with him, and make the crossing to the Pacific first, picking up the fur cache on the way.

He had any number of additional troubling delays he could place inside Hunt's journey. And with all the bad luck Hunt had already encountered, everyone would assume it was due to poor leadership when bad things continued.

Lisa didn't have much time though. He had to get Clark to at least agree to let him set out to get Dorion. But then he would keep going so the Missouri Fur Company—his company—would reach the Columbia first and stir up ill will toward those who would follow among the tribes between here and there. They'd never look to Astor as a future supplier. And he just might add to his riches by unburying those valued furry bank notes. Clark wouldn't go for anything illegal though. So he had to make this sound…official and fair.

William Clark greeted his partner and ushered him into the Missouri Fur Company offices, a part of Clark's well-furnished home. The captain's once lean, soldier's body had spread with his wife's fine cooking. A foot taller and two stones heavier than Lisa, it was obvious marriage agreed with him, though it slowed his once sprightly gait.

"Listen. I've reason to believe Dorion has deliberately attempted to go beyond the law, to avoid paying a debt he owes me," Lisa said when the dark chocolate drink had been served by Clark's new servant.

"He underestimates you."

"I've decided to pursue him, but we may as well make the trip worthwhile. I could shore up trades with the Mandans, a few others." He sipped, wondering how much he should share.

Clark's hickory chair creaked with the man's bulk. He ran his ringed fingers through red hair. "I believe that would be wise, Manuel," he said.

His easy acquiescence was surprising. "I'm…pleased," Lisa said. "I can leave as soon as we're loaded. Of course, the more trade goods I take…"

Clark nodded. "I'll add to the cash reserve, though I fear you will have to bring up your share as well. We might get another investor, but we're not in the best situation right now."

"Listen, twenty thousand will seem like nothing if it returns what I expect."

"Granted," Clark said. "Oh, I've some special cargo for you, assuming you have room."

"We'll make room."

"Good. Also Henry Brackenridge, son of the novelist, has been asking for the chance to go west. He supposes himself a hunter in addition to his note taking about flora and fauna. He won't be ready for a few days, perhaps a week or more. Will that give you time?"

"He'll only add to the legitimacy…of the expedition. But we must move quickly. Hunt has already left and—"

"You'll need to hurry then," Clark said. He lifted his chocolate cup in a toast. "How I envy you the journey."

Lisa raised his cup, grinned. He'd gone from fury to finesse in less than an hour. Yes, Lisa's Indian, that Dorion, had served him well, and the louse didn't even know it.

Marie woke with a throbbing head. How long had she slept? Where were the children? She sat up, first panic then pain piercing the dizziness. Her mouth tasted thick as though she'd eaten bitter roots when she hadn't. She tried to open her eyes, pressed away the stickiness, scanned for her sons.

She touched a tender place below her eye. She could at least see, enough to know that Baptiste slept, exhausted from the dark night that kept them wakeful, walking. Paul sat, squeezing a ball of leaves, his legs straight out, his back nestled near the pit of Marie's arm as she lay. He stretched far forward when the glob of leaves dropped, and then whimpered as he struggled to sit back up. He couldn't. Instead, his chest lay flat against the earth, between his short legs. He whimpered louder.

"You are pressed like a poor fur," Marie told him, gently easing him back into a sitting position as she sat up beside him. He rocked on his bottom then, waving his arms as though to get her to lift the ball of leaves for him. *"Non."* She gentled dark hair from his eyes, pushed it behind his ears. A wild cowlick like grass growing around a post sprang up from the back of his head. She spit on her hand and pressed it, but it had a life of its own. Paul still rocked, then eased to the side and fell, failing to put his hand out to collect himself. He cried.

Her husband would have let the boy cry. "Teach what happens when he forgets to set a hand out," Pierre might say. Marie saw it differently. Her own mother's spirit had been smooth as a premium beaver hide. She would never allow a child to cry if she could stop it with her touch. Her mother's sisters and brothers shared those gentle ways. Marie never heard her mother raise her voice except to hold off wolves at a buffalo hunt. And that last time when she'd told Marie to stay behind.

Marie had been loved into being who she was, and she wanted the same for her sons. Another name of her people, Ioway, meant "sleepy ones." It was surely a mother name, for no crying child would ever find sweet sleep.

Marie sat now, steadied herself. She lifted Paul to her lap. So small he was, so fragile compared to the solid bone and bulk of Baptiste. How different brothers could be. Sisters, too, she remembered. Sisters, too.

She bounced the child on her hip, then offered him her breast. He quieted and looked at her, slowly closed his eyes while he continued to suckle. At least he was not yet walking so he couldn't wander off.

But he should be walking by now. She counted. Fifteen months.

Baptiste had walked by then. Baptiste just moved more quickly. Thank goodness he remained close by now. He could find things to distract himself—crayfish and butterflies, snakes and snails—and he peppered her with questions. When they lay down to rest, he usually kept her awake. She must not fall asleep with the boys still awake, she reminded herself. She would have to be more careful, make sure the children were safe no matter what happened with her husband. She shuddered as she recalled his actions of the night before. Paul's eyes startled open.

"*Va dormir,*" she said. "Sleep." She sang a song as much to soothe herself as her son. Her eye ached. And in the quiet, the images came back like the sharp slap of an open hand.

When Pierre first tipped the willow-covered jar up to his lips the night before, she had thought their moving away from him would keep them safe. But with that act of drinking whiskey, he repeated what he knew, as though he took a familiar arrow from his parfleche and placed it in the bow. She hoped he wouldn't pierce her with it, hoped he would fall asleep before he found blame. She'd been so sure he wouldn't risk rye so soon after learning of Lisa's warrant, so soon after Hunt's helping them make their escape. That he wouldn't want to explain the bruising of his *femme's* face.

Her only place of safety on this journey was to disappear. It was hard to know which risked her sons' lives more: staying with their father when he was like that or going away as they had.

She'd thought her husband's anger would settle like leaves after a spring storm. She'd underestimated him. She'd stumbled.

The whiskey formed Pierre into something from a nightmare. Bad dreams filled with dark blows and hatchets arrived to her too, when the hut became too warm or the robes too heavy in her sleep. But the nightmares became real when she ignored the looks in Pierre's slate-gray eyes, when the amber liquid slipped between his lips. She should have taken the drink from him.

"This will not be easy, *femme,*" he'd told her when he stood behind her.

Her heart pounded. Paul coughed; Baptiste pulled at her, asking her a frantic question about what? A turtle or a leaf?

Perhaps she could have cajoled Pierre out of his mood, helped him fall asleep. She'd tried to give him the dried meat, but he grabbed at it, tore off a piece with his teeth, and stared at her. She held her arm up to ward off his abruptness, to keep Paul safe.

Pierre struck at her.

"You did not pay Lisa," she said when she got her breath back.

Pierre bit and chewed the dried meat.

"After all Hunt allows, letting us come, paying you well. After all this, you still do not pay off a debt?" She should have known her words would set him off, challenging him so. But she'd gone on, her mouth heedless to her wisdom, her mind wanting to be right. She'd been nursing Paul, rocking her child against her breast as she spoke. The child fussed, had trouble suckling. He pulled away and crawled to lie beside his older brother pressed against a robe. Both boys sat, still as a raindrop on a flat leaf. She watched Paul suck at his thumb. Did the children always huddle when their father tipped his whiskey? Were they just waiting for the rustle of wind to die down, for the still water to drop? Maybe her angry voice frightened them as much as their father's clenched fists.

"Why should I pay for what is not my debt?" Pierre told her. He wiped the back of his hand across his mouth. "This is not a military mission. We make choices as we see fit, not because some Captain Clark or Lewis tells us so. Hunt hired me for what I know." He jabbed at his chest with his fingers. "Me! And what I know is that Lisa did not deserve the payment." He drank again, stared at her. How could his eyes already be glazed...unless he had been drinking much earlier. "What I know is that you are here only because I let you be here, Ma-ree." He spoke her name. Not as she wished it, not as a mother word with hush and respect, but as though spittle collected at the corner of his mouth. "Ma-ree." He said the name again. He laughed.

We are named by our choices, she thought. Her name was "Coward," keeping quiet.

"Do you still have the money then?" she said at last.

If he did, they could perhaps send someone back with it, to pay Lisa so he would not come after Pierre.

"Perhaps your father spends the money so he *cannot* pay his debt," she said to Baptiste, careful to make her words a quiet comment not a challenge. "Perhaps he buys whiskey with the money."

The whiskey had already joined his anger, so quick she did not see it coming.

"What do you expect?" he said to her. "Pushing me into a corner before the partners, Lisa, bringing out falsehoods against me, against the Astorians as a whole, of which I am one."

"I'm an Astorian too, now," she reminded him. Pierre only stared at her, one eye drooping more than the other. Words had failed him then, and he'd used the palm of his hands, his knuckles, to teach her the lesson she refused to learn. She'd covered herself from the blows at her head.

"I'll take the children, meet Hunt's boats without you," she shouted.

"Ma-ree," he'd snorted.

An owl lifted.

"We'll find protection among Astor's men," she said. He'd struck her again, then stumbled over a tree root. He groaned then fell into a snoring sleep.

Her heart pounding, she lifted Paul, the baby screaming now, and rocked him still. A flush of woodcocks exploding in the underbrush broke the silence. Baptiste sat beside her, patting her shoulder as she rocked her younger son through his fears.

She, who came from a line of warriors who battled bears with their hands, who could outrun deer, had merely covered her head to ward off the blows, grateful Pierre failed to turn on her sons.

She waited in the darkness, shaking from the pain of her poor choices as much as from the cool March night. The moon had failed her too, hiding beneath dark clouds.

Eventually, Pierre's snores filled the night air, and she sneaked back inside the tent. She thought to grab the baby board but wanted no sudden noise to wake Pierre.

"Where will we sleep?" Baptiste whispered behind her.

She'd motioned silence with her hand, then eased the robe out, letting her husband's face lie flat against the ground, drool pooling from his open mouth.

"We go," she whispered. She and Baptiste dragged the heavy robe while Paul rode on her hip. The horse neighed low, pawed at the oak it was tied to. Should she take the horse? No, it belonged to Nuttall or Bradbury. They would need it when they stopped to pick Pierre up. She wanted no cause to claim she had cheated anyone.

A pair of snipes rustled in the underbrush, and Paul grabbed her neck. She felt for her ears. The earrings were missing! A small loss in this night of losses, she thought, as the trio let the escaping moonlight lead them deeper into trees.

Water lapped against the heavy boats, and Pierre could hear the mix of French and English as the *voyageurs* shouted to each other.

Pierre stroked his beard, acted calm.

She had done this just to make him look bad, to trouble Hunt now and make it appear that he, Pierre, could not control his own family. How then would he help control bands of Minatare or Blackfeet, keep both from trading with the British? Did she think the Americans would care if a woman had bruised eyes? The Americans understood the need to settle disputes as a man must. It may not be a military expedition, but men understood the place of discipline behind the tent flap. Did she think they'd bother with the whereabouts of a mere woman? With children? No, this would only bring uncertainty to Hunt, a man already edgy with delays. Pierre would have to reassure.

"Aye, and the dogs'll be enjoying a run, Wilson," Mackenzie shouted to Hunt. The big man made his way to stand beside Hunt, the hounds sniffing and lifting their legs at shrubs and new scents. "Here Blest! Here Blowed!" Mackenzie called as the dogs barked and moved out into the underbrush.

"Don't suppose the hounds can track her?" Hunt said. "Be good for something."

"The lass and laddies can't be far afield."

If his *femme* did not appear now, then no matter. She would live by her own choices. Perhaps she'd already come to her senses and headed back to St. Louis. He'd have to make up some story if they picked them up along the way, signal to her what he'd told them. And if they arrived at Nodaway and she never arrived? The thought hit him like a punch to his stomach.

"The woman does not need dogs tracking her," Pierre told them. "She and the boys decided to go by foot for a time. It will harden her for the journey. The woman didn't want to hold us back. As I told young Toupin there, she'll follow the river. She's a strong woman. No warrant arrived then?"

Hunt didn't answer. Instead, he motioned for a man to leave the *bateau.*

Carriere stood beside Hunt, tightening his red sash at his waist. Sweat beaded on his forehead beneath the band around his head. "See if you can find them," Hunt told the man. "Take the horse."

"*Oui,*" the *voyageur* said. "It is some time since I ride the horse. You can take my place, Dorion." He grinned.

"No, no," Pierre protested to Hunt. His head ached, his mouth still felt thick. Did Hunt intend for his interpreter to press his flesh against the oars? "I'll find deer along the way while I look after them. It is my problem. No need to spare a *voyageur* to pursue a foolish woman."

"Take the horse, Carriere," Hunt repeated. "Dorion. Get in the boat. I want you out of Lisa's reach. We're pushing up the river now."

"The woman is fine. Sturdy and stout," Pierre insisted. "She and the boys will be fine."

He almost believed it.

Marie and her sons spent the day crouching through the blackberry vines and chokecherries, stepping over rocks that dribbled toward the water. Once they hovered in the brush to allow a man on horse to pass them while they hid. At first, Marie thought the rider was her husband. She was surprised at how much the thought pleased her, how disappointed she was to discover it was not him but the kind *voyageur* named Carriere. Had this all begun just the day before?

She hoped Pierre would come to find them, to apologize for his temper. He would kiss her swollen eyes, and she would see forgiveness in his face. She would take what part of it was hers, ask that he forgive her demanding ways, her hanging on to things she should let loose of. It was the way they paddled together, the way it had happened before. Who could expect it to be different?

Still, this journey meant a different way. There were others in their lives now that would be there day to day for some time to come. But it had not been her husband on that horse nor on the horse that came later. Instead, the two scientists talked and stopped and looked at bare branches, made tiny writings on paper they wrapped around the stems. No one called her name. The boys stayed silent as rabbits in the shadow of a hawk.

Carriere hunted perhaps, although Marie had not known many *voyageurs* to train as hunters. Their short bodies were bred for *bateaux,* for the heavy work of paddling or pulling boats upstream if need be, for pushing oars into deep water, for moving men with large girths like Mackenzie to their rightful places at a chief factor's table. Carriere had carried a rifle, she thought. Surely he could not have been sent out looking for them. No. Her husband would have come seeking them; no one else would bother.

Perhaps Hunt had not allowed her husband to follow them, the thought crossed her mind.

The boys had turned at the sound of hounds barking, their musical tones carrying through the heat of the day ahead of them. Baptiste stopped his searching for colored rocks momentarily when he heard the dogs. He'd stretched his limbs, cocked his head at her. She nodded. "Yes, *chien*," she told him. "Blest and Blowed."

"Will we see the dogs tonight?" he asked.

"Soon," she said.

What can I do? We can't walk the five hundred miles to Nodaway, even if the trail winds beside the river that far. Crossing side streams, gathering food will delay us further. What was I thinking?

She carried Paul on her hip, careful to shield his face from the new bud branches. His weight wasn't much. The drag of the buffalo robe proved more tiring. She wiggled her nose at her own scent when they rested. Her arms were weak as wet willows from carrying the robe and Paul, too.

By the time the sun was high above them, they no longer heard the dogs. The horsemen had ridden on past. The trail at least was well worn beside the river, and she and the boys could move faster on foot than those in the four keelboats being poled and dragged. Her eyes would be less swollen in a day, she was sure of this, and then she'd show herself. Before, if she and the boys couldn't snare a rabbit. They'd be fine. She and the boys would be fine.

"I am *faim*," Baptiste told her mixing English and French. He rubbed his slender belly.

"We're all hungry."

It was too early for berries. They might make a slingshot quickly, but they had to keep moving. She handed him a small stone, and he placed it in his mouth. It would keep his mouth moist and perhaps trick his stomach into thinking food flowed into it instead of empty juices. She had a small amount of dried meat left in her pouch. She'd planned to eat it when Paul had finished nursing the night before, just before her husband's temper had found its way to her face. She still had the piece and would break it up between the boys when they stopped to rest that night.

Clear streams from melted snow gave them good drink. Water was more important than food; this she'd learned long years before.

Marie offered comments about the birds they saw, the small animals that startled their path. She noted trees and shrubs new to her and told her sons of them. She fashioned a kind of harness for Paul with the belt she'd worn at her waist and that way carried him more easily on her back. Still, the day wore on.

"I will tell a story of a hungry fox," Marie said when Baptiste mentioned again that his stomach spoke to him with discouraging words. "I can hear your stomach," she said. "We can feed it a story while we walk."

"If it has a bear in it too," he said. "And *le chien.* The dog will bite the bear, yes? That's how the story should end."

Marie smiled. She winced, and she felt her lip with her tongue. It was still puffed up like a bloated fish. She shifted Paul, reaching behind her with both hands to raise him higher on her back, his knees draped over her arms. She felt his drool on her neck.

"We will make the dog wise and the bear slow and the fox—"

"Hungry," Baptiste said. "Make him very hungry. But not so hungry he eats the dog."

She laughed. "I'll remember."

"I like stories," Baptiste said. "But I like food more."

"We will tell many stories on our journey west then," Marie said. "And you may be surprised at how the stories fill you up. Maybe better than the buffalo hump or corn."

Baptiste grunted and she began her tale. It was how they walked their way paralleling the river.

This was what mattered then, this being with her sons, helping them learn and grow. If it meant she must stand taller to face an unpredictable man, step over her own fears to make it clear to him that she would keep her children safe, do whatever it took to protect them, then she would do this. Even if it meant disappearing into the woods for a time. Even if it meant speaking up when she must.

Pierre had never struck the children, at least not yet. He played hard, sometimes. And he only brought his fists to her when whiskey passed his lips and he took her challenge as invitation.

She could control this.

Hunt would control the whiskey once they were underway, and she would control what she did and said that aggravated Pierre. It was the pattern, like the expectation of the seasons. She had walked this way before. She could make new paths.

Tomorrow they would walk closer to the river, and the boats would come upon them. She'd be careful, make sure it was Hunt's party before she revealed herself. And her husband would know they could survive without him. Perhaps he would remember before he struck at her again.

Marie broke the jerky into two pieces, and the boys ate, then slept in a heap, the heavy robe curled around them as she leaned against a tree, her legs straight out before her. She had not eaten, but with new vision and watching them safely sleep, Marie felt as though she had.

Pierre said nothing to her when she walked into Hunt's camp the next evening, though he let himself breathe easier. The *engages* greeted her with head nods and tips to their caps. It surprised him, how relieved he felt when he saw her light buckskin dress over tan leggings appear through the dusk. She still dragged the heavy buffalo robe. A child on one hip, the other clasping her hand. Tired. They looked tired.

He nodded to her as though this was as they'd arranged it. No need to let Hunt think otherwise. When the time was right, he would walk to her, see how she had fared, and lift his sons to his arms.

She kept her eyes down as she moved through the *voyageurs*. She lifted them to that boy Toupin, but only when the Canadian spoke to her. She patted a horse at the neck when she walked by. Did she look out the corner of her eye at him? Yes, he thought she had. Pierre nodded with his chin, directing her, and she turned until her eyes found the tent he'd set up without her. It was within sight of the others. His way of telling her she could sleep safely this night.

A part of Pierre wondered if he should make a ruckus of her arrival and insist she go back to St. Louis now, show that he could make her behave. No, he wanted to stay low to the ground for now, hope Hunt would seek him out as needed for advice. Hunt was a young man, maybe twenty-six or so, though that hawk-nose aged him some. Pierre was only five years older. Hunt might not think Pierre had sufficient skill to manage tribal trades if he couldn't handle his own family. He couldn't be sure what Hunt would think about his *femme*'s wanderings, and Pierre wasn't a man to ask.

The truth was, something she'd said about Charbonneau's woman stuck with him. He'd met Sacagawea before his father returned to Washington with the chiefs, sending Pierre away that year. He hadn't thought she'd contribute much to Clark's Corps of Discovery. She was young, looked unhealthy, as he recalled, not a likely candidate to travel to the Pacific and return. But he'd been more interested in Charbonneau and how the man had managed to survive those years with the Mandans with all the jokes made about him when his back was turned. He'd seen both the woman and Charbonneau in later years in St. Louis. A child walked with them, and another, said to be her sister's, joined them too. Clark had bought them a farm, it was said. Sacagawea didn't look like a farmer's wife. She wore English dresses, as though she hungered after the title of factor's wife, a *bourgeois*'s madam, instead of recognizing who she was: a Snake woman, the wife of an interpreter, who had been taken west and had come back to plant seeds into soil.

But his *femme* had said Sacagawea's presence and that of her son gave comfort to the Blackfeet and Crow and other tribes as Lewis and Clark journeyed west. She was right. It offered comfort to her husband, too, no doubt. Pierre's *femme* warmed his bed as no other had, and while he would not tell her so, he was pleased she'd forced her way along. She could be of good use, just as she'd said.

It was just that he could not let her set the limits, make and break the rules. These Ioway women had a way of getting stronger than they should. He'd known that when he'd taken her as his wife.

It was one thing for a husband and wife to be separate in trade, as he knew his mother and father were, men and women earning separate wealth. This he could live with. It was when a wife challenged her husband's wishes, his rule, that he had to take action. His mother, a Sioux woman, and his father, a Frenchman, had struggled to work such things out. His own mother was often strong-minded, and he had vowed his marriage would not be burdened with a too forceful wife.

He had picked his *femme* with those qualities in mind. She'd been young and, like a growing tree, could be bent and shaped at will. She was just sixteen when he spoke the vows with her before his parents. He had wanted a bone-strong woman with a straight back and arms muscular enough to field press hides. He hoped she'd have a good mind so she could learn to understand his words. Who wanted to spend his old age talking only to a post? She should have skills in handling moose and beaver hides so they would not be scarred and found inferior. He wanted her to know how to stretch the hides into the rings that allowed them to be dried and stacked and later baled. She should know how to make a bullboat, the round boats formed from hides that could carry a single man across a raging river.

And he wanted sons. Powerful sons.

And he wanted a woman who could laugh, though not at him. She might tell a story or two, but better would be if she could watch and listen to the stories he told. Most days, he had found all those things within his *femme*.

It was her other side, the ruffled side, he'd been unprepared to find. She needed to learn, and he knew no other way to teach except to strike, just as his father had. Soon his boys would need such lessons too.

Pierre swallowed as he watched her. She pulled Paul from around on her back and now settled the boy on her hip. The child still had an odd look to him, as though his eyes were squeezed out by his mouth. His ears, almost pointed like a cat's, sat lower than they should have. A single tooth jutted out from his lower gum and pushed against his upper lip making it look as though he'd been bitten by a bee. His mother fed him often from the fruit of her body, but he still looked lean as bone.

Perhaps Holy Rainbow had been right—perhaps the child had not been meant to live. And yet Paul had.

"Hunt found you then," Marie said, interrupting his thought as she approached him. "And Lisa did not."

Pierre nodded. A light rain fell gaining strength as they spoke. Men scattered for cover, mud spitting as their moccasins dug into dirt. He would tell her now that he had requested a surprise for her. It would be his offering of apology, his penance without using words. "When the partners acquire horses," he said, "I have asked for one."

"Because you are too weak to walk?" she asked.

This woman could make him burn so. He rubbed at his knuckles. A hot light seared through him. He tried to do good things for her, he tried. "No, because my hands are sore from the tending of a woman who does not listen to her husband." He held his fist up closer to her face now, as though examining his knuckles, but with the threat clear. Rain washed over the puffiness on her cheeks.

"Then you should seek *Le Fou's* herbs, get Nuttall to give you a glove with a poultice to soothe your hands, not a saddle that will rub you raw in wrong places," she said.

"You, woman…" He stood nose to nose with her.

"Yes, I am," she said.

Only Pierre could hear her low chuckle. It was not a friendly sound, not the laughter that told him they could start anew with his rules in force. His life with this woman would not be so easy as that. No, it was a sound of challenge, a ruffled feather in his face.

He couldn't predict which way his *femme* would go when he set his limits. "Paddle-minded," his mother had called her, moving from one side to the other, depending on the ripples of the river.

It was true. His wife did often move from one side to another, but she always made a distance in a day.

5

Family Matters

"Femme," Pierre whispered in her ear. "Come with me." She hesitated, wary. Her face still wore knuckle prints of blue, tender to the touch. Still, his voice sounded kind, invitational. The cool night brushed her face as his hand reached for hers in the darkness and his fingers tugged at her, gentle, until she stood beside him, outside the tent. A two-point blanket wrapped her shoulders. "Look." He pointed upward, and she gasped.

The sky was washed with the flicker of lights. The northernmost star looked so bright and close she raised her hand as though to touch it. "The Mysterious One sweeps a dark hearth," Marie said, "and leaves silver dust behind."

"You think the One who makes this is a sweeping woman?" Pierre said.

She shrugged her shoulders. The image had come to her from her mother, words carried in a basket of memories she sometimes plucked up without thinking. "My mother said women do the work of cleaning the hearth, keeping the fires burning warm so her family won't wish to go too far from the heat." She pointed to a section of sky where the night like black strands of hair cut through the thickness of silvery strings. "Can't you see where the broom's straw separates the stars?"

Pierre grunted.

A friar's verse came to her then, and she said it aloud in the way she remembered, "What woman having ten pieces of silver, if she lose one, does not light a candle and sweep the house and look till she finds it and then calls her friends saying rejoice, for I have found the piece which I had lost."

Pierre said nothing, pulled her closer, his arms around her as she leaned into his chest, both staring up at the sky.

"Sometimes I long for the gathering when what was lost is found," she said. Her husband still had not spoken. "If it is not a swept hearth, then what is it for you?"

He thought for so long Marie wondered if he had heard her. "My mother would say it is a baptized sky," he finally spoke, "that the stars are dribbles of water where God has dipped his fingers and sprinkled them across the night, christening the earth as his own. As a friar christens us." Pierre cleared his throat. "Women's things," he said.

"The night was like this when your mother named me," Marie said quietly. "You sat with her at the center fire while she wove new sinew through snowshoes. You didn't defend me," Marie said.

"You refused the friar's water, eh? You are Her to Be Baptized."

"She said I made poor choices, that she wondered what kind of mother I might be."

"You are here on a journey of risk," he said. "Should she wonder?"

"Do you?"

He stayed silent a long time again. "Our two children are well," he said. "You have lost neither of them to the woods or water."

"There will be three before we reach the Columbia," she said. She hadn't been sure it was the time to tell him. It was early, but she knew the signs.

"Keep it from Hunt and Mackenzie," he said. "They already have much to worry over."

"With no interest in how far someone moved away from the hearth," she said. Before Pierre could respond, horses nickered low in the rope corral, and Pierre and Marie turned to see what had roused the animals from their sleep. "The boys? Did Baptiste wake up?" Marie asked, stepping away from her husband.

Pierre shook his head, pointed to a slender form patting a horse's neck. "Toupin," Pierre said. "He watches you."

"He feeds the horses," she said.

"Beneath a night sky?"

"Now you worry overmuch," she teased.

"Toupin has aspirations."

Pierre left her standing as he ducked back into their tent.

"He is just a boy," she said as she crawled back under the robe with him, listened to the snores of her sons.

"Don't feed his interests, *femme*. You have no food to spare."

Hunt had the English camp boy, George Gay, cut his hair so there'd be less chance of lice. His hair thinned anyway and itched beneath the felt hat. Maybe it was all the rain, the constant moisture that fed the vermin. He scratched at his head even though George assured him he hadn't found a single nit. Just thinking about them made him itch. In the sliver of mirror he hung on the tree, he caught his reflection. Hairline just to the collar. Perfect.

At least they were making gains, his thoughts returned to the journey. That evening, they should reach the village of Cote sans Dessein. Beyond this place, Dorion said, there'd be no evidence of a village populated with any white people—except for the wintering camp at Nodaway, of course. This village, then the Osage camp and finally Nodaway. He'd begin wearing leggings and leathers then.

Dorion had proved to be reliable, except for that stint with his wife missing. He still thought the man had lied about what had happened. Or else the woman was as willful and stubborn as Jonah, avoiding for days the directives of God. Pierre Dorion probably had the market on stubborn, however. Hunt still marveled at the man's foolhardiness to refuse to pay Lisa, even after he was told to. At least they'd outwitted that one! McClellan, one of the Nodaway partners, would be relieved to hear that when they met up. Still, Hunt had to admire the man just a bit: He'd found a way to warm his bed at night and keep his advance.

The *engagés* beached the *bateaux*, built a fire, and fed the party in less than an hour. Hunt marveled at their pace. They were anxious to visit the little village, a last touch of civilization. "See what you can find out about the warring factions," Hunt told Dorion. He needed to know what river rumors preceded them even this far out.

Manuel Lisa pushed the supplier, Moorhead, as hard as he dared. He'd called in all his favors and threatened to withhold others if he didn't get needed loans and the blankets and knives they'd purchase.

And it had worked. Even his father-in-law had invested.

"I wish you didn't feel the need to go," Loette Lisa told him, her hand sharply on his chest.

"It is my work, Señora Lisa."

She coughed, covered her mouth. His wife was sickly, always had been. More, now that she carried a child. Maybe this child would live.

"Listen to me," he said, dark eyes flashing. "I'll return, richer than even you can imagine."

"But not sooner than I'd wish," she said, her brown eyes tearing.

He patted her hand, dismissing her. "I've work to do. I'll be back late."

He left to pursue the taverns of St. Louis, seeking desperate men strong enough to take a twenty-ton loaded barge upriver yet able to be inspired to catch and counter Hunt. He needed twenty-five such men. At least for him, the race could not get started soon enough.

Dorion had taken his wife and sons to the huts at Cote sans Dessein where he said he had some old friends. The man did seem to know someone no matter where they went. But when he returned, he didn't have good news for Hunt.

"Bands of Ioways, Sauks, Sioux, and Potawatomis camp nearby."

"Your wife is an Ioway, correct? Would she know any of them?"

"Those Ioways are as thick as gnats together, so she likely does. But one of their chiefs pushes for more English goods, so if there's trouble they'll go with the French-Canadians," Dorion told him. "Softened by the British goods. That bunch has no interest in the American trade."

"So we've nothing to worry over then." Sometimes it seemed to Hunt that Dorion made mountains out of beaver mounds or else he just wanted Hunt to stumble, to make his own abilities have more weight with Hunt.

"They could raid us here, just because we have goods. That would shift the balance farther upriver," Dorion told him. Was Dorion...lecturing him? Hunt wondered if he spoke to Mackenzie that way or if the Scotsman would already know these intricacies. No matter. He was a quick learner, and Dorion obviously felt like instructing.

Dorion continued, "We don't want the Ioways or Sioux or the others to have any extra goods when they start arguing with the Osage. If they appear too tough, because they have some of our goods, they'll pester the Osage, like a fat dog waving a meaty bone in front of a hungry pup. By the time we roll by, the Osage'll be more than annoyed. They'll be looking for a tussle and might find it in our little expedition, blaming us for the Ioways and Sauks looking too good. And we'll have even fewer goods to help the Osage change their minds."

Hunt scratched at his head. "Any skirmish here will mean poor trade and make us ripe for raiding later on too. Is that right?" Hunt asked.

Dorion nodded. "It's all about a grand entry, Mister Hunt."

"You mean when the Indians ride into the forts all dressed up, shouting and singing and what not?"

Dorion nodded. "It's not just in what's done but how it looks."

"Even way out here," Hunt said. "Indeed. I see no waxed walls of government or commerce beneath these willows, but I feel the politics just the same. Well. I suggest we post extra guards so we don't lose even a blue bead. Is that what you'd suggest, Dorion?"

Dorion grinned. "Indeed," he said. Hunt nodded in approval.

"Maybe I know some of the Ioways," Marie offered. If they were from a band she knew, she might be of assistance to her husband, like Sacagawea was to hers.

"You stay out of these things. Hunt will forgive the ruckus you caused earlier," Pierre said, "with your wandering off, if you listen to your husband now."

"I could help," she said.

"Extra guards help."

"The *voyageurs* don't like to carry guns. They prefer paddles and pushing hard over water, to escape."

"Worried over your little Toupin?" he said.

"He is not my little Toupin. None of the French-Canadians want to be on land. The hunters, the partners, they can defend better than the *engages*."

"You think I don't know this, eh?"

Marie shrugged. "If we moved faster, the tribes would know we are not here to trade with their enemies. When we make only a few miles each day, it causes a wonder."

"Stay where you belong, *femme*," he said. "These are not mother things." Pierre stretched his arms behind his neck. "Hunt's pleased he spent extra to have me along." He scratched at his back. "See if I'm lousy, will you?" Marie moved his hair at the neck while he sat. She looked.

"Insect bites," she said. "Not lice."

Pierre grunted. "Hope Hunt packed plenty of tobacco leaves for steeping. We're all bound to get lousy before this trip is over. Unless the louts drown before we do, with all this rain."

"If we had a nanny goat, I could make the itching stop," she told him.

"Nanny plum soup, eh?" Pierre grinned at her, scratched again. "Those on the *Tonquin* ship will have nanny manure for making soup to put on their lice. The ship's crew is to resupply at the Sandwich Islands and pick up goats and pigs and whatever else for the post at the Columbia. We'll have fresh pork and goat then. Before winter." He reached over and tickled Paul's belly, and the child laughed. "Before your brother even arrives. Then your mother will have no time to meddle into men's trades."

Baptiste's arms hung around his father's neck; Pierre stood and pulled the child now, tossing him upside down, then holding him by his ankles and swinging him, his head barely above the earth floor. The boy seemed to like the rough play. Baptiste actually laughed. "Again," he said.

Pierre plopped him down. The boy whined.

"Are you all right, Baptiste?" Marie said. "Go now. To your mat. Sleep." Baptiste whined again, and Pierre reached his hand as though to strike him.

"No, Pierre," she said, pushing his hand down. "This is my work."

He brushed her aside. "He fools you, *femme*," Pierre said as she placed herself between her husband and Baptiste.

As Marie folded her son to her, Baptiste smirked. The feeling left her lacking.

Toupin rubbed the horses down with a piece of soft hide. At least *Le Fou* brought things along to tend to the animals. He'd heard Mackenzie say the expedition would be acquiring many more horses farther upriver. He'd thought this was a river journey, with only a short hike over the Shining Mountains before they carved out canoes and finished the journey in *bateaux*.

Now the partners talked about horses. A lot of horses. Not that Toupin didn't like the animals. He found that he did. But no one was interested in cooling even the few they had now after a day's ride nor in finding good grazing for them near campsites. Few of the *voyageurs* seemed to know what a horse needed. The five animals they had with them took up a good share of grass. It was probably wise that the hunters, a Virginian named John Day and even Pierre Dorion once or twice, stayed out overnight sometimes, ranging farther along the river to bring in deer meat to supplement the dried foodstuffs they carried in the *bateaux*.

Truth was, when Dorion hunted, Toupin felt extra importance. He'd made it his personal mission to look after Madame Dorion. Not so anyone would notice. He certainly didn't want *her* to notice. Taking care of things, from a distance, was what a gentlemen did.

The Dorion boys liked his company as far as he could tell. Little Paul didn't say much, just gurgled and wore a big silly grin most of the time. He guessed he was just a happy baby. Baptiste would sometimes watch while Jean rubbed a horse down or scampered to bring more firewood if Toupin was the cook's help that day. And his being with the boys seemed to comfort the woman.

She sure didn't get any comfort from that husband of hers, getting her up in the night to stand in the cold and look at stars. Toupin noticed that since her overnight foray that one time, she now stayed a little farther behind her husband when they walked somewhere, as though he pulled her like a boat. And she had had a bluish tint to her cheeks when she'd returned. He didn't trust that man, at least when it came to how he dealt with a woman.

Ici, even when Dorion did have a horse to use for hunting, he might have let the woman ride. She might have liked the break from sitting on the water.

Or maybe, like Toupin, she preferred the boats.

At least Hunt had cared enough to send someone out to look for her. That surprised Toupin. Most partners of an expedition didn't even notice the Indian women or their children, let alone care enough about what happened to them to send a search party out. He'd never known a Hudson's Bay man or a North Wester to do something like that. Too expensive. Took up too much time, they would've said.

Hunt didn't seem bothered by time.

They spent much longer at nooning than he would have were he in charge. And he noticed that Madame Dorion always had time to slip to a *confidentiel* place near the river, returning with her hair damp and a fresh glow to her skin. Every day, before they left.

Still, Hunt was a good man. He'd ordered extra guards, too, and while Toupin didn't like carrying a fusil, it gave him reason to keep his eyes on the Dorion tent.

As though she read his mind, Madame Dorion approached now, carrying something that the setting sun glinted against. He was aware of her closeness, could smell the scent of herbs in her hair.

"In your household, did your mother or your father use the scissors?" she asked. She held a pair out. "I managed to get a sewing kit from the village," she said. "They're old, but they cut well enough."

Toupin stood up, reached up under the horse's neck to pat beneath the animal's mane. "Ah, my mother," he said as his voice cracked. He dropped his eyes. Something about looking at her made his throat scratchy as coarse wool. "I cut my younger brothers' hair myself before I left for Montreal."

"It makes it easier to manage the lice, I find. Especially if there isn't tobacco juice to rinse the hair with."

"And no goats for their spicy soup," he offered, then laughed. She laughed too, a sound like the tiny bells the altar boys rang at high mass.

"If you want me to cut yours, I will," she offered.

"*Ici!* You think I'm lousy?" he said, standing up straight. He ran his finger through the loose, curly hair bringing the dark strands over his shoulder to peer at the ends.

"I didn't mean…it's just that you have no mother here…I should have…*pardon*," she said, dropping her eyes.

"I don't…" he cleared his throat. He blushed now, he was sure of it, and so bent to rub the horse's leg, lift up its hoof as though to remove a stone. "*Merci.* For the offer," he said. "But they haven't struck me yet. And the longer the locks, the easier to shake the mosquitoes away…when that time comes."

"If you change your mind..." she said, then walked away. Toupin rubbed harder at the horse's hoof, aware that blood rushed to his head. Probably because he leaned over the horse's hoof, he told himself.

He'd met a few other Ioways as far north as Fort William on Lake Superior. Good people, though they could be a warring bunch, too. The men said that Ioway women were honored for their honesty, mothering, generosity, and courage. Madame Dorion wore all those qualities. He scratched vigorously at his neck. He wouldn't be able to sit still if she were to cut his hair. Still, like his mother, she probably wouldn't like knowing that he'd lied about the lice.

Marie worried over it for several days before she found Hunt mixing powder and ink so he could write. Gathering her courage, she spoke with a combination of French and English, asking if he had a moment for her. She carried Paul on her hip.

"Indeed," Hunt said, setting his writing lap desk down. "Will your husband be joining us?" He laid the quill pen beside thin paper.

She shook her head. "He's posted at guard," she said.

"Ah, yes, that's right. What can I do for you, then?" He reached out to tickle Paul's chin, and the toddler reached for Hunt's glasses. Hunt jerked back. "Curious, little thing, isn't he?"

"All children are," she said.

Hunt looked at her then. She cleared her throat, looked at her fingers, cold and white as bone. "When my husband has...whiskey, his mind does not do as it otherwise would. He—"

"The rations are controlled, and will be, throughout the expedition. You've no need to worry. At least not from Dorion's whiskey consumption."

Marie lowered her eyes, not wanting to challenge. "He...sometimes finds supplies. Of his own. He—"

"Knows everyone. Indeed." Hunt picked up the quill pen, tapped it. "But as we continue, even your husband will be in country where no one knows his name. Being a Dorion will not help him then. He'll be forced to be more…civilized in the wilderness. Learn to live without the spirits." Hunt reached for a lace-edged handkerchief from the inside of his sleeve, dabbed at the back of his neck. "Indeed. Until then, I will watch the rationing closely," Hunt said. "And you, you just try to please your husband and look after your sons."

For her part, she would keep to her husband's wishes, not be trouble to him, learn to stuff her words inside her mouth. She would be like the bird-and-plant men, Nuttall and Bradbury, and fill in what she did not know by using her eyes, her nose, the feel of the wind at her face, and what she remembered, not by bothering Pierre. She could not write things down as they did, but she could store the images in her mind.

She walked back past the horse rope corral. Young Toupin tossed rocks into puddles with Baptiste. Please her husband, Hunt had told her. Pierre had, in his way, promised her a horse. It was a way of apology for his hurting her, and she had sniffed at him. One must never discount an apology gift, she could hear her mother-in-law's words. Saying "I'm sorry" was never as important as the giving of a gift.

When and if Hunt went overland, a horse would be a valued gift. She had been too quick to turn away. With her sons she noticed that what she praised, they did more of. She would try that with her husband now, pay attention more when he offered kindness instead of jabbing him because he did not give it her way.

She waited for her husband to come in from his watch. He untied his moccasin, squeezed rainwater from the leather.

"You will be a big help to Hunt," she told Pierre.

Pierre lifted his eyes to her, his lips parting in a smile. His beard glistened with tiny raindrops, like stars thrust against a dark sky.

"You think so?"

She smiled back. She would make it so he would not miss the whiskey.

Oh, the sweet, sweet stillness of a morning! Marie's heart spoke the words as her moccasins moved silently over the path dampened with dew. A breath of light, pale as a butterfly's wing, gave glow to moss-lined trees; a woodpecker thudded out its words of warning to intruders. She squatted beside a willow. Even acts within a *confidentiel* place brought peace beneath dew-softened leaves. She watched while squirrels stilled then stared, alerted before speeding along a tree fall. Some unknown place called them, and they answered, their tails of fur a tender brush to paint the air before they disappeared. A bug whined against her ear. She shook her head, missed the copper tinkling of her earrings. She would try to trade for a pair, though what a baby needed would be of greater importance.

She should hurry back, not leave Pierre tending the boys for long.

The air smelled of spring earth and well it should. They'd had steady rain for days now, making the work of this expedition greater than any had imagined. Rain soaked the moccasins so her feet felt squishy and cold. Water seeped around their ankles as they huddled in the keelboats. At the last evening meal when the rain had finally stopped, the bread still smelled like moldy earth. Wilson Hunt had ordered it thrown out. Marie wondered if someday they might all be hungry enough to remember they'd thrown food away.

She did no cooking on this journey. As in the fur posts, men were designated to prepare the twice-daily meals. Toupin, Carriere, and several other Canadians tended to that task. But here, the mixed-bloods, the *metis*—her family—ate with the others. Marie helped as she could, grinding corn, washing up. But the babies occupied her. She'd spoken with John Reed, the clerk who managed the supplies, and had gotten sinew to repair tears in Baptiste's moccasins, had added to her sewing kit, putting the costs on Pierre's account.

She gathered moss and dried it in the smoky fires so she could use it on Paul's bottom. Soon he'd learn to tend to this himself. He had to, with another infant on its way.

She looked out at the swollen river. A log, set free by the higher spring water, bobbed by in the main channel. The *engagés* would have their work today, easing boats past log piles clustered like discarded kindling, or rowing and pushing with long poles against the current, around sand bars that split the stream like spears. They were already so late in the season yet Hunt seemed unrushed.

She geared herself for the trials of the day. At least it was now impossible for Lisa to catch up with them. He would have had to outfit canoes and drag the same swollen river that had kept them at a snail's pace.

They reached Fort Osage on April 8, the flag flying from the blockhouse instead of the long pole just inside the palisade. Marie had heard Pierre call the fort by Clark's name and also as the Fiery Prairie Fort, the image of distant flames vivid in her mind. "We trade among the Osage. This is where the greatest wealth is. Greatest risk, too," Pierre told her as they left the keelboats to walk through the high wooden gates of the fort. Marie carried a leather parfleche. Paul burrowed in a willow board on her back.

Several from the wintering party met them there and ten additional *voyageurs*.

"They just got tired of waiting on you," Crooks said to Hunt. Marie thought the New Jersey man bristled.

"We've had our share of delays," Hunt told him.

"Well, good news. The Osage at least aren't interested in giving us any trouble," Crooks told him.

"No. They're eyeing the Ioways and Sauks," Hunt said. "Dorion here's alerted us. It will suit us to get what we need quickly and move on, before trouble starts between these tribes."

Men moved about the fort with knives at their belts. Trappers leaned on flintlock fusils exchanging news with what they thought was a spring brigade, the first trading group up from St. Louis bringing goods. Marie suspected they hoped Hunt's party brought in fresh supplies in return for pelts being aired and pressed that would be taken back East. They'd be disappointed with Hunt's explanation that they were headed west to find water trade routes all the way to the Pacific and that what they carried with them was meant to help them win the tribes' loyalties to Americans over the British, not to refurbish the free trappers' meager supplies or reward Osage men for bringing pelts to trade.

Marie would avoid them, the Osage. Her people had always tried to avoid the Osages, so full of power and weaving alliances like strands of sturdy rope. They looked down on Ioways, mere growers of corn. They never saw the Ioway as warriors or worthy.

Her eyes scanned the natives at the fort. She wondered if she'd see any of the Ioways camped nearby, recognize a distant cousin if she did. It would be pleasant for Baptiste to meet a relative, but so many close relatives had died with the pox that year, the year Pierre had found her still living in their hut, she wondered if any remained. Baptiste fast-walked beside his father who took long strides in front of her and Paul.

She had trouble catching her breath. Any Ioways here would be only remnants of relations, if she saw any at all. A last image of her mother, leaving, telling her to stay and take care of her sister, came to her, and she halted, felt dizzy for a moment, then shook her head of it.

"Are you all right, Madame Dorion?" Jean Toupin asked her. The boy was a firefly at times, appearing from the air, at her arm. He bent over beside her.

"Just remembering," she told him. She looked over at him and smiled.

"Are you coming, *femme?* Or do you look after one of your pups?" Pierre glared. She squared her shoulders, shook her head no, and hurried away from Toupin. She caught up with Pierre who quickly involved himself in conversations with trappers, Hunt and Crooks, and Mackenzie, too, asking questions, their eyes moving toward fingers pointed west. Someone scratched lines in the dirt. Hunt called to Toupin who raced past them, back to the canoes, returning with a roll of parchment Marie suspected was a map.

She turned her attention to the fort's women and children and trappers' horses and the dogs, lots of dogs.

It would be good to talk with another woman, Marie thought. Perhaps she could make a trade for some hazelnuts or dried nettles, things she'd need to stay healthy with new life forming within.

They were the country wives of *metis* men or free trappers, not affiliated with either British or Canadian or American. They went wherever beaver lived and sold to the highest bidder, with no pressure to choose a side if war should come. And there was talk of war, even here.

Still Marie found connections with the mothers and wives. It was like unwinding a loose string back from a blanket of many threads to discover where they'd been dyed, who else belonged to the weaving.

"My auntie, Waits for Him, was once married to Aird at Prairie du Chien," a round-faced woman named Winter Blanket told Marie. "You know this man?"

Marie nodded. "But not your auntie. He had no wife when I knew him."

"Ah. Before her then. Or maybe he sets her off," Winter Blanket said, her dark eyes growing wide. Winter Blanket carried surprise not judgment in those eyes. For Marie, if Aird had set his wife off, her regard for the old man who had visited them at St. Louis would have moved to a lower place. Winter Blanket worked beside a woman shaped like a ball of dough. They both gummed the seams of a birch bark canoe with their sticks. The second woman said nothing, just kept to her work. "We are sister wives," Winter Blanket said. "Chipewyan. We return soon to the far north." The younger of the two wore her hair in braids that looped at each shoulder and disappeared back into hair the color of night. "Maybe we will travel with your party," she said to Marie.

Marie set Paul against a tree trunk where he could look out from his board. She gestured to Winter Blanket, offered to press the gum at the seam on the side where she stood, while wondering what it would be like to share her husband with another. Would that be better than being set off? Is that why some women chose to stay when a younger, stronger woman was brought to a husband's bed?

"Where do you go next?" Winter Blanket persisted.

"To the Pacific."

The older of the two women looked up. "Like the Shoshone slave did?" she asked.

Marie nodded.

"You are a slave then?"

"No, I chose to go. With my two sons and my husband."

The younger woman nodded. "He would set you off otherwise."

"No! I chose to go, for my children."

"However you see the sunrise," Winter Blanket told her, shrugging.

Marie watched to see whether Baptiste had found a playmate in the fort's children. She pressed her fingers at her back, easing the ache there. She scanned. No Baptiste. Where was her son?

Almost before she thought the words she heard the snarls and barks. Squinting into the distance, she heard the wail, then bounded toward the knot of skinny-tailed dogs tearing at a carcass, her son screaming in their midst. The dogs scattered at her shouts, leaving Baptiste, sitting.

She grabbed her son, yanking the deer bone from his hand, tossed it to the dogs. Blood poured from his nose, his forehead. She pulled at the gurrah cloth at her bodice and pressed the cloth against his face, the light material turning red. Winter Blanket puffed beside her, shouted at the dogs, then pointed toward the post. "Water," she said. "Then we find Doctor Murray."

"The way is difficult," First Wife told her later when tiny stitches marred the boy's face. He looked so fragile, his bushy eyebrow now sliced by a dog's jagged tooth. Still in his board, Paul stared at his brother. Baptiste's trouble had captured him in seconds. Marie would have taken him out, but she worried what trouble her younger son might find. "I take care of my sons," Marie said. She held Baptiste in her arms. He slept now, the fort doctor's medicine still working to ease his pain. Tiny black threads pulled swollen skin over the ridge of his nose.

"Hard to do alone," the older woman said. "They scurry, these children. You go alone there, no other trappers' wives, no grandmothers. No one has gone first to make a way." She looked to the west where the sun set. "Few have crossed there. I know no stories of a short portage across the mountains to the big river. I think these men create such stories. No women have gone that way."

"Except the Shoshone slave," Marie reminded.

"She did not try to take two young ones with her. She knew the dangers of the trail."

Marie's heart thudded in her chest. She said nothing, looked away.

Pierre heard the screaming and singing as he came out of a dark sleep. He felt for Marie. She wasn't beside him. He didn't think the scream came from a woman. No, it was a man's whooping. He listened again. Now women trilled with loss and victory songs. There must have been a raid. Those Osage. Hunt hadn't moved out fast enough.

Where was his wife? He looked around. The boys slept, but she wasn't there.

They'd been at Fiery Prairie Fort long enough to resupply. The fiasco with the dogs and Baptiste was blown bigger than needed. Hunt had remained another day, "resting *engages*," he said. The expedition should have already headed out. He listened to the high-pitched singing while he crawled out from the robe, slipped on a shirt over his britches, tied his leggings on.

The moon shone through slivers of clouds, but he could see light from a large fire that appeared just outside the walls. Men with muskets stood staring. Crooks and Hunt were dressed along with several others, watching through the open gates, long pistols at their sides, ready to help close the heavy doors at any threatening movement, from the looks of their stance. Pierre approached, listened to the intonations, the songs and cries, the drumming sequence. He shook his head, still groggy from the ration of rye.

"Just about to rouse you, Dorion," Hunt said. "What do you make of it?"

"Scalp dance," Pierre said. "There's been a battle. Osage've had success, eh?"

"Guess that's better than having 'em mad because they lost," the hunter John Day said.

"They've had casualties," Pierre said. "Their women cry."

"Exactly," Hunt said. "That should keep them from worrying over us when we head out in the morning." Hunt hesitated, asked Pierre, "What is a scalp dance exactly?"

"An honoring dance for those who survived and returned; and a grieving dance for those they lost. They'll make trades—the wages of this war in exchange for an earlier loss. Give a scalp to a grieving widow or mother, to vent her weeping on."

Hunt seemed satisfied, and Pierre used the pause to look around, to see if he could find his *femme* in the shadows. Surely she hadn't joined the dance. She'd spent too much time distracted by other women. She did best when she just looked after him, kept her eyes on their sons.

He was tall enough that he could see over the heads of several standing around the dance circle. No Marie. She wouldn't be here. She hated the Osage. No, she must have gone to a *confidentiel* place. He'd go back. Nothing to worry over. She was probably already under the birch bark strips that formed their tent, checking on Baptiste and nursing Paul to sleep. She'd just gotten up in the night. He'd crossed her path. He hoped so. He didn't need another challenge to his rules.

He headed back, his eyes searching the darkness to see if the drums had roused that nosy *engagé*, Toupin. He couldn't find him either.

Marie rocked, her arms around herself as she listened to the drums. She'd been foolish, selfish. She could not keep her sons safe, could not bear a child along that trail. Not without another woman, not alone. Why had she thought she could? Even with women close by, a dog had bitten Baptiste. What chance did she have to raise her boys, to keep them living all across the mountains? She remembered Holy Rainbow's words questioning her mothering. "Anyone who will not choose the friars' water, how will you give your sons the strength they need?" her mother-in-law had said. She blinked back tears.

But the woman had been good to her, had taken her in as a young girl, orphaned, alone. She hadn't made her a slave but a daughter, one of her own.

And Marie had disappointed, refused the friars' water.

"I will pray for you," Holy Rainbow told her. "Remember. Wherever you are, God is there. He does not leave you alone."

It was just as she'd thought. God tracked her down, brought punishment for her willful ways that put her children at risk.

She and her sons would have to remain, stay here at this outpost until Pierre returned. She could gum boats for her keep, sew things. A doctor stayed here. Pierre would have to understand. She knew now he'd been right all along. She'd tell him that. She had pushed her way into a man's world. She didn't belong.

"You think I care that the Astor's men hear you?" Pierre shouted to her. "Go! Now! Get into the boat. Get your sons and prepare to leave." A wet fog draped over the morning, kept the fires close to the ground so she coughed out as she cried. Pierre kicked at her, his foot piercing her side.

She caught her breath. He'd forgotten about the baby! He would never hurt the baby! "I can't, my *époux,* I can't go." She was on her knees now, pleading with him, her hands at his belt, her fingers white as bone. "*Les garçons…* You were right. I can't keep them safe. You'll be better without me. I should have listened."

"Now you listen to me?" He stormed around her, pushed her back, his fingers pressing into her shoulders as he leaned over her, the sweat of his rage heavier than the rain. "You defy me? Get into the boat!"

She sobbed without stopping, aware that her eyes burned and her nose hurt from the crying. Pierre jerked her, holding both shoulders and shaking her until her neck ached. She could hear Paul crying and Baptiste screaming, "*Non, Papa. Non!*" The child pulled at the fringe on his father's shirt.

"Mama, Mama, Mama!" Paul kept repeating the only word he knew.

Pierre swung at Baptiste, but the boy was too quick and skirted behind him. Then Pierre swatted Paul's face and the child's fear turned to rage.

"No no," Marie cried, reaching for her son in his board. She couldn't stop crying, even to comfort them, even though her tears seemed to frighten them more. Protect them; she had to protect them, from what they were seeing, from their father's anger. Her fault. It was always her fault.

Her eyes scanned them, these men. Heavy greased canvas slicked over their shoulders and the loaded keelboats to repel the rain falling. They made no move to help. Those *engagés* ready to pull with the towropes already at their shoulders wiped rain from their eyes, stood curious, almost. *Voyageurs* wandered from the storehouse, picking up last-minute handkerchiefs and tomahawks. She was aware that Crooks scowled, rain running off the brim of his everyday beaver hat. Hunters and marksmen stood slack-jawed, but unmoving. Bradbury, the scientist, even Nuttall, *Le Fou,* just stared. Astorians all, who only stood and watched.

Even Murray the doctor had taken refuge inside the blockhouse, but Marie imagined him staring out through the open doorway, watching a mere woman sink into mud.

In the distance Marie saw Winter Blanket huddled behind the older Chipewyan woman, fingers at her mouth.

She lived a nightmare, only this time she could not wake up by the mere force of her will.

From the side, Hunt approached. She felt a brief flutter of hope. The expedition leader cleared his throat. "We need to be underway, Dorion. Do what you must, but hurry along."

She felt Pierre's hands on her then, Paul's board torn from her arms. He lifted her, tossed her into the *bateau*. Her knees scraped against the side. She thought she heard Jean Toupin shout from the blockhouse, hoped she hadn't. Pierre would take his interest wrongly, would be fueled by false jealousy. The cries of her sons as Pierre dropped them onto her took her attention, Paul's board thumping into her arm. Baptiste whimpered beside her. She brought both sons inside the swell of her arms. She did not look up. She shook.

"You are my wife," Pierre hissed. He leaned into her, his face so close she could see the wide pores in his skin as the rainwater washed over him, the gray slate of his eyes narrowed like a wolf's. "You are an Astorian, responsible for the success of this journey as much as anyone. Remember that. You rolled your children into the hands of harm; you roll all of us. Remember this. Being here was what you wanted."

Hunt gave the order, and the first keelboat set out. Pierre rode in the one behind hers. Marie shivered as the boat eased its way into the heavy current, the smell of flotsam and dirty stream breaking through her stuffy nose. The downpour matched her spirits.

Pierre was right. It was what she'd asked for by pushing her way along with her children in tow. *Astorians.* It was a name she wished she hadn't chosen. It meant family now. Whether she liked it or not.

6

Spring Currents

At the Nodaway camp, Marie added a fold of new-dyed linen she put into her parfleche, something she would save for when her time came. It was good to organize, to plan ahead for a child.

She and Pierre spoke little since his "outrage at the Osage," which is how she'd come to think of it. He busied himself with talking to men, finding out from trappers coming down from Rupert's land north what news they had of tribes and the supply of beaver. Their group had grown to sixty-eight Astorians and more partners with Scot names. The men encouraged themselves in the evening camps with the talk of what awaited them, paid no attention to a woman huddled with her sons, considering her choices.

Marie's lip healed well with a piece of salt pork applied to it gingerly each morning. The tiny stitches from Baptiste's face she'd taken out with the old scissors and her fingertips. *Le Fou* Nuttall had given her some herbs she'd steeped, then placed like a poultice to ease the swelling. "Good for, ah, bruising, too," Nuttall told her, his eyes dropping.

Yes, he'd stood by and watched too. It was her shame she must cover though. She hadn't kept her son safe from the dogs or her husband. Baptiste had huddled, fear on his face, watching his father hurt his mother. Her selfish demands brought them all here, exposed her sons to that.

She'd press Pierre for nothing, she resolved yet again. She would tend to her sons, keep them together, keep them alive, answer only when spoken to by her husband. Offer no thoughts. That was what she must do. That was what any good mother would do.

"Extra guards? Here? Why, lad? Aren't we miles from the Sioux yet?" Mackenzie said.

They'd moved upriver, left the bustle of Nodaway behind. For Hunt, it felt as though the expedition with all its many men was now complete and finally begun. Mackenzie threw sticks to his dogs that they groveled over, then returned. Donald never seemed to give Hunt his full attention, always spoke standing sideways, his focus on the dogs.

Hunt spoke distinctly, made sure his voice sounded strong, firm. "Dorion says he sees signs of Sioux." Hunt motioned to the riverbanks high on either side.

Mackenzie snorted, threw another stick. The dogs howled their high-pitched sound as they ran.

"I find the man does have some sense, Donald. He hasn't steered us wrong so far."

"No, only brought the Spaniard to tail us and his wife and sons to drag us."

"That's been tended to, his wife's been…no trouble. And surely Lisa's been discouraged, or he'd have caught us by now."

"I wouldn't be believing that as fact, laddie. At least not yet. Lisa's ruthless. Suggest we poll the partners, see if posting guards or pushing on farther is the better course."

Hunt clapped his hands once. "It's not open for discussion. We'll stay the night here, post extra guards, as Dorion says." Hunt walked away, his new buckskins chafing at his thighs.

Dorion showed them how to make piles of sticks and branches in a circle around the camp. Portions of gun powder were set in each pile.

"They'll come in under cover of darkness. Tell the *engages* not to get trigger happy," Dorion told him. "Nor your partners either, eh?"

"Is this one of your…drama things, Dorion?" Hunt asked. "The costuming is as important as the performance itself?"

"You'll see," Dorion told him.

It was a moonless night. In the distance, Hunt thought he saw movement. Dorion signaled him to silence. Now Hunt was sure of it, Sioux warriors moving near the riverbanks, their horses silent as falling snow. His heart pounded in his ears. He wondered if Mackenzie and the others felt the edge of fear mingled with excitement.

Suddenly Hunt felt more than heard the explosion of sound, of horses and hooves, men screaming and shouting, of high-pitched trilling. Dorion must have fired the first shot, right into the damp bundles, bursting them into flame. In the flashing light, he could see men with tomahawks, waving them wildly as they bent to slash at empty tents.

Hunt's hands were so sweaty he missed his target on his first shot. Then the fusil discharged, setting a second then third and fourth pile of branches into flame. Horses reared. Indians slipped off, twisting and turning until the Sioux mingled in a circle held together by the fusils pointed at them by nervous *engages*. One or two warriors had run away and were now well on their way to spread the news.

They'd taken prisoners! Indeed. Hunt couldn't tell who looked more startled to be standing where they were: the French-Canadian boatmen or these Sioux.

"I say we kill them," Mackenzie said coming to Hunt and Dorion. Other partners approached, slapped each other on the back.

"Really, Donald. And what would that gain us?"

"It would be telling the larger tribes we're not to be trifled with. Teach them a lesson. You can't coddle them like children, Hunt. Some of us have experience with the way these…people think. Force. Strong force. That's what they listen to."

"Dorion?" Hunt turned to his interpreter for his advice.

"Let them go but first tell them we're just moving through, eh?" Dorion said. "Tell them that next year and the year after, we Americans'll return. *Americans*," he emphasized the word, "from the Pacific Fur Company, will come with many valuable goods. We'll pay top price for their pelts and hides. We're not here to fight or arm their enemies. They can trust Americans." He turned to Hunt. "Always say Americans." He looked over at Mackenzie, then back to Hunt. "Next year, we'll trade for their pelts, if they'll trap for the Americans; and we'll bring their women vermilion and blue beads and treasures they've never known. Offer to smoke with them, Hunt, and pull the smoke with your hands in toward your throat. That's how they know you speak the truth."

"Make trading partners out of them that would kill us?" Mackenzie said. He pulled at his red beard, shook his head. "Sounds like what a half-breed would suggest."

Hunt squeezed his hands together, paced. He was still getting used to the moccasins he'd begun wearing at Nodaway. He clapped his hands in decision. "It's what Mister Astor wishes us to do, Donald. To negotiate trade routes. Treat people with respect and they'll return it. It's the Golden Rule, Donald. Even way out here."

He may be a novice, but the mark of a good leader was knowing who to take advice from, and when. Dorion had done well. Hunt would put his trust in him.

Marie had heard the speeches before. She made sure the children behaved during the pipe smoking, the talk-talking. The warriors would sometimes find her eyes, and she knew they were of a tribe who listened to a woman's counsel. Perhaps they wondered why she didn't sit beside the men. What did her presence say to them? She wouldn't admit it, but she felt a certain pride watching her husband seated beside Hunt, passing the pipe and using his words and wisdom to make their way west. She'd never seen him look more fit, as though a moccasin had formed itself perfectly to a foot. He was a handsome man, leaner now than when they'd begun their journey, his facial features sharply defined in the firelight, as if cut with English scissors. Once he looked over at her, lifted his chin in recognition. A wave of warmth moved through her.

The men finished their smoking, and with some ceremony Hunt's men returned their tomahawks to them. They ate together then, and when finished the warriors mounted their horses and rode out. Mackenzie wore a half-smile the whole time.

A week later, one of the warriors returned, riding hard into their camp. His eyes searched, stopped at Pierre. It was one of the men they'd set free. Pierre listened, spoke. Marie could understand much of the Sioux herself, and she caught her breath, pulled her boys closer to her.

Pierre turned to Hunt, though the other partners had all gathered around. "The man says the Teton Sioux plan to steal our boats near the Ponca Village on the Niobrara River," Pierre told them. "They'll blockade the river and allow no one to go north without paying a price of trade goods. They could easily clean us out, Hunt. End this expedition. Or they'll try to kill us."

"So, Wilson," Mackenzie said. "What does all your experience tell you to do now?"

Hunt looked at Pierre but answered for himself. "I say we determine how to place the boats so the best marksmen are spread out. We reload the boats. Heaviest cargo in the last canoes. Have the hunters shoot some charges into the shoreline. Make a show of force."

Pierre nodded. "Let them know we won't be buffaloed, eh?"

"Exactly," Hunt said.

Marie smiled, patted Baptiste's shoulder, brought Paul from her hip to help him stand. At least Hunt could see her husband's value and was not afraid to note it before the other men.

"Who's that?" Baptiste said, pointing to a rider appearing on a frothed horse.

They all turned, Marie included, as the new rider dismounted, gasped his breath and waved what looked like parchment. He wore *voyageurs* clothing, but the fusil he carried said he could handle trouble even riding alone. "Wilson Hunt?" the rider said.

"Indeed," Hunt answered, stepping forward. "That's me."

"I've a letter," he said, still gasping. "From Manuel Lisa."

Marie bent to pick up Paul who'd fallen, felt her heart thump in her chest.

Mackenzie and McClellan, Joseph Miller and Hunt, Crooks, even Bradbury hovered over the letter. When Pierre approached, Marie watched Hunt turn his back. *So they won't allow Pierre to even read it?* The partners all moved then toward the boats. The Sioux who'd warned them of the Teton attack rode off with a wave to Pierre, who paced.

She could hear the partners' loud shouts, with the name of Lisa spit out most often by McClellan, and supported by the gruff voice of Crooks. Finally Hunt came forward.

"Lisa is but a day or two behind," Hunt said. "I…would have you join us, but where Lisa is concerned, you aren't always…rational, Dorion." He patted Pierre's arm and walked back to where the others were still talking, their words wrestling on top of each other.

"How can that be?" Marie asked after Hunt left.

"Silence, *femme*." He stood, hands on his hips. "That Spaniard…" Pierre said, his arms crossed over his chest. "He must have driven his *voyageurs* to near death to be so close behind."

"Maybe he brings trade goods, is just part of the spring brigade."

Pierre snorted. "What do you know, woman? We have been on the river two months. He's outfitted his barge, hired men, and forced them upriver. He is this close." Pierre held his fingers an inch apart, in front of Marie's face. "He is within a day, maybe two behind us."

"He'll catch you," she said. "What will he do?" Her eyes pooled with tears.

Pierre gazed downriver. "We must figure how to use him."

His words struck her like a stone. It was always about using people, making tools of words and men to get what they wished. She was no better.

"Shouldn't you be in there speaking with the partners? You have knowledge of Lisa. Surely this is about your not paying—"

"They don't include me because I am not their color," he said. He spit. "Mackenzie only wants European blood making these choices."

Mackenzie's dog Blowed, the smaller of the two Porcelaines, sniffed and sneezed in the brush. Marie called to it but it acted deaf. Young Toupin whistled with no success either. Marie turned her back to her husband. She bounced Paul in front of her, holding both of his hands up over his head while his little knees bent then straightened, like an overused coil.

Eventually, Hunt returned and signaled to Lisa's rider who had drunk from a jar and wiped the water from his dark beard. He chewed on jerky now.

Mackenzie signaled his dogs with his hands, and they trotted to him. He scratched at Blowed's neck.

"Tell Mr. Lisa that we will do as he asks," Hunt said. "Tell him we'll wait here for him, right at this spot. You'll recognize it? Lisa's quite right. There is strength in numbers as we go through the Teton Sioux. Tell him there's to be a blockade, and we'll need all our efforts together to break through it. We are, of course, quite amazed that he has come so far so quickly. His *engages* must be near death with the effort. We had no idea he was in…pursuit. No, not pursuit. As his letter says, he seeks a cooperative effort and to find his missing employee." He looked at the letter, slapped it in his palm. He glanced at Pierre. "He seeks his employee named Henry, he says, who left last spring and never came back."

"You don't trust that, do you, Hunt? The man's not—" Dorion said.

Hunt clapped his white hands to quiet Pierre. "It was good of Señor Lisa to advise us, to warn us, as he has. We'll be a stronger force together. We'll await his arrival. You say he's one, two days back?" Hunt asked the question as though wondering about the weather.

"Maybe less," Lisa's man said.

"Good, good," Hunt told him. "We'll be waiting. You best head back now. Can we give you some whiskey? Perhaps some fresh venison before you go?" The man shook his head. "No? Well, please put Señor Lisa at ease. We'll be here waiting."

As soon as the emissary rode out of sight, Hunt shouted to the *engages,* "Break camp quickly, as though your mother's on her way and she's just discovered your darkest secret."

Hunt shouted orders. The dogs bounded into boats. Tents were struck and rolled into loose bundles.

"I thought we were waiting," Marie told Pierre as her husband threw things into the cloth bags, ordered her to roll the birch up, as he folded items into parfleches. *Engages* carried barrels on their shoulders, their red belts blowing in the breeze. The dogs barked their musical tones as they waited for Mackenzie, front feet on the edge of the boat. Marie adjusted the baby board with Paul in it onto her back. She hurried Baptiste into the boat. Within minutes, they were into the flow of the river.

Hunt had lied. He'd excluded her husband from an important discussion and he'd lied.

"Pierre, shouldn't—" Marie began.

"Ask no questions, *femme,*" Pierre said.

"But Hunt has lied."

"He does what he must."

Hunt gave directions as though telling people where to sit at his holiday table. He felt relaxed, calm. As long as there was always a choice, he could find any crisis intriguing, something new to discover and write about later. The *engages* had responded to his orders, pulled the boat with the swivel gun and two small howitzer guns into the Missouri. The men had moved with remarkable speed, seemingly pleased to be told what to do. There was something to be said for simply following orders. Lewis and Clark must have known that and thus formed their military expedition.

They'd make good time, pull up as they neared the Tetons, and he'd get Dorion to approach so they could talk. Mackenzie might not share Hunt's confidence in Dorion, but in matters of these Indians, Pierre was their best bet. Now when it came to the Spaniard, well, Donald could be right about keeping Dorion more than a pistol-shot distance away. Mackenzie had even suggested they leave Dorion to wait for Lisa, see if the Spaniard was really coming just for him.

"And then how would we make it through the Teton Sioux, Donald? Tell me that?" Hunt had said.

"If Lisa gets within gunshot of Dorion, we may have to find that out anyway," Donald had answered.

Hunt felt the wind on his face, then heard shouts. He looked up. Could they be near the Tetons already? He heard the thunder of hooves, then noticed McClellan and Crooks waving at three grizzled riders that looked more like bears than men racing toward them on horseback.

Hunt signaled for the boats to be beached again. The wintering partners were already shoulder-slapping the riders as Hunt approached. The riders shouted, as though unaccustomed to speaking in normal tones close to people. They smelled of bear grease and dirt.

"Robinson, Hoback, and Reznor," Dorion told him.

"You know these men?"

"We may be tugging at the ropes to be on our way, but these three've been living in the country we're heading to for the past three years. They know the routes. They could be a gift from God," Pierre said.

The three started immediately to give them directions. "Go north first, get yourself some horses from the Arikaras, if you can," Robinson said. "Then go overland. One mountain, not a whole string like the Shining Mountains, not even all that big a ridge and you hit a branch of the Columbia River. Just like that. A little overland hop and you'll hit rivers."

"That easily?" Hunt asked. "You've been there?"

"Just follow the Wind River. Don't have to take that northern route the way Lewis and Clark did. Avoid the warring tribes, those Blackfeet for sure. But you got to get the Arikaras to trade you horses. You need lots of horses."

"Two per man," Hunt said.

"Three each," Robinson said. "They'll tire and you got lots of goods." The grizzled man scanned the boats.

"Those Arikaras'll make it hard on ya," Reznor said. "They save their horses for trade with the Cheyenne so's they can get food." He lacked front teeth, and when he grinned, Hunt could nearly see inside the man's throat.

"Clark did say he thought there was a better route south, below the Yellow Stone River," McClellan said, excitement in his cultured voice.

"There be," Jacob Reznor said. "We just come from the Wind River country. Be glad to take you back—"

"Indeed!"

"If we wasn't heading home. Tired of the mountains, we are."

"Unfortunate," Hunt said. "We could use your wisdom, gentlemen. And your marksmanship, if needed."

"Sure and you can't wait another year before heading back to St. Louis?" Mackenzie said, coming up from behind. He scratched at Blest's ears, the dog moaning softly in appreciation. "Haven't missed much in St. Louis. Bathtubs and all. Still made of tin. This is where there's action. In the wilds, laddies."

Hoback nodded. He wore a colorful scarf across one side of his head, a jagged red scar peered out from it near his eye. He had a habit of pulling it down to cover the scar, to no avail. "Almost scalped once," he said when he noticed Baptiste's stare, then dropped his eyes rather than look at the boy.

Hunt tried to sort the many voices converging as the rivers did, one on top of the other before blending into one stream. If he could get these men to turn around with them, they'd have both experienced hunters and guides who knew the trails. If Lisa caught up with them, these skilled shooters could help hold him off until they made their way through the Sioux. *A shorter way. Overland. On horseback.* Historians would write of this adventure, yes they would!

"We're moving out, gentlemen," Hunt said. "So perhaps you'll ride with us upriver and share a meal at least. Hopefully, not a last one." He laughed.

"We might be obliged to share your victuals," Robinson said. "I see you got a fiddle there. Ain't heard much music for a time."

"Nope. We're aheading home," Hoback said. "Can't wait to sleep on a feather bed again." He readjusted his dirty red scarf. "Besides, I don't want to meet up with no Sioux tomahawk."

Hunt grimaced. "Seems a crime Mr. Astor's dream of an overland shortcut will be left wanting for the love of a feather bed."

Toupin's eyes scanned the riverbanks. All this rush and whispering bothered him. The Sioux attack, though no one had died, still gave him a cold sweat just to remember it. Hunt had changed with the addition of the other partners. Small shifts, the way a pup grows as you watch until one day it's a growling mass of wolf. There seemed no single, steady Astorian now, no calm in this river of white rapids. With all the partners holding varying views, wild-looking men with scarred heads saying go here and there, Lisa sending emissaries that Hunt lied to, how would they decide the important things like whether to try a new channel, which route to choose? Which of those men they met really knew the way of a mountain or whether a ridge path was a tribal trading trail or just took someone to a fishing place? He and George had even talked about returning to St. Louis after the attack. But he'd given his word, and besides, if he didn't keep his eye out for Madame Dorion, he didn't know who would.

Hunt's party traveled five days farther upriver, each mile filled with scanning of riverbanks, the *voyageurs* jumping at the splash of a beaver's tail, the rush of wood ducks scattering at the river's edge. Near the mouth of the Niobrara River, Pierre finally found a time to talk with Hunt alone. He told Marie and the boys to stay out of the boats but where they could be seen from the high riverbanks.

"We stop here," Pierre said. Sand bars and islands marked the Missouri like finger swipes of green in the midst of dusky blue. High ridges on either side made the way narrow. Hawks flew from the bluff tops, dipping and lifting in the air currents. "Makes a man wonder if the birds are not alone watching us," Pierre said.

"You've seen Teton signs?" Hunt asked.

Before Pierre could answer, several braves began shouting at them from the bluff tops.

"Are we under attack, Dorion?"

"What I've been trying to tell you. Bring them in," he told Hunt. "See if they're friends or not."

"What makes you think they won't shoot first?" Hunt asked.

"It isn't their way," Pierre told them.

Pierre signaled and the six Sioux men rode into the Astorians' camp. Pierre translated to the partners, then made his way to Marie as though to fill her in, but also to be sure the Tetons saw her and his sons there with them.

"There are nearly three hundred lodges waiting for us," he told Marie. "Yanktons, Brules, and Miniconjous. The Tetons want no one to trade with the Arikaras or the Mandans. Not us for horses, not Lisa for his geegaws and rifles."

"You told them about Lisa?" Marie asked.

"They want to handle getting the pumpkins and corn from the Rees to the Sioux themselves. I tried to let Hunt know that the Tetons are like middlemen—they charge a tax for helping bring food from one place to the other. I don't know if the partners really understand it. Sometimes I think that they think the tribes are like beavers, easily trapped because they have so few ways. Our being here meddles in the Tetons' way, especially if they think we're bringing food to trade. It's not just about American or British goods with them; it's about messing up their trading partnerships."

"What will Hunt do?" Marie asked. She wiped Paul's bottom with leaves as they spoke beside the *bateau*. Baptiste had found his way to Jean Toupin, and both moved close to Mackenzie's dogs.

Pierre wrinkled his nose.

"Something the child ate troubles his bowels," Marie said. "I've no way to stop it. No goat's milk to scald or blackberries to steep into a tea. If he does not improve, I will ask Hunt for brandy. Or you could make a trade with the Tetons for something for a child's stomach. They'd know for sure then that we are not a warring party."

"Hunt's going to try to parley with the main group of Tetons, when we reach the blockade. Maybe scare them a bit with the howitzers." Marie raised her eyebrows. "Only powder, no shot. Not unlike what we did with the piles of branches." Pierre tossed small pebbles toward an imaginary target at the side of the wooden boat.

"Hunt's going to tell all the Tetons that he's looking for his brothers at the Great Salt Lake and he's crying to see them. Been a whole year, he's going to tell them, since he's seen his brothers, and he'll kill anyone who tries to prevent his reuniting with his family. He says I need to make it sound real mournful, his not seeing his kin. Like I did this parley group. And for you to be where the Tetons can see you."

"You lied to them?" she said.

"Saved our scalps," Pierre told her.

"The *engage* Toupin says an interpreter must never lie. It will cut away his strength the way a river carves a bank in spring, leaving nothing to stand on later."

"Your little Toupin knows nothing about negotiations. He's a boy who only steers where another tells him. You want to hear what we'll be doing by someone responsible to make it happen or listen to a boy's mourning?" She bit her tongue to keep quiet, nodded. "Hunt will offer them tobacco and corn and see if they'll be appeased, as he puts it. They'll see you, the boys, and think, *oui,* these people come for a gathering of family not to trade or harm. 'Course we got to get the chance to talk, or all the storytelling will fall on dead ears. Ours."

"Honesty is a good boat to carry one over troubled waters," Marie said as she lifted Paul to her hip and walked to where Baptiste played with the dogs and Toupin.

Pierre felt his face grow hot, his jaws clench. The woman could aggravate him beyond all reason. Like a blast of heat from a fire, he'd explode as she picked at him, pushed, jabbed. He never meant to strike her. The whiskey made him weak at times. Sometimes, even when they wrestled in jest, he'd sense a burning on his skin, firing through him if she threatened to best him with the strength of her arms and her legs. His father always said such women needed breaking even if they were strong as bone. But some of them—like his mother—grew stronger in the mending.

Several hundred braves rode along the river on the opposite bank. Hunt ordered the boats pulled in and the howitzer shot toward a gathering now of nearly six hundred armed braves. Powder only. Noise only. No lead. It was a gamble.

The explosion frightened Paul and he screamed, pulling on his ears. What must the warriors have thought of the noise? When the smoke and the milling about of the warriors cleared, Pierre saw the Indians waving buffalo robes as a sign of halt, a sign of talk. He pointed the signal out to Hunt.

Hunt clapped his hands. "Well done, Dorion," he said. "Well done."

The partners met then, deciding whether to shoot lead at the warriors they'd just frightened or let them talk.

"They signaled to talk," Pierre told them, for the first time worried that if they failed to listen to him, they might all die. "Hunt?"

"McClellan, Crooks, Dorion, and I will cross the river. If anything happens to us, you give the word to fire, Donald. I've no doubt you'll be able to do it. Dorion, make sure your wife is where she can be seen."

Donald tipped his fingers to his beaver hat and nodded while the others stepped into one of the canoes, *engages* poling them across the water.

Marie could see her husband in the Tetons' circle after they smoked the tobacco. They were a handsome people, these Tetons. As tall as her husband, most of them. Well fed though lean. Their horses were well tended too.

Pierre's hands and arms moved like a dancer's as he talked with them. She wondered what he struggled more with: the words of the Tetons or Hunt's lies he had to tell. She wished she could have been there. The work of those left behind was to wait and do what they were told. She hated waiting, sometimes hated doing what she was told.

Mackenzie let the dogs scamper, making it look like an outing. Toupin squatted near the water's edge. He turned every now and then to nod at Marie who stood, arms at her side, watching while her children played, within sight of the Sioux.

Marie wondered if her husband felt the agitation of the *engages* who sat with pistols and rifles across their knees instead of towlines and oars. They'd give their lives on a difficult portage, carry heavy boats over boulders and rocks. But their fingers fumbled with a fusil at their shoulders, sometimes with even a knife or an ax. They were good men, these Canadians, who would return from this journey not with the wealth of Hunt or Lisa but only meager wages—if they hadn't added too much to their account—and with stories to tie their experiences together into some kind of meaning.

"When's Papa coming back?" Baptiste asked.

"When he has done what he can to save our meager hides," an *engage,* Antoine Clappine, told the boy. The man had a barrel chest and chewed his lower lip each time before he spoke. He and Carriere both sported red-and-green striped sashes at their waists, as though one color was not enough.

"The partners need your papa," Jean Toupin said.

It seemed hours and perhaps was. Pierre and the partners returned unharmed, and Hunt ordered the party to make camp.

"If they're gone in the morning," Pierre told Marie, "we'll know they bought the lie."

They spent a sleepless night with double guards. In the morning the river mist rose to empty banks. Pierre told her quietly, "We told them there's a boat behind us with goods. Assured them this new trader is whom they'll have to bargain with to stay out of their way." Pierre grinned. "We suggested they hit him fast and hard. That should keep Lisa occupied for a time." Hunt had the *engages* set off tobacco and bags of corn onto the shore as payment for their safety, and they eased the boats up the river. "I don't see anyone there to pick it up," Marie said.

"They're there, all right," Pierre told her. "If we hadn't left the corn, they'd be riding down hard on us right now."

"If they strike Lisa, will we hear it?" Marie said.

"Depends on if that man's discovered that we didn't wait for him yet and whether his *engages* are still willing to kill themselves to catch us."

"Not that way. Can't you see how the water darkens?" It was Mackenzie arguing with Hunt about the split in the river, which channel they should take to get closer to the Arikaras. Hunt won out but, within hours, they realized they'd gone the wrong way and had to turn back to take the other channel.

"Just gave Lisa some catch-up time," Pierre complained.

"Maybe Mackenzie does it on purpose," Marie said. "Tells Hunt to go one way assuming he will disagree and go another."

"How would you know this, a woman?"

"They don't agree to things," Marie said. A part of her wondered if Mackenzie would lie as Hunt had ordered her husband to. Perhaps honesty didn't carry the weight for a Scot, a New Jersian, as it did for an Ioway woman.

"Women stumble over rocks no one else ever sees," Pierre said.

"But we see snakes when you think what's lying on the path is only a stick. No one gets bitten by a stick."

"Señor Lisa, please. The men need to rest. Some of them will die without it. We've pushed so hard so quickly. I'm ready to collapse myself," Henry Brackenridge tried to reason with the Spanish trader. "And the woman, she's very tired and she's not well."

"We've come this far this fast by my standards, my knowledge, my driving," Lisa said. "You think I don't know it's a nearly impossible feat? It does not matter, my friend. All that matters is that we reach Hunt's party together, before they encounter the Tetons and the Arikaras. Hunt does not know it, but he needs us. If he relies too heavily on his interpreter, he'll be sorry. Dorion is no genius. He's a drunk. Hunt needs us."

"But you're bent on Hunt's destruction. Even I can see that."

Lisa laughed, clicked his boots at the heels, and bowed at the waist. "Ah, you have the imagination of your novelist father," he said. "No, no, no. No destruction. The West is large enough for us all. I merely hope to find my employee Mr. Henry, deliver Mr. Clark's cargo to the Mandans, and then come home."

"With twenty thousand dollars' worth of trade goods in your hold and howitzers for what, their flotation qualities?"

Lisa smiled. "Rumors of investments are often like dramas others create," he told his guest. "Manuel Lisa is merely on a journey to find a friend. That is all. With a woman along to assure the Tetons that we're making a friendly journey."

Brackenridge looked up and past him. "You best put her where she can be seen then," he said. "Because I'd say those were several hundred Sioux come to call." He tilted his head toward the ridges dotted now with an army of horses.

Five days later, in early June, Hunt reached the Arikara village. He and the partners would have to come to some decision here, not one that could be turned back so easily as going up the wrong arm of a stream. He'd felt like a fool pushing to go up the narrower channel, but the water was muddied and he assumed that meant other streams fed it. Well, Donald had been right about it.

But here, in this lush land with horses tearing at grass, here they must decide, once and for all, whether to risk a different trail than Clark's, whether to go overland with horses—if the Arikaras would trade for horses—or continue on by boat, hoping to trade later as Clark did, for Shoshone or Snake horses. He had already decided: If he could secure the horses here, they'd take their chances with the overland route, break away from the shadow of the Corps of Discovery.

The air felt warm as he walked from the boat to the camp of rounded huts and tents. He rather liked how his feet felt now, no bunion rubbed by hard leather but by soft moccasins that gave comfort. Wildflowers dotted the riverbank; the Dorion boy picked some for his mother. He guessed all children did such things. He envied the child's pleasure in play. "Train up a child in the way he should go: and when he is old, he will not depart from it." Hunt thought of his mother's lessons in Proverbs. The lies did bother him. But he had so many counting on him, and it had seemed the best way.

Dorion said they were late already. They still had Lisa breathing down their necks. And here stood another people with sharp eyes, skilled negotiators. Astor had been right in telling them not to underestimate the Indian people: They were no dried leaves easily blown out of the way. He would pray for guidance, hope Providence would forgive his…lapse.

Dorion made the connection. The Arikaras acted friendly, which surprised Hunt. They accepted the powder, shot, and knives offered. They didn't even look too upset when Hunt had Dorion repeatedly tell them, "No guns."

"Tomorrow," Dorion told him as they left the day's parley, "we can go for the horses or move out on the river."

"I have asked for guidance," Hunt said. "We go for horses. We need no fewer than three hundred. Get your rest tonight. You'll need to be sharp—"

"Monsieur Hunt, Monsieur Hunt!" It was young Toupin, running toward him.

"What is it, boy?"

Toupin pointed to a barge breaking the water, caught his breath. "Lisa! Señor," Toupin gulped, his voice cracking, "Lisa has caught up!"

"Don't talk with Lisa; don't let him meet with the Arikaras before we get the horse thing settled," Pierre warned the partners.

"Move upriver," Crooks said. "Tell the Arikaras we need to move upriver to talk better. Lisa will say anything to get what he wants."

All of them will, Marie thought. *All of these men will say whatever comes to them to get what they want.* Perhaps it was the way of men. Her too, letting herself be "seen" as a tool to trick the Tetons. And hadn't she lied to Angelique way back in St. Louis, just so the woman would not know how her rumor that Pierre intended to leave her behind for another wife had hurt her? But perhaps lying to set off pain was not so great an error as lies to make a gain.

For the next four days Lisa's *voyageurs* moved the barge up one side of the river and Hunt's team poled their craft up the other side, talking with the Arikaras in the evenings. Lisa camped far enough away that Marie couldn't see how many men he had with him. Then one night at dusk, Lisa's emissary—the one who had brought the message earlier to Hunt—approached the Astorian side of the shore. Marie watched the man pole across the water. This time when the *voyageur* left the boat, he did not head for Hunt's tent. He made straight for theirs.

Lisa had a "present" for him, the *engage* told Pierre, but he must come to Lisa's barge to get it. "Join him for a smoke on his side of the river. He has whiskey he says he will give you, between friends. Bury the bad bones of the past."

"Don't go," Marie said.

"I need no advice from you, *femme*," Pierre said. He chewed at the side of his nails. "This is a man's affair."

"Why risk? Hunt will explode if he finds out. He tries to arrest—"

"He can't enforce it here. No, I find out what he's up to; that's why I go. Gather information. It's my duty."

Marie mended moccasins, pulled the sinew tighter than intended. The leather puckered tight at the toes.

"Maybe he offers me five hundred dollars, eh?" Pierre said. Marie looked up at him. He picked at his teeth with his knife, wiped the blade on his leggings, dropped it back into its shaft on his belt.

"For what?" she said. "If he only comes here to find his employee—as he tells Hunt—he'll return to St. Louis soon. Besides, he needs no interpreter. He's gotten this far without one."

"You know nothing," Pierre told her. "Lisa has a sign-talker with him." Marie raised her eyebrows. "Old Toussaint Charbonneau, who went with Lewis and Clark, he rides in his boat, eh?" Marie put her fingers to her mouth. "*Oui.* The emissary brings a feast of news. And his little slave woman is with them too. You are not the only woman going overland. Lisa brings the Shoshone slave, Sacagawea."

7

Savage and Sweet

"Are your eyes getting so old you missed seeing the woman?" Pierre asked. "Charbonneau could not talk for Lisa with the Tetons. They had to use signs." Pierre smiled.

"Who tells you this?" Marie said.

Pierre nodded with his chin. "He does. The messenger. He comes over quiet, before this. He tells me much."

Lisa's party had made brief contact with the Astorians earlier in the day. Marie had seen *Le Fou* Nuttall and Bradbury greet a man they called "Henry" and, for a moment, she thought he was Lisa's lost employee. But later the name "Brackenridge" was spoken in tones that meant "old friend." Bradbury and Brackenridge walked upriver, scratching on paper, talking. So far, theirs was the only contact she'd noticed—until the emissary arrived to gather her Pierre.

She wondered what the Arikaras thought of this, two parties easing up either side of the river, both with a woman with them!

"Charbonneau is old," Pierre continued. "He does not speak as I do. Maybe I come back and Hunt has to pay me more, *n'est ce-pas?* More earrings, *femme?* I could buy you more." He fingered the outer rim of her ear. "When did you stop wearing them?" She jerked her head away.

"Why do you risk what is known for what's uncertain?"

"You think like a woman," he said. He pushed at the air as though to silence her. He untangled his crossed legs and stood. "I go. Enough is said."

"So, we meet again at last," Manuel Lisa said. He reached his wide hand out in greeting to Pierre. Pierre stepped out of the *bateau* and onto the deck of the twenty-ton barge Lisa had badgered his *engages* into towing upriver. Pierre acted as though he needed to balance, didn't take Lisa's hand. The Spanish man wasn't as tall as Pierre, and he was softer. The leather thongs of his shirt pulled at his rounded belly. "Listen. You will take a whiskey with me then, like old times." Lisa smiled, showing straight, white ferret teeth in his dark face.

Pierre nodded. He would stop after one small sip, so he could listen to what Lisa failed to say as much as what he did. Pierre followed Lisa into the cabin, noticing the brass blunderbusses pointed out the windows. He accepted the mug Lisa handed him, tipped it up. The liquid slid down his throat, as familiar and comforting as an old song. He took another.

His eyes scanned the barge cabin. They were alone. All Lisa's party camped on shore. He didn't see either Charbonneau or his *femme.* Maybe the emissary lied? Clearly only this *bourgeois* slept on board.

"And your gift?" Pierre said. "Your emissary says you have a gift for me."

"Always, you go to the heart of it, *mi amigo,*" Lisa said. "Even after all these years we ride together you do not wait for the…amenities."

"I took a risk coming here," Pierre told him. Lisa refilled his mug. *I won't drink it; just let Lisa think I will.*

"Why, my good company," Lisa said. "Isn't that a gift?" He wore a single ring on his pinky finger, with a blue stone inside. It flashed in the oil lamplight. "My good company…and your choice of my trade goods. Something for your señora."

"Do you have much left after the Teton trades?" Pierre smiled.

"That was clever of you. It was your idea, yes? Hunt would not know to suggest it."

"You told them you came to find Henry, n'est ce-pas?" Pierre took a drink from the mug. The whiskey calmed a heartbeat he hadn't realized still raced. "You don't carry much in trade to choose from, eh? As far as I could see looking at your barrels and packs. That must have helped convince the Tetons you wouldn't undercut their bank."

Lisa smiled, set his mug down on a small table covered with a white cloth. "Come with me," Lisa said, turning, then when he noticed Pierre setting his glass down, "No, no. Take your drink with you. Let me refill."

Lisa refilled Pierre's mug and led him outside on the deck. Pierre's eyes adjusted to the night as he followed Lisa to an area in the center of the barge cabin. Lisa lifted a door in the floor. Pierre half expected to see another swivel gun pointed at him, to match the one he'd seen at the bow. Instead, he saw crates of goods, hidden from any prying eyes, unopened. Enough to stock a storehouse, enough to trade with a dozen tribes with room to bring back thousands in pelts.

"Rifles, powder, steel traps, beads, tobacco, bags of corn, and even dried pumpkins." Lisa laughed. "If the wise-eyed Tetons had seen those they'd have had our hides for sure."

"You got through with all this?" Pierre said.

It was a stunning, cunning coup. Lisa did indeed intend to compete with Astor, to be the first to get to the tribes along the Columbia. He had many more goods than Hunt. If he wanted horses, Hunt would lose and the Missouri Fur Company of Lewis and Clark would be their traders for all time. Pierre took another drink. His hand shook. It was obvious Lisa had no intention of turning back when he found Henry. If he even looked for the man at all.

"I told them we sought a lost employee, that we're friendly. It's why we have a woman with us. You tell them the same, sí?"

The man wanted someone to know of his daring, Pierre thought.

He wanted Hunt to be told of this scheme to bring goods on a barge past the Tetons and all the rest. He needed Pierre not to interpret, but to let Hunt know what Lisa'd accomplished, how clever he truly was.

"So. You see, I will be here setting trade while you and the Astorians wander your way to the ocean. Maybe you arrive there. Maybe not." Lisa grabbed the helve of an ax, hit a crate with the blade to open it. The splinter of the wood broke the night silence. "But I will already be trading fine American goods with the Mandans and the Shoshones and even Crow and Blackfeet as I go west to the river tribes. Your Hunt dribbles little trinkets with promises that ships will send better goods up the Columbia. The next year maybe. When you come again, you discover I have already made the contacts needed to undo you. I broke into trade in St. Louis; I can do it here. The tribes will already be happy with what Manuel Lisa brings them. They will never look toward the Columbia for their goods."

Maybe he did intend to stop at the Shining Mountains. Pierre couldn't be sure.

Lisa opened another bottle, put his arm around Pierre's shoulder, and poured. "Why not stay with me, Dorion? You know these tribes. Why waste your time with men like Hunt, who will likely die before he sees the Pacific? It is already so late to start out…"

"You have Charbonneau."

Lisa shrugged. "He takes his wife back to her people. Clark pays for their journey. Clark always was one to go with her wishes. Not like you. You can send your woman back with Hoback. You saw those three mountain men camped out there?" He pointed into the darkness. Pierre heard horses stomp. "They join Lisa." He drifted his fingers over the lace of his shirt. "Me, they come upriver with, when Hunt could not even make them think twice about staying." He squeezed Pierre's shoulder. "They know the overland route. They tell me. Details. Hoback goes back and can take your wife. Now." He released his grip. "They bog you down here. There will be other women, Dorion. You know this. More docile ones." He laughed. "Oh. Your wife does not tell you? I keep it a secret too then." He laughed. "Take her a gift, that wife of yours. She likes earrings, *sí?*" He swept his hand across the crate.

Pierre's mug never emptied. He'd had only one, maybe two swallows. He looked toward the box. How would Lisa know his *femme* liked earrings? He felt his ears grow hot. "I go now," Pierre said. He reached as though to take a fine-bladed stiletto from the opened box.

"Yes, yes. From little St. Louis," Lisa said. "Your woman will recognize it. Misses her homeland, I suspect."

"Or she knows it will defend her against the likes of you," Pierre said.

Quick as a mink, Lisa slammed the lid down. Pierre jerked back his hand. "Then you will simply have to pay for what you already owe to me before I permit more quality goods to leave in your hands."

"Your warrant will do no good here," Pierre said, rubbing his fingertips. "No one will enforce it." He took another drink to soothe the pain.

"There is more than one kind of law, Dorion." Lisa no longer smiled. "You owe me $200. You will pay the currency, or you will work the debt as my interpreter on my expedition. Justice will not be stopped, even this far from St. Louis. "

Pierre swung toward the man who stumbled back, laughing. The space felt close, small. Pierre heard his heart pound as he moved away from the barge hold. He leaped onto the deck. The night air cleared his head only briefly, but the water that splashed up on him as he hit the river startled him. He heard dogs bark, headed for the flickering lights on the far bank. The image of a black snake slithered through his thoughts. He must stay as far away from Lisa as he could. This lesson was the gift that Lisa gave him.

Marie busied herself settling the tent trying not to worry over what Lisa might rile Pierre into doing. Did Lisa offer liquor? Her mind replayed her conversation with Pierre, made herself consider something else. So another woman rode these waters. She'd like to talk with her, ask her about these expedition men, white men, full of themselves yet using those of mixed blood to make their way. Maybe ask why Sacagawea had gone on with them all the way to the ocean, taken her son. Why had she kept going after she'd found her own people, her brother among the Shoshone?

Maybe Sacagawea saw herself as part of something larger than just her own family, her husband and son. Marie swallowed. Was that a reason she had risked *her* sons to come, to be a part of something grand? What was grand about a baby's cries or her son's now scarred face? What kind of mother was she?

"Papa comes back soon?" Baptiste asked.

"I don't know," Marie said, her voice harsher than intended. His lower lip slipped out, and she could see his eyes pool. "We must be patient," she told her son, her voice gentling. "Go to sleep now." Instead he scanned the space until his eyes found the soft alder he'd picked up in the woods. He sat cross-legged, pulled a British clasp knife from his sheath, pushed the catch on the tang so the blade would stay open and began to scrape at the stick.

Paul woke then. She hadn't bound him in a board to sleep, hoping he would rest better without it. He whined, crawled toward his brother. "Baptiste," she said. Her older son refused to look at her. "Be careful. Your brother is close, he reaches. His hand—"

Baptiste pushed the child aside.

"No, Baptiste! He's your brother," Marie scolded.

Paul wailed then, and Marie lifted him, patted his back in comfort. "You must not hurt your brother, Baptiste. He counts on you. Sh-sh, now." She bounced the boy on her hip, her hand at the back of his head. He smelled of smoke and pitch. He pulled at her bodice as she held him. *"Non!"* She told him. "You are a big boy now!" She held his fingers, kissed the knuckles that seemed always to be cupped up like knees, never straight. Paul pursed his mouth as though to spit at her but didn't. Instead, his attention went to her ears and he smiled. So quickly he became distracted. He pulled on them gently, then at her hair until it came out of its knot at her neck. He ran his fingers through the long strands, his eyes almost crossing as he pulled the hair toward his face. His small fingers bent as he combed, over and over. The movement soothed him until he fell asleep.

Boys fought with each other. This happened in a family. But Paul was so small and Baptiste so large, the older might hurt the younger without knowing. Baptiste needed to be more responsible, especially with another baby on its way.

She calculated. She expected a child in January. Yet she had a husband who flirted with danger at this moment. Her eyes watered. If only Pierre had let her stay at the Osage camp. It was too difficult, this journey, too many uncertainties. It would only get more difficult as her baby grew within her.

When the Ioways had a baby, they rested nearly a full moon, giving time for a baby to know its mother. No traveling for nearly four weeks. She felt the warm June night. Even if the three mountain men were right, Hunt could never reach the Pacific before snow. She stroked her son's face, listened to the bullfrogs croaking in the night. She heard a splash, some shouts at the river. She moved to the tent opening, stepped out. A shadow crossed the moonlight. Her husband, drenched, soon pushed past her.

"The man is doing what I said he would," he told her, peeling wet clothes from his body. He reeked of whiskey, and she stepped back. "He competes. His barge is filled with trade goods, below the false bottom. Oh, he is a clever one, that one. And he insists I owe the debt."

"What did you—?" Too much. He'd had too much.

"Silence absolu." Pierre motioned for her to be quiet, holding his fist up. She flinched. "You hear that?" he whispered. "Lisa. He has followed me. He is here. Come to take me back."

Pierre listened. Lisa asked one of their *engages* for a towline! A stupid reason to come to the Astorians. He had towlines at his own camp. It was a trick, to get him, Pierre Dorion. Lisa had everything he needed, even an interpreter.

Pierre grabbed dry clothes, wobbled. His *femme* reached for him. "No. You have whiskey on your breath," she said. "You do foolish things!"

Baptiste hunched back in the robe, cowering.

Pierre pushed her aside. With four long steps, he reached Lisa, who was talking face to face with Hunt. Pierre spun him around and struck his fist into Lisa's face, savoring the surprise in the man's eyes. Hunt grabbed at Pierre's shoulders. Pierre could barely see him for his own rage, but he heard Lisa breathe hard, shout, "Give me a knife!"

Pierre lunged for him, was pulled back by Hunt.

"I will meet you back here with my knife, *mi amigo,*" Lisa shouted, stumbling toward his boat. "We will settle this now."

Pistols! Pierre needed pistols! He turned to his tent, pushed past his wife. "My pistols. Where are they, *femme?*" He'd find them. Once retrieved, he shoved them at her. "See!" he said. "See? I protect you." She stood with her sons behind her as he headed to where Crooks and McClellan stood.

"He deserves whatever you have to give him," Crooks said as Pierre approached.

"Been asking for it all along," McClellan added.

A crowd of *engages* and *voyageurs* gathered. Pierre paced, shouted for Lisa to come and face him. He turned to see Marie pushing Baptiste's head back inside the tent.

"Let him see his father tend to business," Pierre shouted to her, swinging the pistol and motioning her out. "Let him see his father put an end to this Lisa, this trickster. Judgment will happen here on the Missouri."

He had trouble standing straight. How much had he drunk? No matter. The pistols were his strength. He paced, barely hearing Crooks rant on about Lisa, his bad ways, listing the wrongs of the man. Crooks did not matter. McClellan did not matter. Lisa mattered. Lisa and his suggestion that he send his *femme* back, wanting him to work off a debt he did not owe.

He saw the crowd separate, and Lisa stood before him, hand on his knife. This would be easy, this settling with Lisa.

Hunt stepped up between them. "Get yourself a pistol, Lisa," Hunt said. "I'll not tolerate a duel without equal weapons, even between savages."

"I say, Wilson, do you think this is…wise?" Bradbury spoke. Then to Lisa, *Le Fou* said, "What will his death gain you, Manuel?"

"They're grown men," Hunt said. "I'm not responsible for their squabbles. This is not a military expedition."

Their words ran together in his head, these men, these…partners. Lisa was a coward, that's what he was. Pierre tried to form the words but couldn't.

"He's drunk," Bradbury said. "There's no way to make the duel fair."

Lisa paused. "I will get my pistols," he said and waved for an *engage* to take him across the water. Bradbury followed him, and another American Pierre didn't recognize waited near Lisa's boat. Pierre heard them telling Lisa it was not worth the deaths, his or Lisa's. "There must be a way for us to work this together," Pierre heard *Le Fou* say.

Pierre stood for a long time, his heart pounding, his breath coming fast. He was ready. Now. His mind was clear. Lisa's death would settle everything.

Pierre paced, his pistol jabbing the air as though making a point. Marie watched his face each time he passed the center fire, his eyes dark sockets, his nostrils flared in fury. It would be a long night, one that might end with his outrage spent on her—if he lived. Her fingertips touched that tender spot beneath her eyes. *Nothing foolish. Nothing foolish. Please, God, nothing foolish.* She didn't know if it was a prayer for him or a promise to herself.

"You get him, Dorion." Crooks or McClellan spurred her husband on. Did they like to see men kill? Was it because they were both of color, a Spaniard and an Indian? These…men, these partners who asked others to fight their battles for them: What name did they choose for themselves by their choices? Even Hunt did nothing to interfere.

A tool. That's what her husband was, a way for those who hated Lisa to rid themselves of him without getting blisters on their hands. Rid themselves of Pierre, maybe, too. They could use Charbonneau and his Snake wife to assist them.

Hunt had merely wanted to make the weapons equal for the "savages." He used the word to mean animals walking about in human shapes. But what they did to each other, these men with their trimmed hair, these men who scraped at their fingernails with fine files, who refused to intervene to help, no savage would do this, not if they had better tools to use, not when words would do as well.

Even the scientists, walking away with sweet, soothing voices would know that a death now, in the midst of negotiations, would only put their own hides at risk. Then she recalled that all the Astorians had stood and watched while Pierre struck her that morning at the Osage camp. Yet they walked into the night with Lisa to calm him, to keep him from being injured.

Pierre says I am paddle-minded, Marie thought. She shook her head, looked back at her boys who slept. Keeping them safe with no grandmother about. Helping them all stay alive in this uncertain place surrounded by men who looked out only for themselves, that was what mattered. There were such men everywhere. Even going back to St. Louis would never change that.

Pierre could die here. She could be widowed. Was she strong enough to raise her sons alone? She pulled the blanket around her shoulders. She clucked her tongue at no one, just the squandering of it all. Like boys throwing sand at each other, like Baptiste bullying his brother, that's what this was about. Over what? She didn't know. At least when her people raided an enemy camp they returned with goods from baskets to horses, wealth to distribute to help others. Lisa's death might bring Wilson Hunt the wealth of the Spaniard's trade goods but at the risk of the Tetons' smelling the bad blood and taking advantage? No, Pierre's death meant loss to them all, not just for her.

Marie watched the ranting. She quieted the boys when they whimpered in their sleep. She stayed out of sight as her husband's rage increased, his threats spoken in Sioux and French and English, mixed.

She considered calling out to him, to soothe him, remind him of an honorable way out. An Ioway warrior found such ways to settle things. Her husband could claim third honor as *Ushkaon,* a name that meant he was a coup striker, had made first contact when he fisted Lisa. That was enough. It could end there.

Marie sat at the opening of their tent. Should she go out to bring him back? Or would he shoot at her?

Marie watched until the embers of the fire burned to ash. As the moon rose, her husband's words, the swinging of his pistol, slowed. Sparks from the flames drifted up into darkness. The partners eventually tired of craning their necks to see if Lisa would return. They bent to their tents instead when looks at their pocket watches brought shakes to their heads but no entertainment. The *engages* began singing soft sleeping songs. Crickets, loud enough she could no longer hear the voices of the plant men still in Lisa's camp, muted the night like the stroking of soft fur. Her hips ached from squatting, and she stood.

Le Fou had shown the most wisdom, Marie decided. He wasn't a fool. He'd be the Buffalo Bundle Doctor among her people, helping heal and drain impurities away. In the morning—if her husband still lived—she would have to thank him.

She stepped into the moonlight.

"Come, husband," she whispered. Pierre turned glassy eyes at her. "All have gone to sleep, see?"

His eyes looked pinched and foggy as he gazed around the empty camp. She watched his shoulders drop, and while her heart pounded with uncertainty and her small hands glistened with sweat, she led her husband to his bed where she held him in her arms.

Pierre snored. Marie stroked his tight curls, his beard, the way she patted Paul's small head when he lay troubled and tossed. His body would jerk as though surprised by something inside his dreams. Pierre's body did this now, and his startle frightened her for just a moment.

How could she love a man who could be so foolish, who could hurt as much as he gave hope? It was a choice. She chose the name wife.

A dog whined in the distance. The boys turned in their sleep. Paul smacked his lips.

Her name was mother, too. She would raise her sons to be warriors, but better to seek the prophet status, men who did not raise arms against another in battle but who rode with a war party, with no intent to fight with weapons. A prophet used his wisdom to predict victory. And he could call the battle off if he saw great loss ahead, call off the battle without losing face.

They needed a prophet here, Marie thought as she slid her husband's heavy head from her chest and curled herself around sleep.

Loaded, Lisa's and Hunt's parties began to move out, separately, in their boats drenched by a driving rain. They would head for the main concentration of Arikara Indians and, hopefully, trade at last for horses.

"These small groups we've been talking with will tell the others what we're about," Pierre told Hunt as he rubbed at the back of his neck. Pierre was aware that his *femme* listened while she readied the boys, took down the tent and rolled the birch into bundles tied with rawhide. He stood straighter knowing she listened, even if sometimes Hunt didn't.

Marie had not snapped her dark eyes at him this morning, had spoken with gentle words, so he must not have harmed her in the night. He wished he could remember. The whiskey gave him strength, then stole his memory.

He looked across to Lisa's barge. There'd been a visit. He remembered that. Not much else.

"We're first on the river, my good man," Hunt said. "Arikaras will be dealing with us before Lisa, Providence willing."

"The tribes will know before we get there that there are two groups easing their way into their land," Pierre said.

"We look like soaked rats," Hunt said. Rainwater ran off his hat. "Certainly can't appear to be a threat to them this way." Water drenched his leather britches, deepening the wet, spreading stain. Some of the other partners still wore the slender pants and stiff collars of a portrait pose.

"Just so they believe we only want horses and that we won't interfere with their other trades. They need the foodstuffs of the Cheyenne and Sioux." This would be Pierre's hardest work so far, the one Lisa wanted him for most, the one that would prove to Hunt that he had made the right choice in choosing Pierre Dorion and allowing him to bring his family with him.

Pierre had suggested Hunt send a small party overland to make sure Hunt's group got to the Arikara villages before Lisa could.

"Indeed. I'll send them, Dorion, but there's really nothing to worry over now. I've…tended to things with Señor Lisa."

"How?" Pierre demanded. That Lisa was slippery. "I've seen all the trade goods he intends to use to foul us up. You can't—"

"I have the matter under control, Dorion." Hunt diverted his glance, avoiding Pierre's eyes. "I've paid your debt, added it to your ledger sheet. It was what should have been done in St. Louis."

"It won't stop—"

"Enough, now. It's settled."

The two sent out had come back saying the land was too rugged.

McClellan grunted. "If Lisa reaches them first, Wilson, he'll talk them out of letting us through and getting horses. We'll be without animals even if our Dorion here and the howitzers are skilled enough to help take us through their barricade."

"What is it with you and Lisa?" Hunt asked. He rubbed at the glass of his pocket watch. Pierre could see beads of water inside the glass case.

"You don't want to know," McClellan said. "Just remember this. If Lisa crosses the river before us to talk trade with them, I'll shoot him. You can tell Bradbury I said that, by the way."

"I hope you were right about the Arikaras, Dorion. They didn't support Lewis and Clark. We might have made a good dent in their party back there, hitting them with the howitzer and not just scaring them with smoke."

"Six hundred braves retaliating would have dented us, too," Pierre said. "They'll see we aren't coming to arm their enemies. My *femme's* presence assures them of that."

By midday, they'd moved upriver farther and the rain had stopped. Warm sun on the river sent plumes of steam rising to an azure sky. Both Lisa's party and the Astorians beached their boats on the same side of the Missouri, across from the villages that Pierre could see had Hidatsas and Mandan parties in them. He'd heard rumors that both those tribes held the Americans in contempt right now, but that the Arikaras, never liking to take the side of the Hidatsas, would stand with the Americans and let them through—if they paid a river passage price. He was counting on Hunt meeting the price.

Pierre and Hunt watched as two chiefs approached their beached *bateaux* with the Arikara trader, a man Pierre knew. He greeted the Frenchman, and the trader told them that the two headmen were Big Man and LeGauche, one a war chief and the other a civil chief. Both announced no passage through unless many presents were paid.

"We have such presents," Pierre said. "But if we give away too many, we will have none left to trade for horses. We want none of your furs. We're not a spring brigade taking furs back East. We're heading west." He swallowed to prepare for the lie. "To find a friend near the Great Salt Lake. Later, Americans will come to set up your own trader who will deal only with the Arikaras as you wish him to trade. We'll bring American goods, not the inferior cloths and knives of the British that break. A war may come, back East. There will be no British goods then. But for now, we want only to find a friend." To Hunt Pierre said, "Just nod politely. Give them time to check us out."

"No going through without paying a present price," the trader said. "And you can't trade for horses or anything else until the price is paid." He said something to the chiefs, then, who pressed reins against their ponies' necks and left without changing expression. Pierre watched the chiefs' horses throw mud on the well-worn trail beside the river. Lisa stood in the distance, watching from beside his barge. It would be a long day.

Marie had begun pulling things from the *bateaux*, their tent, her parfleche. Everything looked soaked. She adjusted Paul on her back. She should let the boy walk more. Pierre was sure the boy's grandmother, Holy Rainbow, would have. Grandmothers knew best about such things. Paul should walk. It would toughen him for the journey. Pierre would talk to Marie. But not today. She was in good spirits today, and talk of changing her care of the children bristled her like a bee-stung mare.

"Geese'll be flying before we even reach the mountains if we don't get trading for those horses, eh?" Pierre said.

"Let me understand," Hunt said. "We can't trade anything unless we pay the passage price? Not even show them what we have, dazzle them with our goods so they'll consider trading their horses?"

"Not if those two chiefs don't approve," Pierre said.

"Everything is wet," Marie complained.

"What?" Pierre tuned to her. "You worried over a little rain, woman? Go set up."

"We should lay things out to dry first, husband," she persisted.

Pierre looked at her. How could the woman think of such things at a time like this? He looked at Hunt.

"Forgive my comfort-seeking wife."

He noticed villagers topping the riverbank, staring at them. Their trader and the headmen had ridden downriver, talked with Lisa now.

"They're watching us close," Pierre said. "Not as many as I'd have thought, but more than I'd want to take on."

"Are they sick, do you think?" Hunt asked. "Diseased? There aren't many women and children."

"Still enough men to take us if they choose."

Marie said, "Lay out all the soaked goods. Everything needs drying."

"*Femme.* What point is this? We are doing work here."

"Their women may find something they like while the sun works. Their interest will feed the trade for horses." She smiled.

Pierre stared at her.

"Have the *engages* unload," Hunt told him. He clapped his hands. "Be sure they put out beads and blankets and kettles and vermilion, just to dry, mind you. Maybe even some of the baskets and powder. Sun needs to bake them, too. She's right. Everything got soaked. Can't accuse us of trading if we're just using the sun to air out wet socks."

Toupin and Carriere began opening the barrels and canvas bags. Other French-Canadians untied parfleches and bales of soaked trade goods. Villagers like hungry geese arched their necks to see. Women in soft moccasins pressed their feet into the mud at the water's edge, peered at the drying items, chattering and talking.

A smallish woman whispered something to a big man with rings on his muscled forearms. He nodded, looked upriver, then rode down over the bank to Pierre. "I am a chief," he signed.

"What's he saying?" Hunt asked as Pierre watched, then moved his hands to respond.

"He says he owns horses and he'll talk and trade whenever we're ready. Whenever we set the price so he can get some of our dried goods in exchange for his mounts."

"Indeed," Hunt grinned. "Let's begin then with our new definition of 'dry goods.'"

Pierre exhaled. He hadn't realized he'd been holding his breath.

Marie watched her husband and the partners being poled across the river to a meeting set up with the headman and the Arikaras' trader. They'd begun small trades, and she took no small pleasure in having initiated it.

Now, in a second boat Lisa came alone, though he would join them in the main lodge for the meeting. The Arikara trader had insisted on it. The Arikaras didn't want to dawdle with two sets of traders. They saw all these white men as one.

She swallowed hard. She had no confidence that Hunt would keep McClellan and Crooks and Mackenzie and the other partners from urging her husband into bad choices with Lisa present.

"At least we'll know what Lisa tells them," Pierre told the partners. "Charbonneau can't translate so well, and their trader will correct to suit himself. Better for us if we all crowd inside to pass the pipe together."

Even the plant men were going along, to sit in the council of men. *Engages* and *voyageurs,* women and children, would be left behind while these men walked through the hot rocks of headmen and chiefs, not sure when a spark would ignite a flame and set the whole thing afire.

No women would be allowed to enter. Women, who probably owned the lodge they'd meet in, who had surely tanned the hides and sewed them together and even painted the vermilion pictures on the outside. Women, who would tell the stories to their children.

Bradbury would now be introduced with an Omaha name, Wakendaga, meaning physician. "To make him sound more like one of them. They'll like having a plant healer there with us," Pierre told her. "No war party would bring a plant healer along. His presence signals peace."

"My presence would paint a picture of a trade party and not a war gathering. As would your sons' being there."

"You push too far, *femme.* They might think we come to trade you away, eh?" He lifted her chin as gentle as a butterfly landing. "Best you wrap up your dry treasures before the next rains come. Leave men's business to men." He started out of the tent, then turned back. "I will take the boy," he said. "It will be a good lesson for him."

She flinched, brushed at tears stinging as she urged Baptiste to his father's side.

Let the men do as they wish. Let them smoke pipes and make trades, treat a small boy as though he held more value than a woman's wise words. She had things to occupy her time.

She placed Paul on his board and hoisted it onto her back. Then she made her way to Lisa's camp.

Hunt was thoughtful as he waited in the lodge, Lisa visible across the circle. Dorion's woman had come through for them by getting the trade started, and he had settled the business with Dorion's debt, so now they could truly focus on horses.

He wasn't sure what Robert McClellan's problem was with Lisa, but the Spaniard had been quite reasonable when he proposed a stoppage to the uproar by a mere payment of the interpreter's bar debt. Lisa had been cordial after that. He even accepted the payment as sufficient for the stain on his honor the *metis* had made with his fist in the Spaniard's face. Why, Lisa had even offered up Eduard Rose, his own interpreter staying at the Mandan trading house. Quite gracious of him, actually. Lisa was just a man seeking justice over a debt and hoping to find his lost employee. Nothing more. An expedition leader had to discern these things, know when to step into a dried buffalo chip in order to avoid walking into something much messier.

Marie saw her before being seen. Like a soft shadow, the small-waisted Snake woman emerged from beneath overhanging oaks, dressed in calico over leather leggings. Smoke from the cooking fire rose around her ankles so she stood as though drifting through fog. This was the famous Sacagawea, the wife of Charbonneau, interpreter, who went west with

Clark and Reuben Lewis's brother, Meriwether. This was the mother who had carried her son Pomp across the Shining Mountains and returned him to safety.

Marie swallowed, remembering how the woman's eyes had judged her, riding behind her husband near the St. Louis wharf, the day Marie lost Baptiste.

Marie took a deep breath. She was just another mother. What better way to spend an afternoon than with another woman who had journeyed across the land in the company of white men and returned to tell the tale? They were equals here, two mothers traveling with expeditions. Yes, Sacagawea had more stories to tell of going and coming back. Marie had only "going stories." But she would be equal to the telling.

Marie straightened her shoulders, hiked Paul up higher on her back, gaining courage. When she did, she remembered a blessing Holy Rainbow gave to her once when Marie lifted her baby son onto the board. "It is an old blessing given to a man named Benjamin by an elder named Moses who, like you, had walked through wilderness places. 'The beloved of the Lord shall dwell in safety by him,'" Holy Rainbow told her. "'And the Lord shall cover him all the day long, and he shall dwell between his shoulders.' Is that not the image of a child carried on the back of his parent?" she said. "Lifting him through muddy river waters, taking him to safety on the other side?"

"It's a blessing for the beloved," Marie had challenged. "I'm not the beloved. You call me 'Her to Be Baptized.' I didn't have the friars' water. And I am not his."

Holy Rainbow waved her hand, drifting Marie's words away. "It is a promise," Holy Rainbow told her. "All blessings are promises, made by the person giving them. They say the words, then they touch the person who receives the blessing."

Holy Rainbow drew Marie into her arms and held her there, the brush of the elk teeth that decorated the dress of her mother-in-law's bodice pressed against Marie's cheeks.

"It is the Lord's decision to love and bless," she told Marie. "He wishes you to love him back, but his promise is made to each one. Each is worthy. He seeks every one, but they can choose. He attaches no strings of sinew unless you wish it. I make this blessing to you and my son and grandsons, so you will be carried to safety, as you need. You'll make such a blessing someday to your children, hoping they'll love you back as they rest in the groove between your shoulders."

Her mother-in-law had pressed her hands to Marie's face and breathed softly on her closed eyes, repeating the phrase, "The beloved of the Lord shall dwell in safety by him." Marie had felt the warmth of her hands and her heart. The memory comforted her now.

It was strange that those words should come to her when her stomach had begun to flutter and her shoulders ached with the weight of her son while she watched another mother.

Sacagawea wore beads around her neck, and white ermine skins hung from her braids that rested on her chest. Like Marie, she carried a knife at her hip. Her choices spoke of paddle-minded ways too, Marie thought—white women's clothes and the hides of weasels.

Marie scoffed at herself. Didn't all women walk in two worlds? That of their husbands and that of their mothers. So. Indian women linked to men with mixed blood walked in three worlds, and when their children grew to manhood, there were four worlds to negotiate. Mixed-blood children were invisible to those company owners who refused to acknowledge their worth by letting their father earn a living, his wife at his side. Such children needed mothers to interpret for them.

Marie scanned the place where they camped. Brackenridge, the plant man who had come up with Lisa, had stayed behind. He squatted beside a plant, running leaves between his fingers. Then he stood, made notes.

No sounds of children. Had she left them behind? *How hard that must be,* Marie thought, *to be here, going home, without her sons.* Sacagawea had always appeared sickly in St. Louis from what Marie had heard. Perhaps sadness was what she had discovered on that expedition while the men were naming streams and mountains after themselves.

Marie stepped on a branch that cracked into the still morning. Birds flittered into the sky. *"Pardon,"* she said, embarrassed. Brackenridge looked up from his book. Sacagawea turned, her mouth an O of surprise. Her dress stretched across her abdomen for just a moment as she twisted. When Marie saw it, she caught her breath. So. They shared this as well.

"À voix douce," Sacagawea said, her own voice as soft and sweet as she claimed Marie's to be.

Now that she'd been spoken to, and given a kindness by the woman, Marie dropped her eyes. They were of the same age in years, but the Snake woman deserved a greater level of respect for what she'd accomplished, living in those worlds with only men, then traveling on to St. Louis, a place of new belonging.

For a moment, Marie wondered if she'd be able to ask her what she wished to know, even if they could find a common language beside the use of their hands. Still, she had made her way west and back with her son. Marie needed to know what had given her strength to make that so.

Paul squealed and rocked himself back and forth against Marie's back. "Sh-sh," Marie told him. *Why does he pick now to behave as though he has never been trained?*

The woman spoke, blended French and Hidatsa. She motioned toward Paul. The Hidatsa sounded like the Yankton Sioux of her husband and Holy Rainbow, and Marie startled to hear the language from a woman's voice after so many years. She squinted in concentration.

The woman cleared her throat, must have assumed the difficulty was her choice of words. She added awkward hand signs, hesitated. "Ah. Our children listen better, ah, with honey words than with sharp ones, *n'est ce-pas?* I try to tell this to Mr. Charbonneau. He wears deaf ears."

Marie nodded, her throat dry. She called her husband mister, as though he sat at tables with white men, his face reflecting wealth in the waxed wood walls. Marie looked down on the top of the woman's head. She was so much shorter than Marie. The part in Sacagawea's hair was perfect, even early in the morning. Her dark hair glistened with grease that smelled sweet.

"Your children are quiet as we travel," Sacagawea continued. "I'm surprised to hear a child's voice here. And a woman's."

She wasn't judging, just being pleasant, as though they scraped a hide together, had known each other in another time. It had been awhile since she had sat beside a woman friend talking and tanning hides.

Marie spoke, surprised at the catch in her throat. She swallowed back tears that rose from some unknown river. "My husband says your husband takes you to the Mandan village. He does not leave you behind."

Sacagawea raised her arched eyebrows in surprise. "Your *époux* speaks of such things with you?"

"Your travel with Lisa has been good?" Marie asked.

"Lisa does not much like the Astor men. And he pushes the river." She coughed then, her fingers over her mouth. Her eyes were deep set, watered, her cheeks thin as Hunt's paper. The woman turned back to the copper pot, stirred the corn that bubbled, then took out a spoonful in a wooden bowl and offered it to Marie.

"Do you know what he will say to the Arikaras?" Marie asked.

Sacagawea smiled, shook her head. "My *époux* has little time for women's words." She looked wistful. "Lisa makes one wary as a disturbed buffalo. Who can predict what he does?" She shrugged her shoulders the way Marie had seen white women do sometimes, as though to end a conversation. But Sacagawea continued, "Who can predict these men? A prophet would grow crippled here, trying to predict success or make a party turn back before disaster."

So she knew of prophets, how they tried to turn away danger. "Only men of wisdom listen to a prophet," Marie said as she pulled Paul from her back.

"Or to women," Sacagawea said. She smiled. Her eyes brightened, though only a bit.

"Or women. And sometimes they must be both the wise one to listen and the prophet who knows what to do about it," Marie said.

The woman had a puzzled look on her face. The language confused, Marie thought, just as it did for her. But her smile showed even teeth, not one who held the hide so that her teeth arched over her lips. This Snake mother did things her own way too, Marie decided.

"You can put your baby there, beside the tree, away from the smoke," she offered, pointing. "It is safe. He must be heavy. It will be nice to hear the chatter of a child. He is your only son?"

Marie shook her head and pointed with her chin. "Men choose small boys to take to council, over the company and wisdom of their mothers. My husband takes Jean Baptiste, who carries only five summers, in with Lisa and Hunt. The men—"

"This is Pomp's first name, my son," Sacagawea said. This time her smile filled up her face. "His name at birth and when he was baptized. It is a prophet's name, Jean," she said.

Marie hadn't known this. But she suspected that had her own mother lived, she would have known it. And more, approved.

Marie smiled as she watched Sacagawea stroke Paul's cheek. She had found someone to help share her load for however briefly they would walk together.

8

The Beaded Belt of Kindness

Putting pigs in a pen was easier than getting partners to agree. Hunt had begun trading with the Arikaras, but after nearly two weeks, only thirty horses had been secured, their tails bobbed to mark who owned them now—Astorians. The partners agreed that three mounts was necessary per person to carry the tools to make canoes once they crossed the mountains. That meant over three hundred animals for carrying supplies and trade goods. Hunt thought that if they got one hundred and fifty they could still do it. Now he wondered if they could get by with half that many. All but the partners would simply have to walk.

The bobbed tails of the geldings and sturdy mares they'd negotiated for grazed nearby. So much haggling and so many chiefs and subchiefs to appease. They were anxious to be off, too, these Arikaras, to make the trades for pumpkins and corn with the Cheyenne. At least Dorion said they were anxious. Hunt couldn't see it by their actions. Negotiations began late each day, after the usual smoking and talking and whatnot before getting down to business. Dorion said they were unhappy about the wild game being depleted by all the Americans. Hunters brought in deer and an occasional elk, taking needed food from the villagers. Well, what were they supposed to do? They needed to eat too. If the Indians wanted to leave to find better food, then they should bargain faster.

Yesterday Dorion had let drop that with all the tribal politics, he wasn't sure if the Arikaras were bargaining hard or simply had no more horses to trade. Then one of the winter partners, McClellan, started spouting about how late in the season it was anyway, that they should go back to the Osage village and wait until next spring. Impossible. War with England could break out. They could be attacked heading back as well as forward. Besides, Astor was counting on him.

Lisa approached from his camp now, springing along like a game-cock, clicking his heels and bending at the waist, acknowledging Hunt as he moved on past. Only one or two of the partners even joined them in the trading. Maybe that was just as well though, since each time he came out to report, a partner would complain about the results.

"You're crazy to have Lisa sit there while you negotiate our needs," one of the partners had told him just this morning.

"Astor gave me authority to do this as I saw fit," Hunt reminded them. "I like knowing where Lisa is and knowing what his trader is saying."

"I doubt even Astor would invite the enemy into camp," Macken-zie said.

"The Arikaras invited him in, Donald. Besides, didn't you say that things are done differently here? Lisa's been nothing but a gentleman since the night with Dorion."

"Deception is deception no matter where or when it shows up," Mackenzie told him.

"So far, Lisa's done nothing to interfere. He hasn't even expressed interest in the Arikaras' mounts, which, if he intends to beat us to the Pacific, he'd surely be needing himself." Hunt was sure now that Lisa had simply come to seek that lost employee of his, and he'd be heading north as they moved out south.

Dorion signaled for them to enter the trade circle. Finally. Hunt looked at his pocket watch. Nearly noon. By the end of the week, he wanted out of here. Even if the partners didn't trust Lisa or the mountain men's words, or Clark's belief of a shorter route, Hunt did. With those grizzled men's drawings, he was sure they could still make the Pacific by fall. *Horses. Just get horses. Keep on course, that is what Astor would want.*

After all, Astor was the only partner he really needed to please, and he felt sure he was doing that.

"Maybe we should nip a mount and head on back with the scientists," George Gay told Jean Toupin. "I'm tired of cooking." The two were skinning a deer the hunter John Day had brought in that morning. Dogs from the Indian village and wide-eyed children hovered close by. The camp boys spent most of their time preparing food now with sixty-eight men to feed twice a day. Toupin had hoped he'd be around for some of the horse trading, but he'd been buried deep in skin and bones. At least at night he had time to mend his socks, tend to necessities. His feet had grown since his mother had knitted those socks for him in Montreal the year before. Nothing fit him. His arms hung out of his sleeves like a garden scarecrow. Some days, he stumbled over his own toes, fell like a child. He wasn't sure what was happening to him. He stood nearly a foot taller now than George. But he knew one thing hadn't changed: His word still meant something, and he'd promised his mother he'd stay.

"Not possible," Toupin told Gay. "My advance is already with my mother." He cut a section of ribs from the carcass, handed it into a child's grubby hands. The Astorians could go with one less rib at the evening meal. The boy kicked up dirt as he scampered away to share his treasure. Three long-tailed dogs jumped at his heels, but he held the raw meat high over his head. Toupin sliced at the deer's hindquarters, gently separated the last of the hide from the carcass, trying not to put cuts into the fur.

George laughed and punched his friend in the shoulder with the back of his palm. "I jostle you, mate," he said. "I don't want to go back, least not on a horse! It makes it a greater adventure, though, to know that we stay like some desert rats on a sinking *bateau.*"

"You and me, we know how to plug a bad *bateau, oui?*" Toupin said.

"I just hope we'll get to ride on something. I'm not relishing a walk all the way west," George told him.

Toupin nodded. He might have to ask Madame Dorion to make

him up some new moccasins if his feet didn't stop growing out of the ones he had on.

"The medal Lewis gave out did it, that's my bet," Pierre told Marie as they walked now, days later, among the horses, Baptiste by her side, Paul on her back. Pierre had said she would have a horse to ride, and he wanted her to choose one. Baptiste pulled on her hand. "Too close," she scolded. "Don't startle them."

"That arrogant little man, Lewis," Pierre told her, "gave Chief Grey Eyes a cheap medal and five years later, we reap the rewards." He shook his head.

Baptiste patted at one of the horses that lowered his head to him, snorted in comfort. Marie ran her fingers over the velvet of the horse's nose. She turned so Paul could feel it too. "Mama, Mama," he said. At least the boy tried to talk. Baptiste patted at the animal's neck.

"That horse is the color of a fall maple. Of red earth," his *femme* said. The animal nickered low as Marie walked around it.

"What will we call him?" Baptiste asked.

"To name a thing is to love it," she said. "We must choose carefully."

"He's gelded already," Pierre said. "Good strong hindquarters. He can carry the weight. I'll tie a marker on his mane. He'll be yours if Hunt approves."

The horse twitched ears forward, lowered its head to her. "We wait to see what name comes," Marie said.

Pierre wished she knew how hard his work was, this negotiating. It took all his concentration for the trades. He watched what each man said of his horse, how the animal behaved and what Hunt did or didn't do. At least Hunt was up to the task, didn't lose his temper with the timing. McClellan or Crooks or Miller would have pushed over the edge.

Of all the partners, Mackenzie seemed the least dismayed by the delays, the most likely to simply accept what was. He talked often with the mountain men who still hovered at Lisa's camp. The big man played with his dogs, rode out and let the scent hounds rustle up prairie chickens he shot, bringing back the birds for plucking and feasting. He puffed up with admiration for his own marksmanship. He even hovered over Pierre's *femme* as she worked the hides the camp boys gave her.

At least his *femme* could work the hides. Once on the trail she'd have no time to strip the sinew for thread or to fashion new parfleches they could use to haul water or store rabbit fur sacks in to warm the children this winter. She seemed happier working at what she knew.

Still, it bothered Pierre to see the man hover so. What man wasted time watching a woman work?

Mackenzie looked to be losing some of his bulk. Maybe as he thinned, so did his influence. Of course, the addition of the other partners seemed to water the stew. It took even longer now to get a decision. "We should already be south, along the Wind River by now. We could encounter storms in the Shining Mountains, even in August," Pierre said. "We mark this horse for you." He lifted the long tail hairs and pulled out his knife to cut them.

His *femme* patted the sorrel horse's neck. She bounced Paul on her back, stretching her buckskin dress across her abdomen. He didn't want Hunt to know yet, that his *femme* expected another. It would be one more thing for the partners to haggle over. Working the hides took her strength. Field pressing the pelts into tight bundles to be tarred at the seams taxed her, made her arms ache as she readied those riches. But showing the boys how to set rabbit snares and pulling stickers from their feet didn't take much fat from her bones. Her body still looked lean and firm. This was good.

"Maybe the other herd will have a horse who speaks more loudly to us," she said.

"What other herd?"

"There are horses at the Mandan post," she said.

"How do you know this?" Pierre asked, stepping from behind the horse. He stared at her.

"I listen," she said.

"Who talks to you?" He finished cutting the tail, handed the black and copper strands to her.

"People who have been with Lisa say this. Brackenridge." She hesitated. "Sacagawea."

"You go to Lisa's camp to gossip? When? Charbonneau's woman tells you this? How? She knows no French, even after all those years with Ol' Charbonneau."

"We talk," she said. "Hidatsa and Sioux have sister sounds. She speaks a few French words, some English. There are women's ways." She rolled the tail hairs she'd use later, twisting into reins or rope. "You tell Hunt there are horses at Lisa's Mandan post. Reuben Lewis is there now. Maybe Lisa's partner will trade horses for Hunt's boats. What use will we have of those boats? And these Arikara people will not wish to trade horses for canoes. Only what's in them."

She never failed to amaze him.

"The partners will be as jumpy as water on the skillet to trade anything to Lisa," Pierre said.

"Hunt is the chief factor."

Pierre laughed. "Yes, but with many subchiefs. The Americans don't run their factories the way the British or North Westers do. But why would Lisa agree to sell? Tell me that, if you know so much?"

"Maybe he tells the truth now. He does not pursue Hunt hoping to have fur posts farther west. Hunt has beaten him, by keeping you. And he has Charbonneau to interpret, and there is another at the post, Sacagawea says. Lisa sees soft money everywhere, in beaver streams, in boats of rivals. He seeks money, that's what drives him. If he can't keep Hunt here," she shrugged, "he will go for the money. There must be money somewhere out there, a fur cache maybe."

Pierre grunted. "Or maybe he sells horses because he needs fewer himself. To follow us. He has fewer men to mount up. Lisa would do nothing to help us unless it helped himself."

"It is just information," she said, shrugging.

Pierre nodded. He raised his chin toward Paul. "Maybe you teach your baby to trade walking for riding on your back."

"He is young yet, but he learns."

Pierre watched her set the boy down in the dusk. The horse had wandered off, ripped at grass inside the stick-and-brush corral. Baptiste found a grasshopper and headed toward the river to try his luck with fishing. Almost immediately, Paul wailed to be lifted again, his arms upstretched. The child wanted too much from her, always wanting. She made him slow to learn, treating him as an infant.

Pierre smacked Paul on his bottom, brought on a harder cry. The child was not tough enough. She coddled him to no good end. Coddled milk always soured. "Leave your mother be," he said and swatted the child again, the sting of flesh against flesh loud even to his own ears. His *femme* whisked the boy up into her arms.

"I have no need of help from you," she hissed. "You go. Do your work to find horses. This is mine."

"What do you mean, Nuttall and Bradbury and the rest are planning to take horses and return to St. Louis?" Hunt tapped his finger against the parchment. He glared at Mackenzie. Behind the big man, the river ran with a greenish cast. Could that be summer moss already forming?

"Laddie, it's not my doing. They think the weather'll be changing too soon." Mackenzie shrugged his shoulders. "We are late, Wilson."

"And Brackenridge? Does he stay with Lisa, or does he ride back with my scientific…men of adventure too?"

"No need to be judging them harshly. We'll be asking much of our *engages,* learning to ride, not being sure where we're headed—"

"We have Clark's map! We have Robinson and Hoback's descriptions. They're out there now drawing maps! Perhaps Providence will compel them to join us yet. Lisa doesn't need them."

"Aye, and there's that question, too."

"What is it, Dorion?" Sometimes the man startled him with his quiet entry.

"I think I've found us the horses we need, eh? Though it'll require negotiating with Mr. Lisa's partner."

Hunt clapped his hands. "Whatever it takes," Hunt said. "Let the scientists run. We'll have our horses and my own notes to record this journey and surprise them all with our success."

Manuel Lisa was a man who could switch his steps quicker than a squirrel twitched a tail. Sometimes, this life work of envisioning change and making it happen felt like the flamenco dance—close and slow, circling one's partner, hot breath flowing between them, then a sudden shift, with feet spinning and clicking until one hardly knew where the dance would take them next.

This was his current dance. He didn't want Hunt to have so few horses that he'd change his mind, decide to spend the summer, turning their journey into a fur exchange after all and cutting into Lisa's territory. But he didn't want Hunt to have enough horses to succeed either. The scientists heading back was a good sign that Hunt wouldn't make it. They'd taken his hints about the dangers ahead, the late start. Now the slow trading helped too. He'd convinced Hoback and the others to join Hunt once they got their horses. Just for a distance, enough to get them well settled down the trail. Then they had their orders, or rather their jobs. Lisa grinned. Nearly everyone could be bought for the right price.

Lisa was even prepared to offer up Eduard Rose as an interpreter who could assist Dorion as they moved into Crow country. Now, how could Hunt or the other partners object to such generosity? Eduard had his own orders to follow, of course. But Hunt would discover those in due time.

The only problem he'd encountered so far came from the Dorion woman. Brackenridge said Clark's little cargo and Dorion's woman had become friends. And she'd learned of Lewis's horses at the Mandan Fort. Now Hunt wanted to trade sooner than Lisa had hoped. He had to get word to Reuben Lewis to limit the number available for Hunt to fewer than fifty animals and to make his dance around why he couldn't spare more animals sound believable. Sometimes one had to count on a partner. But he'd trained Lewis well.

The Snake woman rolled a leather ball to Paul. The giggle when he threw it back sounded like the trickle of spring water that dropped from rock to river near the bluffs of Marie's Des Moines.

"You make days fly," Marie told her, saying the words in Sioux, moving her hands in signs. Marie had heard that Sacagawea's name meant Bird Woman, and she asked her, using a blend of Hidatsa and Sioux, how she named herself.

"Clark calls me Janey," Sacagawea told her, smiling. "An easier word for him to scratch." She made writing motions. "But I am Sacagawea to myself." The women sat together on the grass beside the Missouri, Sacagawea beading a purse she'd laid down to entertain Paul while Marie worked on repairs to Pierre's leggings. She'd bartered for some yarn and mended wool stockings for him too.

Today was one of Sacagawea's good days. Some days, the woman would not come out of her tent, and Marie would walk away. Or she appeared, but kept busy, working on a basket as though in a fever. Once or twice she said she was *malade,* though she didn't look ill. But she was always tender toward the children, never raised her voice nor appeared distressed with them. These weeks together with Sacagawea had been the first real friendship Marie had known as a married woman. Theirs was a savored tie where Marie found she could tend the nicks and flaws in the relationship without allowing tiny tears to rip away the warmth.

They spoke of berries to ward off the soft bone disease, dug roots to do the same. Together they ground up buffalo chips they crumbled in their palms, to "soak up baby bottoms," and peered over each other's shoulders at tanning hides or baskets being woven.

"These grasses?" Marie asked, pointing at slender greens she'd not seen before, wondering if they would be good for basket weaving.

"Not this time of year. Later," Sacagawea said, "some things bring value later."

Once they took the boys to a pool formed in the backwater of the river. The women dropped their clothes to plunge in, not just to bathe but also to swim. It wasn't early morning, when Marie most often frequented the river, private and alone. It was midday. And in the water, they'd pointed to the belly of the other, compared childbearing ripples of their skin, laughed at their shared distortions.

"In St. Louis, I thought of you as a small-waisted woman," Marie told her.

"A small-waist pig," Sacagawea said as she patted her belly.

They'd floated on their backs in the sheltered pool while the boys chased after crayfish, promising white flesh for a stew. Using signs and the few words they shared, they'd talked of babies and travel and men.

"At least while we wait for our *enfants*," Marie said, "we cannot be blamed for attracting the yellow bears into camp. The *engages* will hoist food bags high but not because of us."

"The yellow bears frighten," Sacagawea said. She made gestures of their fierceness and about keeping her children safe. "My *époux* does not worry over such things," she said. Marie wondered if she, too, sometimes felt alone, doing the work of raising children, even though she was surrounded by men.

Their understanding of each other lacked the fluid movement of one shared language, but being with her these weeks, with another mother, another wife of an interpreter, a woman—this woman—had been as soothing as the scent of wind in sweet grass.

Sacagawea had changed since she'd seen her on that pillion riding behind her husband in St. Louis. She now wore a wide beaded belt at her waist that was no longer small, and buckskins replaced calico.

Pierre's attention to the negotiations and the partners' tight control of whiskey had meant more pleasant evenings with her husband, too. He was less demanding of her on days they made progress with the horse trades, and she kept still when he growled at the campfire on dismal days when he didn't. He had shown her no unkindness since they'd been at this Arikara village, and a part of her wished that they could stay. Marie had begun to heal. Time, like burned bone, rubbed even harsh memories into ash.

But it was already July.

Paul wobbled, dropped onto his knees, stood up again, took one or two steps, dropped down. He moved across uneven ground, carried the ball and tossed it again, the forward motion causing him to fall toward the Bird Woman. He caught himself. *He is learning,* Marie thought, *though it takes him longer.* It was a truth she now admitted sitting back and watching him with another woman's hands reaching out to catch him. She could admit the truth with another mother's acceptance of her son.

Blowed, one of Mackenzie's dogs, came up and pulled at Baptiste's shirt in play. Paul shied away from the dog, but Marie thought that a good sign. He remembered what had happened to Baptiste. He'd learned some caution. Baptiste brushed the animal aside, which only excited the dog more. Paul crawled after the dog.

"Again," Baptiste told Sacagawea. He held out his hands to the fine-boned woman who smiled at him. She tossed the ball. The dog jumped for it, which appeared to anger Baptiste, who struck at the dog.

"Go now," Marie said. "Help your brother catch crayfish." She looked around. "Where is Paul?" She cast her eyes right, then left. "Find him," she said, standing.

Baptiste slammed the ball into the ground with a force that surprised Marie. He stomped off, a dark scowl on his face, heading where a trail of flattened grasses marked Paul's likely position. She heard the boy chuckle.

Marie sighed, sat back down. Sacagawea leaned over and patted Marie's hand.

"You abandon me," Marie signed then, forcing her fists open and closed as though shooing away flies. "It makes me cry." Marie raised both index fingers to her eyes, indicating tears.

Sacagawea made the sign for "push" meaning "must" and said, "Go to my people." Then indicated that Marie, too, must move on.

She nodded. There were many "musts" in a woman's life. Some she chose and some came with her being. Marie wished she had a way to ask her how it was for her in the quiet places of her mind. How had she come to take her son west? How did she decide to let her son be baptized in St. Louis, and what did that mean to her? Was she baptized? What was it like to be the only woman among so many men during those years of travel? She'd made this latest river trip north with all white men, except for her husband and Lisa the Spaniard. What had she learned from that?

Marie turned to see Baptiste taking his brother's hand and helping him walk back. Before her, the riverbank was awash in yellow and blue, flowers bending to the breeze.

Sacagawea's husband must have protected her on that journey, Marie decided, took her as a second wife, to keep her safe. Marie had found Charbonneau snoring as often as not when she would make her way midmorning to their camp, and he didn't act much like a shield. A new interpreter named Rose had ridden down from the fort and now joined Pierre in the negotiations so Charbonneau had even less to do. She'd heard tales that he was less than able when it came to crises, too.

Still, Sacagawea stayed with him, and he had not set her off for another. And she now carried his child.

Maybe she should ask Charbonneau to interpret for them since he did little else. But of the things she'd truly like to say, could she? Not with the man as the tool of her thoughts. No, she couldn't ask the things that a woman most wanted to know, about how and when to intervene in the foolish choices of these white men. She wished to know from another *sauvagesse* what she dreamed for her children and if it concerned her that they carried the blood of more than one race.

Marie looked at the profile of the woman as they sat beside the river. Had her cheek been broken, that slender nose? It looked so. What did Janey do if her husband struck her when he drank? And she wanted to know if Sacagawea thought she needed such a man to take care of her and her children. Did she know how to stand alone, strong as bone; or how to mend when she felt broken? Marie wanted to know from her friend how to move back and forth across that bridge of a woman's life, from hungering child to giving mother to strong woman. How could a man translate such questions or convey a woman's answers?

Such personal thoughts could not be asked of another anyway, only willingly shared. The signs of their hands and the stumbling Hidatsa, French, and Sioux worked, if sometimes more slowly than desired. Marie would try again to speak of hard things, share her worries and perhaps discover what she needed to know for this journey west, something that would help keep her sons alive.

"You come to my people," Sacagawea told her. "There is room there."

Was she inviting her for a visit or suggesting she not go with the expedition?

"I go for my children," Marie said and Sacagawea nodded.

Marie pointed to Sacagawea's stomach and her own and signed, "snow." Sacagawea nodded. Marie thought their babies would enter the world at the same time, January, the time when gray snow covered l'Ayvoise huts. Five more moons and they would each have an infant at their breasts. Another baby to bear a winter on the western coast.

Sacagawea had told her once of the climate at the Pacific, making the signs for "falling from clouds" over and over. Both of their journeys should be over then: Sacagawea to her people the Mandans, and Marie along the mouth of the Columbia River and to the sea.

"I go because I cannot stay behind," Marie told her. Sacagawea nodded. "It is…greedy, to want my baby born at this westering place."

Sacagawea shook her head no, then signed and said she wanted her baby born "where he will not confuse the sound of the wind with wagons on a cobbled road."

"You want a boy," Marie said, not making it a question.

"A girl," Sacagawea said. "So she will always be close to my heart."

"We will be at the Pacific then," Marie said. "My child will know water first." Water, carrying her out of her mother into her father's world of rivers and seas.

Sacagawea became excited, and with her hands she described a huge child she'd seen there. Then Marie realized it was a fish she made with her hands, walked off several paces to show the length. "Whale," she said, making Marie repeat the English word.

Marie's eyes grew large in astonishment. "That big?" she said, and Sacagawea nodded, her braids bobbing on her chest. Her eyes sparkled. She told of the great beauty of the water and used the word for "must" again, saying Marie must make the men take her to the sea even though it was a hard two-day journey from where they had built their fort on the big river, Fort Clatsop.

"They will say it is too far for a woman," Sacagawea said. "But you will know you have already come so far. You tell them you will see the sea. Sometimes you must just tell the men or they will overlook you as though you are a blueberry on a thick-leafed bush. It is the color of blue beads, the sea," she said then. "A belt of mine I traded for two sea otter skins Clark hungered for was that color."

Marie pointed to the beadwork on her bag, lying where she'd been sitting. She signed the word for color and then pointed to the blue sky. Sacagawea shook her head, looked around, as though seeking something the perfect blue. She did not find it. "I held on to the memory of the blue water with those beads," she said. The woman's words for memory translated as "heart knows." Her heart would tell her what she remembered.

Sacagawea sat back down and sighed deeply. A sadness washed over her face, cheeks drawn in. She did not look well to Marie. Perhaps she missed her sons more with Marie's boys bounding about.

What was best for her son was what that mother had chosen, leaving him behind with Clark. A mixed-blood son would know a better world with Clark's help—a *bourgeois's* help.

Baptiste sneaked from around a bush, jumped on Sacagawea's back. She winced in pain but pulled him gently over her shoulder. Paul plundered her lap from behind her and the three rolled as children together, the dog barking at the tumbling, his fur wet from the river.

Marie thought she should do that more, not just tell her boys stories but roll with them like puppies. Her children laughed, and her heart knew it as a sound of joy unequaled.

"All Reuben Lewis would spare was fifty horses," Hunt told the partners. He paced. July and they had only eighty-two horses. Barely half of what they needed. He hated to ask the French-Canadians to walk until they reached the great river, but there was no other choice. Hopefully, the horses would be healthy enough to trade away to Indians when they reached the arm of the Columbia. They'd give horses for or make canoes to take them to the ocean from there. Providence would provide. He had to trust that.

"Maybe we should trade with the women," one of the wintering partners said. He spit, pulled tobacco from the tip of his tongue. "Or should I say 'trade the women.' Our sutler, Reed, seems to be doing a good business with his strings of beads and hide scrapers the *engages* are buying. They turn them into lusty evenings. Perhaps we should promise more beads and we'd get more horses."

"You miss what happens there," Pierre told him.

"Oh? And what would that be?"

"It is an exchange of strength. And it is a gift, a kindness to offer warmth to another. That's what the women do."

"That how you got your woman, Dorion? You so special she wanted to keep you warm?" This from another partner.

"It's Dorion who ended up with someone special," Hunt said. Mackenzie raised an eyebrow, glanced at Hunt. "Enough of this chatter," Hunt said. "What matters are horses, and the women here do not own them. The Blackfeet wives have horses, gentlemen, but that warring tribe we hope to avoid. They don't like to trade. They simply kill white men since they've had such poor relationships with the North West Company."

Mackenzie frowned, tossed a deer bone. Blowed scampered after it.

"I say we turn back," another partner said. "This has gone on long enough. It's too late in the year."

"We've been over this. We're going on," Hunt said. "We assign horses to the partners and hunters. The rest we pack."

"And for my wife?" Pierre asked.

One of the partners scoffed.

"She is…with child," Pierre went on.

"What?" McClellan turned on him. "Have you no shame, man?"

"Would you have your mother walk, McClellan?" Hunt snapped. "Your wife will have a horse," Hunt said, raising his hand to indicate silence. "She's earned it. The remaining mounts will be packed or held in reserve for those *engages* who have trouble covering this hard-pack ground. French-Canadians' arms will withstand storms, but their feet are as tender as a baby's bottom. Mackenzie, make sure Reed's got plenty of bear grease and extra hide for moccasins. We're going to need them when we leave…tomorrow."

Marie fidgeted where she sat. Sacagawea worked deer brains into a hide to soften it. She coughed, wiped her mouth with the back of her hand. Marie stuffed the ground buffalo chips into the base of Pierre's moccasins. "If it soaks baby bottoms, it will soak water and keep feet dry," she told her friend.

Sacagawea smiled. Paul pounded chipped stones as though attempting to make an arrowhead as he'd seen his father do. He chattered, carrying on a conversation, but the sounds made no words. He tossed his effort, picked up another. Baptiste rode on a horse with an Arikara child; the two trotted toward them, and Sacagawea pushed against her thighs to stand. She lifted Paul out of the way and smiled up at the mounted boys. She made the sign that meant leaving again, and Marie felt tears pool in her eyes.

No. She must not think this way. She had chosen to go to protect her sons from a life of uncertainty without a father. And because there was no other choice. She could learn the languages at the Columbia, teach it to her boys. She'd discover words to express her thoughts to women of other experiences, to share what ached inside her at a moment like this one, when she watched another woman hold her children to her heart.

The sinew on the moccasins Marie stuffed needed cutting. Marie patted at her waist for her knife, realized she'd misplaced it again, wondered when.

Sacagawea saw her searching. *"Attends un moment!"* she said. Sacagawea reached behind her and pulled a knife from the sheath at her beaded belt, then handed it to Marie.

The knife felt solid as a friendship. Three brass rivets held the two antler handle-halves together, an arched blade extended out between the opaque halves. Marie accepted it, liking its weight in her palm. She turned it over. It was crudely fashioned but sturdy. She cut the sinew pushing the blade away from her, then lifted it to give it back.

Sacagawea raised the palm of her hand to her shoulder, up and down, making the sign for "give."

"For me?" Marie said, patting her fingers on her chest.

"Oui."

"Lew-is," Sacagawea said. "Lewis gave as a gift to people we visited who treated us with kindness. There were many," she said. "The knife is the same, but each tribe, each man is different. Even among whites." She made the sign for someone who wore a hat, a finger drawn across the forehead. "Some are good." She signed, "Level with the heart. Some no. Walk in kindness, even when they choose injury." She nodded with her chin toward the camp where the men stood in clusters, tobacco smoke drifting up over their shoulders as they bent in conversation. Sacagawea swatted the horse's rump, and the boys trotted off.

"Kindness is the beaded belt that binds all together," she signed. "A blue beaded belt."

Marie turned the knife over, fit it into the empty leather holder held at her own waist. Meriwether Lewis had given a knife to Sacagawea. Now she had passed it to Marie.

"You are truly wealthy," Marie said. "To have so much to give away."

Sacagawea dropped her eyes, a deep pink rising to flush her face. The two mothers sat in silence, watching children at play.

"We leave at dawn," Pierre told her. "So if you're wanting to say something to your…the Bird Woman, you best do that." Marie looked up at him. "I'll stay here with *les enfants*," he said.

Her first thought was whether he had whiskey stashed and would use the time when she was gone to consume it. She hesitated. Hunt had given no whiskey out since the horse trades began. "Don't then," he said. His voice softened. "Hunt's giving you that horse. The maple leaf one you liked. It will not go against our account. Said you'd earned it."

"You told him it was me who knew about the horses Lisa and Lewis had?"

"Sometimes woman's talk can be shared." She smiled at him. "Take the lamp," he said, motioning with his chin.

She picked up the oil lamp. "The moon shines. I won't stay long."

He was not a bad man, her Pierre. He made choices. Sometimes choices of kindness. Only when he drank did he—she stopped herself. There had been that one time, in front of the Astorians. She wondered if that was why Hunt had given her a horse to ride west, not because of anything she'd said about the horses but to push aside his shame.

She made her way beneath the cottonwoods, through narrow-leaf willows snuggling the river. She could hear Toupin singing in French, songs that put the *engagés* to bed each night. She hoped they'd keep singing when they left their boats behind, sing on their horses.

Beneath the moonlight, she found Sacagawea's camp and scratched at the flap, then she gave her name. "Charbonneau?" she said. Charbonneau said something in Hidatsa, and Sacagawea opened the flap, confusion on her face. Marie had never come here at night.

She held the lamp up and made the sign for "I go." Charbonneau stood behind her, and Sacagawea spoke in French, easing into what she wished to say, waiting for him to translate.

"We leave tomorrow," Marie began. "Hunt gives me a horse to ride, for me and the children."

"This is a kindness," Sacagawea said, and Charbonneau grunted agreement when he told it to Marie.

She dared to ask a question then. "Will it be enough?" she asked Sacagawea.

"Will the horses be enough for the children to make it so far?" Charbonneau asked, to clarify. Marie nodded. "Not enough," Charbonneau said, even without translating. Sacagawea pulled at his fringed sleeve and said something in Hidatsa. He responded. She said something back, annoyance in her voice.

"It will not be enough," he said. "The Cheyenne may trade you more horses farther along if you meet up with them. They will see you, a woman and children and they may offer to trade rather than war. Assume this is so. The woman says 'expect kindness.' Whatever you give out, it will be returned."

"Will I be enough?" she whispered then, not sure why she chose that phrasing. She had a hundred questions she wished she'd asked, about being a mother, about staying or going, about riding in the company of white men. Yet all she could think to say when she would never see this woman again was a reflection of herself: "Will I be enough?"

The woman smiled at her. She lifted her eyes to Marie's, cupped

Marie's ear gently as though it were a hummingbird. "You are a good mother," Sacagawea said. "You love your sons. They may not always do as you wish. They may not always give in return, but this will not stop you from keeping them safe, from loving them. Your sons come first in your heart. I see this. And you will carry them safely on your back as a mother must."

Marie heard Holy Rainbow's blessing in the words. Before she could collect herself to speak, Sacagawea had thrown her arms around her and they stood, these two women, weeping. Two mothers, filling each other's beaded bags with what their hearts would remember.

"Go now," Charbonneau said. He placed his hand on Marie's shoulder. His voice was old, gentle. "It will not get easier."

Marie nodded, wiped at her eyes. Her words caught in her throat, with the ache and the weight of their parting. Sacagawea pressed her hands to Marie's face, the lamplight reflecting pools in her eyes. "You will be enough," she said in Hidatsa. "And whatever else you need will be provided." Then she turned and slipped inside the tent.

Marie heard deep sobs like that of an infant coming from her own throat. She reached for a calico cloth at her waist to wipe her tears and remembered her gift. She pulled the lost knife from her waist purse. It was a thin stiletto she had brought with her from Des Moines. She'd found it when she'd returned to her tent the day Sacagawea had given her the Lewis knife. She handed it to Charbonneau who took it, nodded. He turned it over in his hands.

"*Femme,*" Charbonneau said, stepping inside their tipi. *Sacagawea is called femme too!* Marie did not wait for her friend to come out, knew she would not. They had said all that could be said now between two women, mothers and chosen friends, tied tenderly forever.

9

Pitch and Roll

The line of *engages* spread out before her, backs bent under heavy packs. Marie walked too, the hard earth jarring, the horse snorting beside her. The horse was a stumbler, but he collected himself quickly. She often let Baptiste ride. Pierre's mount had fallen on one of the ridge trails. One look at its broken leg and Hunt ordered it shot. Toupin and Gay and Carriere turned the animal into stew. Marie ate it, pushing aside the sadness she felt for the loss in favor of nourishing her unborn baby.

One of the supply horses had been given to Pierre to ride when he hunted. Otherwise, the Dorion family had one animal between them, a horse they'd named Hawk. Marie had tied a tiny bird bone in the chestnut colored mane. Sometimes the wind struck it, releasing a kind of whistle like the bird's song.

Paul hung in his board from a skin, its strapping laced over the shoulders of the horse. His dark eyes watched her and sometimes followed the birds that flitted past him. The air draped heavily with dust from the horses ahead. The landscape differed from any Marie had seen before, all rolling, treeless hills and vistas of prairie tumbling toward gray mountains. Where spring rains had once pooled, flowers still bloomed, thickening the valleys in the distance like colorful beaded bags all red and blue.

Paul's eyes crossed when he gazed at the real beads Marie tied to dangle from the rim that bowed over the head of the board. She laid a cloth over the arc to shade his face when the sun beat down. The colored stones she tied with horse hair also hung from the rim to entertain him, poor child. His feet were swollen from the stickers he picked up when he walked this hard-pack ground. He liked to strut his newfound skill of walking upright, racing flatfooted as a buffalo calf after his brother. But he still fell often, getting back up with his face full of scratches.

Dirt caught in her teeth, but Marie's mouth was too dry to spit. Paul squirmed and Marie stumbled. "Mama," he said.

"I'm all right," she said. She should carry him, but that meant shifting the load of their personal belongings on her back. She was tired. Very tired. They'd been walking for weeks. She wanted to spare the horse that the Indians said was five winters, the same age as Baptiste.

Pierre had gone off with two other men, hunting. The truth was Marie had found the first days of Pierre's absence...pleasant. No wondering about his moods, no surprise jabs with his words, no fear of his whiskey. Ever since they'd left the Arikaras, Hunt listened more to what Hoback and Robinson had to say than to anything Pierre offered. Even Rose, the interpreter Lisa "loaned" Hunt, had the chief factor's ears over her husband's words. As a result, Pierre had become irritable, often lashing out at the slightest provocation, growling at the boys like a bear at their smallest complaints.

If he was successful in the hunt, they all hoped he'd come back in a better mood.

This morning, though, marked the sixth day Pierre and two *voyageurs* had been gone. The other good hunter, John Day, had been sent to see if he could intercept some Cheyenne to secure more horses. That had been Rose's idea. She didn't mean to tell Hunt how to do his work, but sending a hunter for horses didn't seem wise to her. And now two *engages,* not accustomed to riding or hunting, and her husband, who was, had been out way too long.

"Rose is right. We can't wait for them," Hunt told her. "We have to keep pushing." He cupped his hands in that way he had, then said, "I'll order up signal fires."

"Only fools would miss the signal," Rose said. He had heavy eyebrows and a low forehead that made caves of his eyes. "But maybe you *got* fools on this trip." Rose laughed as he chewed with his mouth open so bits of tobacco sprayed out. "Maybe it was the horses. They might have flicked those bobbed tails and set their riders off."

"Save your wisdom for the Crow country," Hunt told him.

That night in late August, Hunt ordered a pyre of pine burned at the top of a ridge, and the *engages* kept it fueled all night. Marie sat beside it, her sons asleep under the skies. *What if Rose is right? What if Pierre has been left behind, injured, confused by a fall from a horse?* She should have taken the boys and gone with him. It was always better to be with him than to wonder where he was.

"I sit beside you?" It was Clappine, one of the more cheerful men. "I confess I like the desert. More than the water." He leaned in to whisper then. "I have a little fear of the rivers, though they are my life. Now I find a sea of sand that holds fewer surprises, *eh bien?*"

"That is good," Marie agreed. Clappine had dragged his sore feet along rock-strewn trails, pushing beneath branches bearing wizened fruit without names to this desert landscape. Most *engages,* like Marie, carried heavy leather packs of personal or trade goods. But at least she had a chance to ride at times. Most of the *engages* didn't.

Horses stomped in rest at night, a back leg bent like an elbow marking their sleep. Young Toupin claimed to have spent his life until now on rivers and seas. He rubbed the partners' horses down, and even in the morning Marie noticed the packhorses he loaded stood quiet, trusting.

Trusting. They were all just trusting Hunt, and Hunt trusted Rose. And the words of old trappers to find their way through to the big river, the Columbia.

Antoine Clappine sat on the ground off to the side, his face shadowed by the signal fire. He lifted his leg across his knee, the moccasin soiled and bearing a hole. He pulled at prickly pear and stickers on the bottom of his moccasin, swearing under his breath. He looked up sheepishly. "My legs, they will say 'no, you do not belong to those feet,' they are so different from feet that ride in canoes."

"Maybe we should soak them in tea," Marie suggested as she moved Paul's legs aside so Clappine could sit better. Antoine removed the moccasins, pulled *voyageurs* grease from his pack and rubbed it on his foot, then smeared more on his face to hold off the gnats that plagued their nights and days. He offered her a smear and she took it, dabbing the strong-smelling paste on her dry cheeks, pressing some to Baptiste's then Paul's face, too. "Tea would taste good."

"Can't spare much water," Clappine said. "In this dry place."

"Water comes from more than one place," she said. There might not be drinking water to spare, but she suspected that if they dug in the little dips where flowers bloomed, they might find water. And the urine of the horses and their own could be mixed for a poultice. Urine helped soften hides; it could surely soften feet.

Marie wrapped her arms around her knees.

"He knows his way," Clappine said softly. "Pierre, he will come back. He has too much waiting for him." He stood, stretched, yawned, scratched at his rib cage, then headed for his bedroll.

She did miss Pierre, missed his ways that weren't always gentle, that lacked the polish of smooth-stone men such as Mackenzie and Hunt. She missed his boasts of all they'd do when they reached the Columbia, how Hunt would reward him for all his efforts. Had Pierre volunteered for this hunt? No, he'd been sent.

They set fires again the next two nights, and the following day entered a valley where a herd of buffalo grazed. Food, right here waiting while her husband still hadn't appeared.

She saw dust in the distance. "Maybe Papa?" Baptist asked.

She shook her head. "Too much for three men," she said and then to prove her right, John Day pushed in several horses. The partners and *engages* gathered around, cheering. Marie counted thirty-six. Day quickly remounted a fresh horse and, with several partners, they killed enough buffalo so everyone could feast on fresh hump.

"We can stay here a day or two," Marie told her sons. "Hunt will not waste the buffalo, and I can help handle hides. It will give your father time to catch up."

She walked out to where the men had downed a big bull and were taking the hump. "Careful of the hide," she cautioned.

The partner McClellan looked up at her. "We aren't taking time to tan the hides, woman," he said. "Just having a good meal tonight."

Rose rode up, dismounted.

"We will need meat later, *n'est ce-pas?*" she said to Rose. Surely he would understand why they shouldn't leave this much meat behind. If hungry Indians came upon this waste, they could be angered enough to follow this expedition, serve up their own kind of justice.

"You think because you ride astride like a man instead of as a lady you get to be heard?" Rose said.

Marie's face burned.

"No sense trying to buy time for your man who's too stupid to figure out how to get from here to there. Sooner we get through Crow country, the better," he said. He took the hump offered to him and reined his horse away.

Marie could hardly eat that evening. She chewed slowly, a sickening feeling filling her as she watched small blackbirds sit on the bloated carcasses of the animals, hides still firmly attached.

Hunt walked toward the signal fire where the woman and boys kept watch. The woman had appeal to her, her quiet strength, her uncomplaining ways. The *engages* could take a lesson from such as her. He needed to tell her that they'd have to head out in the morning. They needed to keep going. Rose was right about that. And yet, he had an uneasiness in his stomach over it. Once his mother had said that through his wish to avoid distress, he sometimes created fiction out of actual fact. A part of him wondered if he wasn't doing that now, with

Rose, overlooking something obvious because he didn't want to take on the man anymore than he had by setting up signal fires. No, he decided. He had no actual evidence Rose was doing anything less than his best. They were behind. That was fact. Taking time to dry meat, well, it could jeopardize the entire expedition. Still, it didn't seem wise to leave the carnage open in Crow country. But Rose was familiar with the Crow, so he wouldn't propose doing something dangerous...

"You walk alone," Dorion's wife said in that lilting voice, interrupting Hunt's thoughts.

"Indeed. Just wanted to make sure you had enough pine for the flame."

"We smoke some of the meat while we wait. *Pardon,*" she said. "We could do more if we—"

Hunt shook his head no. "Rose says we should move on. He hears geese heading south, he says, we're so late in the season. The horses are already heavily loaded."

The woman looked up as though to hear geese then turned back to him and said, "Rose is a man of many reflections when he drinks at the river," she said.

She doesn't trust Rose, is that it? "He's served us well."

"He makes sounds like he might leave," she said. "Go to his Crow friends."

"Does he? I hadn't heard. The *voyageurs* tend to exaggerate in their discomfort away from the water," Hunt said. He picked at a rough spot on his buckskin shirt. Inside, his stomach rolled. Rose leave? If the man deserted them while they left good meat lying around, and if they didn't wait for Dorion either, why, all matter of trouble could befoul them. "I think he's done us well," he said.

"He is a man who looks for furry bank notes," the woman said.

"What? What do you mean by that?" Hunt looked at her strong chin, that perfect hair part, even under these conditions.

"If a man has a reward for taking us safely through Crow country, he has more to gain by staying than leaving early."

"No benefit at all in deserting us in this country," Hunt said.

"He has friends here. Maybe Lisa pays him for his work…"

"Sabotage the expedition? Now there's a fanciful suggestion," he said. "Lisa is nowhere around to disrupt, now is he?" Sometimes women missed things all together. Why was he even talking to this woman anyway? "We'll head out in the morning. This'll be our last signal fire. Can't afford to bring on trouble, and your husband will simply have to exercise his skills to find us. Just wanted you to know."

With that he nodded to the two boys, the older standing with his hands on his hips, elbows out. The glare on the child's face cut him like a knife as he fast-walked away.

"Where's Papa?" Baptiste asked her in the morning. More *engages* were mounting up now, though they still lacked horses enough for everyone.

"He'll be back," she said. "He's with the hunters. Remember. I tell you this how many times now?"

"You said when we woke up," Baptiste challenged.

"I was wrong. Maybe today—"

"You don't know," Baptiste said. "I ask Hunt. He tells me."

"Carry your brother for a time," she ordered. "He tires."

Baptiste lifted his brother without gentleness. "Baptiste," she cautioned. "Give him to me. We'll ride Hawk together."

Baptiste ran ahead, found Hunt. The man had taken to his leather clothes as though they were skin. Even his powder horn strapped across his chest never seemed to get in his way while he rode. He leaned down, listened a moment, then motioned the boy away. Marie saw her son seek out Toupin, who sometimes was allowed to ride a dun-colored mount. Baptiste walked too close, she thought. She lifted her chin to shout, thought better of it. She couldn't protect him every moment. She could only teach and hope he solved his problems without fists. Baptiste said something to Toupin, and the *engage* leaned over and pulled the boy up behind him with one arm.

They traveled two more days until reaching a section of canyon and river that required crossing. The rocky, barren ground beyond would make tracking them difficult. "No sense waiting or delaying longer for 'em," Rose told Hunt. Marie turned, stared back. Not a single swirl of distant dust to tell them her husband followed.

"We'll set camp early tonight," Hunt said. "Cross in the morning."

"You're soft," Rose scoffed.

"It'll give our camp boys a chance to fix more of that meat while it's still fresh. Smoke some of it. Might be our hunters will make up the distance. If not…"

"You can always stay here," Rose turned to Marie. "Wait for him."

Hunt scowled, then ordered another signal fire set at the highest point.

Marie made her camp beside it.

It would be sad to discover that you truly loved someone, missed their good qualities far more than you regretted their bad, before you had the chance to tell them, Marie thought. She looked up at the night sky. A full moon. Few stars. Unless something was wrong, he should have been back. Maybe she should stay behind, return to where they'd killed the buffalo. But then what? What if Crow people found her there in that slaughter? What if Pierre intercepted the expedition farther on, never came by the buffalo place, missed them totally? Had Hunt sent whiskey with them? She couldn't stay here. What would be the best thing to do for her sons?

"Let him do nothing foolish," she whispered. "Let me do nothing foolish."

"Mama?" Baptiste asked. "Who do you talk to?"

"I…spoke a prayer," she said. Baptiste nodded. What had Holy Rainbow told her, that she would pray for the safety of Pierre and his *femme,* even if Her to Be Baptized had not chosen the friars' water? She wondered if that woman's prayers could reach into two separate places, so far from the warmth of the center fire.

Jean Toupin brought his knife to the edge of the sharpening stone. He tried to concentrate, but he kept looking at the woman waiting at the fire. His mother had once looked that sad, when his father had died. He'd put his arm around her shoulder, pulled her shawl to her, and she had bent her face to his hand. When he'd kissed her cheek, he'd tasted the salt of her tears.

Toupin missed talking with Madame Dorion, finding out how she saw this landscape, if she could find the hope in it despite the heartache. He might like to ask her what she thought about the rumor that Hunt had offered Rose steel traps and ammunition as a reward, he said, for taking them through Crow country. Toupin wished they'd all have such a fine reward waiting at the Columbia. A man could become an independent trapper with such a start. At least it meant they wouldn't have to carry those traps on their backs any farther than Rose was going. Still, it seemed an odd thing for Hunt to do. Toupin didn't guess Dorion had been offered any such prize just for staying on.

Now, Dorion wasn't anywhere around. Madame Dorion looked that sad. She might want someone to sit beside her…but it couldn't be him. He wouldn't know what to do, what to say! His throat got dry just thinking of it. Maybe tomorrow night. Yes, if she sat out again, and it looked like she cried, he would ask if she wanted company. Courage, he decided, just took time.

Marie heard horses stomping, shouts. Gunfire. They were being attacked! By Crow warriors? She woke her sons, a soft hand over their mouths as she whispered. She felt for her knife. Baptiste rolled over, laid on his stomach, elbows bent beside her as the signal fire burned low. She scanned for the dots of campfire lights. She saw only a few riders racing around the flames. Then she heard men laughing. Pierre's voice, his booming call. *"Femme,"* he shouted. "Where's my *femme?"* The word had never sounded so fine.

She stood, called back to him. The Ioway's welcoming cry rose from her throat; tears spilled, and she failed to wipe them. He would know how much she'd missed him by their presence. She waved as he rode up the knoll toward the fire. He jumped off, swinging her as she laughed, relief surrounded by love.

Marie poked Pierre's shoulder when he finally set her down. He kissed her soundly, released her. She stumbled back, caught herself, pulled at her buckskin dress. "Where have you been, husband?" she said. "What takes you so long?"

"We lost our way, eh?" he said, laughing.

"No. What happened?" she asked.

"We were lost," he said, irritation in his voice.

"For all this time? You missed the signal fires?"

"Get me whiskey," he said. "I've been without."

The men did tell stories of their journey then, at the fire's edge. They had not once seen the signal fires, and yet they'd found their way. "This is what must be remembered, eh? We found our way in this scoop of land. We rode too far back looking for buffalo," Pierre said. "Found a herd, made our kills, and in the morning looked around and not one of us could see even a cloud of dust to say where you were heading. We loaded two of the horses with meat, but that meant walking, and that slowed us too. This is big, big country," Pierre said, shaking his head. "We might have never found you but for our good skill at keeping going."

"You didn't see our dust or tracks?" Hunt asked.

"Only a fool could get lost for so long," Rose said.

Marie watched her husband squint his left eye. She felt her stomach tense. But he must have been too tired. "We weren't really lost, Rose," Pierre said. "Just behind your party, far enough back we didn't have to eat your dust."

"If a man stays far enough behind," Marie whispered to him as they entered their sleeping hut, "it is as if he is on his own trail."

While the boats had provided a level of order—who rode in which, who poled, who pulled, what supplies arrived where—on horseback, no such understandings existed. Hunt made assignments, so at least making and breaking camp became easier. He directed separate eating groups and named more *engages* in charge of cooking and loading up. Marie and Pierre had ended up as part of Hunt's party, with the English boy George Gay as their cook.

Marie noticed her disappointment that young Toupin had not been assigned to them. Gay appeared to enjoy her sons, but she liked hearing Toupin talk of his younger brothers and sisters as he spread sand on tin plates to clean them. George was gentle enough, and he loved to sing too. But child-talk failed to excite him.

"You sit at the factor's table," Toupin told her when she rode beside him while he walked the next day. Marie nodded. She had thought of that, been too shy to say it. "You are fortunate. You don't have to hear the grumbling of the other partners."

"They want to be at Hunt's table?" Marie asked.

Toupin's voice cracked. "They just complain," he said. "About our pace. The trail. The weather turning."

The little bone in Hawk's mane whistled, and it reminded her of her copper earrings, the ones she'd lost. She felt for her hair comb holding the knot at the back of her head. She didn't want to lose it, too. Ahead, Baptiste and one of the dogs wandered toward dry grasses, disappeared inside the landscape. She shouted. Baptiste didn't respond. He was only a boy, after all. How could he be expected to remain on the trail? The landscape offered so much newness.

"Where is your son?" Pierre said, riding up behind her and Toupin, startling her. He led a packhorse behind him.

She pointed. "He explores. It's a way he gains his name."

Pierre grunted. "He could get lost. Attend to your duties, woman," he said, then yanked on the lead rope and passed them by.

She rode off toward the tall, brown grass where she'd seen Baptiste last. She called to him, and this time his head bobbed up. Beside him stood the dog. "Come," she called. She didn't chastise him when he approached. He carried a long black bug with a hard shell. She dismounted, bent to listen to his stories. His pouch was filled with tiny rocks, and Blowed, Mackenzie's dog, panted and sniffed at the pouch when he took it from his neck to show his mother. Her son's eyes sparkled as he told her where he'd picked up each treasure. "You must not wander far from the line of horses and men," Marie told him. "I miss you, wonder where you are. The dog—"

"Mackenzie tells me I can take the dog," Baptiste defended. He scratched at the dog's ears.

"Yes, but we need to know where you are. You are a part of a long snake that makes its way through this land. We must see its head and tail and in between to know it's all here."

"A snake?" he said. Baptiste looked past her. "The horses and men don't look like part of a snake," he said.

"They make up a *débile* snake," Marie told Baptiste. "But we are a part of it, and you must not make it sicker by disappearing."

She pulled Baptiste up beside her and they headed back. Her eyes looked for Pierre. She found him, astride but asleep. Hawk nickered low when she dismounted. She stepped in front of Pierre, grabbing the reins and patting the horse's nose as she looked up at her husband. The warm sun beat on his face. She poked at Pierre's leg when the horse walked past, perhaps a little harder than intended.

"What?" Pierre said, jerking awake. He blinked, grinned. "Lucky I didn't fall off, eh, *femme?*"

"Where would I be then?" she said.

The terrain had changed slowly. Fewer shading trees, more shrubs, more dust and rock to trouble their toes. Sticky heat and insects bothered them by day; mosquitoes raged against them at night so that the children had tiny welts all over their bodies. Marie put mudpacks on the bites when they had a good water supply—something that had been dwindling of late. She used tallow and grease on their faces, too. That morning, though, she'd been chilled beneath the buffalo robe. The weather promised change. They must be nearing the time of turning leaves.

Pierre disappeared into a thicket of brush ahead, and Marie pushed her way through the tangle of vines. Mackenzie and the others stopped periodically to look at a compass and confer with Hoback and Robinson and occasionally her husband, but always Eduard Rose.

Baptiste and Paul rode Hawk, Marie walking beside them. "Ow!" she said, reaching down to press at her toes that had stubbed on a rock. Pierre turned his horse.

Marie did not mind walking. It kept the swelling in her legs down. They hurt less than when dangling over the belly of a horse. But it seemed to bother Hunt when she walked instead of rode. She supposed because he thought it would slow them, but she could outpace any of the *engages,* even carrying a baby. Pierre said she could "walk a hole in the wind." In this country, she was making that true.

"You hurt, Mama?" Baptiste shouted. He twisted to see her.

"No mal," she said. "Don't worry."

Pierre rode up closer. "Want I should find some water?" he asked. "Make it feel better, eh?"

"We grow short of water."

"I can get Hunt to release some." He made his way up the line toward the leader. Marie *was* thirsty. It would be good to have a drink even if it tasted brackish. All the water did now.

Pierre and Hunt exchanged words, and Hunt looked back toward Marie. Others had stopped too. How could one woman's feet bother so many? Paul started to cry. She knew Pierre would be distressed by the sound of it. He rode back, thumped the boy on his head with his reins. *To distract,* Marie thought. To Baptiste he said, "Get off. Your mother will ride now."

"Let the boy—" Marie began to protest.

"Mount up, *femme.*"

Hawk switched at flies with his tail while they stood.

Pierre lifted his leg over his horse's neck and hopped off. "Go ahead. Get on. You carry Baptiste. I will carry Paul."

"The horse tires easily," she said. Hawk twisted his neck to look at her, ears forward as though he eavesdropped. "I thought you went to get me water," she said, glancing up at Hunt.

"We slow things. You will ride from now on. All the time." He held his hands for her to step into. She stepped up and sat astride.

"It is no help," she said, "that you fix a thing that wasn't wrong."

They were lost, not just behind. Hunt was sure of it. He swallowed hard. As long as he had a direction, a next step, the feeling of disaster he'd become aware of lately could be kept at bay. But as they moved, faster now with the woman and children riding, he still couldn't shake the discomfort.

The woman didn't understand it, but the *engages* had been looking out for her and those boys without realizing it. Rose had pointed it out to him, suggesting they might make better time if the children didn't wander off, if the woman didn't stumble as she walked. Hunt was surprised by his observation, in part because up until then he'd been wondering if Rose wasn't sometimes doing things to slow them down himself, like pushing longer to negotiate for horses with the Arikaras when Dorion was sure those people had given up all they could.

Dorion was suspicious of Rose, he knew, but Hunt thought the man was fine. He simply hadn't wanted to wait for Dorion because he trusted that the man could catch up. And Rose had rushed them before they'd gotten all the buffalo meat they could have dried for trade if not to eat, because, he claimed, he didn't want them to be targets for Crow or Shoshone arrows. Dorion was being foolish. What possible ulterior motive could Rose have to sabotage this journey? It was his throat, too, if they didn't make it to the Pacific before snow.

Hunt pulled the horse up, took a drink from the glass bottle covered with hide. Just a sip. They were running low. What if they didn't find the river? The worry edged toward him again.

His own mother had said that at times he could become quite morose as a boy, imagining bad news as though doing so could somehow prevent it. Hunt chuckled to himself. He remembered trying to imagine all the things that could go wrong as he prepared for an evening with a young lady, believing that whatever he conjured up could then not come to pass.

It did seem to work, though any number of minor disasters he hadn't thought of occurred anyway, from spilling cherries on the woman's dress to the horse's expressing indigestion at the worst possible moment. And out here, there were as many things to go wrong as stars in the heavens. Blisters and bugs were annoyances, but mixed-bloods and pregnant women could bring down grown men.

They'd made sometimes twenty miles a day, from his calculations. But neither Hoback nor Robinson acted confident whenever he asked how much farther it would be before they hit the mountains, let alone how much beyond them it would take to get back on water.

Young Toupin looked gaunt. The *engages* needed fat, more than he would have thought. The elk and venison the other hunters brought in had little fat. They should've jerked more buffalo from that big kill. The men complained of hunger constantly. Even though they worked their muscles less, no longer pulling the heavy *bateaux* up the rivers, they still craved food that satisfied. They just weren't broken to the land.

Even the horses looked leaner, and the grasses dried with little nutrition to offer. And water. Each time they filled their water bags he breathed a prayer of gratitude followed by one heavy with pleading it wouldn't be their last drink. He wondered if Astor realized when he sent them out that the landscape would be more troubling than the tribes.

As if his thinking of Indians made them appear, Rose pointed out a line of dust in the distance. Horses milling around.

Shoshone it looked like, maybe twenty. A handsome people. All these plains Indians were. Tall, strong, like Dorion's Ioway woman.

"They're intimidating us," Rose shouted. "Or trying to. Just look fierce as you can. We don't have to put up with them. We outnumber them two to one."

Dorion rode up then, gave that one-eyed squint he had when he was looking at a distance. "No rifles, Rose. Maybe they have some jerky to trade."

Rose held his horse's reins up high in front of him, arching his horse's neck. The animal backed around, tried pulling against him. The moment gave Hunt time to think.

"Let's bring your woman and children around," he said. "Set them up front here. Have them sit high."

Pierre had ridden back, and his wife had dutifully followed him. The Shoshones' milling stopped, and a small contingent rode in, eyeing the woman and boys.

"Ask them if they know how far it is to the large river over the mountains," Hunt told Rose while the Indians offered jerky to trade.

"They won't likely know," Rose said. "Doubt they've been there. These tribes don't travel that far afield."

"You talk with them then, Dorion. Seems as though you know someone almost everywhere."

Rose sat right beside Dorion, and Hunt watched the face of Dorion as he spoke and worked his hands. He never challenged, always gave respect. The braves left and Hunt said, "What did they say?"

"We're headed right. But they don't know of any big river that goes directly to the sea."

"Well, they spoke of one, an arm of the Snake River," Rose said.

"One to avoid, the way I read their words," Dorion said. "And nothing that's just right over the mountains."

"We're headed in the correct direction though, right? That's all we can hope for then," Hunt said. Dorion nodded. "At least we aren't lost."

Hunt put them on tighter water rations. Pierre had suggested it earlier, though Rose had said he was being "unduly worrisome."

They were consuming much more water than before, Pierre thought. The days were hot for September. Maybe the climate of the northern Sioux country made him soft. Men got silly if they had no water, wandered about and acted as though their minds were gone. Just yesterday, Michel Carierre had been leading his horse and got off course, dazed and confused as though looking for something. His own little Baptiste had pointed him out, and Mackenzie had ridden out to get him, his two Porcelaine dogs sniffing at every sagebrush and rock outcropping in between. The horses' heads hung low, and Pierre knew they'd have to find some way to get water soon or they'd all be crazy or dead.

He looked behind him. His *femme* never complained, at least not where any of them could hear her. She never made him look bad. He gave her credit for that. She'd even convinced the *voyageurs* and John Reed to make up tea with horse urine for the men to soak their feet in, refreshing them for the mornings. Mackenzie even put the salve on his dogs' feet.

She could spit tacks at him with her eyes though. Like when he told her to keep Paul from sticking his hands into his mush in the morning while he ate. A man needed a little time to himself without a child constantly underfoot. And she could pierce his heart with the way she raised her chin, turned her back on him. It hadn't been his fault she was here, dealing with this dust and dryness and duty.

"You can bet Rose's got extra water hid somewhere. Watch him close," Pierre told his *femme*.

Pierre watched him too. And his own sons. It was a terrible thing for a father to watch his sons' thirst, claw at their mother's breast as though they were still babies.

Mackenzie's dog died in late September. It was the one he called Blowed, the one who had trotted off with his Baptiste most often. Even digging the hole to bury the dog had rankled two of the wintering partners, for taking up too much energy, too much time.

"I will do it myself," Mackenzie blustered. The flesh below his chin quivered while he dug, and Pierre offered to help make the shallow impression for the dog. The man was still large, though the limited rations had carved out a jawbone on his face that had once been flesh chin to neck. Pierre thought the man's horse would have been the first to die, not his dog, given the load it had to bear.

Pierre noticed it was the first time Mackenzie seemed to be concerned about what was happening to them all. He'd been content to let Hunt make the choices, make the mistakes. Now, with Blowed's death, the man looked around as if he was just now noticing where he was.

"My dear sister asked my father not to drink his tea from the saucer nor to say a prayer on a night when she brought a beau home for supper," Mackenzie said as Pierre scraped at the ground with a shoulder-blade shovel. "His prayers were overly long, I'm afraid." He spoke in French, and Pierre noticed Marie and the boys standing close. "They sat to eat; Papa fidgeting with his hands with no prayer allowed. They had a fine meal, and my dear mother served the tea." Mackenzie wiped his forehead, gasped as he talked. "Papa usually cooled tea, in the saucer, but he'd promised not to that night. So he took a sip. Sure and it burned the old man's tongue!" Mackenzie smiled. "Papa spit a spray of hot tea that wet the suitor's suit. 'Glory be!' Papa said. 'The tea was neither blest nor blowed. No wonder it burned.'"

Mackenzie smiled, his eyes watery. "So I named the dogs that way. Blest and Blowed." His voice caught. Blest sniffed and whined at the lifeless form in the shallow pit. Mackenzie couldn't finish. He waved to Pierre to proceed and walked back to the camp.

Old men's eyes grow leaky, Pierre thought, *crying over dogs.* Baptiste showed no emotion at all over the dog's death. A sign of strength, Pierre decided. There was nothing to be done for the loss. Tears never fixed a thing.

Marie had laid her hide knife down, the one Sacagawea had given her, and lost it. She thought she'd left it beside the big buffalo cow, but she'd completed a second carcass after that, so she must have laid it beside that last bull.

She'd cut the liver and hump, and Antoine Clappine had promised to cut it into steaks for the "partners' table and maybe a little left over for the French dog." He smiled at her.

In fact, near the Powder River, the *engages* had glutted themselves on the buffalo despite Hunt's warning to eat slowly and sparingly after so long without fresh meat. But they hadn't listened, and they ached and groaned with stomach cramps still this morning.

They'd gotten another course correction from a small band of Shoshone. Pierre had signed what they searched for and had been told that they traveled too far north to reach the twisting river. They sighted a stream later where the Indians had said it would be, relief showing on all of their wet faces.

Then Crows had surprised them, riding in, dressed in full regalia. The vibrations of the thundering hooves woke the children, and Marie stepped outside of the hut, her hand shading her eyes. When the dust cleared, she saw horses! All the horses Hunt could need. Fresh ones, not drained by thirst and hunger.

Negotiations would begin, she could see that. Then they'd been blessed with a buffalo herd, and the Crows had remained to hunt with them. Rose seemed to know some of the Crows. Well, of course he'd been this way before with the employee Lisa said was missing. Maybe he asked them questions about the man.

Marie retraced her steps to the big bull shot early that morning by her husband. She didn't like leaving the hides, but she knew the Crow women would process them, stretch and tan them. The Astorians had time only to cut and fire dry the meat to prepare for their ascent into the mountains. Marie longed to talk with the women. She missed the lilt and lowing of a woman's voice. But now Hunt hurried them to leave Crow country.

She pushed against the heavy bull carcass. The knife had to be there. Why was she so unsettled in her mind as to lay important things down and forget where she placed them? Once she'd even dreamed that she threw Paul away as he lay in a pile of buffalo bones. She realized it too late, all her frantic searching through the dog scraps revealing nothing of her lost child. She'd awoken with a start, sweating, and was relieved to find him safe when she checked on him.

She'd begun the task of scraping the hide from the carcass. It had been some months since she'd done this kind of heavy work, and then she had been neither pregnant nor weakened from poor food and little water. She'd scraped and held the knife with her teeth, while she pulled with both hands, yanking the flesh from the meat. Then she'd cut again, slowly ripping the sinew from its hold on the meat, working carefully to avoid holes or cuts in the hide. Some Crow woman would remember her care with that hide.

Yet sometime during the day, she'd laid her knife down.

She pushed at the big bull with her shoulder, sweat dripping down inside her buckskins at the base of her breasts. She was shorter in breath now. Surely the whole time she carried this new child she wouldn't be having trouble breathing! Perhaps it was the nearness to the mountains.

She pushed again and saw the glint of sunlight on the blade. Yes, there it was! She stretched, reaching beneath the heavy hide and patting with her free hand, her fingers gripping the blade. She pulled it free and let the carcass push down against her. Pieces of sticky meat hung on the blade, and she rubbed it against her leggings to clean it off, then slipped it inside her sheath. If she just retraced her steps she could find things. She'd remember, when something was lost, she had to go back to where she started before she could go on.

They'd traveled another month, encountering small bands of Crows, Shoshones, Flatheads. Everyone had ideas about where they should go. Just the day before, Pierre had communicated with some Flatheads who said they could not reach the river to the ocean, at least not in the way they planned. She wished she could talk to the women who rode with the Flathead party, to see if any of them had crossed the mountains this way, to assure her that the Mad River, the one that snaked its way to the ocean, was one they could ride on all the way to the sea.

Rose remained with these Crow, and Marie watched as traps and rifles were handed over to him. Pierre said they weren't to trade guns to the tribes. Hunt must have thought only Rose would use them. The steel traps might have been good trade items later when they needed canoes to run the Columbia. In a way, Hunt had listened to her, though, offering up something to keep Rose with them until he was no longer needed. She wondered if Hunt might reward Pierre that way too someday, though Hunt had no fear of Pierre deserting.

As for the trail, they'd have to rely now on those mountain men… and Pierre's skills…and whatever influence Hunt had with Providence.

Her sons' eyes sank farther into their heads. Once again, they needed fat. She read into the Flathead women's looks questions she couldn't answer like: *Where are the hides you will need to stay warm in the snow? Who are you to be traveling so far into the unfamiliar? Who are you to put your sons at risk?*

They reached a big river in October. Marie felt her heart rise with excitement. There were trees near. They could make canoes. This must be the river! But they followed it into a narrow canyon only to retrace their steps.

That night, Marie listened to the arguments between the partners about whether they should have gone north to the Togwotee Pass instead of where they were now. They argued about whether the Indians had given them good advice; they talked on top of each other's words, didn't listen. Why did these men bother over what they "should have done" or if they now trusted information they'd already acted on? It was wasted fat to chew on things already decided. They were here now.

In the morning, they moved on, away from the river. White-barked trees with golden leaves dotted the ravines of mountains with sharp peaks and spires like giant versions of stones she'd seen dripping down and growing up inside caves near the Mississippi River. Sagebrush scratched Paul's board that hung at the side of Hawk, so Marie had taken to having him ride in front of her while Baptiste rode behind. Pierre said the boy fidgeted too much riding with him. "He is better with his mother."

Her abdomen pushed forward now. She had a third child already, carried on a horse. Sometimes she had to remind Paul not to throw himself back at her. "The baby," she told Paul. "You will hurt the baby."

"I the baby," he said, and she smiled.

Red stones like the peaks of tallow candles split a blue sky. The sight was so breathtaking, so unlike anything Marie had ever seen she could not even make up a story for the boys about these rocks.

"Reminds me of drawings of European castles," Mackenzie told her as he rode up beside her, Blest panting across the saddle's pommel where the dog rode now.

"*Pardon.* What is a castle?"

"A place where lords and ladies live," he said. "A home, of sorts. For royalty, kings, popes."

"If these stones mark the home of a lord," she said. "He must be great indeed."

At the Green River, Hunt ordered a camp, and from the smile on his thin face Marie could see that his spirits ran high. He recognized this river, he told Pierre, from what the Shoshone told him. "It goes direct to the Mad River, just over that next ridge. Only a few days away. And from there it's an easy run to the Columbia. We'll make it before the snow flies yet."

Two days later, at the banks of a wide river, Marie's heart sank. Another band of Shoshone came upon them and shook their heads at Pierre's questions about running the river in canoes. Marie could tell by looking at its dark waters that it was a deep and secretive river, holding currents and twists beneath its surface. Swift with rocky rapids, only boulders lined its banks, its rage and rush crushing out any plant that dared to sprout. The Des Moines, the Missouri River, all had rapid twists, but they also had warm carpets of green to contain them, to offer up grass for the horses, places to set tents for rest. Sometimes the rivers left rich, deep circles of soil as they meandered around, signs of nourishment in their midst. The Ioways often farmed those rich middle places.

Not this river. The islands were narrow and sliced the river like open wounds. Even the *voyageurs* frowned when they saw it. The Canadians had talked of nothing but how good it would be to return to the water. Now they mumbled to each other, shook their heads.

"There are no good trees for canoes," Michel Carriere said when Marie asked what troubled them. "Cottonwood does not make good boats. The wood is slick, hard to work. It is not a good sign that there are no good trees here. This cannot be right. If it was the river the American, Clark, said we could take to the ocean, there would be canoe trees here."

Hunt ordered them to spread out, to find suitable boat material. Then he sent Pierre, John Day, and the Irish sutler, John Reed, to scout the deep canyon to see if canoes of any kind could carry them through. A cold, October rain spit at them as the men saddled up to leave. " 'Tis the season of unstable weather," Mackenzie said. "Hot then cold."

"Like this expedition's successes," McClellan grumbled.

His words made Marie's stomach roll.

10

Witness

Lisa let the girl rub warm oil on his back. He lay on his belly, his face resting on his forearm on a buffalo robe, his britches still on, shirt off. The Omaha woman-child was a beauty, though shy as a pine marten. He'd wanted to secure an alliance with the peaceful Omaha people. A marriage-of-the-country with this señorita would do that…if she showed any interest at all…as the youngest daughter of the chief.

The guest lodge fire cracked, and he felt sleepy, snug, while cold winds blew outside. His eyes drooped. It had been his best year of trades. And he still had supplies enough to last the winter here and then head back west to Henry's Fort where the cache of furs might still be found. He'd be remembered always for his chase of Hunt, his river feat. In one twenty-four-hour period his *voyageurs* made seventy-five miles, three times the distance of a good river day. All because he knew what drove men.

And the best was yet to come: when word came back from Rose or the mountain men that Hunt had failed, took another wrong turn. He smiled to himself. It had all worked out so well. He was close to a magnificent cache, had ample goods for trade, had ruined the hopes of the richest man in America, John Jacob Astor. And if successful, this young woman, Mitain, would one day warm his bed. No one could beat Manuel Lisa.

"Listen, a little ache in the shoulder, you can work that area, *sí?*"

Silence greeted him. The girl was said to understand some English. "Mitain?" He rolled over.

He was alone in the guest lodge, with only the buffalo robe and his memories to warm his bed this night.

Hunt expected Dorion, John Day, and John Reed to explore the river for four days. They returned in two.

Dorion's eyes held a vacant look, cavernous. He rubbed his hands in what had turned into a drizzling cold.

"Are we close then?" his wife asked before Hunt could.

Dorion shook his head. "Many bitter blasts await. The riverbanks in places are walls of rocks. They overlook rapids like hungry tongues moving in and out of a growling mouth."

"No place to beach boats?" Hunt asked. "No—"

"We can't run that river, Wilson," Reed told him.

"Head north," Hoback, the mountain man, said. "We know that country better. Maybe we'll find some game that way."

Robinson shook his head no. "We'd never make it through the snow on the pass."

"There's a river there," Hoback said, ignoring Robinson. "Ain't never been explored, but chances are it gets you to the Columbia. We was at that river with Lisa's employee he was looking for. Henry. We can get you there. We've been there."

Hunt frowned. Why was it so hard to decide? Was he too tired, too hungry? Everyone looked beaten. The partners offered no help at all, just left it to him.

"Can that river fork take us to the Columbia?" Hunt asked Hoback.

"Better river than this one." Hoback nodded.

Hunt sighed. "If it accepts a canoe we can claim it for Astor, for the company's future. That is what this expedition is about, gentlemen," Hunt said. "Taking steps for the future."

"No, it's about getting somewhere alive," one of the partners said.

"We're going north," Hunt decided and the weary caravan changed direction.

They made it through the mountain pass. The *engages* wrapped their feet in furs. But at the banks of what Hoback said was the Teton River boiling with white water, one of the partners, Miller, threw up his hands. "I want out of this expedition. Look at us. Starved and wizened. On a river that'll kill us. I won't be a party to it."

Hunt could feel his stomach knotting. He hadn't anticipated any of the *partners* wanting out. Only an *engage* or two or those mountain men. But they'd remained faithful. Why now, when things looked hopeful again? Hunt's heart pounded. His hands sweated inside his gloves. *Let them desert,* Hunt thought bitterly. That's how he'd note it too, if the expedition failed. Desertion. What was he saying, if it failed. It couldn't. He just couldn't.

The party tromped along, *voyageurs* loaded with axes and tomahawks, blankets and beads. They carried what they'd need to trade for food and canoes once they reached the Columbia. The weight burned more fat from their already challenged bones. Marie could see her breath as she puffed in the cold October morning. Both boys complained of hunger.

"Quiet," she said. "We ride Hawk while others walk. We must not complain." Marie noticed even the horse had thinned on this journey. She patted his neck, ran fingers through his mane as they plodded up narrow trails scattering pebbles as they passed.

At the Canoe River, they halted. "See! I told ya so!" Hoback pointed out two old cabins they'd built the season before with Henry while in Lisa's employ. "I know this river, yes sir, I do." The wooden palisades were deserted now, but reassuring for Marie's eyes. Hunt christened the river "Henry's Fork" and called the dribble of huts "Henry's Fort." At least they'd found something they had set out to find.

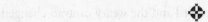

While the hunters brought in game to supplement their supplies, the *engagés* built canoes from the stands of fir and pine. Fifteen boats in all. It took many days. The horses they then left in the care of a band of Shoshone who appeared out of the morning fog. Hunt gave them some trade goods, hesitating over how much smoked venison to offer up. He refused to give them rifles but promised more beads and little bells when a return party came back for the horses in the spring.

Marie patted the neck of Hawk, fingered the tiny whistle in his mane. She retied the rawhide so it would stay, though she knew it unlikely she'd see the horse again. The gelding lowered his big head, nickered low. Baptiste wiped his eyes, as though he understood the leaving.

"It's all right to cry," she said. "Our people are good criers. It cleans the soul." Baptiste did cry then, burying his face in the dark mane he'd hung on to when he sat in front of his mother. Paul, too, patted the animal.

"So, so," she told the horse. "You stay and we go." He pushed against her, and she pressed her cheek to the big animal's head, breathing in his scent. She shifted Paul to her other hip, pulled out a twig in Hawk's mane. His ears twitched back and forth. "We named you Hawk, but you named yourself as a good friend, strong and faithful."

A Shoshone woman, built lean like Sacagawea, nodded to her as she handed her Hawk's lead rope. She made the sign for bird, made a diving motion with her hand, the word for hawk. Then moved her hand level with his heart. "Good," Marie said. The woman nodded, signed "good" back to her and added the words "big heart."

Marie saw them last as they loaded the canoe. Hawk stood beside five or six other horses on a ridge, ripping snow-dusted grass, the wind separating his tail hairs.

Nestled inside the canoes, Marie and her sons whisked now past the gray rocky ridges lining what Hunt called the Canoe River. Floating on water, she felt safe in the hands of *engages* like Michel Carriere, young Toupin, and the others. They could read rivers. She trusted that, tried to forget the pricks of worry circling the men's words at the evening fires. None had seen any waters such as this Canoe River was, with its narrow gorges that kept them from easily beaching for a portage and promised swift currents that twisted them, unsuspecting.

When the sun hit their faces, the days were warm. But the deep canyons shadowed, bringing chills beneath their buckskin clothes.

"Even in Rupert's land," Jean Toupin told Marie, "I never saw such a twisting, growling river."

Black rocks that looked burned jutted out of froth as white as a trillium while ebony water surged around them. On this river, men whom she'd come to recognize by their voices shouted from behind, signaling directions of how to take a rapid, learning from the sink and boil of boats crashing through before them. She found small comfort in their calls, her arms holding her children tightly while water baptized her face.

At a calm section of river, she'd look over the side to watch a leaf picking up speed, promising an approach to the sound of a distant roar. "Beach 'em!" someone would shout, and the *engages'* muscles would bulge in the effort of bringing the wooden boats to a place where men could get out, catch their breath before walking ahead to see what more they faced.

Often, they portaged. Men stood then, assessing the white water that split the surging rush, making whirlpools and hiding rocks and unforgiving ridges. Marie shivered in the drizzle. She pushed a fox skin around Paul's face, tied a wolf hide around Baptiste's shoulders and neck, but still the wind whipped at their faces, chapping them raw. She tied her belt around her own belly, surprised that the baby did not push out more. Even the ties at her rawhide dress had not been loosened. Could she be losing weight and the baby still gain? Her own fingertips looked white more often than not, and she exhaled onto them, stuffed them into a wad of rabbit fur until they tingled with pink.

On shore, she watched while the supply-laden canoes were eased through a narrows by rope made of twists of braided buffalo hide. On one day two canoes were swamped, all provisions lost. That night, they ate ducks Pierre and John Day shot to supplement their dwindling venison jerky. Marie's teeth hurt, and she wondered if the lack of fruit could make her gums ache so. She must ask if Reed had cider vinegar left and drink some. It might help her babies, too.

They camped beneath a stand of cottonwood, the night air cold. Reed commented at the partners' meal that he was low on tobacco. "Seems every man wants something to soothe him after this sort of day. Had quite a rush on chews."

"Lucky we didn't lose your stores then," one of the partners said. "Lost just mere buffalo robes and jerky."

No one laughed.

"This is a mad river," Clappine told Marie and Pierre later when they stood with the boys at the fire. "No matter that Hunt chooses to call it the Canoe River. Even in the calm, it churns beneath. An angry, dark snake of a river, it is. Mad."

"Can I go in your boat tomorrow?" Baptiste asked the *engage*.

The Canadian brushed the boy's dark hair. "It would be a good change from the coughs of that partner Ramsey Crooks," he said. "To hear a boy's voice. But—"

"Please?" Baptiste turned to Marie.

"Let him," Pierre said.

She could use a rest from the child's constant tending, leave her more time for Paul, perhaps allow him free of the board. But having both her sons within reach seemed comforting to her, as selfish as that might be.

"It'll toughen him to be away from his mother, eh?"

"Your brother will be distressed if he sees you too far ahead."

"Papa says."

"No!" she said, squeezing his arm harder than intended. She glared at Pierre.

"You never let me—" Baptiste began.

"Your mother may need you to keep her safe," Clappine said and took the moment to depart.

Frost lined the canoes the next morning.

They entered a narrow canyon midday. Clappine had gone ahead with others to assess the need to portage. They'd returned saying they could go a distance but then would need to carry the boats to avoid a long and dangerous rapid. As they approached the portage point, Marie could see the river boil as though in a long trough of iron, spraying and spilling, stirred by the Evil One's fork. Ahead, Clappine maneuvered a canoe with the partner Ramsey Crooks and several other *engages* when the canoe shifted sideways to the sound of splintering wood.

Suddenly squares of merchandise baled for transport disappeared beneath the roll of white water. Shouts and screams echoed in the canyon. Marie's heart pounded as she watched *engages* struggle to handle their own canoes while attempting to reach men in the water. Clappine and two others clung to a rock, their fingers white. "Hang on!" Hunt shouted.

Hunt ordered boats pressed to the shoreline while ropes were tossed. Too short! Then too late as the remains of the canoe swung around, crushing Clappine and pulling him under. Four other men sped like dry sticks sucked down the rapids, spilling out below. Marie pushed Paul's face into her breast.

"Mama, Antoine swims." Baptiste pointed.

Marie stared. Could it be? Was he all right?

Men bobbed, swirling and bumping into rocks. Shivering *voyageurs* were picked up downstream. Then fires were built and a count taken. Baptiste sucked on his thumb, something he hadn't done for years. All Hunt's men were present, save one: the *engage,* Antoine Clappine.

❖

It was clear they could not make passage to the sea by this Canoe River. "I had hoped it was a way," Hunt said. He chewed the inside of his cheek. The partners' eyes glanced uneasily between them.

Pierre watched Hunt in the firelight. Were his eyes pooling? No. Surely no leader had watered eyes. It was enough that Mackenzie grieved his dog, that his own sons had cried when they left that Hawk horse behind with the Shoshones, and again when Antoine Clappine was lost to his watery grave.

But a leader should never cry; it only disheartened his followers. Even Pierre knew that.

These men, these partners, were soft. They had trouble making the hard decisions. Sometimes things did not work out, but a thing had to be decided, just the same. If not for all these men, then each one for himself. A leader must give hope. Hunt kept sending parties out, looking for information as though some right and perfect piece of news would be brought back to tell him exactly what to do next.

A leader had to gather up what he could and twine it like a bridge over an empty chasm, moving from where he was to where he needed to be. A man's strength was the courage it took to cross that gorge, not in the gathering up of information about how to do it.

"Dorion, head on up, you and an *engage* or two. See if the rapids cease after a few miles."

"Wilson…" Mackenzie said.

"Do it!" Hunt ordered.

The men obeyed, found that the river still twisted and snaked. When they were alone, Hunt said to Pierre, "This is a branch of Lewis's River, then, not the Canoe at all. Just the Mad River that snakes to the Columbia, I know. It can't be floated, not from here. We've come upon it too far north." A light snow fell as they talked.

"We will go back, winter at Henry's Fort?" Pierre suggested.

Hunt chewed on his cheek. "No. Let's see if we can't find some way of putting canoes in and out on the south bank. We've turned back enough."

At the campfire with the partners, Hunt prepared them for the south bank approach. "Rations are getting low," he said. "We've no horses now. We've got to split up. Some of us have to chance the river. The south bank may prove more agreeable to our little crafts."

Marie and Pierre and the boys were part of the river group joining sixteen Canadians in four of the best canoes. Toupin was not in their party. Just as well, Pierre decided. His *femme* had enough boys to mother.

The sutler, John Reed, no longer needed to hand out meager supplies—he had none to spare—so Hunt assigned him to take several men overland seeking to trade for horses again, and food, and bring both back to Hunt's party if they succeeded. The partner Ramsey Crooks volunteered to return to Henry's Fort, to retrieve the horses left there—if the snows weren't too deep—and then meet up with the main party. The mountain men would go with him. Donald Mackenzie took four men north to find the Columbia, away from the river on foot going by compass points. Toupin was chosen by him. The final group, McClellan's, would follow the river easterly with the same orders: to find the Columbia, horses, or food, and bring them back for the others who would simply walk along the river's shores.

"Get a good night's rest, gentlemen. Lady," Hunt ordered, tilting his head to Marie. "Tomorrow tells the tale."

In the morning, the four groups separated. Hunt's group lowered the canoes into the river hoping to cross, hoping the terrain on the other side would be less hostile. If they could portage, maybe they would find a branch of the river they could navigate father along. They began passing, one by one, using a rope to take the supply canoe through a rapid.

The boat capsized spilling precious cargo.

Only three canoes remained, not enough to transport all of Hunt's divided party.

"We cache the canoes here," Hunt said. "And anything we don't need to trade for food or for canoes once we reach the Columbia. We carry only what we need." That done, they began the long walk above the river.

Hunt's party moved now through a place made up only of sharp, black rocks with not even an old blade of grass sticking through. Falling snow eased their parched throats some. They were on small rations of dried meat.

Even scrubby sage is looking good to eat, Hunt thought, as the wind whipped snow from the land, pitting his face with cold sand.

Marie felt the painful kicks. Her baby wrestled from within her, protested. Hunger gnawed at her, at this baby, her sons. She felt tears in her eyes as she watched Baptiste dragging his feet; Paul was so light that when she lifted him it was as though she were winnowing seeds.

She kept walking. Hunt's party continued on, intercepted after a few days by Reed. He'd turned back only to describe a desolate land, no sign of Indians or food or horses. Then Crooks came, thwarted by weather and the realization that a return to Henry's Fort without horses and trying to come back to Hunt would take him too long. The snows would consume them. Only Mackenzie's group had kept going.

"We need to split into smaller parties," Pierre said. "A group this large will cause any Indians to hide for fear we'll eat up all they have. Fewer is better, eh? You may have missed signs of Indians, Reed."

"You go out there then," Reed said. "'Tis not so easy a task."

"Now, gentlemen. We'll make a base camp here," Hunt said. "We're all a bit irritable, and now is not the time for squabbles."

There were trees at least at this place where the Mad River could be crossed if not canoed. It was a *boise* or woodsy place, Marie called it. Odd to find it here when they'd come across so many miles of rocky land longing to be touched by trees.

"Looks like wormwood trees," Mackenzie said.

Within a few days, even the smaller parties returned. The news didn't vary. No one had seen Indians, horses, or food.

"*Pardon.* Could we winter here then, at this *boise* place?" Marie asked. The trees would permit shelter. In a moon or so, her baby could be born, and she could rest.

"*Non,*" Pierre said. "We speared all night by torchlight and caught only one sturgeon. How long could we live on that? No, we keep going, I say. There are Indian people out there. We'll find them. They'll help."

Hunt nodded, agreed, told Reed, "We trapped eight beaver. We dried some for you and ate the rest. Still it is not enough to feed all of us for four, five months."

"We advance on foot," Pierre said.

"Who's giving the orders?" Crooks said.

"I am," Hunt answered. "And we do what Dorion says."

Hunt's party numbered twenty-two, including Pierre, Marie, and the boys. They took the north bank of the river; Crooks led his party on the south. Pierre thought Mackenzie the wisest of all the partners to simply follow a compass point north. But Hunt was perhaps the most in need of Pierre's service. And if they made it, it would be Hunt who would recognize Pierre's contributions.

Survival supplies were toted as were trinkets, his *femme* called them, things needed for trade if they encountered Indians with food or horses. And still *engages* carried heavy loads of powder, lead, knives, tomahawks needed for trades once they reached the Columbia, and tools to make more canoes. It was a balance to know how much to carry for trading, yet not so much the weight of it could hurt the bearers.

Hunt's group walked without following the river now. Few trees dotted the landscape. At times, they could hear the roar of rapids, see the sliver of water in the distance. They could not canoe it. They couldn't even drink from it. They took sips from pools of rainwater or melted snow left in the clefts of the sharp rocks. They could see across, once or twice, to follow Crooks's progress. Gradually, the Mad River's canyon widened, and Hunt's small party walked on alone.

Through it all, Hunt did not scowl or blame. Neither did Pierre's *femme*. He may not have been with the most skilled overland group, but at least grumbling did not drain them. He wondered if his *femme*'s disposition shamed the men, kept them from complaining when they heard nothing from her, a woman who carried a baby. It was not what they needed, this baby. Not now. Pierre frowned as he watched his *femme* pick up Paul and slip him around to carry him on her back. She must have miscalculated when the baby would arrive, for her hips had barely widened.

When they stumbled onto a Snake Indian camp, their presence so startled the families that even the women ran off, leaving their children hidden beneath straw.

"How could they leave their children?" Hunt said.

"They have little food, even for themselves," Pierre replied. "Maybe they hope we'll follow them so their babies at least can eat."

Hunt nodded as Marie squatted to talk to the children.

"Stand up," Pierre instructed. "Stay where you can be seen, *femme*. Let the boys move about too. If their fathers are looking, we want them to see that we mean no harm to them."

"They have a knife," Marie nodded toward a blade lying on the ground. "One of our trade goods."

"Maybe McClellan came this way, sent them back to us," Hunt said, excitement in his voice.

Hunt moved next to Pierre then. "There's a man watching through the bushes. Can you speak with him?" Hunt asked. "Tell him anything you think will make him willing to trade for food, then information."

Pierre nodded, appreciating that Hunt permitted a man to think for himself, without telling him how to accomplish a thing. Pierre plucked his cupped fingers twice at his heart. Then lowering his hand to his waist, he made a motion back and forth as though being cut in two. A man stepped forward, and Pierre exchanged signs with him.

"They have little to spare," Pierre told Hunt. "They will let us have a dog. But then we must move on. They say we are going in the right direction, to the Big River."

The Snake Indian man eased out of the brush, slipped sideways, bending inside his tipi.

When he stepped back outside and offered Pierre's *femme* dried fish, she took it, tore off pieces to give to her boys. Hunt nodded for her to eat what was left.

Pierre signed more.

"What did you tell him?" Hunt asked.

"That the mother was hungry," Pierre said. "He says we can stay just this night."

"Good enough. Now convince him that she has many children so all our bellies can be fed."

In November they came upon a small Shoshone family traveling through. They offered directions too when Pierre signed, looking warily at so many hungry Astorians.

"They want us gone," Pierre said to Hunt. "Not sure I trust their information."

"What choice do we have?"

Marie could hardly listen now when they encountered Shoshones, or Snake Indians, as Pierre had taken to calling them. She couldn't think straight. Her boys whined. Her stomach growled. She pressed her small hands to her belly. The baby was so tiny. It barely moved, her infant, even when she lay down at night, her back arched into hunger. She fed it with soft words, but never enough food. It was her only choice.

She had hoped her milk might return so Paul and Baptiste could have something to sustain them, but her body gave up only a pale liquid and that not for long.

"The boys will toughen," Pierre told her.

She imagined he told her this to make her feel better about not having any milk, not that he was indifferent to the suffering of his children.

Then she began to see things. In the distance, a cluster of cottonwoods beckoned and Marie dreamed of food, of steaming buffalo hump and moist cornmeal laced with plump chokecherries. She thought of grainy corn bread drenched with honey. A thick-stemmed sagebrush reminded her of back strap, the tender loin along an elk's back that nearly melted in her mouth after a quick stick at the fire. Blue sky made her think of huckleberries and then beads and a meal shared with a friend beside the Missouri River. She longed for something solid and warm inside her stomach. So she didn't at first trust what she saw ahead.

Gray points like tallow candles dotted the distance, emerging eventually as tipis near a river surrounded by dogs and several dozen horses.

They gave them fish to eat, dried and chewy, in exchange for some blankets. Hunt bartered for five dogs and tried to trade for a horse they could roast.

"Can't they see we're starving?" Hunt asked as he and Pierre left a tipi.

"They don't eat horses," Pierre said. "Only dogs."

"Maybe you've gotten them to change their mind," Hunt said, motioning toward a Shoshone brave leading a spotted pony their way. "At last," Hunt said. "Meat." He swallowed.

But the Shoshone walked past him and handed the lead rope to Marie. "Mother rides," the man signed. "You move on."

The following day, Hunt's party ate two of the dogs they'd traded for, supplementing the food with dried chokecherries one of the Shoshone women had given to Marie. They ate another, boiling even the bones into a weak soup the day after. It did not go far with so many men to feed.

Marie had not allowed herself to name the Shoshone horse she'd ridden now for several days, sure it would be asked to give its life. The horse had been a gift of kindness to her, to relieve her children of some fatigue and give her rest as she straddled the horse's bony back. She patted its soft nose as it twisted its head to gaze at her.

"Your horse," Hunt said, nodding to the animal after several more days as men chewed on old leather and slurped up soup made of water and herbs. "We must eat your horse." He stared at her. "Tomorrow."

A wind-driven snowstorm pushed against Marie's eyes. She moved the fur of a wolf pelt circling her face that draped over Paul as he settled between the shoulder blades of her back. She remembered as she did long years before, when she was just a child. She'd found herself alone inside a blizzard once along the Mississippi River. Each time she thought she'd falter, just sit down and sleep, she would take one more step. *As long as I can still remember three old stories told around the winter fire, I will stay awake, take another step. As long as I can recite the friars' beads, from beginning to end, I will stay awake, take one more step.* She kept giving herself challenges. *As long as I can tell my own sons three more stories, I can take another step.* She continued on.

The gift horse nickered.

Her stomach growled in hunger. She heard other stomachs too, watched the shaky hands of men, their faces raw from wind, eyes sunken in starvation. Had Sacagawea and her child endured such hunger? Marie wondered. Her friend had survived, found a way through.

"We can eat the horse, or let the woman continue to ride," Hunt said that evening.

"*Non,*" Pierre said.

"We vote. Everyone has a vote, including the woman."

How could she deprive them of this food? *And yet,* she thought, *as long as there is another step I have not taken, I can go on.* Perhaps that was so for the men, too.

Not a single Astorian voted to eat Marie's horse.

"You give them hope," Pierre told her that night. "That's why they vote to let you ride. So long as food walks beside them, they can dream of the next meal. Hope," he said. "You give it. Hunt doesn't." Keeping the horse alive was a gift of kindness to them all.

The next day, a small celebration broke out when they came across a family of Shoshones who said they'd seen a white man traveling with a brown-and-white, long-tailed dog.

"Blest!" Marie gasped, finger to her mouth.

"They are indeed," Hunt told her, but he smiled, knowing. "It's good news," he said. "They're still alive and must have gotten fish or fowl somehow if that dog still lives."

"Mackenzie would never eat that dog," Marie said.

"Indeed. He has the luxury of living off the fat of his jowls for a while yet, so he won't have to make that choice." Hunt laughed. Marie thought the sound of it was almost as filling as fish.

They reached a twisting river. At first Hunt thought it might be the Columbia, and the *engages* stood straighter, one even broke out in song. But as they approached, he could see it wasn't wide enough, not as Clark had described the Columbia. He unscrolled the map, his voice cracked with emotion.

"It's the Snake River. Again," Hunt said.

"Mama, look!" Baptiste pointed. Hunt turned to look, seeing faint color through the snow. Men moved.

"It's Crooks!" Pierre Dorion shouted. The forms halted, and Hunt heard them shouting back.

"I had thought they would be at the Columbia by now," Hunt said, his voice tight. "Make up a boat from one of the buffalo robes," he ordered.

Dorion's woman used her skills at making the round boat formed from buffalo bull hide. Her fingers moved stiffly in the cold. She rolled out a buffalo hide, telling Pierre to gather willows, which she twisted with rawhide into two hoops, one slightly smaller than the other. The fur side of the hide would ride in the water. On the inside of the hide, she laid the largest hoop then pulled a foot of it up over the top hoop. Around the edge, she used her knife to cut holes in the hide every few inches.

"Hold it," she told Pierre. She braced the sides with sticks. Then, with rawhide, she worked the strands through the holes, pulling the sides up. It was like lacing up leggings. Finally, she had a round bowl wide enough for two men to kneel in and paddle. The boat could be pulled behind a canoe or paddled by itself. The buffalo's tail still attached would drag along behind in the water.

"If there was time, I would hold it over a fire, to shrink it tight to the frame," she said.

Hunt shook his head.

Dorion got in, paddled across, and picked up Crooks, who was thin as an oar. He stuttered from hunger and the effects of exposure. Hunt had Dorion make two more passes to pick up men, bring them together on the same side, Hoback, Reznor, and Robinson among them. Now Hunt had too many starving people staring at each other.

"You can't go farther," Crooks told Hunt when he'd consumed the small portion of dried fish Hunt gave him. "We've all got to go back, to some stream. For fish. For beaver. Kill some horses." He looked at the Dorion woman's mount, wiped his mouth.

"Back? But we must be just a few days from the Columbia."

Crooks snorted. "This river...too far. Wait until spring." He coughed, wiped blood from his palm onto his leggings. His hands shook.

"But we're so close—"

"We're not close," Crooks said. His voice cracking. "Best bet is to go back, find a place to winter over."

"You can't go anywhere, sick as you are," Hunt said. He paced, squeezing his hands.

"*Pardon.* The *boise* area," Dorion's wife offered. "It is where we last had food we caught for ourselves."

The woman was right. Hunt stared at the eyes of Crooks, his men, the children. How had it come to this? All the trading, of powder or trinkets for food, of traveling north or south, of canoes or blistering feet, eating horses or dogs. It was his doing. He somehow had to salvage what he could of this, bring as many through alive, regardless of when.

"We go back then. To that woodsy area. We had beaver there. We could make shelters. And there were friendly Indians."

"Won't stay that way if we use up their good will," Dorion said. "All of us trying to winter there—"

"I realize you disagree," Hunt continued. "We'll leave John Day to hunt for you, Mr. Crooks, and that *engage* who also looks too weak to travel." He nodded to LeClerc, a once robust silversmith who spoke of learning a blacksmith trade when they reached the fort. "When you feel up to it, you can follow us back. It's my decision. And you three...mountain men?" Hunt said it as though he'd eaten spoiled meat.

"We're staying right here," Hoback said. "Fewer we are the more likely some friendly Indians'll take pity on us. Make the best of it negotiating with the locals in this frozen place, then head back to St. Louis come spring."

For just a moment, Hunt wished that he had negotiated to go with the ever-moving red-haired Scotsman Mackenzie. Surely the man was a better leader than he was. Mackenzie must have been in the best shape of them all. He hadn't even eaten his dog.

Pierre shook his head. They were back at the *boise* place, after weeks of retreat through snow and rock. Hunt now sat with his hands around a tin cup, hot water steaming. A few flakes of dried leaves floated at the top, pretending to be tea. Pierre looked at him, wiped his nose with his hand. He hoped he wasn't seeing his own reflection in Hunt's defeated eyes. They just had to survive the winter. Lucky for them, they had shelters here and some food. Baptiste had snared a rabbit—his son!—and an *engagé* had trapped another beaver.

Pierre hunted farther from the camp the next day. He made a lucky shot through a cluster of trees. Then, with the carcass of the small buck draped across his shoulder, he stumbled into even more good fortune: a friendly Shoshone camp.

"They say they know the way to the Columbia," Pierre told Hunt. "Come spring."

"Can you get them to guide us?" Hunt held his fork poised to poke at another piece of hot venison. He chewed slowly. His eyes, earlier vacant as caves, now showed some light.

"They say we're crazy to try it now," Pierre said. "Wouldn't have told you if I thought you'd try to leave now. My *femme*—"

"You take me to the Shoshone. I'll shame them into taking us. Can a woman carrying a baby be tougher than one of them? Ha! I'll get us a guide if I have to trade your woman's horse for him."

Pierre bristled. "It is her horse," he said. "Not yours to trade."

Hunt lifted his chin. "Indeed. It's a Pacific Fur Company horse," he said. "An Astorian horse. Everything belongs to the company. Best you not forget it."

In the end, three Shoshones agreed to take them and offered up parfleches of dried food in addition. "It is advent," Hunt said. "The time of anticipation. The perfect time to travel since we have three wise guides to show us."

The party once again set out.

They reached the place where they'd left Crooks and found more of Crooks's original party.

"Bring us across for some of your food," an *engage* called.

"We'll bring some to you in a bullboat. No need for you to cross," Hunt shouted back. Again the bullboat was unrolled, rehooped, and food put into it along with an *engage* to row it across. But one man, so deranged from starvation, thrust himself into the boat, throwing his would-be rescuer out. Within seconds his weak state was overtaken by the water, and he slipped under, losing his life, the food, and the boat. Robinson, one of the mountain men who had gotten separated from Crooks, shouted across that they would stay where they were, pray some Indians might provide them with food.

"We ought to stay together," Hunt said, pulling at his beard.

But there were thirty-two now, plus Pierre's wife and sons, and three Indians all still miles from the Columbia if what the Shoshones said was true. No one had seen Crooks or John Day or the hopeful blacksmith, LeClerc. Hunt shook his head. They were nearly ten months on the trail and still weeks from their destination.

"All of us will not make it," Pierre told him. "It is better we divide."

"And keep going," Hunt said. "Let these Indians guide us."

For the first time, Pierre let himself wonder what would happen if they didn't survive. He saw himself digging shallow graves for his wife and children, all because he owed a debt to Lisa so long ago, a debt he'd refused to pay.

The pains started as a backache.

"She would not wish to hold the party up," Pierre had told Hunt. "We will catch up, eh? In one day."

Pierre's sending Hunt and the rest of the party ahead bothered Marie. Why, she couldn't say for sure. It was true she didn't want to hold the now-divided group up. She didn't worry that they might somehow miss them in the snow. Pierre was a good tracker. This was woman's work, this heaving and squatting new life into being.

Several days after the *engage* had drowned, the Shoshone guides had led them into a wide valley with clusters of trees and mountain ridges standing as sentinels. The sun felt almost warm on her face as she pulled branches into place, rolled out the hide to line the bottom and the shelter's rounded top. In between sharp pains, she stood, took soft furs from her leather pouch. She still had the swatch of linen purchased at the Osage camp in the company of Winter Blanket.

The baby's coming early must have been what made her uneasy. It should not be ready to face the world yet. *So small.* Perhaps her infant grew hungry inside with so little food, so little comfort these past months and now made its name by its choice to come early. She could offer it so little. She hoped she would have milk.

Being alone with her children, husband, and horse, did not distress her. But the arrival of a being whose life had already been placed at risk by her selfishness, she who did not want to be left behind in St. Louis, this concerned her.

"Your wife's a strong woman," she'd heard Hunt tell Pierre. "Not a peep of whining from her the whole time. Quite remarkable. I didn't realize it was her…time."

She did not think of herself as a strong woman, no. She named herself as uncomplaining. How could she complain? She had chosen this. She had asked for the ache of hunger for her sons. She had requested this cold place for the arrival of her infant.

She hoped it would be a boy. A son would be welcomed. A boy would grow to manhood to take care of his mother if his father died. A son might forgive what his mother had done to him in bringing him to this place, this grand valley, to be born early into cold.

A girl would remember that her mother put her own needs first.

Marie prepared the place for birthing while Pierre built a fire at the open face of their mounded hut. The boys huddled near it, trying to get warm before they dozed. Sleep came easily to the hungry. Marie turned herself, patted the area as though it was a nest. Outside, snow fell. It reminded her of the month of gray snows, when Holy Rainbow said, "A special child was born." She told her, "Celebrate. Fill up with the presence of the infant, given as a gift."

Advent, Hunt had called the season. Waiting with anticipation.

Marie celebrated with a single cry when a tiny, wailing girl slipped out almost without notice. She picked the slippery infant up and held her to her breast, caressed her face and dark hair.

Pierre bent back inside the hut, having stoked the fire. A slender cord strung between her and this baby as she lifted the child up for him to see. He nodded, didn't smile. She bit the cord, tying it tight before laying the baby at her breast. The baby fit into her two palms, she was so small.

Did Marie dare to name her?

"It is a good sign," Pierre said, leaning over her.

"That she breathes? That she is born early?" Marie said. "What?" She heard the horse stomp beside the lean-to of branches they huddled in. Baptiste awoke, poked his brother. She could see by the tallow candle the wide eyes of the boys huddled in the hut, watching their new sister. "What is a good sign?" Marie repeated.

"That it is a girl," Pierre whispered.

"You wished a girl?" It surprised her.

He cleared his throat, looked over at the boys. "I will take it, Marie. Let me do this." He put his hands out to receive the infant.

"You would swaddle the child, a girl? You would do this?"

"*Non.*"

She felt her world suspended like a spider from a single strand of web. Every scent, the horse, the afterbirth, the sweaty warmth, the touch of skin to skin. She hung on every sound of breath: her sons', the horse's, her husband's, this infant girl's, waving in a startling wind.

"*Non,*" she whimpered, knowing then. "*Pardon!* No!"

"It will not live, *femme.* You must know this. It will only make the dying harder. You must think of this infant, not yourself, Marie."

"She has come this far. She has come early. Yes." Marie swallowed. "*Oui*, but she wants to breathe the air we breathe, to be out of the water. See? Her tiny nose, it moves, it takes in…" She clutched the baby to her breast, fumbled to put the tiny face to the nipple, her fingers bone white with cold. "See. She eats. She eats."

"Marie," he said. He touched her face gently with his chapped fingers, brushed at the wetness on her face. He did not look at the child. "It will not live. Let me do this thing for you. To keep three babies alive—it will be too hard. To keep this one when you have no milk…it is selfish, risks the others."

"She eats. She eats. See, she opens her eyes. She looks at me. She already knows me. She's strong. She'll live." Pierre placed his hands over hers. "The friars would not want…" she insisted, "No, no, no, no…"

This was her fault. She took this child on a river journey full of rapids and starvation, long before it chose to breathe the air. What had she done to bring such fragile life into a place where no hands reached out in hope, where one who shared her blood would stop the flow of it?

"Look at you, so thin, your bones push out." Pierre's voice was kind, kinder than she had ever heard him speak to her before. "Even if it was a boy, we would need to do this, *femme*. You cannot keep yourself and these two and now this one alive."

Her mind swirled. *What have I done? What have I done? If only I had stayed in St. Louis. If only, if only…*

"When she dies, it will not grieve you so much. A girl will not carry the weight of grief as a boy child. That is why it is a good sign. Give her to me, Marie."

He called me Marie, she realized, saying her mother name as she wished to hear it, full of kindness and with love. Marie. Her mother name. Tears formed at her eyes. She knew. The baby could not live in this cold world with so little stored up before its arrival, so much bitterness to face to even take a breath. Was Pierre right? Would she grieve her daughter's death less than a son's? She pressed her lips to the infant's forehead, smooth as a river rock, a slight taste of salt upon her tongue. A daughter's life was hard. It required tending, loving, living often without notice of the effort given. A girl, a woman, might be the mere reflection of her work, what she accomplished, nothing more, to some. But Pierre was wrong. The world around them might not value female children, but that did not make them of less worth. Each child she bore arrived with equal weight inside her heart, inside the Up-In-Being's sight. She was sure of this, as sure as Holy Rainbow was that she was loved. Marie's memory, her "heart knowing," as Sacagawea had signed it, would know no difference in the grieving if she lost a daughter or a son.

"This is why you sent Hunt on without us," she whispered. He knew what he would do, had planned it. Yet his eyes were kind, so very kind. His hands looked weathered, but gentle.

"Give me the *enfant*," he said. "It is better we do not make it suffer more."

She pressed the child to her, rocking and rocking until he pried her fingers from the bundle. "Marie," he said. "My Marie."

She was so weak. So very weak.

11

Providence

Pierre led the horse, striding out, pounding his feet like nails into the cold ground. They reached Hunt's group twenty miles farther into the valley, a single day's ride for Marie and the children. Pierre shook his head, surprised to see the camp. The man was soft. He had halted after all.

"To celebrate New Year's Day," Hunt told Pierre when they arrived in the mountain-circled valley.

"It is the Canadians' favorite day," Marie said, her voice like a loon's, sighing and low.

"So it is. We'd earned a rest. You, too, I see."

He peered into the bundle she held in her arms.

"It is a girl," Pierre's *femme* said.

"And you've named her what?"

"Vivacité," she said. "It means deep feeling. Intensity. A wish to live. She named herself." As if on cue, the infant cried a high-pitched wail.

"She should be called Defiant," Pierre said. "She will keep us all awake with the passion of her living. We can only hope she does not have her mother's defiant ways." He thought he saw the color of his *femme*'s face deepen from more than just the cold chapping of her cheeks.

She'd said she was weak, but it was he. He just couldn't do it, not when the woman begged as she did. Yet his weakness would bring her more pain later, he knew this. An infant barely bigger than the palm of his hand could not live. Marie's breast was larger than the whole child. How could it suckle? He was weak. Still, the look on Marie's face as she smiled at him now warmed him in this winter place.

For seven precious days, Marie nestled Vivacité at her breast. Pale-sky liquid dribbled into the infant's mouth, stopping the weak crying only for short times. As she rode, Marie held the child close to her, showing her tiny face to Paul and Baptiste who merely glanced, then hung their heads in fatigue. Paul now rode between his mother and brother. Marie could hardly look at her husband, and yet she knew: He was a prophet in this war to survive, trying to tell her a disaster lay ahead.

Even now she could hear the pain arriving in the infant's weakening cries. So hard to hear her cries and have no way to stop them.

She thought of Holy Rainbow's God. Could he hear Vivacité? Did he care less that this infant was a girl? Would he have kept a boy child alive? She spoke into the moonlit night, wondered if her l'Ayvoise words would be understood by Holy Rainbow's God.

"Can you carry this child in the cleft of your back?" she whispered as Vivacité lay in the crook of her arm, only slightly heavier than the fur that surrounded her. "Is she your beloved? Will you keep her from hunger when I can't? Just a few more days, the guides say. Just a few more drops of milk to keep her alive, that's all we need. Or will you make her dying be a message to her selfish mother?"

The morning Hunt said was January 6, 1812, broke with sunshine over the tree-covered hills. Sweet-scented smoke drifted over the camp. Led by the three guides, the party wove from the valley through a cleft in the high ridges. They'd started upward. Ice clustered at the edge of a fast-flowing creek. Marie's horse was bony and slow. He drank along with the Shoshones' mounts. The sunshine warmed Marie's spirits, though it did not fill her belly. Still Marie heard her boys laugh and point at a hawk high above as they trudged upward following the stream.

Vivacité tugged at Marie's breast with less vigor than the night before; her dark eyes stared into Marie's face now as the horse carried them along. The infant seemed to peer through her. Her body did not move. She didn't cry. Her face no longer pinched in hunger. Still pools of water formed in her staring eyes. She blinked eyelashes the width of horse hairs. Blinked once, twice.

Marie sang softly. She could almost feel the closeness of food and shelter. Vivacité moved her tiny tongue out between lips smaller than pumpkin seeds. A hint of blue circled her mouth. Marie thought she saw the flutter of a butterfly's wings inside her daughter's eyes. So small, with just the slightest wink of letting go. Glassy eyes, like tiny dark beads, lids softly closing and then open wide.

The hawk screeched overhead and Marie looked up to see it soar. When she looked back, she knew her world had changed. Marie pressed the fox fur away from the tiny chin. She brought the baby close and kissed her forehead, nose, those tiny lashes. She gazed again. So blue, she could almost see through her skin as thin and webbed as a birch leaf. The child drifted away. The hawk screeched again, a kind of whistle to its throat. *You have done what you could,* those eyes seemed to say. *You have been a good mother. Now let me go.*

They placed the infant in a shallow grave dug by the *engagés* and Pierre. Marie kicked at frozen rocks to loosen them, piled them over the tiny shroud of fur. Pierre crossed himself, mumbled, made the sign of the cross again. "Come, *femme,*" he said. "She is not of our world now."

He took her elbow, helped her onto the horse, and they headed out. Leggy goats watched them from high in the surrounding rocks. She smelled elk scent, but the men were too weary to pursue it. The Shoshone guides said they were close now. Soon. Very soon they would see the river that would take them to the sea.

Two days later Hunt's party overlooked a valley that spread like a gold-and-brown blanket patched with white. Snow-dusted tipis rimmed the flat below, surrounded by a thousand horses. And beyond flowed a river, a vivid ribbon of blue.

Marie turned to her husband. Tears formed in his eyes. If only they hadn't turned back. If only.

"Providence. I cannot sufficiently express my gratitude to Providence for having let us reach here," Hunt said. He sniffed and rubbed at his nose with his handkerchief. He'd said the words first when they'd gazed down from the mounded ridge above this camp. He'd repeated the words several times since.

For the first time in months, the Astorians had enough food and water and friendly people offering shelter. "Providence provides," Hunt told the straggling survivors.

Where was Providence two days ago? Marie thought. If she could have kept her child alive just hours longer, her daughter would have seen these handsome Cayuse people, would have been nourished by the milk of a Cayuse mother. Two more days and Marie could have gained strength to make her own milk again. If Providence was so all-seeing, all-loving, why had Hunt been blinded to the right rivers, the best choice?

Just two more bitter days. Providence hadn't found a way to keep her alive. Her daughter would have gurgled as the women admired those tiny fingers and lashes. Her child would have ridden on one of the more than two thousand horses grazing in the plains beside the river they would follow to the Columbia that would take them to the sea.

But it was not to be. Providence wore the faces of the Shoshone guides and used the hands of these friendly people to deliver these men to their precious river. But Providence had not been large enough to save one tiny female child.

Like the Shoshone, the Cayuse refused to eat horse meat and used their dogs to transport goods, lap their faces. But seeing the gaunt men, Pierre said they'd understood Hunt's party would eat the dogs and accepted these white men's ways…at least until they had strength to hunt elk and deer. The Cayuse shared their fish with them, plenty of fish.

Hunt had purchased eight horses and two colts as soon as the Cayuse allowed the trade. Venison was in short supply, and the Cayuse mostly lived on dried fish and berries. Hunt wanted to limit how much of the Cayuse provision they ate, especially when they'd given them shelter as well. So he'd ordered colts stewed for the Astorians.

"You must eat now, Marie," Pierre told her. He offered her meat from the stew pot Hunt had ordered prepared.

"Why should I eat?" Marie said.

"Your sons need you to be strong for the rest of this journey. We are not there yet, my Marie."

"You are within reach," she said. "Hunt's Providence will get you there without my help. There is no need of my eating now. My boys will live with their father's help." In truth, she did not want to take food from a man who had wished his daughter dead. She wanted to punish him as much as she wanted to punish herself for her selfish choices.

"Then eat as a gift to these people," he told her. "They open their lodges to us. It is a kindness. Receiving it acknowledges their wealth, *femme*. You know this." He took a bite of the stew meat stuck on the end of his knife. "These people could turn on us," Pierre went on, "decide we are not worthy of their generosity. Where would your sons be then?"

"Providence will provide," she said.

"Marie," he said. "Do you want to die here, among strangers, because you refused their kindness?"

Marie thought of Sacagawea's words. Wealth meant one had enough to give away. *Providence must not be wealthy,* she thought. Providence kept her baby who needed just tiny breaths of air to fill up.

"Your sons need you. A mother must think of her sons," Pierre said.

She narrowed her eyes at him, tired of the journey, forgetful of her reasons for coming at all. "I no longer wear the name of mother. I take it off." She tossed her robe to the cold ground and stomped on it.

"The name belongs to you," he said. "You chose it." He chewed the meat, staring at her. "See? You have sons."

"What mother would expose her children to such empty stomachs?

211

What mother would not give up enough milk to keep her child alive?" She hissed the words at him. What kind of mother could still love the father of children allowed to suffer? "You should take back your father name too," she said.

Pierre picked up the robe. A cold east wind blew across the plain, and Marie shivered. "It does no good to lay blame, Marie. The wind hits us, sometimes because we rode to a place where the wind always blows. Sometimes because we are pushed by storms that come only once to a place. It is a poor bet to say we should not have been there. We are there. Now what to do? How to stay warm? Who will hold us in the storm, eh? That's all we can ask with the hope of an answer." He bent and picked up the robe, motioned for her to put it around her shoulders.

"Now what to do?" she said as she took it, mocking his words.

"Your sons," he said, looking past her. She turned.

Baptiste carried a piece of dried salmon in one hand and pulled his little brother with the other. His hollow cheeks were puffed out now, stuffed with the meat and already filling out after only four days with these people, barely a week since her daughter had died. Bits of salmon stuck in his teeth. "Eat this," the boy said handing it to her. "I am full."

Already giving her directions, just as his father did. Someone was taking care of them. Someone would look after them if she died in this place. Let Providence do it.

"I'm not hungry," she told her son and walked away.

Hunt gave two of the sturdy mounts to the Shoshone guides who had brought them to this place on the Umatilla River. Pierre had been afraid that Hunt would offer the guides nothing but trinkets or a shirt as he'd heard Lewis did, adding insult to intrusion. But Hunt had given something of value and thus honored both the guides and the Astorians.

This was good, Pierre thought as he rode out, hunting. This Northwest was big, wide country allowing the eye to see for miles while on either side mounds of ridges rose up. Yet deer seemed to disappear into little dips and knolls of the rolling grasslands. Pierre hadn't gotten close enough to shoot any, but his eyes had feasted on the landscape. No wonder the Canadians from the North West Company pushed into this country. David Thompson already had a lodge constructed he called "Spokane House," on a river north. Rumor was he prepared to collect furs to ship to the Far East, too. Competition.

Snow dusted the mountains in the distance. They had to be full of beaver and elk and deer and fox. No wonder Astor had invested thousands in this expedition. This place had as many or more riches as the waters that reached to the great Hudson's Bay.

And here he was, stepping into this commercial canoe before it was even loaded, before anyone really knew how much richness it could hold. Pierre felt his heart race. It was an adventure, taking hold of this new land. Hardly anyone here yet, except one lone man from Rupert's land—David Thompson—and now Astor's crew. And him.

And all these Indians. It surprised him, his thinking of himself as "one of Hunt's men," an Astorian, before recognizing his mixed blood. But he *was* an Astorian now, for better or worse. He was. It hadn't been his fault that the Astorians wandered for so long, not finding a shorter water route as planned. Hunt had listened to Rose and the other partners more than to him. But he, Pierre, had negotiated at that *boise* place where a smaller river met the mad one. There he'd secured the Astorians good guides. His words had encouraged the *engages* to persist over mountains, despite their weakened state, reminding them that little children and a mere woman trudged beside them. He shamed them into staying alive. And he'd done his best to protect his *femme* from the pain of the baby's early birth.

He'd failed at that. She'd suffered for a week watching her child die. He should have taken the infant while she slept, placed a hand over its mouth so it would not have suffered. But he couldn't face his *femme's* eyes. Neither the child's.

The girl might have lived. Paul had lived despite his troubled start. Pierre's own mother had intervened then, and the boy grew, learned at his own stuttering pace.

Pierre's horse stumbled and recovered. They had to be just a short distance from the Pacific. He was sure of this. And Wilson Hunt listened to him and learned the ways of these Cayuse, the Shoshone, and others. Hunt wasn't rigid like some of the partners, nor…bored, as Mackenzie had been. Hunt learned. He didn't expect things to happen only one way. He understood that the ways of the Indians here might be similar to how the Eastern tribes did things, but there were important little differences that he best pay attention to.

Pierre noticed the differences. The Ioways and Sauks and Foxes had taught him to watch keenly. His *femme*'s people's ways were not his ways. Even the burial of their *enfant* would have been done differently among the Sioux.

A sharp pain came with the memory. Rocks marked Vivacité's grave in this land, not the presence of a cradleboard swinging from a tree or the sound of wind sighing through the remains of a high funeral pyre. His mother would have laid a cross there.

He thought of when his father died. He'd been gone on a hunting trip. When he returned and stood at his father's grave, Holy Rainbow showed little sadness, and it occurred to him then that it was because she, too, knew it was the way of all living things.

"The Friars say we will see him again," Holy Rainbow had told him. "In another place and time. Not like a spirit that returns to roam the earth. Not like that. But as a child opening his arms to those in his family who have wandered and now return home." Her eyes had been filled with tears when she turned to him. "It is a hope," she said, "and the promise of a good father."

Why had he thought of that now? He was a good father, even if he couldn't get his sons' mother to eat. Pierre fidgeted in the saddle. His mother once said that his acceptance of baptismal water was a sign that his heart had changed. Maybe it had, more than he knew.

His *femme* would want to go back to that grave. He knew this. She'd place things there, perhaps shape dirt around it into the form of a beaver or a horse as her people did. Maybe on the return trip east, when they went back they could do this. In the spring, if they returned. He'd always thought he would return, until his family came along.

He heard a noise off to his side. A deer with large ears and a rack of horns raised its head. Pierre lifted his rifle from across the pommel of the saddle, loaded the powder then eased it onto his shoulder. The deer bounded off. He whistled and the animal stopped, turned to locate the sound. It was a pattern he'd learned in this new place. He closed one eye, sighted and shot. As he rode up, he spoke an honoring prayer for the animal who gave up its life for his *femme.* Dying was a part of living, didn't she know this?

Marie no longer dreamed of food. Pierre poked the venison chunk from the hot fire, blew on it, and handed it to her still stuck on his knife. She'd smelled the meat roasting slowly, the animal cooked by one of the *engages,* Michel Carriere.

"Is very good," Michel insisted.

Her hipbones stuck out as though elbows; her hair felt brittle and dry. Her small hands looked like chicken bones wrapped with flesh held together with blue strings of veins. But the hunger that gnawed at her did not live in her stomach anymore.

"I take some to *les enfants* then," the *engage* said, lifting his palms toward Pierre with a look that said, "I have done all I can."

"The woman is stubborn," Pierre said as they left the tipi together.

Marie lay on a robe, weak. She wondered idly where the boys were, yet she couldn't seem to work up a worry. She should have been making repairs on their clothes, doing what she knew how to do. The buck's hide needed tending, but she had no strength. It would take energy to scrape clean and shape the hide, no doubt stiffened by the cold.

She sat up to do something, couldn't remember what. Maybe find Baptiste, see if he and Paul were together. Were they sleeping in someone else's tent? Toupin, what had happened to that boy with the acorn eyes? She couldn't remember.

She noticed her knife, picked it up, and turned it over in her hand. What had she been planning to do? She knelt back down, her palms drowsy on her thighs. She sat, not sure for how long.

She felt air from the flap opening at the hide-covered lodge they'd been given to use. Paul waddled toward her. He pulled on her skirt. "Mama," he said. "You come?"

"Not now," she said.

"Go," Pierre told her, coming in behind the boy. It was an order. She wasn't sure if she had the strength to go or to resist his order. "Take your robe. It's cold."

She sighed, stood, pulled the robe around her. She let Paul lead her outside. No clouds roamed the blue sky. She could see her breath, but the air didn't feel cold through to her bones. Smoke from the tipis drifted above them as Paul led her to where a woman stood. How did Paul know this woman? Marie looked down at him. His tiny fingers opened to show a palm with dark roots piled inside. He smiled that large grin of his that squeezed his eyes shut and made his thin lips disappear.

The Cayuse woman lowered her robe, motioned with her hands, signing, "eat" and "good," her hand level with her heart. The woman was nearly as tall as Marie, though one shoulder sagged more than the other.

"*Petit,*" Marie said. She held her fingers to show "just a little." Some of the men had been sickened by the root's richness after so long a time without food.

The woman nodded, and before Marie could tell him it was all right, Paul pushed the soft roots into his mouth, his palm mashing them around his face. Soot marked the edges, ringing his smile.

The Cayuse woman's fingers covered her lips, suppressing a giggle. Marie allowed a small uplifting of her own lips. The woman had a kind face, doelike eyes. Maybe this woman had been looking after Paul while Pierre had been out hunting. He seemed at ease with her. Paul laughed.

The woman signed "all gone."

With dirty fingers, he scratched at a pouch hanging around his neck. He pulled another cooked root out. "Mama eat?" he said.

She stared at him.

"The boy wishes you to live," Pierre told her, coming up from behind.

Paul's lower lip moved out as she shook her head no.

Pierre signed something to the woman then, his hands working so quickly Marie had trouble following it. She motioned for Marie to follow.

"Go, Marie," Pierre told her. "I will watch the *garçon* and Baptiste. Go now. They will be safe with me."

His voice held gentleness, lacked blame. When had that started? After the death of their baby? Did he think she could forgive him so easily? Did he think her so paddle-minded she would not remember what he said about the arrival of a female child, about naming Marie as a mother who did not love enough? Who could love a man who loved a woman like her?

The Cayuse woman said something Marie failed to understand, then motioned again for her to follow. Her moccasins pressed along a patchy snow-covered path marked with mud. It led to a small hut next to another tipi. Footprints indicated frequent use. The woman pulled back the flap of a tipi and motioned Marie inside.

Marie could hear the rush of water from the icy stream beyond. Water. It would take them soon to the mouth of the Columbia and whatever waited for them there—if she chose to go. Maybe she would just stay behind, disappear inside her mind.

Inside the tipi, Marie listened to bare branches of willow brush against the lodge's leather. The woman motioned for her to undress. Marie hesitated, but the woman unwrapped her own robe, slipped off her leggings, her moccasins, and then pulled her buckskin dress up over her head. She picked up a copper pot Marie recognized as a trade item they had brought. It had water inside. She pointed to a low lodge just outside, then made the signs for "mysterious" and "unknown."

"Medicine," Marie said. The woman stepped out.

It would feel good to be clean, to let the heat of the hot rocks inside penetrate her aching body, ease her wounded spirit, bring color back to her fingertips. It had been a long time since she had sat with women, listening to their breathing, taking in the comfort that arrived on soft chatter spoken without demand. When had she last inhaled the peace of women's presence in a warm lodge?

Long before St. Louis. Long before she had come this westward way. It had been with Holy Rainbow and some other Yankton Sioux mothers. Before Pierre took her as his wife. She'd been surrounded by women there, mothers and sisters she'd grown to care for. Holy Rainbow had used her name inside that sheltered place, Her to Be Baptized. It had been a loving place, a hut for holding things she had not known she'd need for her journey into marriage.

She wouldn't understand what these Umatilla River people said. She did not hold them as friends. Their world was different from her own. If she lived, she would be going to another world with men and women who knew different ways. She felt tired. If her daughter had lived, Marie would have introduced her to such newness. Together they could have come to know this land as a woman would.

These...sisters weren't here to help her begin a long journey into marriage, into what the future held. She wore a new name now, a mother name. *A mother name.* How had she earned such a title? Just by giving birth?

She had placed her children at great risk; she'd been too weak to stand alone. She had a long journey to make before she could respond to the word "Mama" without wincing from the judgment.

What mother needed the judging eyes of other mothers? She did that one job well herself. Her husband had begun to call her gently by the very name she'd wished, yet now it held no truth.

The Cayuse woman returned, steam lifting from her body. She must have plunged into the river after sweating in the hut and was returning now to feel the heat some more. The woman touched the sheath at Marie's waist, Sacagawea's gift. *"Bon couteau,"* the woman said, motioning "good knife" with her hands. She indicated the knife would be safe in the lodge, then signed, "Question. You called?"

She'd asked for Marie's name.

Marie shook her head as though she didn't understand. It was too raw, this question.

"Called Calming Water," the woman said, pressing her fingers to her own breast. "Question, you called?" she signed again.

Marie turned. She knew it was rude, but she hoped her beginning to undress would make the woman think she had not heard.

She removed her knife and sheath, pulled her clothes from her body, folded them, then stepped between the two lodges and bent inside the smaller. Several women huddled. Marie could see them just before the flap closed behind her leaving them all in total darkness. She smelled the warmth of the firepit, the fresh scent of something like cedar or pine. It was like a womb, she thought, dark and moist and safe. She let herself sink into the curls of buffalo robe she felt against her thighs. She leaned her back against another that lined the hut. The heat bristled wet at the base of her neck, at her hairline. Warmth permeated into her hips, her spine.

Calming Water dipped her fingers into the copper pot, threw a spray of water onto the rocks burning beside the entrance, and the steam rose. Marie could see the woman's face in the fleeting firelight; two others sat beside her.

They were kind faces. Mother faces, offering comfort as a mother does. It was who they were, named by their choices. She thought of Paul's look when she declined his root, of Baptiste's when she turned from his venison chunk. It was all they'd had to offer, and she'd refused. A mother should never refuse food offered by a child.

Calming Water touched her hand in the darkness. Marie felt the woman crawl toward the opening, then motion to Marie. In the sliver of light let in by the opening flap, she signed, *"petit,"* and Marie knew that on an empty stomach, she must not stay inside the heat for long.

Marie crawled to follow, aware now of a deeper hunger. She stood, wobbly. Calming Water led her the short distance to the cold stream, and they plunged in, hand in hand. The shock of it sent shivers of pain like porcupine pokes all over her. Marie gasped, taking in air as she stood, water cascading down her shoulders and back. She sputtered, tossed her hair onto her back. Calming Water looked at her, and together the women laughed. It felt so good to laugh.

Hunt said Providence had led them all here. Perhaps Providence wore these women's faces, their caring hands. Perhaps Providence would fill her up.

A light snow fell on her and Calming Water, big flakes streaking dark hair with white. Marie was an Ioway woman of the Gray Snow people; gray like the stuff that strengthened bones.

They had no more need of the Shoshone guides. Now they'd consult the writings of William Clark to make their way. Pierre could hunt more than guide from here on, but he still had gifts to offer Wilson Hunt, gifts of his experience, of languages and the subtleties of commerce he picked up. And he would have to do that without the aid of whiskey.

It had been weeks now. The shakiness of the loss of liquor had mixed into hunger shakes beside the Snake River and the mountains. He couldn't tell the one gnawing from the other for a time. The Cayuse had no whiskey. Not even the North West Company dared trade in that.

But now that his stomach was full, his mouth longed for that other comfort. It helped settle his mind. Hunt had no more whiskey. John Reed's supplies—and perhaps Reed himself—were depleted. Pierre would have to do his work without the benefit of the counsel of rye.

Hunt bent over Clark's map laid out on a rock. The scratching gave no help as Hunt moved his finger through the deep canyons of the mad Snake River and turned back to that *boise* place. But now that they knew where they were, the maps could guide them to the sea.

Hunt pointed to a place on Clark's sketch. "See here," Hunt told Pierre. "That river there must be the Wallow Wallow. Wonder why they repeat some words?" Hunt underlined the word with his finger.

"It makes the word smaller," Pierre told him. "The word for dog is two sounds of the word for horse, meaning a dog is a small horse. *K'usik'usi*."

"Indeed," Hunt said. "So Wallow Wallow means…?"

"Wallow or *walatse* as some say, means 'running water.' That river," he pointed, "is a small running water, compared to the Snake there. Or the Columbia. See, where Clark marked it."

"Our Canoe River must have been Clark's Mad River. The Snake by another name. If only we had known." Hunt shook his head.

"Nez Perce are there, where that river comes in." Pierre pointed. "We've entered downriver, but found friendly people, too."

"Providence," Hunt said. He pointed back to the east. "We've crossed a range of mountains Clark and Lewis never encountered, I suspect."

"River rapids they didn't know either," Pierre said. "One that's Antoine Clappine's grave."

Hunt cleared his throat. "Indeed. We have already lost more men than Clark did. I am sorry for that. And not knowing what's happened to Crooks and Day and Mackenzie and Reed does not permit easy sleeping, even on a full stomach this past week, thanks to your efforts." Pierre heard the sound of children, laughter in the distance. "At least your family is still intact, Dorion," Hunt said. He pronounced it the way Pierre did, as though it rhymed with Des Moines. "That is, the family you started out with." He cleared his throat. "I regret…your wife…she is—"

"She is a good mother."

"She is that," Hunt said. The men stood silent for a moment before Hunt continued, "Now then. I believe we should head out this way, don't you think?" He pointed to the map again. "See if we can get information about canoe material and what sort of difficulties we may have making passage through these narrows Clark makes notations about. Celilo Falls. I'm counting on your efforts, Dorion, to keep us alive through them. Astor worried about the river tribes more than any of the others."

"Have you seen Carriere?" Marie asked Pierre later when they'd finished eating. "He said he'd sing, put the boys to rest."

"He went out hunting with some of the Snake Indians." Pierre nodded his head in a direction where a small band of the Indians had camped. "I'll look around."

No one had seen Michel for several hours even though he knew they planned to leave.

"We will just depart?" Marie said the next morning. Pierre tightened the rawhide around the parfleche.

"We can't wait," Pierre said.

"You would just leave him," she breathed.

"Don't say it as though we commit some crime," he said. "He may have chosen to stay behind."

"When you were lost, Hunt put up signal fires."

"For all the good it did."

"But he—"

"Carriere knows where we head. He can find us from here."

But Hunt delayed the expedition. Pierre's ears burned red when Hunt told him his wife had made a good case for an additional search. His *femme* had gotten her tongue back, and it entangled his work.

He and another *engage* who'd recovered quickly spread out to look for signs of the French-Canadian who loved singing to children. The Cayuse people told him that the Snakes did not easily mix, chose warring over words. They'd seen the French-Canadian ride off with them, laughing, when the Snakes broke their camp. Pierre even followed part of the trail of the Shoshone guides back toward the *boise* through what the Cayuse called the Shawpatin Mountains. The Blues. No sign of their Astorian.

"He might need help, and we do not bring it." Pierre's *femme* rocked forward as she knelt in the hut, then back, a low moan forming. "Would you leave me this way? Would you say, 'Oh, she wandered off. It was her wish'?"

"Marie, I—"

"Did your father not say a man should bring a body from a strange land? Take it to rest at home where it belonged?"

Her words stung. He had heard his father once say this. He had given such promises to old traders and trappers himself, had even made such comments about his own body, should he be found dead.

"He would look for you," she whispered. "He would not leave your bones to be found by wolves in a faraway place with no one to mourn them."

"It's not—" And suddenly he knew: This was not about a missing *engage* or putting a man's bones to rest. She had not insisted they walk the banks of that Mad River hoping to find the drowning victim. His mouth felt dry.

If only he had a touch of rye to ease into this. He took a deep breath. "Maybe the French-Canadian goes to our Vivacité," he said softly. "Maybe she welcomes him and he carries her…"

Her rocking stopped. She stared at him.

He heard her moans then, rising to a keen of grief, a death song she had been too weak to sing when they placed that girl-child in the grave.

He leaned toward her, whispered into her ear, his lips missing the feel of the copper earrings that once dangled there. "Some seeds are planted that never grow, my Marie. And others, they grow, but not how you expect." He breathed in the scent of her hair. Cedar. She had been cleansed in the women's hut. "We go now. To the sea. With two young plants who need their mother. For that is what you are."

He put his arms around her, wondered if she'd let him rock her back and forth. She did.

He knelt beside her, no longer craving rye.

12

Destiny and Desire

Beaver splashed abundant along the willow-lined stream. Fresh horses carried their goods, Marie, and the children; Pierre and Hunt rode as well. "It's a land of plenty," Hunt repeated as he pointed. "Too bad we had to cache the steel traps back there." He pulled out his hunter's watch, clicked open the hard case. "It is already seventeen, January." He stuffed it back inside his shirt. "Our desire now is to move down this Umatilla or the Eu-o-tal-la River, that's what you say they call it, Dorion? Indeed, until we encounter the Columbia, make our trades for canoes and our final destination."

"We can make canoes?" Marie asked.

Pierre shook his head. "Clark says the bluffs close to the Columbia have few trees on them. The Indians have traded well for their canoes, and we'll have to lure them with big hooks to catch big boats. Clark says these tribes have all they want, eh?"

Marie thought of all they'd cached hoping Hunt had sorted well. Did they carry what rich Indians would want?

The climate felt mild here. The ground muddied as they rode. Even that evening, the air though cold did not bring an ache to her feet. The buffalo robe wrapped around them felt almost suffocating in the close space where her sons breathed in sleep beside her and Pierre. This was strange country, this flat plain, this winding river. Not freezing and yet it was the month they would hunt bear at home, wrestle them with their hands. She'd seen her father do this once long years past. She fell asleep remembering.

Marie heard the rumble in the distance, followed by soft pats of rain against the tent they'd pitched in the willows. The tap-tap became a torrent followed by cracks of thunder. A flash of lightning and the horse whinnied and stomped. Marie sat up, pulled her dress on over leggings and moccasins, and tied her knife to her belt. She'd just check the horse to make sure it was tethered. As she stood she felt the tent side bulge against her shoulders. The hide draped around the lodge pole collapsed, sending a cascade inside.

"Pierre!"

He already sputtered from the wet that quickly rose around his ankles. He pulled on clothes, grabbed at the children. "Give me Paul," she shouted above the rage of rain and something else, some other rushing sound. Paul clung to her hip, his fingers grabbing. "Go," she told Pierre. "Help the others." He almost threw Baptiste at her then, sloshed out, rousing Hunt.

When the lightning flashed, Marie could see that they were mere lily pads inside a wind-driven sea. Water pressed against her calves as she hoisted Baptiste onto her back, reached with her one free hand for what she could grab. A basket swirled past like a snowflake in the wind. She snatched a leather parfleche, pulled on it. She turned around, thinking of what to take: a trade blanket. What else? Another flash and she caught a glimpse of Pierre as he disappeared into the darkness.

She sloshed away from the willows, heard the shouts of men and horses. A crash of thunder followed by lightning allowing her to see what made the roar: the rising Umatilla, pushing mud and branches and small trees their way.

They could get away faster on the horse, she thought. She turned, couldn't see it. It would risk the boys to spend time searching for it. "High ground!" she heard someone shout in French. Hunt barked orders.

She pushed water with her knees, her thighs, the children crying, the darkness like a grave of blackness. *At least Vivacité missed this. She'd been prevented from dying in this.* Marie stumbled, righted herself. Her feet touched a bench of higher ground. Shallower water. She kicked at a bundle of trade goods floating in the water, pushed it with her foot, then grabbed at the muddy bank before her. She scrambled up, slipping, water pulling at her skin dress. Mud caked beneath her fingernails as she clawed, Paul's hands around her throat nearly choking her. Baptiste slid off her side to make his own way up the slick bank. His leaving gave Marie a spurt of force. Her toes dug into the soft mud as she clutched at clumps of grass at the top. She peeled Paul's fingers from her throat. More lightning. Baptiste stood off to her side. They were on safe ground. "Watch him," she said to Baptiste as she set Paul on the ground, then turned back to grab a parfleche, another bale of goods before the rush of the water swept everything away.

She felt the sting of tears then, brushed at them with muddy fingers. To her right men shouted. She listened for Pierre, tried to locate him in the darkness. The rumble moved away. Light split the night in the distance, a drizzle fell.

Perhaps she'd seen her husband for the last time. Perhaps she would be a widowed mother now, as lost and alone as though he'd set her off back in St. Louis. Maybe her sons, too, would succumb to this harsh land. And it would be by her hand, being at a place where wind and water washed to shape her as though she were mere stone.

"Hey there!" Pierre said. He raised his rifle in a wave at Marie and the children. Her shoulders straightened as relief flooded through her.

Marie shivered, her children huddled on her knees, and Pierre moved through the *engages,* checking on supplies. When the darkness gave way to feeble dawn, she saw the river of mud that had swept through their camp. Men huddled together farther down the bench, trying to start a fire with scraps of waterlogged wood. Someone had saved a string of tobacco. Wispy smoke rose over his head. Pierre motioned her toward them. He led two horses. Neither was hers.

Marie stood from the squat she'd been in, her legs numb from holding both boys huddled on her knees. Prickles stung her calves, slowed her approach to him. He grinned at her, his face pocked with mud.

"*Cheval!*" Paul shouted. He lurched toward the animals.

He rested his hand on Baptiste's shoulder. "Sorry I could not save your horse," he told Marie.

"We all live," she said. "So we are rich Indians, with little left to carry."

The next day, they sighted the Columbia.

They stared at the wide-flowing river that had been the object of their desire these many months. The high banks reminded her of the bluffs of her Des Moines, though these ridges lay like layers of dark molasses poured across flat cakes. Higher on the north side, the ridges were dusted partway down with snow. Hunt's party stood on crusty mud. A pair of geese honked downriver, then settled in lichen-covered rocks within sight of the stream. Ice like strings of pale beads nestled at the edges of blue-gray water that looked smooth as a lake. It would now take them to the sea.

All they needed were canoes.

They traveled on the south side, though Hunt kept saying they needed to cross over. "The trail Clark marked is on the north side," Hunt said.

But the river ran nearly a mile wide, and when the wind blew, white tops dotted the waves.

At dusk, Pierre pointed to dark forms near the water. A family of Indians huddled near a fish-smelling fire built between two crude dugout canoes. Their eyes held hungry looks. "Those won't get us to the sea," Pierre nodded with his chin to the burned-out logs. "But they might ferry us across."

They traded the two horses to ride across the Columbia River. Marie and the boys rode in the last ferry. She marked the journey in her memory as they bobbed like a stick in the choppy water. This river had lured them nearly twelve moons now, from the time Pierre had admitted his desire through signing on with Hunt. Her desire had taken her here too, to this river, to this life.

Mallards paddled close to the shore as the Astorians beached, then carried what trade goods they'd salvaged on their backs now. They'd need them all. Even Marie could see that. The bare hillsides meant wood would be precious and raise the cost of any ride to the sea.

"Mackenzie and McClellan have passed through," Pierre told Hunt after hand-talking with a group of wide-faced Indians they encountered on the trail midday.

"They have?"

Men, women, and children stood before the long-thatched huts, watching them.

"They describe a fort at the mouth of Nici-Wana River. That's this river."

"They…they've seen it? These Indians have seen the fort Astor's men built?"

Pierre shook his head no. "Some who've been there have come back this way and described events. Some troubles, too."

"Indeed. They can communicate such distances?" Hunt asked, eyes searching.

The air smelled of fish. Fish bones littered the riverbanks. Fish skins burned in firepits. "Another party came through too," Pierre said. "Overland like us. Not carrying much."

"Truly? That's got to be Mackenzie or Crooks," Hunt said. "So they made it." Hunt clasped his hands as though holding something precious. "And Astor's ship, too."

"*Pardon*, the dog?" Marie asked, Paul again riding on her back. "They see Mackenzie's white dog?"

Pierre signed and nodded. "With a tall man, though apparently not so big as we remember him," Pierre translated. "But all of us are thin compared to these people."

The Indian Pierre spoke with had round shoulders, a wide face, but

Marie did not think any of them fat, as Mackenzie had been, just short and wide. "They've got no canoes to trade either," Pierre finished. "Says we need the Wish-ram people for that, downriver."

Marie could tell as they approached the Wish-ram village that these were trading people. Canoes turned upside down next to wood-roofed lodges were made of a heavy tree that matched none they'd seen. A few horses grazed nearby. Fishing spears leaned against the lodges. "They have houses that don't move," Marie told her husband. Pierre nodded. "They have enough food just staying where they are each season." These were wealthy people indeed! They'd found a way to stay in one place, not have to ride horses here and there following buffalo or bear. Getting them to trade the sleek boats away would take some doing.

Pierre sign-talked a few moments, then a Wish-ram man motioned him into his house. The wood roof sloped almost to the ground like a ramp from a river dock to a boat. It was the same angle as some of the people's foreheads. Marie watched Pierre and Hunt climb down a small ladder and disappear inside. She set the boys down, told them to stay close.

Round-faced people stared at her from the corners of their eyes as they carried baskets. Men and women with the high, sloping foreheads gave the orders.

In a few minutes Pierre signaled Marie. "Bring the children," he said. "They are curious over you."

She joined another ten or twelve people who lined the perimeter of the large lodge. Some moved about, others rested on mats, some sat with children in cradleboards with what looked like weights on their children's heads. They were shaping their heads to create that sharp angle! The women did not cower back, but looked at Marie with open curiosity. One stood to finger Marie's hair comb and the holes in Marie's ears. Several of the women had broken teeth. A few, even though about Marie's age, had no teeth at all, though none covered their lips when they laughed. The women were shorter than Marie and wore a kind of woven skirt that didn't reach their knees.

They chattered to each other with words Marie didn't understand, lifted the fringe of Paul's shirt and ran their fingers through Baptiste's thick, black hair that never seemed to snarl, even now, windblown and long.

A dusky-scented oil burned in a cleft of rock creating a shadowy light. Coiled bags hung from the wooden rafters, and a woman with a long, clean scar across her cheek stood and took what looked like red meat from one, handing pieces to the Astor party, including Marie and the children.

Marie turned it over in her hand while the boys ripped and chewed. *Pemmican, from salmon, not from buffalo,* Marie realized, staring down at it. Dark blue berries and nuts were ground into it. The woman pointed to a stack of it and held fingers up. Marie raised her hands to show she had nothing to exchange.

The woman pointed to the knife at Marie's side. Marie shook her head, handed the pemmican back. The woman grunted, rejected that, signed something that seemed to mean it was given to her now.

"She says she has enough food to give away," Pierre told her. "And that you are a poor woman who has nothing to swap."

The woman shrugged and pushed the pemmican close to Hunt's face then, said something boldly as she gestured that her body was available for trade. The men beside her laughed.

Hunt's face turned a deep red, noticeable even in the dusky light.

"You may not need me for the interpreting," Pierre said.

"These women trade themselves in front of their husbands?" Hunt said.

"Here they do."

"Let the negotiations for canoes begin," Hunt said sternly. "This is why Providence has led us here."

Now the serious discussions began. A calumet was filled, the smoke a different scent to the fish-filled lodge. The men drew the smoke toward their throat, the place of commitment and trust. No women smoked, but they sat behind their men, leaning and whispering words.

One or two Wish-ram men, sometimes a woman, looked over the open bales of goods Hunt had the *engages* bring in. They'd point to a string of tobacco or a clasp knife, most interested in the lead boxes they could melt down for bullets. A woman spotted a paper of vermilion. Someone pointed to buttons, another to a sandstone pipe. Even Marie could see these were slight items compared to the canoes Hunt needed. Dogs barked in the distance. Her sons had dropped off to sleep.

Marie forgot her hunger as she watched. She noticed that the men did not correct these women or bark at them nor send them back into silence. Women took turns listening then interjecting words their husbands appeared to hear. To the side, several women continued to touch Marie's skin dress and point to her leggings and their baskets. She watched someone dip hot water from one, the weave so tight it could hold both soup and hot stones. Someone pointed to the basket and Marie's knife and she remembered Sacagawea's saying what she had given up for Clark to have his robe of sea otter skins. If necessary, she would give Pierre the knife to trade for a canoe.

Suddenly a man signaled and the women moved to sit beside their men, not behind. *Women, coming beside their men, as a femme should,* Marie thought.

Pierre announced they'd traded the tomahawks, gunpowder, lead, and the last of their blankets for two of the long canoes. It was enough. The proceedings were finished.

Marie stood as her husband signaled when an older Wish-ram man held his hand up.

"You are welcomed," the man said in English.

"English?" Hunt said. "Did he use English? Has he known what we've said all this time, Dorion?"

Pierre sign-talked; the man responded. "They know of English-speakers, on the upper Columbia, Okanogan area," Pierre translated.

"David Stuart," the Indian said.

"He knows our partner Stuart?" Hunt nearly danced a jig.

"This man spent some time with him," Pierre said.

"Indeed, that is good news! That means the *Tonquin* arrived with her stores intact and the partners are trading already with interior tribes. Stuart, McDougall, and McKay. They must all be alive! We are the first then to claim this country for America! We've beaten the North Westers at their game. Astor knew what he was doing. And we've done it." He clapped his hands. "I'll be a wealthy man," he said. "You too, Dorion. You'll be able to support your fine family in fashion. And we've done it. We have."

"Wait," Pierre held up his hand. Marie listened to the Wish-ram man's mix of English and French words. "The ship blew up? The *Tonquin's* destroyed?"

"What?" Hunt said, his voice screeched like a parrot's. "What's he saying?"

"The *Tonquin* was lost," Pierre continued. "The Captain took it north after unloading at the Columbia, hoping to trade with coastal people for pelts and—"

"Boom!" the Wish-ram man said, raising his hands to show a violent upsurge into the sky, dribbled debris falling on his fingertips.

"Who? How? Does he say how?" Hunt asked.

"Indians," the Wish-ram man said. "They die with ship."

"I pray no partners were on board," Hunt said. "The loss of the ship will be challenge enough." Hunt straightened his powder horn over his chest.

Pierre said something more, and the man nodded. "One or two of Astor's men die, but mostly shipmates and Indians."

"At least there's still a post at the mouth," Hunt said. "We must focus on that success and not on what those savages tried to take from it. At least most of Astor's wishes will be met. Success over the North West company is still ours."

Pierre looked at Marie. He nodded his chin toward Hunt, touched his finger to the side of his temple.

Hunt's expedition did not lose so many men as a sunken ship, Marie thought. *But he does not honor you, husband, for your part in getting us through to see Astor's success.*

Baptiste rubbed a dirty finger on Hunt's page before Marie could stop him.

"Pardon," she said.

"It's all right," Hunt said. "It's just my accounting of our trade today. And of Providence's provision. I'll read to the boy." Hunt imagined the boy might like that. He spoke louder, so all could hear. " 'We traveled 1,751 miles. We endured all the hardships imaginable. With difficulty I express the joy at sight of this river, for so long the goal of our desires.' This is what the written word says," Hunt said.

Baptiste looked at him with questioning eyes. "Remember this." He brushed the boy's black hair back from his eyes, closed his book. "Desire accomplished is sweet to the soul."

The boy nodded as though he understood, then wandered off to speak with an *engage.* The men were singing again as they set up camp. French songs. Other *voyageurs* talked now of dreams and wishes as though getting closer to a goal permitted open hope.

If Mackenzie had made it and the Stuarts were already trading, then they'd accomplished Astor's goal—trade from the West to Asia could happen. And Hunt had done what he'd set out to do. A warm sense of contentment filled him.

The proverb spoke to him as he pulled a blanket around him to sleep near the canoes. *Desire realized was indeed sweet to the soul.*

Marie made herself remember what she was seeing, to tell the children in stories for when they grew older. The telling would tie these experiences together like the lacing of a treasured necklace.

They portaged around a cascading falls where the whole Columbia narrowed through cuts of black rock. Indians stood on platforms, leaning out over the shooting foam, tied with ropes at their wide waists to keep them from falling; they speared giant fish with long flint spikes. Beside them, men held circle nets as round as the bullboats pulled behind canoes. Long slabs of fish dried on spears near fires or smoked while hung over branches like wide, lazy leaves. Abundance danced with the landscape.

When they beached the canoes to portage the rapids, new people invited Hunt's party into fish-scented lodges. Marie watched as men and women played games, hiding small animal bones in their hands while others pointed and guessed who hid them. Flashy feathers and elk teeth and trinkets were thrown onto blankets and picked up by the winners who guessed correctly.

In the morning, the Indians helped them portage. Pierre said these Wascos would take nothing for their help, only traded entertainment for their efforts.

"Clark said these were the ones to watch for, slipping in to steal things in the night," Hunt said to Marie and Pierre. "One benefit of having no goods to pilfer, I guess."

Marie noticed that each member of Hunt's party was taller than any of the men or women here. Even Marie bent to look into these round faces. And her features were different from theirs, her face longer. The women wore their hair loose or in braids, while Marie kept hers with the dark knot at the back. Her skin color was lighter too. Rocks of the hill bluffs that lined the Columbia here sloped like the sides of a tipi, and these women's foreheads did too—except for a few that Pierre told her were slaves. "Captives aren't allowed to have their heads pressed," he said. "Looks like they trade in more than just baskets and boats. Better behave, *femme*, or I'll see how much I can get for you." He grinned at her.

"I might get rich for you," she said.

These women displayed baskets for trade but didn't enter into talks as the Wish-ram women had. The landscape changed as much as the people, Marie decided. Barren hills of deep ravines and rivers with long rocky ridges requiring portages gave way to wooded areas, the river ever widening. Rushing streams entered from the sides. Waterfalls higher than those back in her Ouisconsin homeland cascaded hundreds of feet, plunging over mossy ridges to disappear into pools and streams that pushed out to the river. And always in the distance rose a white mountain, higher than anything Marie had ever seen. "Hood's Mountain," Hunt said when Marie asked if it had a name.

"Wy'East," a Wasco woman said louder, nodding to the snow-capped peak.

Rain drizzled on them in the morning, mist lifting to reveal rocky islands and sometimes island spears of green. A cough from an *engage* set blue herons lifting from the water's edge. Massive fir trees dusted with snow at the ridge tops blackened their way to the sandy shoreline. Mud flats appeared and sank away with the tide. They had to be nearing the ocean.

They eased past a series of villages, homes made of logs that could not be moved as Marie's Ioway tipis. "Multnomahs," Pierre told her, "same as what Clark called that big river entering from the south."

That day, they beached on an island, and on the north side of the Columbia, Hunt noted a good-sized village. Several men wearing British jackets with gold buttons approached. "Wherever did they get British wear?" Hunt said.

Pierre tried sign-talking, but their leader shook his head.

"From the ships," Pierre told Hunt. "They say they've seen lots of ships, and he tells me this in English and a kind of French. They are Wappato people."

"Indeed," Hunt said. "There are many more tribes here than I believe even Astor imagined. And British influence…"

Hunt walked away, chewing the side of his cheek.

Pierre continued with his talk, and the men nodded and returned to their lodges.

"They're savvy traders," Pierre told Marie. "This competition for Astor to rule the trade of these Indians will not slide as easy as an otter down a riverbank. *Non.* Outwitting Lisa will be remembered as easy compared to what lies ahead."

Dark rains fell daily. Once or twice the sun warmed through dense clouds. Marie's fingers, as she folded them around her sons', were no longer white with cold. They wore the color she'd been born with, a solid acorn brown. No cold snow-covered huts here. Reddish boards gleamed wet instead. She had never been in terrain like this, in a climate so wet. It unsettled. At least she thought it was the weather; it might have been Hunt's hunched shoulders and the worry lines forming at his eyes.

After several days in their thick-sided bark canoes, the river widened almost to the size of a bay. Around a bend, Marie noticed four canoes moored on the south shore and a craft with masts. *Another village?* she wondered.

Suddenly shouts went up from the *engages,* from Hunt. Pierre shot his rifle once into the air. Marie turned, startled. Where was the enemy? She clutched her sons closer.

"Don't alarm them, Dorion," Hunt cautioned. "Don't want them thinking we're the enemy."

Someone yelled, "Palisade!" And Marie turned as an *engage* pointed up the bank of the south shore. French-Canadian accents speared the air. Men ran down the bank as Hunt ordered their flotilla beached.

"Astor's Post," Hunt sighed. "At last."

Blest, the white dog, bounded toward them. As Marie lifted the boys from the boat, the dog jumped and licked at her face. *"Le chien,"* she cried, lowering Paul from her back, setting his spindly legs on the grassy riverbanks at this place Hunt said was truly Astor's.

An overcast sun cooled the air, and Marie stretched her legs, aching after kneeling these past weeks since they'd located canoes. It felt almost as though they should plant seeds soon, the breeze warmed so balmy.

She smelled a cooking fire, could see tiny flowers blooming on the forest floor.

Logs with sharp points set high on a ridge marked Astor's fort. So this was it then, all they'd been seeking.

Men surged through thick foliage along a path where the shoreline had been cleared of trees. Shouts and waves preceded them. Her boys squealed and chased after Mackenzie's dog. *Engagés* broke into song.

"He brings you blessings from Astoria on this February day," Mackenzie said to Marie in French. The Porcelaine hound sniffed at her, long tail wagging high. "The dog missed you."

Mackenzie was the partner who always spoke French with her, and now it was nearly all she recognized of the man, that and his hair the color of a blazing sunset. He had no jowls to shake when he talked; his cheeks were caverns, but his eyes sparkled with recognition, almost with a kindness. "You have arrived."

Hunt reached out to shake Mackenzie's extended hand, but the taller man grabbed him and kissed him on both cheeks instead. Soon McClellan appeared, dressed in fresh buckskins, though the hide seemed to hang from his bony frame. The sutler and supplier, the Irishman, Reed, smiled when he greeted them, his eyes tired. They all looked different, as though surviving had smoothed them around previously rough places. Marie wondered if Hunt's party looked as strange to them as they did to her.

Marie looked around and realized she searched for Jean Toupin. She hoped the boy and his friend George had made it. Her scan was distracted by a man named McDougall being introduced to Hunt by Mackenzie. He'd come by ship. He, too, had hollow cheeks. Everyone did, she noticed. Could food be scarce here in this abundant-looking land where salmon swam, where Multnomahs and Wish-ram people ate well enough to stay in one place?

Her insides growled and she pressed her hands against her stomach, hoping to stop the sound. Still bony. She must look bony. She had not seen herself in a mirror since St. Louis. Now she looked down at her feet. Her moccasins were soiled from the dark mud. Dried globs of dirt clutched at her buckskin dress. She hadn't tried to remove stains for months, not since Reed said he had no more chalk to give her. New cuts and scrapes roughened the leather. She'd repaired only essentials on this journey. At least now, finding an awl to rethread would be easier at the store supplied by Astor's ship. Everything would be better now with replenishment from the ship's provisions.

She captured only small sinews of news threaded with fast-spoken English and very little French as the partners talked with Hunt. Faces appeared open and full to the sun. Then she watched Gay and young Toupin set upon the canoes, unloading what few supplies they had. Jean Toupin nodded his head to her in greeting, then lifted a parfleche to his shoulders and headed to the fort. *Good*, she thought. *Hunt will not have to write to his mother to tell her bad news.*

Two men introduced to Hunt as clerks, Gabriel Franchere and Alexander Ross, spoke in English, the former with a French accent. Still, so many talked, and Marie was so tired from the journey, from finally arriving, that she couldn't keep all the conversations straight. She would have to get Pierre to tell her later what she'd missed.

"What?" Hunt said. "Thompson's been here? When?" He stood beside the canoes as the camp boys unloaded them. "How could that be?"

"Nothing to worry over, Wilson," Mackenzie said.

"Indeed. Having a North West Company man just arrive here, this doesn't concern you? What with the *Tonquin* lost, we'll have to work twice the hours besting those North Westers."

"Indians took the *Tonquin*," Duncan McDougall said. "At least that's what the Clatsops have told us."

"McDougall's become attached to an Indian lass," Mackenzie said. "Gets his news from her."

McDougall bristled. "It is a formidable alliance we may well need, Donald."

"She's formidable, all right, that Ilchee," Mackenzie said.

"She's a princess, a daughter of a Chinook chief and—"

"But what about Thompson?" Hunt asked, with that parrotlike screech of agitation. "What's his being here mean?"

"I told Donald we were entirely too accommodating to the Brit," McClellan said.

Mackenzie pushed his hands at the air as though to soften it. "Let's set this aside for now. Much to be decided later, not now."

"Let the British get in too far and they're like a tick, hard to back out," Dorion said.

"And you are?" McDougall asked.

"Dorion's our interpreter," Hunt said.

"We've no need of his opinion about the British—or much else here," McDougall said.

"Maybe he can hunt," Mackenzie said. "If he doesn't get himself lost."

"Oh, I imagine there's a report Astor will need hearing of," McDougall said. "Dorion, pick up and help."

Hunt and the partners turned to walk up the grassy bank to the knoll...over the water.

"I'll join you at the factory soon as I settle my family," Dorion said, following behind.

Hunt opened his mouth to speak but Donald interrupted. "Take your time," Mackenzie told Dorion. "We haven't much need of your ...elite services now."

Hunt's eye caught the woman's. He turned away as though to scan the river view. *Dorion.* Donald was right. He didn't have need of him now, not really. McDougall could apparently converse well with the local people; there were more than enough clerks here already. And Dorion had been a fair amount of trouble now that he thought of it, what with his debt and delays. He'd chased what he brewed back in St.

Louis with an even stiffer swallow of distress on the overland journey, getting lost and whatnot, not to mention the needs of the woman and children. Things were different here. Tools were meant to be used, then put away or sent to another site. Things changed.

"Hunt…" Dorion said.

"I think your duty lies with your family now," Hunt said, turning toward the mixed-blood man. "Just as you said. Perhaps later we can see what the hunting needs are here so we can address your outstanding debt." Then he turned back to Mackenzie and said, "I don't like it, Donald. They're our competition. Astor wouldn't—"

"Aye. You're worrying overmuch, taxed by the journey, you are. The rules are different way out here, Wilson. We should celebrate now. Reed's here. You've arrived intact."

What could this mean, the Englishman Thompson having been here first? Hunt wondered. "Did he try to claim this place for England?"

"Oh, he didn't go into any of that. Shared a little whiskey is all. What we should do ourselves now. Celebrate. It might set us all to a better tune," Mackenzie said.

"We'll celebrate, all right. Celebrate Providence delivering us despite the Manuel Lisas, the Eduard Roses, the mountain men, the Indians, and now a North Western man appearing on our shore." Yes, things were different here. Dorion would have to learn that lesson too. Hunt just hoped he could forget the look in the woman's eyes and that they weren't at this moment burning holes into the small of his back.

Baptiste and Paul skipped on the banks, happy to be freed of the confining canoes. Marie watched them, the afternoon sun warm on her face in this area cleared for the new fur post. It would be good to stay in one place for a time. Here, they would be a part of Astor's plan to change the trade routes. Here, they would change what Pierre could do. It seemed many of the men who had come on board ship had been introduced as "clerks." Did they need so many clerks? Marie wondered

She looked around. There was no large ship anchored here, no huge storehouse called the *Tonquin* that Hunt described as carrying all they would need. That smaller craft, one called the *Dolly*, must have been the ship Hunt said had been carried in the *Tonquin* hold, brought in small pieces to be assembled here. A second ship, the *Beaver*, was to resupply them, then take furs out of a warehouse to Sitka and Canton. Still, this did not look like the bustling port and fur trade post she had expected to find.

Perhaps the ships could not come in this far, would have to anchor at the far sea; maybe this was just a bay and they were not yet at the Pacific. That was where the true fort would be. Maybe this was a simple warehouse. No, the Wappatos had said British ships went that far upriver. This fort must be all there was. The wide bay must be the sea.

As if to reassure her, sea gulls scratched white wings against the sky, taking Marie's eyes in a westward direction.

Jean Toupin returned from carrying a load. He hoisted a last parfleche onto his shoulder.

"That's McDougall," Jean Toupin told her, nodding toward a man wearing a wool suit and vest coat as he walked down toward the partners. Toupin had gotten taller and stood lean as a bacon strip. He nodded to the big man bending beneath low branches of towering trees. "McDougall is the chief factor here, of all the partners."

"That will change," Marie said. "Now that Hunt is here."

"*Eh bien,*" Etienne, another *engage*, said, coming up from behind. "That would be good. They have many who act as chief factor. Too many. And McDougall, he counts each pelt twice and never stops giving orders."

The ground looked soft, matted with brown spruce needles. Shrubs with shiny leaves bordered a path worming its way upward. Blest sniffed along behind Mackenzie, his tail wagging.

Marie turned back to the river, a gnawing in her stomach. Something had changed—the partners, MacKenzie's tone, Hunt's…

Paul clung to her skirts, his thumb in his mouth. Baptiste pulled at her hand, "Are we at the *océan*?" he asked. "I want to see the *océan*."

"So, so. In a little bit," she said. Both boys moved away from her, exploring.

Pierre stood beside the canoe. He stared at the partners ascending the bank without him. Hunt and McDougall conversed, the latter gestured toward the canoes.

Hunt turned. "Hurry up then, Dorion!" Hunt motioned with his arm.

Her husband straightened, grinned, took long strides to approach.

"No, no, man," Hunt said, disgusted. "Hurry, load your rifle. Go out hunting. The hunter here is ill. Hurry on now. There's work to be done."

Marie felt her face burn for her husband's shame.

He should have gone in with them, Marie thought, *to talk of what they'd learned, of what he'd found out, of what had upset Hunt.*

Pierre spoke with the Canadians now, hurrying. He loaded his rifle, talked louder than usual. Some of these new men he must have known from his journeys north to Mackinaw when he'd traded there years before. He exchanged words with a wide-faced man whom one of the resident *engages* said was named Jeremie. The man shivered slightly as he ran his hands along the sleek canoe. Marie thought it might be the damp air. "He's Oweyhee, from the Sandwich Islands," Toupin said.

"He and the other Kanakas, that's what they call them, tend the goats and pigs the *Tonquin* picked up at the islands," Etienne said.

"You have little to carry, Madame Dorion," Toupin said.

"Lost a batch of those hogs in a fierce storm," Etienne continued. "Jeremie says what survived had to be rowed across the bay to the north side in a canoe. McDougall, he wants things tidy here, and the pigs disagree. They have the best idea. It is a disagreeable place this Astoria."

Baptiste made his way back toward Marie. "I miss you," he told Toupin.

The *engage* ruffled the child's head.

Pierre approached. "There should be another ship."

"It was exploded," Etienne told him. "The captain died with it. Very bad, he was. Indians blew it up. We have problems. Plenty. Why we have the palisades built and the cannons at the corners."

"Maybe you can talk some sense to those relations of yours, Dorion," another *engage* suggested, his voice jesting. "Good to have a mixed-blood around now for such things."

Marie saw Pierre's hands clench and unclench on the rifle stock.

"Our Iroquois hunter can't control 'em; don't see why this one should," said another.

"Not Shonowane's job to interpret. He just needs to get healthy and get us some meat," another said. "Maybe Shonowane's just playing sick."

"Hunt and you look the most shriveled and took the longest to get here, 'cept for poor Crooks and John Day," another said. "Who knows what happened to them. Doesn't say much for your guiding, Dorion."

"Astoria is doomed, that is my truth," Etienne said. "Sooner I leave here, the better."

"I want to see the *océan*, Mama," Baptiste said.

"We must find your brother."

Jeremie, the Sandwich Islander, moved like a crab, walking sideways with a limp. He had Paul in tow and handed him to Marie. "I leave soon. You, woman, you should go too," he told her.

"Paul," she said, speaking to her son, but the Kanakan's eyes lifted in recognition.

"You know the name my mother gives me?" he said.

"Paul is my son's name," she said.

"You're a Christian then."

"My mother-in-law gave him the name."

"This is no place for Christians," Paul Jeremie told her. "You will find this out. Like me, you will desire to get out. No one should stay behind here." He headed up the path.

"I want to see *océan*, I want to see *océan*," Baptiste chanted, tugging on Marie now. Paul pulled loose from her, ran to squat close to the water. "*Océan. Océan!*" Baptiste chanted.

"Come join me, little one," Toupin called to Baptiste and started toward him.

Pierre took two steps toward Baptiste. He struck the child's face with the back of his hand, splitting the boy's lip. Pierre turned to Toupin. "You will stay away from my family. My *femme* has enough children to take care of." Baptiste screamed in the background, blood on the hand he pressed to his face.

"Be still," Pierre barked at his son, his eyes narrowed. Baptiste wailed, and Pierre struck the boy again.

"Non," Toupin said, his arm on Pierre's.

Pierre brushed him off.

"Pardon," Toupin said, "It has been a long—"

Pierre swirled, his rifle raised as Marie shoved between them, reaching for her son. She watched Paul run away along the bank. Her heart pounded. "Husband—"

"You keep your son silent," Pierre shouted to her. "You. *Femme.* Go find a place to set up our tent away from these people, all these people." He glared at Toupin who had stepped back, his face a ruddy red.

"Inside the dwelling house—"

"We'll make our own way," he said, his nostrils flaring like a winded horse's.

"What do you desire of us, husband?" she said, eyes dropped. Her hands rested on Baptiste's head.

"Do whatever you de-sire, Ma-ree," he said, dragging the word out. "I have more important work to do. To hunt. But first, I go see if Reed's whiskey is restored. This climate cools too much." He stomped up the path and disappeared through the wooden gates.

Do what you desire, Pierre had said. Her desire had been to become a *bourgeois's* wife, to move her husband up to partner, to be known by a new name. She desired to be a good mother, keep her sons safe. Maybe that could not be in this Astoria place.

Desire. The word tore a hole open in her heart.

Part 2

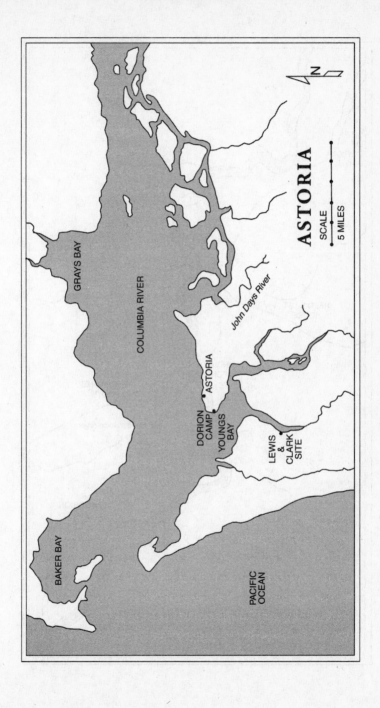

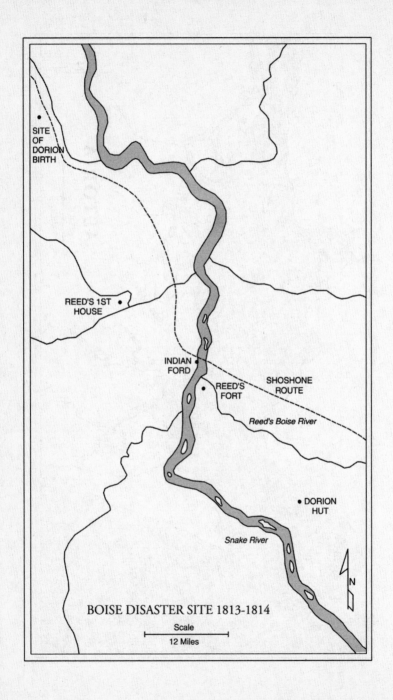

SITE
OF
DORION
BIRTH

REED'S 1ST
HOUSE

INDIAN
FORD

REED'S
FORT

SHOSHONE
ROUTE

Reed's Boise River

DORION
HUT

Snake River

N

BOISE DISASTER SITE 1813-1814

Scale

12 Miles

13

Astoria

Marie knew that if ever the partners dispensed liquor, it would be this night, even if the stores were low. Celebrations came rarely, and Hunt's party had missed their New Year's revelry, making their stop minus whiskey and rum. Marie sighed at the memory of Vivacité living through the New Year. She must not think of her. She needed to find a place to protect her sons now, give herself time to console her husband. Hunt had made better decisions without the party of partners around. He had treated her husband as someone worthy, a future leader. Perhaps he recognized Pierre's longing to be a clerk. He knew firsthand his skills, and yet now that they were in Astoria he treated him like a pesky dog.

She'd had a role on the journey too, offering a sign of safety to the Indians by just being there with her children. Perhaps in their destitute state, Hunt remembered that men and women were not just tools to dig and gouge with, to accomplish his own desires, but that they had hopes and wishes too that could be formed like a good stew if they worked together.

They'd arrived here in this place, just that way.

But now, already, she knew this Astoria would be different. These Astorians dressed themselves in the attitudes of St. Louis, wore high hats to shadow their eyes as they had back in the Osage camp. Once again, her husband was just a tool, not someone worthy of increase.

Once again, she was just his Indian *sauvagesse* said in that unkind way. Here, what a mixed-blood man did to his Indian wife would be no concern of theirs.

It was a concern of hers.

Water lapped against boats. Wind flapped at the sails of a small sloop moored downstream. At the palisades, cannons stared out in quiet accusation. Marie walked up the bank, both boys in tow, her personal parfleche looped over her shoulder. They passed a fenced area. Inside the timbered gates Baptiste stopped to watch Etienne, and Marie let Paul down off her hip, still holding on to his hand. She spied what she thought would be the dwelling house, blacksmith's shop, trading post, and the largest building which would be the chief merchant's house. The *engages* and *voyageurs,* craftsmen and hunters, would be mashed together into a sleeping room. She must find a place apart—but not too far.

She looked for Pierre. He'd stand taller than most of the men who had returned to tasks in the afternoon sun. She lifted the knot of hair at the back of her neck. Sweat worked its way there. It felt warm in this February month. Back home, gray snow embraced the lodges of the Ioways. She could hear a scrape-scrape sound beside her. The *engage* Etienne pulled the drawknife toward his waist. Chips of wood lay in a fresh heap at his feet. Making ax handles, Marie thought. She turned to watch an *engage* fashion a ladder. Other men with red kerchiefs around their heads cleared ground of shrubs and thick-barked trees. Despite the disruption of their arrival, work had returned to routine.

Perhaps her husband had gone inside. Perhaps the partners patted him on his back now and the clerks offered him a chair. Perhaps they acknowledged their oversight, remembered he had been a clerk back in St. Louis, that he had been hired as an interpreter, given high wages, and had done good work all the way. He would calm himself. She might hope for this.

But just in case, she would check the smaller storage huts. If tools spilled about, stacks of hides or marked bales were set in there, if no pipes, no barrels held brandy or rum, then she would place the boys there for safekeeping while she sought food for them and tried to reason with her husband.

So much to do. She turned then, startled by the view.

Shades of green washed toward the water's edge. And the sky, a sky her daughter would never see, rippled water so blue…as blue as…she couldn't find the words. Then she remembered Sacagawea's effort to describe this place of wide skies and vast waters and imagined the blue beaded belt she had given Clark in trade.

"Look," she called to Baptiste. "See how the water shimmers like cut-glass beads?"

"Is it the *océan?*" he asked, still holding his mouth.

"A part of it," she said.

She heard raised voices then, one her husband's, loud, from inside the post. She couldn't make out the words, but the tone sent prickles down her neck.

Hurrying, she looked about, spied a small shed to the right of the entrance. It would be the receiving room, to hold things the river Indians brought in for trade. She pushed open the plank door. A spider web brushed at her face as her eyes adjusted to the dark. In the well-chinked walls, the partially opened door gave the only light. A ring, a beaver hide stretcher, hung on the wall. Coopered barrels leaned against each other like pale, round men sleeping off too much rum. It smelled fishy in the room. Strings of rawhide hung from nails; a broken oar and ax handles leaned against the walls. Several deer hides stretched out on frames. It was not an active receiving room, she thought. Either the Indians did not bring much in or the Astorians had little to give in trade.

Marie pulled her older son inside, lifted Paul over the stoop, and plopped him down beside Baptiste. "You wait here," she told them, her hand circling their chins. "Be very still. Touch nothing. Don't open the door unless you hear me. I'll find us food."

Paul started a whimper. *"Non!"* she said. "It will be dark when I close the door, but you will be safe here if you stay. Don't follow me."

"I want to play with Blest," Baptiste whined.

"Not now." She took a breath. "It will be as night. I will tell you a night story when I return. For now, pretend you are readying to sleep and wait for stars to fill the sky. Don't follow me. Your papa…just stay."

Paul flopped backward, bumping his head against a keg. The hollow thump echoed in the small room and he screamed. "No, no," she said. She pulled the door shut behind her to block the sound. "Listen," she whispered, her hands around Paul's thin arm. He cried louder. She shook him by the shoulders. *"Silence absolu!"* She hissed now. *"Maintenant!"* Why did they always demand when she was least able to give?

"Mama…" She could hear tears forming in Baptiste's voice. She couldn't see him, felt for the features of his face, the swollen lip. She took a deep breath. "Come here," she said, then reached for both boys, rocking them at her breast. "So now, quiet. I'll stay."

She sang softly to them. And as they quieted, she wondered how it had come to be, that she sat in a fishy place protecting children from their father? How had she made such a long journey to end up here? It was an experience worthy of remembering if only she found the meaning in it.

They breathed the rhythm of sleep. She kissed each forehead, unwrapped the robe she'd carried in and laid them gently on the earth floor. They would spend the night here, though Pierre would be furious when he searched for where she'd set their tent and didn't find it. She hoped his anger would be spent by morning. Her eyelids drooped heavy.

"Femme!"

She startled. He was just outside the door.

Jean Toupin wished he could look for the woman and her sons. They'd be hungry. He should find them, tell them where to find food. That Dorion was a madman, he was. To strike a child that way and for what? And Jean had done nothing to stop it.

In the cookhouse Toupin sliced at the fish with his knife. He'd been less careful than he knew he should be. He slowed himself. Duncan McDougall had chewed at him and George, telling them they must never, ever cut across the fish, and to always treat it with care.

"The Indians will not trade with us if we cut the fish poorly or they think we have no respect for it. Cut always as a long filet. Do it as I say."

"Do it as I say. Do it as I say," he and George would mimic McDougall out of his hearing. The boys had arrived with Mackenzie's group just a month previous, but McDougall allowed little time to learn how to do things "as I say," always hurrying on to the next thing. New orders and ideas.

Toupin had thought the arrival at the fort would ease their days with a roof over their heads, plenty to eat. The Indians ate well, and Jean was sure the fort stocked enough cornmeal and cloth to swap for the oily fish that filled. Instead, they relied more heavily on the one hunter they had, Shonowane, who yesterday cut his foot while chopping a log and now recovered in the sick room.

What could be so hard about catching these big fish? Toupin wondered. Maybe if he and George learned how, the Astorians wouldn't have to depend on the ship's stores to exchange for food. He'd ask Madame Dorion about that. She was an Indian woman. She'd know how to learn from these river people, even if the Astorians didn't seem interested. He finished fileting one of the large salmon, laying the firm flesh gently on the table. He should ask her now. Wasn't it part of his responsibility as a cook's mate to find a better way to feed these men? He wiped his hands on his leather apron and walked outside.

Marie's heart pounded. She wanted more time to help Pierre see that he didn't need to let these Astorians set the pattern of his life, that he could transform their power into something good, what they might accomplish in this Astoria.

She heard cursing, and then the door slammed open. A painted oar slid to the ground. "I bet I find you. Is this stink place where you think I will spend my night? Do you not hear me, woman?"

She could smell the rum. He hadn't been gone that long, had he? He pulled the door shut, the broken oar holding it slightly ajar.

It was as dark as a deep river cave. Marie kept herself between the children and her husband. She shuddered in silence, not defending, keeping her breathing calm. In time, his anger would burn out like a hot fire set in a wet place. But not before his fists ripped at her face with rage, not before they pummeled her shoulders. She bit her lip trying not to cry, to alarm the boys whose eyes were big as stones. Pierre grabbed her hair, yanked at the nape of her neck. He cursed her as he struck as though she were a dog needing whipping.

He didn't strike the boys, but they witnessed the diminishing of their mother which might well inflict a deeper pain.

Finally spent, Pierre stumbled against the barrel, rolled onto the floor, and slept.

Marie held her children until they, too, slept. How was it that what looked to be good always had another side, like the bark of a tree being eaten away by termites from within? What had she been thinking of those months before, wanting to be known as a *bourgeois's* wife?

She must find a way so her boys would never know this kind of night again. *Help me, please.* What tools did she have? Pierre lay there, rum still reeking through his pores. What choices did she have? How did a mother weave her family safely together? Had her own mother prayed for her daughters' protection?

The thought came to her from nowhere.

Marie got up. She must work quickly before the liquor wore off. She cracked the door open farther. The moon now cast enough light to shadow the hides, her parfleche. She located the sewing needles. She eased her way on hands and knees to the sidewall. With Sacagawea's knife, she sliced the sinew stretching a hide to the frame. It would be large enough. She'd need all four. Pierre was a big man.

Hunt slept poorly. In the cool moments of the morning dark, he felt undefended, adrift in a way he hadn't known during the journey west. Perhaps it was the achieving of a goal and not knowing now what should drive him next that made him lie awake and wonder. Providence had provided so much. Why did he feel so…defeated?

He got up, lit an oil lamp, and took out his quill pen. Writing often helped him sort things out. He pulled out his Testament, turned to Jeremiah 33:3, "Call unto me, and I will answer thee, and shew thee great and mighty things." They'd arrived here, hadn't they? Even the woman and the children.

But the *Tonquin* had been destroyed and all those men lost. He got mixed reports on whether the Indians were really that hostile or if the captain had incited them to such disaster. Either way, men had died. And now the ship was not available to take furs on to Canton. There was still so much to be done to complete Astor's plan, to defeat the Brits and men like David Thompson.

He wondered how he could find out if Mackenzie had kept his British citizenship, his ties to the North West Company. That would explain his congeniality toward Thompson. One of the *engages* let drop that the sick hunter was a Iroquois man who'd come with Thompson, then stayed behind when Thompson left. Could he be a spy? Maybe he deliberately hurt himself so that the Astorians would be even more at risk, have less food. They'd have to pay out more for the Indian's provisions that way. No supply ship. No *Tonquin*. Men with British affiliation. Perhaps the whole fort was pimpled with spies.

He'd write his worries down, reread the prophet Jeremiah. Great and mighty things he'd see, if only he would ask. That's what he'd do then: claim that promise still. How a man responded to trials marked him, not how few trials he faced. He'd ask Providence for help then, and ask around to find out what was really going on here. He blew out the light, sure now he could sleep.

Marie's fingers moved quickly. She cut holes in the hide, sewed them into one large piece, then laid them beside Pierre. She listened to his breathing and when he inhaled for a deep snore, she rolled him onto the hides. He lay flat on top. She pulled the skins across his back and she began to stitch it up, with Pierre snug inside. She felt as sure as a fast-rushing stream heading to the sea. The boys slept soundly. Good. She could finish.

When Pierre opened his eyes midmorning, she knelt beside him, the broken oar in her hand. *"Femme,"* he said, looking up at her, confusion in his voice, his one eye sticky and closed.

She stiffened, lifted the oar. She felt cold inside, a gray snow cold. She would not run a river with a man so easily wounded by the acts of partners, merchants, and factors. Pierre had traded away his power. She would not.

She brought the oar down across his thighs.

"Ow!" He grunted, both eyes flying open, accusing. He tried to move his arms, realized he was tied inside a hide cocoon. Then recognition hit. She poked him in the ribs, hard. He struggled then, pushed with his elbows, panted in effort.

"What are you doing, *femme?*" he said. The knot in her chest was a rope that had tightened through the night. "Are you mad?"

"Your fists have struck me for the last time. You've injured our sons for the last time." Thin shafts of light formed through the door cracks.

He struggled against the skins again, his arms tight down beside him as though he were Paul tied in his board. Pierre wrenched his knees, tried to sit up. He couldn't.

She jabbed at his chest now with the oar, raised it over his head as though to strike.

"Whoa, now!" he pleaded. "Hunt and the others, they angered me. I needed a place to work away the scraps they throw me. How else will

I win their favor, help them see what I can do for them? I do it for us. They treat me—"

"How they treat you does not allow you to treat me like I am a tool of yours. I am not here for your pounding. No, I am not a nail," she said. She jabbed at him.

"*Femme*, I…"

"My name is Marie. A mother name. I have named myself. A mother should not need to protect her sons from their father, but a good mother does this. To be the wife of a chief factor, if that is you, is too high a price. I will not pay it. I will not pay that way for you to find your place at the partners' table. I will make a different way."

"You would partner with someone else?" he said, his voice as quiet as she'd ever heard it.

"You do not know me," she said. "After all this time, you do not know me."

She pushed to stand, the movement made the room spin. She stopped, swallowed, saw that the boys stirred. "I would stay with you all the days of my life, but only if they are safe, only if I don't trade myself away."

"I can get another," he said, boastful.

"Good. You will have all your tools then," she said. "If you survive what I will do to you." She struck his knees, watched him wince. Paul whimpered. This was not good for them to see.

Her hands shook, and she felt dizzy. Perhaps he *had* hurt something in her mind. She squatted, caught herself, unsteady. She was just hungry. The boys would be hungry. "Time to rise now," she said, keeping her voice calm as she stood. "Boys, go outside."

Pierre would miss them, and he did not know it. Perhaps he didn't think he deserved the good, the love, they offered. She hated at this moment that she loved him, hoped only she was strong enough to do what she must. "We go now."

"You can't leave me here *fem*—Marie. What will you do without me? Where will you go?" She pushed against him to stand, used him. She turned away.

She heard him strain against the hides again, kicking and scraping with his heels toward the door. "What will you do?" He said it as though she were a child again, making poor choices. She pushed open the door. The light hurt her eyes. "*Femme*. Marie…" His voice had changed. Was that fear she heard or just the pounding of her heart? Her eyes felt pinched. "I will never do it again. Just free me now, Marie." Dust danced in shards of light that met the dirt floor. He nearly whispered the words. "With God as my witness. What must I promise?"

Did she have the courage to place her terms? And if he failed, then what? Would she follow through?

"To never touch the rum or brandy or whiskey again," she said. "And you must never use your fist on them ever," she pointed to her sons. "Or me. Or I will sew you up again, and this time I will trade whatever I must to get *engages*, Astorians, to use this oar, an ax handle, their fists, to do to you what you have done to us. I will do this, Pierre. You'll have wounds worse than if you wrestled down a bear. Are you strong enough to keep that promise? Or will you be like Hunt, using promises only to get what you want?"

The cool morning air stung her bruised face. She was a fool to ask this, a fool to believe anything would change. His silence proved it.

She took a deep breath. "Come, boys," she said and they rambled past her, spilled out into the daylight.

Someone stood in the doorway blocking her way. The face was shadowed, dark against bright sunlight. Was she seeing things? Had the blows to her head taken her to some new place?

"Wait. I will do what you say. Marie, I will do this."

"No boast," she said, not turning around. "You will only take this rapid once." *Is that a woman standing there? Why doesn't she speak?* Marie thought. She seemed to radiate warmth, strength. For her? For him?

"I'll do what you say," Pierre insisted. "Don't leave. Don't...don't go."

She lifted Paul, placed him in the center of her back. His fingers clutched at her neck. She turned then. "You will help me, please," Pierre whispered. "I can do this if you're strong."

She stared at him, lying there, wrapped inside that skin. It was her chance to be free of him. Was he saying what she wanted to hear just to be set free?

"No more whiskey. No more. I promise this. My throat makes this promise."

She hesitated, then felt sure of her next step. Paul's weight moved with her while she bent to cut the sinews and freed Pierre. She stepped back, half expecting him to grab her and throw her down now that he could. He rose slowly. She smelled the damp scent of the hut mixed with fear. And then she smelled the leather of her husband's shirt as he reached for her. She hesitated, then let him pat her head onto his shoulder. *"Pardon, pardon,"* he whispered. "We will find a way here, without the likes of Hunt."

At that moment, she knew that she would never be a *bourgeois*'s wife and realized she didn't want to be. She only wanted to be loved as a woman, a wife, and for her children to see their father loved their mother. "You are a strong woman," he said. "A good mother." She felt herself sink into his arms, welcoming tears flowing down her cheeks. What was her name if not strong?

Sarah Shonowane, a Chipewyan woman, was the woman in the light. Marie had not expected to find another woman at the post, especially not one who knew of beaver skins and buffalo hides, though Sarah knew more of caribou and moose. She was the wife of the Iroquois hunter, Ignace Shonowane, and they had been at Astoria only a short time, she told Marie. Sarah spoke some French, taught by the Jesuits

when she lived near Hudson's Bay. Her husband spoke French and English, too. And both had been baptized.

Sarah and her husband had come across Canada's mountains and
joined up with David Thompson, the North Wester, arriving with him
to build Spokane House on Kettle Falls, north, near the Columbia
River. When the Astorian Robert Stuart came inland from Astoria, he
told stories that lured Ignace Shonowane and his family to this sea place.
They stayed. Ignace was a freeman. "He is an Indian who belongs to no
one but the Lord," Sarah said. "And the Lord shares him with me."

That February day, Sarah had come to take her husband off
McDougall's sick list. Sarah had watched a child spill out of the storage
hut and stood then in the doorway, as surprised as Marie to see another
Indian woman, tall, like her, with an oval face. Sarah had two boys,
older yet not old enough to hunt without their father.

"We live apart from Astor's post, on Young's Bay, a mile or so west,"
she told Marie and Pierre. "Hunting is better there," Sarah said. "And
there are not so many chief factor do-as-I-say rules there." Sarah sewed
the hides she tanned and softened. She traded them for fish and baskets,
things she wanted.

The morning the women met, Pierre stepped into the sun beside
Marie. Sarah spoke. "I hear a child's voice," she said to answer the surprised look in Marie's eyes. "You will come to Young's Bay. We have
fresh fish where I am. And meat. You will be safe."

Pierre had told her to go, that he would speak with Hunt about his
status and join them.

"Don't argue with him," Marie warned Pierre.

"Will Papa be all right?" Baptiste asked.

"Yes. He has promised," Marie told him, hoped she told the truth.

"Look, Dorion," Hunt began. "I may have…suggested greater things
than are possible now. You see the conditions here. Many clerks, supply

problems." Hunt sat behind a crude desk, making the separation between himself and this mixed-blood man clear. He tapped his quill pen. "When the Stuarts return from the Okanogan area, we may well have enough furs to transport to Sitka and beyond. Or when the supply ship arrives, we may have less need of hunters and want your services more to, ah, trade with the Indians. Or perhaps we'll send you off to explore some of the streams…as a clerk, perhaps, leading a small expedition. Assess for beaver. Translate. But for now…" Hunt dropped his eyes.

"I clerked back in St. Louis. These people don't sign much here, use a mix of Indian and French. I can learn to speak it. You know what I can do, eh?"

"I know I need to keep the whiskey locked," Hunt said. "You did yourself no favors—"

"I made a mistake." Dorion rubbed at his elbow, wrapped his arms around his chest.

The man did look remorseful.

"I have paid my debt to the Pacific Fur Company," Dorion said. "I am entitled to the last one hundred dollars."

"Well, there's a little problem there, too, Dorion," Hunt said. He'd dreaded this moment. "Your expenses, those of your wife and children for food and supplies have more than eaten up your final payment, not to mention the damage to the remaining rum supply you invaded yesterday." Hunt cleared his throat. "Indeed, you now owe the company. Not just that hundred dollars, but…" Hunt perused the ledger book, though he already knew. McDougall had already insisted. "An additional three hundred dollars has been added to your account."

"For what?"

He'd have to be careful. The man could be volatile. "The rum. And the matter of Señor Lisa," Hunt said. "You didn't think he just…succumbed, did you? After challenging him to a duel, he couldn't just wither away. No, a trade was worked out. Isn't that the way it's done, even by savages?" He spoke rapidly now, wanting it over. "I paid the two-hundred-dollar fine so the warrant would not be issued, so you would come west as you'd agreed to and Astor's plan would not be held up further. And you did well, Dorion. Let me say that here and now, but yet, you must work off the debt, as the company sees fit. We need a hunter, pure and simple. You'll be allowed to put things on account for your family. It's a trade. I realize it's—"

"A white man's trade," Dorion said. "An Indian'd call it slavery."

Hunt stood. "Here, here," he said as Dorion stomped out the door. Hunt sank back down, relieved the man was gone. Hunt put his head in his hands. Dorion spoke the truth. He hoped he hadn't just betrayed the only man who'd been truly loyal to him in this fort.

"They'll advance me ammunition," Pierre told Marie. "I have met my obligation as interpreter."

"So we do not need to remain here?"

Pierre shifted. "And I tell him no rum on my account," Pierre said. "Did you?"

"He says, 'There is none,' but I tell him, even when the stores are full, I will have none." Pierre hesitated. "He pays Lisa's bill. So I am indebted now to him. More than I thought."

It didn't even surprise her, these white men's way of trapping people into doing things they otherwise wouldn't.

"So. How will we pay this?" she said.

"Maybe McDougall and Hunt agree to let us keep some of the hides of what we kill for the post for meat. We can tan and trade them ourselves."

It would take a long time to pay the debt. But maybe she could help. She would ask Sarah, the Chipewyan woman. They were known as teachers, a skill that increased with wisdom, unlike many men's skills of strength that faded with old age.

Pierre picked at his tooth with his knife. Marie worked on a hide as Sarah had shown her. Nearly three months had passed since Pierre's promise. He kept it still—at least where she could see him. Sometimes he and Ignace Shonowane would be gone for days and she couldn't be sure. But Ignace never spoke of rum or whiskey, and he wore a cross around his neck.

"I still don't understand why David Thompson came and left those Iroquois behind," Marie said.

"You are always asking questions, Marie," Pierre said. "Could be David Thompson checked out what was here, how well fortified we are, in case there's a war. Here, you boys," he said to Baptiste and Paul, "get away from that shrub pile. Snakes there. You poke around, you better catch 'em for the stew pot."

Marie raised her eyes, saw that the boys listened to their father. They jabbed instead now at bugs thriving in a stump. Paul would have three years when the leaves turned this fall, and he followed his brother like a bullboat behind a moving canoe. Most of the trees around the fort had already been cut and the *engages* had to travel farther and farther for wood. Here at Young's Bay, the two Indian families had fewer stumps to maneuver around.

"But why would Ignace and Sarah remain behind?" Marie asked. "Isn't he a free Iroquois who can go anywhere he chooses?"

"He chooses to hunt for the Astorians," Pierre said.

"Maybe he wishes to be a clerk or factor someday."

Pierre laughed, then lowered his voice as though their huts had been built too close to each other instead of several paces distant. "They do not trust him," he said. Marie lifted her eyebrows in question, kept her hands busy, scraping then picking at the bits of meat still clinging to the hide. "The Astorians need him—he is a good hunter. John Day has not shown up yet nor those mountain men who stayed behind with Crooks's bunch. They could all be used here. The partners, they think if there's trouble with the Indian tribes, that being an Indian, Ignace will side with the Clatsop and Chinook."

"They let him live outside the post," she said. "They're not watching him."

Pierre grunted. "The Sandwich Islanders aren't inside the protection of the factory either. But these Astorians trust no one who is not their color, eh?" He sharpened his knife with a stone. "No Indian can be a factor," he said. "Not even a clerk. Maybe not even a mixed-blood could rise so far."

"Manuel Lisa," Marie said. "He is—"

"A Spaniard. And he shares power with other partners, Clark and Reuben Lewis. No, men like Astor, Hunt, they're wary of *metis,* Marie. You should help our sons know this. Our sons must be strong to live in such a mixed world."

"So the Astorians not only let us live outside the palisades. It's where they *want* us."

"Ah, you are a wise woman indeed."

The Easter season, with its short rations, as the men called it, was Pierre's first real test of his commitment. McDougall offered grog, molasses, and rice to the men. It was spare fare to celebrate such an occasion. "It's either feast or famine here," McDougall said. He'd come out on the *Tonquin* and always wore a vest coat and dark breeches and a tall beaver hat when he spoke to the men in the courtyard. "Once the fish runs begin in earnest, we'll have better eating than these wretched fixings."

Marie thought he must never have known starvation, or McDougall would not rate rice and molasses to supplement fish as "wretched fixings." What did it matter? She had found a way to supplement her family's larder.

Jean Toupin had first told her there was no reason for short rations. True, the storehouse had little to offer that the wealthy Chinook wanted. "But we could make fish weirs out of willows and collect at least some fish on our own," Toupin told her. He stood, hands on hips, at Young's Bay while she heated a thin rice soup. "If they weren't so proud, Madame Dorion," Toupin continued, "the Astorians could let the Indians teach them. See, the big fish swim upriver, close to shore. I've been watching. We could make nets, weirs. You know how to weave such things from willow?"

Marie nodded. "I will go where the Indians gather up their fish, then see what I can do. But don't come back here to Young's Bay," she told him. "Pierre thinks I have enough to do."

Toupin's ears turned red. "I take care of myself, Madame."

"So, so," she said. "I know this. We must be quiet as starlight though. If what you say is true, we will shine brightly when we have fish enough to give away."

On the days when Marie came to the post, she watched Clatsop or Chinook Indians pass through the gates, walk right by the cannon platform, and bring in sturgeon or dried salmon. The hunters were often successful, though the elk and deer made slender portions for so many men, now over one hundred. McDougall spoke of the anticipation of a garden harvest and ripe berries eventually. And all would have grains, when the supply ship came.

Marie and Toupin and now Sarah, too, set the weirs shaped like a whirlwind on its side near the shore where the salmon ran. The boys helped too. The big fish swam into the wide openings but got their noses caught as the willows narrowed and they tried to pull back out. It was difficult work, and it often took two of them to spear and net the heavy fish. Then they had to filet and smoke dry. Marie made sure Toupin took some of each catch for himself to supplement the men's spare fare.

"But we will not get rich this way," she told Toupin. "We need the big nets and canoes to bring in the catch as the Chinook do." Toupin agreed. Few *engages* would risk this river to handle nets—even if they had them.

"It will be enough to sometimes eat fish," he said. "And know your boys are well fed."

The Easter grog was offered up and poured.

Though Pierre ground his teeth and scowled at the banter of the silversmith—LeClerc—and Etienne and other *engages,* no one drank enough to lose control. And none commented on the wave of his hand when the cup got passed over him to the next man.

Marie had smiled at her husband, placed and replaced the ivory comb at the back of her neck, eyes dropped. He'd done what he'd said. It was all she could ask for, once, and then once again.

By the time she and Pierre reached their home at Young's Bay that Easter Day, his arm around her had tightened. He'd sent the boys to look for crayfish in the water, telling Baptiste to "watch your brother." And when they bent into the small log hut, Pierre challenged her to a leg wrestle that had ended in sweet love.

"I have things under control here, Wilson," McDougall told him. The men sat at the *bourgeois* table, a vivid sunset reflected through a rippled-glass window. McDougall walked to it, peered out. "I'll have the Owyhee wash this tomorrow. Bugs and all."

"The window's fine. Indeed. The men need time for rest," Hunt said. "They've no grains nor greens. We've slaughtered no pork—"

"Lost three sows with that storm due to the poorly tended fence," McDougall said. "I told those lazy men to fix—"

"They're exhausted. I think they might have scurvy as well."

"Nonsense!"

"Reed says we're out of vinegar. All the dried apples are depleted too. I've seen the scabs. It makes the men accident prone."

"Carelessness causes cuts. Lack of proper planning results in rolling logs that pin men's legs."

"Even you can't have missed the growing number on the sick list," Hunt said.

"Malingering, as I see it. Put them in irons. That's the way to deal with your so-called scurvy."

Hunt sighed. He couldn't get the other partners behind him in anything. McClellan even said he wanted out completely. Hunt could see what was happening. The attitude wasn't right here. And he didn't have confidence their outlook would improve with the supply ship. Why, he'd even learned that the Dorion woman had brought in dried fish to trade and no one had even asked her how she'd gotten them. If she could fish, why couldn't the men? He supposed he should be pleased they'd been accepted into Reed's stores. It would cut down on the trade deficit with these wily Clatsop and Chinook people. He'd make sure the fish were credited to Dorion's account.

"I think we need to send out more brigades," Hunt said. "Set a clerk with several men to trap. We can use the furs. The game will be better farther out. There'll be fewer men to feed here and reduce demand on supplies."

"The Indians' disposition toward us isn't known on the Multnomah River," McDougall said.

"Wollamat," Mackenzie corrected, entering without knocking as a partner could. "The word for the river is Wollamat, as the Indians say."

"Indeed."

"Wilson thinks we should send more brigades out, cut back on the supply drain here."

"For all we know, something has happened to the *Beaver*. We may never be resupplied from it...or any other," Hunt spoke his fear aloud.

"You're not giving up on Astor's dream, laddie, are you?" Mackenzie sat hard on the chair as though he still held much weight. He crossed his ankles and leaned back, arms behind his head.

"It's a balance. To keep the men strong enough to trap and trade or carry rifles against the Indians, the Brits...the North West Company, for all we know. And bring in pelts for shipment to Sitka—if the ship does arrive."

"And if it doesn't, we'll be needing the good will of the North Westers," Mackenzie said. Hunt bristled. Mackenzie dropped his feet, reached for a twist of tobacco. "Leadership is like the assayer's scale, something to be balancing all the time," Mackenzie said.

Hunt paced, hands behind his back. "If the ship does arrive, I'll load it with pelts and take it north. You partners can run things here. Meanwhile you, Donald, prepare to take a brigade up the Wollamat or Multnomah River or whatever it's called. You may as well be trapping as…putting extra weight on the leadership scales."

More brigades away meant fewer hunters were needed to supply the fort with food.

So Pierre and Ignace had been assigned the task of building canoes. Pierre took *engages* to find trees that would work better for the dugouts locating a place they called Oak Point. Several partners left for excursions inland, including Mackenzie who took his Porcelaine hound with him. Even a few clerks ranged out with small brigades, north and south.

For Marie, it seemed Hunt was just a clerk now, no longer making any major choices, merely staying behind the peeled-log walls. Yet she realized she and Pierre were little different. They all paddled as though going nowhere in slow water.

"It will get better when the boat gets here," Pierre told her. "Better then."

They might have peas and grain then, but many workers would leave, go back East with the ship. For the first time, she thought of Toupin's leaving. She'd miss the boy, young man, really. He had a good heart. His mother should be proud.

But the ship coming in wouldn't change what happened for her and Pierre. Maybe she was just tired. She had yet to finish a pair of moccasins the way Sarah had shown her. Her ancestors had been potters, working in clay and the ash of old bones. This beading onto the moccasins took time. She found herself irritable, annoyed with her sons. Sometimes, even Sarah's humming while she worked her awl beside her bothered Marie. It was like that now.

"I will walk to the post," Marie decided, putting her beadwork down. "Baptiste can stay with you?" Sarah had arched teeth that hung over her lower lip.

"See if the burning fish are in," Sarah said. She rarely put things into question, just directed. "You should get some for yourself, too." Marie nodded. "Don't leave your beads there. Some squirrel will chew it," Sarah said.

"If he can do it faster, maybe he deserves to," Marie told her.

Sarah looked at her, puzzled, as Marie rolled the leather and took it inside the hut.

Close to the fort's palisade, she neared the garden being tended by the Sandwich Islanders, Jeremie and Bob. Already tiny sprouts of turnip greens poked through the black soil. Mounds for potatoes dotted one end. She'd learned that the corn had not done well, and neither had the cucumbers. But the rapeseed had. The leafy green plant offered up both roughage and a kind of cooking oil to give variety from the fish. A tethered goat bleated at her as she passed.

A few hogs that hadn't been caught and shipped across the bay rooted in the soft, black earth. Two sheep ripped grass at a clearing. Soon they might have to eat the breeding stock. Just last week, a wolf had killed a hog that had torn through the pen, and a sow consumed a set of piglets before anyone could stop her.

"Must have been something wrong with them," Sarah said when Marie told her. "Pigs do that if the young are maimed. Think it's their duty if they see disaster ahead." Marie shivered at that, wondered about a mother eating its young. Why did Vivacité's face come to mind?

Through the gates of the log wall, Marie smelled the blacksmith's forge. Beside it rose a large trading store and the first dwelling house. A second, under construction, now dominated activity at this fur factory. Men and a few Clatsop Indians moved in and out. Young Toupin worked the small herd of horses the Astorians had acquired. Marie avoided the eyes of *engages* placed in irons in the sun as McDougall's punishment for something they'd done.

Inside, the post's shelves looked bare now. Just one stack of white blankets with two black threads assigning their points and one fathom of gurrah, the fine India cloth the Indians liked. Some colored calico and a roll of corduroy stacked the backboards. Marie had watched the thin gurrah cloth reappear wrapped as decoration on the necks of Chinook Indian women when they joined their men in trade.

"Are there Uthlechans yet?" she asked Reed as the clerk turned to her. She made the sign for "day" meaning "light." Candlefish, the men called them, fish that swam up the river at certain times of the year. They dried them and burned them for light.

"Aye." He reached into a barrel, handed her a stack of the small oily fish. "Sure and when the *Beaver* comes, we'll have the smell of beeswax with our light. "'Tis a scent I never thought I'd miss."

Fish that burned. It was one of many things she'd learned in this new place. She'd always found comfort in the learning of things.

"You've planted then?" Reed said. He gestured, made the signs for "corn" and "work." "You need turnip seeds? Potatoes? You and Missus Shonowane got quite a plot dug out, I hear."

She could understand more English than she could speak, but she was learning this, too. She wished to teach English to her sons. "Fish," she said, "fill us."

"Yes, yes, the Lord does provide. We are fortunate at that. Your boys…?" His eyes looked around as though to see them.

A horn blew then from the direction of the sea. "'Tis the *Beaver!*" Reed shouted as he moved toward the door. "Cargo's coming in at last. Now our lives will change!"

The men making wheelbarrows, working on house frames or rolling logs, stopped and looked toward the river. Even the men in irons raised their weary eyes with hope.

Somehow, Marie knew the ship would not bring much for her, nor did she want to wait upon the larder of others. She wouldn't stay long in this place, not when there were lands they'd come through with beaver and buffalo to spare, lands of plenty. Pierre had kept his word. He could keep it in a better place once the debt was paid. They could leave, go where they pleased. They would provide for themselves, not depend on others.

Marie felt the twist of hair at the back of her neck. She still had her hair comb and Sacagawea's knife. She would give them up, if she had to, for her sons, for Pierre. She touched the knife at her waist. As long as she had it, she told herself, she had a means to provide for her family, to tie them together, and so would not lose hope.

14

Her Way

A tangle of trees and flowering shrubs framed the view outside the door of their windowless hut. Marie bent through the door, then stood to gaze at the sight. A glimpse of the Columbia River, wide as a bay here, sparkled when the breeze pushed blackberry bushes away. Ferns thickened beside the paths along with the fading white blossoms of sorrel. This was a good place, separate from the fort and the growing irritations that plagued the men like the scurvy scabs pocking their faces.

When she picked up the last of the cornmeal ration allowed them from Reed's storehouse, she learned of fights at the charcoal pits and that the daily ration of grog had grown so small it now resulted in brawls. The orders were constant, she learned, a dozen different clerks and almost as many partners saying, *Do this and that. Frame up this wall. Get more firewood.* The men returned exhausted, yet were told to prepare to go south twenty miles to gather salt. On Sunday, when Paul Jeremie, the Sandwich Islander, had been accused of taking too long to raise the flag, he barked back at McDougall and was threatened with the irons in the open stockade. Marie had even seen more than one *voyageur*'s laundry hanging and knew by the holes they'd had no time to even mend their socks. More often now, the men simply sat down with fatigue. This Astoria was no place of freedom.

Things had gotten worse instead of better with the arrival of the *Beaver.*

First, the *Beaver*'s stores had taken days to pass over the bar because of the strong seas. The men could see the ship bobbing beyond the mouth of the Columbia. They anticipated, hoped, but tempers grew short with waiting. Finally, McDougall ordered the little transport ship, the *Dolly*, to risk the rolling waves. It brought in enough supplies so the men feasted with one full ration. By the time the *Beaver* docked, the partners were already on to other things: sending small work parties off here and there, intensifying orders and routines.

Weekly now a group of ten or twenty repacked and loaded canoes to bring in the furry bank notes of beaver pelts as the partners wanted a full shipment readied for Sitka and Canton as soon as they could, to best the North Westers bent on the same trade.

Marie walked the mile or so to the fort, Paul beside her. He still stumbled when he walk-ran, and she didn't dare loose his little hand from hers or he'd be into trouble. He was like a scent hound in finding trouble.

Paul pulled back on her and bent to pick a purple bloom that looked much like the thistles they had at home. *Home,* she thought. This didn't feel like home, even though she had her family with her.

"No, Paul," she said. "Let it be."

But the child pulled on it anyway, and he slipped away, ran farther into the foliage.

"Not now," she said. He could be so quick to disappear. Sometimes if she made a game of it, he'd return.

"Oh, Paul," she said, pushing back greenery. She made her voice sound light.

She could hear a giggle, and then the laughter stopped, followed by a wail.

"Are you all right? Paul?" She pushed at salmonberry bushes, then bracken ferns until she found him, sitting in the middle of a circle of women.

"Mama," he cried when he saw her now, and the women moved aside to let him through. They carried baskets and motioned her forward.

They must be Chinook. Their foreheads had the pitch of a steep roof. Would they think her a slave with her round head?

Marie lifted her son and smiled at them and at their urging peered into the baskets. She'd seen some of the plants they gathered. She touched her mouth to indicate eating, and the largest woman nodded yes. Her plants were the thistles Paul had wanted to pick.

Now the other women came close, and Marie realized Paul had just been surprised by them; they meant no harm. Instead they pointed to the leaves of a shrub and pretended to cough.

"Oh, that's good for a cold?" Marie said. She pointed back to the thistles. "These?"

The woman who appeared to be in charge broke the root, rubbed it of dirt, and bit it, chewing with delight. "Ilchee," she said.

"The plant? It is named Ilchee?" Marie said, mixing French and English and pointing.

Her companions giggled, fingers over their mouths. The woman in charge repeated the word "Ilchee" but tapped her own chest instead.

They seemed to delight in showing her their plants and uses, especially Ilchee, who beamed the brightest when she found a blooming yellow rose. She pointed to a sore on Paul's arm. It looked like the ones the men had from craving cider vinegar.

"Help *garçon,*" Ilchee said in what sounded like a mixture of Indian words and French.

"Help his mother, too," Marie said. She could supplement her family's diet and improve their health. And she'd made new friends, both the gathering of women and the plants. People and learning their ways was what would make this foreign place her own.

McDougall would be taking the *Beaver* north instead of Hunt. That was the new rumor. And Marie was relieved. That partner looked through her, his tiny glasses no help to see her when she happened upon him in the courtyard, had to step aside quickly as he charged past the hog pens on his way to some busyness. She was indistinguishable from the lone

Sandwich Island woman who arrived on the *Beaver,* nothing more than the faceless Clatsop and Chinook women who came in trading their baskets and canoes and sometimes themselves to the Astorians. Some of the men became sick with that lustful disease, and McDougall blamed the women as though they could make such trades without the men. He scowled at Marie as though she were at fault. He'd set a time when the gates would close each evening, and any woman around had to camp outside or return across the bay. Marie hoped once McDougall set sail, that this Astoria would be run more like the expedition, with one wolf to lead the pack, the rest in submission but noted for their strengths. She didn't like being indistinguishable from other Indian women, as if she had contributed nothing to their crossing. Somehow she would have to explain to her sons someday that white men could not separate acorn colored faces from one another. They thought all streams that fed the ocean were alike.

On a June day, Marie gathered her items from Reed's storehouse, watched him make marks on his ledger sheet. He spoke to her in English, as she'd asked, to practice. Paul squatted near her, watching a beetle's progress across the dirt floor.

Marie noted all she'd picked up, the value of the hides and two dried fish she'd brought in. Dried beef, coffee, flour, biscuits, and even precious cone sugar filled her pouch. She would save the sugar for special trades. She'd found another sweet source. *Providence provides,* she thought.

She'd heard Hunt say it often enough and how else could she explain Pierre's kept promise, her finding a friend in Sarah, and her stumbling upon the women whose advice had cleared up Paul's sores, even before she restocked the vinegar. Providence. Hunt's word for God, becoming her word too. She pulled the cattail leaves.

Pierre demanded sweeter things now. It was something new. She found he calmed though when she gave him tiny drops of amber-colored sweets formed at the undersides of cattail leaves. Just as in the back-waters of the Des Moines, the slender leaves gave up the tiny sweets when dried then shaken onto cloth. Inside tea, it was enough to soothe Pierre some days.

He still snapped at her when the biscuits browned too much, barked at the boys. Especially Paul. Once, when the child threw food at a skinny-tailed dog that followed him home from the fort, Pierre said, "We should eat that dog."

Marie frowned. "He makes a friend for Paul."

"Make good stew," he said. Paul's eyes pooled. Pierre said, "No crying or I give you something worthy of tears." He held the back of his hand as though to hit him. He didn't.

"Take these fish bones," Marie told Paul, moving quickly between father and son. "Dig a hole in the garden for them. It will make the pumpkins grow." Both Paul and Baptiste scrambled out, the latter heading for the water. He loved to fish and once brought back a speared salmon Ignace said were called Blue Backs.

"And you," Pierre continued, "why are there so few hides ready? I make two canoes in the time you take to soften only four hides, woman."

"Softening takes time," she told him. "A man can kill ten buffalo in one day, but a woman must work all winter to save and preserve them. His wealth comes from that, not from just the kills."

"These puny deer and elk are not buffalo hides," he said. "You should take less time to prepare them for trade."

She bit her tongue in silence. He wanted her to argue. She'd give him no fuel for this fire that burned inside him, that settled with sweets, if only for a moment.

"Sarah finishes faster," he said then.

Why did he bait her like a bear?

He ripped at the piece of venison he'd poked with his knife, watched her at the firepit where they sat, the breeze blowing the low smoke toward the sea. "She uses her teeth as she needs, does what she must for her family."

The words stung. It was a vanity of Marie's, she knew, to not hold the hides the way she'd been taught by her mother. She resisted the look of wide teeth over lower lips, the look of her mother-in-law, of Sarah. That look named their work.

She ought to give that up, do as he asked. It did not matter what a hunter's wife looked like; only a factor's wife would wish to have straight teeth.

"You say you want to remove the debt, yet you do nothing to make that happen," he accused.

She felt her face grow hot. "I find a new way," she said.

She laced the hide to a post, pulled against the wood when she worked. Later, she'd hang the hides in frames to work them, her back sweating with the effort. "My work is good. The hides are soft."

"We will never be free of the debt," he said, "unless we have more to trade. You must do your part, woman. You must do your part."

She stared at him. In the months since they'd arrived in Astoria, he had kept his word. The Shonowanes' presence helped too—Ignace had no need for liquor. Marie never heard him bark at Sarah. He wore the Jesuit's cross around his neck, told Marie his beliefs in the Christian God gave him strength.

"Is he the same as Hunt's Providence?" Marie once asked.

Ignace furrowed his brow in thought. "If Providence is the God who gives his Son."

She heard the Shonowanes laugh together, their voices lifting through the still summer nights. She and Pierre did not laugh much together.

"He's gentle where we can see and hear," Pierre said when Marie commented later. "Who knows what goes on behind their walls? You're sweet to me where others see you too, eh?" he said. "You make big demands when we're alone."

Big demands, she thought. *He makes big demands.* She opened her mouth to itemize them but stopped herself. Their words had not gone on to fire that day. She had held her tongue. She chose to be happy rather than right.

She remembered that now. "I do my part," she said. She blew air through her nose, opened her mouth to tell him more, stopped. They were alone behind closed doors. She could say what she wished but didn't—just to prove him wrong, just to prove that she, too, could change.

"I see that Toupin hovering here," Pierre said. "Why does he skulk about?"

"He works the garden. The trees, they shaded the fort's garden so much the corn refused to grow. We try something different here at Young's Bay. He helps. He likes being near children."

"Those *engages* are so tired they cannot mend their socks, but one can dig weeds for you? Toupin brings you a horse? No? Then tell him to stay away." When she didn't respond, just kept patting the corn into a flat bread, he said, "He plants trouble, not just seeds, *femme.* He does nothing to help us."

It was just Pierre's way of learning how to live without the whiskey, without the close conversations of Hunt, she decided. The more she defended, the angrier he got. If he had more responsibility like the other clerks, like that Wallace, Cox, and Franchere, perhaps then his mood would lift.

The clerks made more money too. Toupin told her. They could cancel debts more easily, had more to say about what work they did or didn't do. Astor had sent even more clerks out on the *Beaver,* and she hadn't heard of any of them leaving. They had a good clerk in her husband, Pierre. The Astorians simply overlooked what they had.

"There is more than one way to be sure no one else wins you in the wrestle," Sarah said.

Marie nodded, listened close. The two women sat tying sinew at the toes of moccasins. They could see their children chasing the dog, squealing as the black pup shook itself of water from the bay. Only Sarah's older son was absent. He'd joined his father and Pierre on another foray out for canoe logs. Sarah's younger son ran with only a breechcloth to cover his brown body.

Sarah scrutinized Marie's stitches like a cougar teaching her cub. Marie waited for the boxing she'd receive if the work did not meet Sarah's terms. With the stitching, the moccasins would be finished, and the women given credit for them at Reed's storehouse. The Chinook women liked the soft hide work covered with tiny glass beads. A few more, and Marie would see the debt lessen. A desire realized would come to pass. As the garden produced, she could take spare potatoes and the rape oil and trade for dyed cloth. From it, she'd make a covering dress she could trade to Clatsop women in exchange for one of the tightly woven bags she admired. She'd take it apart, see how it was made. Then she'd make one herself. The Clatsops got blankets and rings and cloth for those bags. Marie could do that too, then trade up for steel traps for Pierre.

Today she was learning to stitch the tight way of the Chipewyan women. To pass the time, Marie had asked Sarah about a Chipewyan practice she'd heard of, about men choosing marriage partners and then losing them to chance.

"I have heard your women have no choice," Marie said. "That a man simply challenges a wrestle for you and you must take the winner to your bed."

"There are always choices." Sarah smiled to herself. "One must be clear about what matters and then be courageous to secure it. I knew a woman who cut her husband's hair when she learned of the challenge." Her eyes sparkled with the memory. "She took that man's topknot and chopped it with a knife just before her husband squatted to defend." She made the cutting motion with her hand.

"Ignace was surprised but pleased," Sarah continued. "He accepted my help and the man had no hold to pull him down. I greased Ignace once too. Bear grease all over him. He won that wrestling challenge. I tell Ignace when I tire of him, I will grease the challenger." She laughed. "There is always another way if a thing matters," Sarah said. "We women know this."

Marie wondered how much older than she Sarah was, what she'd come through to decide there was always another way. Sarah stitched, her fingers callused from pushing the bone needle through the tough leather. A pileated woodpecker thumped against a hollow tree. Marie looked up to see if she could find the flash of red that marked it.

"It is one reason we leave the Hudson's Bay place and travel to the Okanogan River and then come with David Thompson here. We are one, Ignace and me, one family. We tired of the challenges for false affection. We believed the Jesuit's words when we said our vows. He said our promise was not just to each other but to God, that we must trust God to be enough to keep us together, even in troubled times. God blesses the marriage, but we make the vows. We pray," she said, saying it as though it was like breathing, a part of her being. "We wished to bring these words to other Indian people, to give them hope as we have known, for how to live forever here and after death."

Marie fidgeted. "My husband says men like Hunt and McDougall fear the Iroquois because they'll tell the river tribes of how the white men harmed our people in the East. He says nothing of your sharing Jesus stories."

"Some may come here to stir hot trouble stew. Not us. We wished for more, for something different. You come here too for more."

Such blunt assurance Sarah had.

She and Pierre had come because Marie pushed it, because she didn't want to be left behind, because she wanted better trade goods, to be noticed, to get more for her husband and her sons. Isn't that why she'd come here? She stitched in silence for a time.

"I want my sons to grow exposed to sunlight without the shadows of tall white weeds," Marie said then. "In St. Louis, their chances..."

She shrugged her shoulders. "They would get choked out there." Perhaps these wishes for her sons were false challenges, like the Chipewyan's wrestle.

"Such weeds will find them," Sarah said. "Even in this far place."

"So. We must find a way to live beside each other, Indian and non? Is this what you say?"

"You must learn to listen and let yourself be guided," she said. "You make your beads in a good design." She signed for Marie, using the word *work* for "make." "You make them different, your own way." She ran her fingers across the brown-and-white floral pattern stitched so tight not even her fingernail could slip between the rows. She grunted her approval.

The warmth that came with that attention surprised her. Was Marie so empty that a woman's grunt could fill her up? What did it matter what this woman thought of her work, her choices or what she "made"? Did she think her work named her?

Marie reached over, exchanged the compliment. "Oh," she said, fingering Sarah's moccasin. "Your work is always good."

Sarah looked at her. "It is not necessary to give back before you do the work of taking in," she said. Marie frowned. "It is also a gift when you receive," Sarah said. "We learn to fill our basket when we practice letting little bits build up inside before we give it all away. It is a choice we make, how to fill our basket and whether or not to empty it too quickly.

"He will not let you come along," Pierre said. "It is only an early party, to see if building a fur house is warranted." Marie knelt amidst a soft pile of goose feathers, sharpening the ends to a nib for pens. Clerks used many pens that Reed took from her in trade. She held Sacagawea's knife loosely, gently cut the quill.

"I can do the work," she said. "McDougall decides this, that I cannot go?"

Marie missed the tasks of preparing buffalo hides and all that went before: the hunt, the celebrations, the women's gatherings to process and prepare all winter long. She missed the trapping, cleaning, stretching beaver hides, and the satisfaction of seeing the bales marked for transport and knowing she had done this, had made this happen with her hands. Had worked beside her mother and sister as they laughed and talked. Her heart melted with the memories.

Canoe making at distant places and going off to hunt for those who trapped at inland streams was not the work her husband wanted. He buried his desires.

"Wallace goes," he told her. "I go along as hunter and maybe interpreter to the Kalapuyas who live that way. Or so say the Clatsops who know everyone. Maybe it's a way to show Wallace I can do what needs doing, and he'll tell McDougall and Hunt, eh? It'll make a better place for us."

"So. The time has come," she said, re-sheathing her knife, stacking the finished quills. "I will ask Hunt to see if you can become clerk."

Pierre shook his head.

"You can lead an expedition out," Marie said, "tell men what to do and when. You can do this."

"You could too," he said. He grinned. "No. A woman can't tell Hunt what to do, even a good woman like you. He won't listen. I'll help Wallace on the Wollamat River, maybe earn his respect, and then we'll see what that gains us."

"It takes you away, and we make no gains on the debt," she said.

"You just don't like being left," he said, his fingers lifting her chin.

"Hunt's taking the ship north. We leave tomorrow." Jean Toupin leaned against his hoe, deciding now was a good a time as any to tell Madame Dorion. She'd been so kind to him, darning his socks, sharing vinegar from her own stores, even showing him how to weave the weirs, though he doubted he'd ever use that skill again. Some activities were clearly women's work. But tomorrow, he and George Gay, and any number of others allowed, would be leaving.

"I thought McDougall would go, not Hunt," she said. "I suppose taking the furs to Canton is the biggest responsibility. It should go to the chief factor."

She knelt on the ground, ripped at the weeds in the garden like an angry goat. Toupin didn't like leaving, not with Dorion gone now too. But he'd finished his agreement and like George Gay, he was tired of "Do as I say" all day.

"I imagine you miss your mother," Marie said. "And your brothers and sisters."

"Being with *les garçons* has eased that some," he said. "I'll tell my mother of you." That seemed to make Madame Dorion smile.

He laid the hoe down and licked his lips of the salty sweat. Taking a deep breath, he said, "I made something for you." He felt his ears grow hot when she looked up at him. "Well, I had LeClerc make it." He pulled a pouch that hung across his chest over his head, loosened the drawstrings, and lifted out something wrapped in a square of calico.

"For me? It is not necessary," she said. Her words the same as his mother's whenever he gave her a gift. He rocked from foot to foot as she unfolded it. He probably shouldn't have done it, but she'd been so kind to him. His mother'd want him to acknowledge her care. She wasn't saying a thing. Was she crying? He'd made her cry?

"Bon," she said then, dabbing at her eyes with her fingertips.

"You…you like them, *oui?"*

"They're beautiful."

"I noticed you had the holes in your ears, those three on each side like that," he pointed, careful not to touch. "And I'd seen some made of little tubes of copper. Maybe you even had some like them. Maybe that's where I saw them, that day when I got little Baptiste up from under the dock." He was jabbering. Even his voice ran up and down, out of control. He swallowed, slowed. "I traded some of the fish. For the piece of copper sheet. LeClerc gave his time for nothing. Said it was the least he could do for you, bringing him that salve for his chapped hands. I hope you'll wear them," he said. "Or save them for…another daughter you might have one day."

He watched a shadow cross her face, as fleeting as a sigh. He could have kicked himself, bringing that up now when he'd never said a word to her about it after one of the *engages* had told him of it.

"I'll wear them," she said, putting the pins through the rim of her ear, then the lobes below. The copper dangled. "And every time they sing within a breeze, I'll remember you and your gifts of kindness to me and to my family." She finished putting them on, shook her head. He could hear the tinkling. "But I have nothing to give you," she said.

"To see you smile and wear them, that's my gift, Madame Dorion. One I'll long remember."

Hunt finished placing his personal items in a leather satchel brought out by one of the clerks on board ship. He wasn't looking forward to the voyage. He'd always gotten sick on the high seas. Canoes were one thing, but the lurch and roll of a big ship without the sight of land to ground him, made him "exceedingly ill."

But as McDougall and the Stuarts had pointed out to him while the partners discussed who should go, delivery of the furs and restocking with goods the interior Indians would trade for were the most important components of Astor's success. "Anyone can build a fort and figure out how to motivate a hundred men," McDougall said. "But not just anyone can ensure that several thousand dollars worth of goods arrive where intended."

Hunt did wonder if they patronized him just a bit. He was the youngest of the partners, but he'd proved himself—with Providence's help.

He hoped the current price of four dollars per beaver skin held. The Astorians hadn't had much time for trapping, what with building the fort. Losing the *Tonquin* not only delayed this Sitka trip, but it meant fewer goods to trade for the skins the river tribes had accumulated.

Hunt had been surprised to see so many British-made items in the hands of the Chinook and Clatsop and even farther upriver when they'd beached near the Wappatos and Multnomahs. Had Astor known the English ships had been coming in these waters for years? Why, Hunt had even seen some red-haired Indian children. He remembered that Mackenzie had said, "A Scotsman or two has jumped an English ship then." It must have been why developing trade with the inland tribes—those west of the Shining Mountain—was so important.

So considering the limited time and all the demands, loading as many full packs of pelts as they had would make Astor proud. Especially once they reached Sitka. These pelts would then be transferred to another ship and with the northern pelts added, taken on to Canton and sold. The Western expansion would come full circle.

Hunt's plan was to return to Astoria with the *Beaver* resupplied with trade goods so they could begin in earnest to convince the Umatillas and Nez Perce and Cayuse and all the other inland tribes to trap for the Astorians and stay away from the likes of David Thompson.

At least he could leave knowing he'd influenced that decision. McDougall had agreed to his suggestions about the clerk-led brigades, and the food shortages had lessened. Perhaps he had been too worried. True, he wasn't accustomed to keeping a fur factory going. Running an expedition through unknown country was different than maintaining a daily regime. McDougall was right about that. Innovation and maintenance were distinctly unique.

And frankly, with Mackenzie now on a river somewhere trapping, Hunt felt better about leaving. The man hadn't completed his assignment to take secured letters back to Astor. Instead, at those dalles along the Columbia, he'd gotten into an argument with the Wascos and the missive meant for Astor now lay in the bottom of the river. With no word from Hunt to take back, Mackenzie had returned to Astoria. For all Astor knew, they were all dead here in the West, his investments drowned. At least when Hunt reached Sitka, he could send letters on via ship.

Hunt put the new goose-quill pens into the bottom drawer of his writing box. Someone had sharpened them to a fine point. He closed the carrying case, finished putting his collar box into the satchel, and snapped the clasp. He looked out the window.

Dorion's woman ran after that young one, what was his name? Paul. The fringe of her leggings fluttered as she kicked up her heels. She caught the child just as he reached the hog pens. She picked him up and swung him around, the boy's head leaned back, his wide mouth open in laughter. The woman laughed too. He hoped Dorion knew what he had in her—a good mother, a woman loyal despite the trials Dorion brought her into. Loyalty mattered in a marriage, in a partnership, too.

He lifted the case, scanned his small room for forgotten items, then headed toward the open courtyard. The mother had endured well their remarkable journey, her losses. It would remind him when he got "exceedingly ill" that much more than seasickness could be endured.

Marie had tethered Paul to herself with one of the long vines the Indian women used for making baskets and sometimes pounded to a pulp and used to caulk canoes. It was tough and allowed the child to move about in a wide circle but stay well within her sight. Pierre had gone with Ignace and his sons who accompanied a work party gathering salt where Lewis and Clark had once boiled the seawater. He'd be gone for at least four days.

As Marie hoed and sewed and told stories to her children, she'd begun to plan. She had not been without Pierre for this long since before Paul's birth, nearly three years earlier. It had only been a month. *I must be missing him,* she thought and wondered what her life would be like if she lost him, if he did not come back.

She'd realized how tentative their place was here when *engages* working with Mackenzie's brigade brought bad news back. Mackenzie trapped near the big falls north of where Pierre served, and there'd been trouble. Caches of hides had been stolen, an Indian chief killed. Mackenzie himself supposedly survived the skirmish. His dog had been lost, but he still reported his brigade was successful. They'd even encountered Ramsey Crooks and John Day, the last division of Hunt's overland party.

A canoe had brought Crooks and John Day and several other *engages* back. The mountain men, Hoback and Reznor, and a few others had stayed behind. "They found themselves some friendly Indians and they're staying there until they get well," the Virginian Day told her.

He also shared a tale of tragedy and starvation beyond what any of the others of Hunt's party had endured. Even now Day shivered when he stood, his hands spilled the coffee mug he gripped, and his eyes moved from side to side as though he expected someone to jump him from behind.

"Don't trust 'em," Day told her. "Don't trust any of 'em. They'll take your clothes and run you naked in the cold."

"You're safe here," she said, patting his hand as if he were a child, hoping she told the truth.

She wondered if Pierre was safe.

Marie increased her efforts to tan hides, even holding them with her teeth now. It both irritated and pleased her that the work went faster. "You be good. I will have no time to chase you," she told Paul. She needed goods, trade goods. They would buy her information, a canoe, dried foods that she didn't have.

Her efforts often kept her from the fort, so when she finished in the garden and walked with Paul to the post carrying several pairs of the moccasins, she was surprised by the clusters of men talking quietly, tension in the air. When she walked to Reed's stores to see what trade goods she could acquire for the moccasins, she spied the Sandwich Islander, Paul Jeremie, in irons.

"Brought him back, they did," Reed said. "Put him off on canoes and the Clatsops brought him to McDougall." Reed usually smiled when he saw her, but today he scowled. "There is no way out. He signed a contract," Reed said. "These…these…" Reed glanced at her. "These *employees* seem to think it has no meaning, saying they'll do a thing and then 'tis something else they do. A man's word is his bond," Reed said. "His word has to mean something."

Like Hunt's words did? Marie wondered. Hunt promised someday Pierre would be rich, then abandoned him as though he were a troublesome dog.

She didn't even look at Jeremie when she passed by carrying her awls and two-point blankets and fathoms of gurrah with her. These were things the Clatsop women liked. These and the fancy moccasins she'd made and kept at Young's Bay. These and her shrewd ways would get her a canoe, well stocked, and she'd leave this place and go to Pierre. They would not bother to pursue a woman to bring her back.

"Papa!" Paul said, pulling against the vine rope that held him.

"Papa's not here now," she told the boy. "But soon. Soon we'll be with him. We have been separated enough."

Paul pointed and pulled against her, both hands yanking on the vine tied at their waists. "I'm not setting you free to run to the hog's pen again." She grinned at him. "You are tied to me as when you were born," she said. "When you were a baby, I cut your cord and tied it there, in your pouch," she said and patted the leather bag he wore around his neck. "We are tied together and will always be."

"Papa!" he insisted, and this time he pointed toward the shoreline where Marie spotted a canoe brigade beaching.

"Papa!" Paul shouted and ran to the shore, tugging Marie along on the vine.

But Pierre was not with them.

"Don't you worry now," the clerk named Wallace told her when she walked to the canoes. "He's got plenty of supplies. A couple of *voyageurs* stayed too. They'll treat themselves well without a company man watching. You'll be going back with me, you and the children and ten or twenty more. In November. Get your tanning hands ready. They'll be working."

"He ordered this?" she asked.

Wallace bristled. "McDougall's named me clerk," he said. "We return within the month to build Wallace House." He stepped away, reached for McDougall's hand, then one of the Stuarts reached out in greeting. "We'll build a factory on that river," she heard Wallace say as the men walked away. "That land's as rich as I've ever seen. Indians're friendly, beaver thick as ticks. Hardly needed the rye to please the boys, everything went so well, though they do like their refreshments…"

His words faded away. Marie picked up her son, gripped him perhaps a little too harshly.

The departure was hurried, leaving little time to say what she wished to Sarah and Ignace.

"You will come back to Young's Bay," Sarah said. "You just go to a wintering place for a time. You'll be back."

"Maybe," Marie shrugged. She didn't want to say what she had planned, what she would try to convince her husband of that would take them far away. "I will remember you," Marie said and she signed the words for "heart knowing."

Sarah's upper teeth rested lightly on her lower lip. "My heart knows you too," she said. She handed Marie a pair of moccasins.

The leather was as soft as any Marie had ever felt. The hide had been smoked with an alder wood, and Marie inhaled the scent. She always took time to inhale the smell of new leather. She rubbed it against her cheek, had Paul do the same. The bead design was one of Sarah's newest. Sprays of colored beads rushed like streams of water into a blue circle of lake. Some of the sprays were double rows and long, and some were single sets of beads that barely reached the circle. "These are all of us," Sarah said, pointing to the streams. "Many colors. Many lengths. Many depths."

"It looks as though some do not make it," Marie said. "They fall short."

Sarah brushed away her observation with her hands. "The length of the stream does not matter. Only that it's there and flows toward the circle that forms the lake we all live in. Sometimes streams go underground so we can't see how far they reach. We can't know what effort they make to find the lake. Rivers serve and every stream matters. You remember this," she said. "Your family is that lake. These people in this post are a part of it too. The river Indians. We are all part of the lake together."

Marie nodded, her eyes brimming. She would remember, especially the way the sun caught the cut-bead design, mixed with her tears.

Wallace's canoe brigade with Marie and her children on board left in early November 1812 for Wollamat Falls. The site was south of the Columbia River, inland several miles. The *voyageurs* oared up the Columbia, often pulling against the heavy current. They poled their way around a long island where geese lifted from the water, giving them fresh fowl to eat when they made camp that evening. Marie watched every item of landscape, memorizing. She collected the quills and the goose down, too.

The Wollamat River ran north near the Multnomahs' big village. At the mouth, Wallace's party headed south. They'd been out from Astoria four nights. Her children had been like fireflies in daylight, being no trouble, hardly noticed by Wallace. They portaged around a deep and thundering falls where Indians fished, then put back into the river to the serenade of sea gulls. Surely they were close now.

Two more days they traveled until sunset dappled gold on the ripples. The thump of oar and pole against the wood, the sound of water lapping at the canoes comforted. Trees arched over the river in places, creating an echo for their voices. In sections too perfect to be random, Marie could see a distance beneath the trees on the shoreline as lush green grass made its way to the roots and trunks of tall cedars and firs. She pointed. "Indians burn the ground," Wallace told her. "Brings out the deer to graze." He pointed to a shape that lifted its head as the *voyageurs* eased close to the shore. The deer held fresh browse in its mouth, nibbled as they passed, not startled by the Canadians' paddle songs.

"Almost there now," Wallace told the boys. "Your pa'll be glad to see you."

They rounded a bend, and the *voyageurs* scraped the crafts onto a sandy beach. "Through that stand of trees there you should see the beginnings of our post. Oh, and there they are."

Wallace pointed and Marie squinted. Next to a fir she spotted her husband. She waved, wings of joy lifting her heart, the cry of the Ioway greeting song forming on her lips.

Her husband raised his arm as though to wave, then staggered back and stumbled against a tree. Was he drunk? Then like mud oozing down a saturated bank, Pierre slid down the trunk, his head flopping forward onto his chest.

15

Under Cover of Snow

Marie rode in the last canoe. Words and choices swam in her head like the candlefish, pushing upstream as the boat drew near the shore. Why hadn't she left earlier to find Pierre on her own? She could have made this trip, found the stream that took them here to this place William Wallace and John Halsey selected. She should have insisted she come in the beginning, just as she had back in St. Louis, not let him be alone.

She fussed at the cloth sack cradling Paul on her back, pushed him up higher with her hands. The dog whined. "Be still!" she hissed. Her husband should have gone on the journey with Mackenzie and the Stuarts to take news back to Astor. Maybe if her husband had been there, their journey would have been successful, the thefts and wounding that returned the men to Astoria before they'd even been gone two weeks might not have happened. Her husband could have guided them back, guided them through. What were these partners thinking of to ignore men like her husband?

All this ran through her head as she pulled herself up from the canoe, her son on her back, all this while blaming herself. She could have kept her husband from his poor choices. And her own.

Wallace should never have left him whiskey and rum. No. She had no time for blame.

"Wait," Wallace ordered when she moved to leave the pirogue. He scanned the shoreline. Marie squinted, trying to see what he could see near the tree where her husband staggered in his drunkard state. She squinted, shrubs and trees obscuring her view in the distance.

Wallace gripped his rifle. He nodded to the *devant* steering at the front of the canoe. The man laid the wooden oar quietly in the boat, its thump a hollow sound that matched the emptiness in Marie's heart.

An overhang of willows echoed back the sounds of water against wood. Wind chopped the river, brushing her earrings. A cloud chased the sun, and now a light rain fell from a gray sky leaving pocks on the river.

Pierre's one leg stiffened before him; the other twisted under, and his head lolled onto his chest. He'd let his rifle drop onto the mat of fir needles beneath the trees. He always tended his rifle carefully…unless he drank rye. Red and orange leaves dotted the ground around him.

"There could be more," Wallace whispered.

"More what?" Marie asked in English.

"Quiet!" Wallace told her.

Her face burned. She signaled silence to Baptiste, her eyes as the men's, scanning the river's edge. For what? Then Marie knew what Wallace knew: Her husband wasn't drunk but wounded.

She could hear her heart pound. She felt Paul stir and scowled a warning at him to be quiet. She prayed he would, prayed that Pierre still lived, humbled by her rush to judgment.

Wallace and two *engages* eased from the boat then, their pant legs darkened by the swift flowing waters. They crouched toward Pierre. Still, patient as a heron, they waited. A dark form moved across Marie's vision from the shrubs. She caught her breath.

"Don't shoot!" the man said. "It's Halsey!"

They scrambled from the boats while the second clerk hunkered toward Pierre, pressed his head to Pierre's chest and shouted: "He lives!"

A *voyageur* grabbed a leather pack, tossed it to Marie, who ran toward Pierre. Paul bounced on her back. She opened the leather parfleche, folded back the corners and tore out the thin gurrah cloth. She rolled the strip into a wad. But when she lifted his leather shirt stained dark, she saw he had a bandage there already, blood oozing from beneath. His thighbone appeared twisted. She attempted to straighten it, but he shuddered in pain.

"Must have cracked a bone," Halsey said. "Just now. When he fell."

"What happened?" Wallace asked. He leaned over Marie and Halsey, whose hands turned red from Pierre's blood as he tore off the old binding, then took the fresh dressing Marie handed him.

"Misunderstandings," Halsey said. "Always misunderstandings."

"The Kalapuya?" Wallace said.

Halsey shook his head. "No," he said. "Those Indians are harmless enough."

"Mackenzie's had trouble with them."

Marie heard the sounds of *engages,* felt more than saw them bring bales of supplies up the sloped bank from the canoe. "Pierre," she whispered, "can you hear me?" The black dog sniffed at Pierre's wounds. She stroked her husband's sunken cheeks.

"They hunted," Halsey said. "It was a mistake. He was struck. Yesterday. We dressed the wound and told him to stay down, but he heard you, the *engages* as they approached. He will heal now, better, that you are here," Halsey told Marie.

Marie cut away the seams of Pierre's leggings. Halsey whistled. "He won't be much good for a while."

"We need to bind it," she said.

"Did Wallace bring more whiskey?" Halsey looked at Marie. Then as though he realized his mistake in asking her about supplies a clerk had packed, he pressed his hands against his thighs and stood. "We need to ease his pain. That's what whiskey does. Don't know anything else that'll do it."

Marie hung to the wisp of Pierre's breath she could feel against her cheek when she leaned into him. She cleaned the chest wound and changed the bandages, washing out the cloth in a copper pot. She'd set Paul off her back, directed Baptiste to watch him.

Wallace brought long sticks to hold the leg straight, and Marie's fingers searched the muscle, the bone, found the place where it had separated, and she yanked with all her strength to get it straight.

Pierre gasped deep with the pain but didn't regain awareness.

"I will find out who did this to Papa," Baptiste said, scowling, his little arms crossed over his chest the way the *engages* often stood as they scanned the rivers while waiting on shore. "I will kill them."

Marie turned to him. *"Non,"* she said. "Halsey says it's an accident. It's not meant."

"They hurt Papa," Baptiste insisted. His tone startled her. She turned from her husband's still form and stared at the boy. His eyes had a glassy gaze. She felt a shiver inside her. So much anger on his little face, so much hate for one so young.

"Hold the sticks steady while I tie them," she said. Baptiste complied, and his eyes lost the hardness as he helped her. "Good," she said. "Papa will be better. We'll see to that." To Wallace she said, "We are ready to move him to a hut."

That evening Marie brought out dried fish, smoked venison. She heated water for the cornmeal that bubbled and thickened. Etienne Lucier, the *engage* they'd first met in Astoria, crawled into the low hut where she and the boys hovered over Pierre. He handed her hard biscuits made at the larger log building where the men all stayed, where the factory on the Wollamat River would rise.

"We need no special treatment," she told Etienne in French. "We'll be no bother here. Tell Wallace and Halsey that. I'll go out and trap as soon as Pierre is better. I can hunt. Baptiste will watch Pierre while I work."

Etienne's mustache framed a kind face. He reached out to touch her shoulder. "No one expects this," he said.

"They expect it," she said, nodding toward where Wallace and Halsey had their camp. "They don't say it, but they wear…disappointment if we don't do our part. You should know this too," she warned. "Even a woman knows this."

"No," Etienne told her. "We trap and John Day hunts. You can scrape the deer hides and dress the pelts to prepare for packing. As we bring in beaver, you'll have your hands full. Only one woman to do so much woman's work," he said, then smiled. "I must take a wife. Just to help you out."

Marie shook her head. John Day still quivered hot coffee. He'd have trouble steadying the espontoon that held the rifle, let alone priming and powdering well enough to shoot. No, they'd need a hunter *and* someone to handle hides. For these partners, it would not be enough. It was never enough.

She woke with a start, her hands still wrapped in the singed side of the hide. She'd fallen asleep at her work. Rain fell steady against the hut, a sound she'd grown to expect in the few days since they'd been there.

Wallace had ordered men to begin immediately felling trees for the proposed warehouse. Other men spread out to trap the small streams of the beaver. Earlier, she'd squeezed a venison-soup soaked rag into the corners of Pierre's mouth. She had some snowberries her Chinook friends said eased the pain of burns. Deer fern, if Pierre could chew, might help too. The swelling in his leg had lessened, but a bone break as this one was would take time for healing. It meant someone else had to bring him food and care for him. Healed bones were signs of deep devotion.

She cleaned Paul's little bottom, casting aside the irritation she felt with his lack of knowing enough ahead of time when his body moved. She clucked to herself. At least an abundance of the soft moss she used to clean him with grew within a few feet of their hut. Providence provided. The boy was three already. She wiped her hands on wet leaves and Paul scampered out. There were more important things to worry over now than how quickly a small child learned to listen to his body's callings.

The scent of meat and corn lingered in the dimly lit place. She prepared all the meals in their small hut, making sure Halsey noted on his ledger paper what she took. She would repay this. She wanted no one thinking they received without giving back. She prepared food twice daily for her family, kept them together. Except when Etienne or LeClerc came for Baptiste. Then she allowed the boy to go. Her inquisitive son appeared to make the men laugh. And without Baptiste in the hut, Paul played quietly beside her, letting the small dog draw up snug beside Pierre.

One morning, Marie told Baptiste she was leaving, to watch and call her if Pierre awoke. With Pierre's rifle and the iron espontoon, she headed out. She wondered if LeClerc had made this iron tool. The seams were well formed and solid, and there was a twist at the top as though to decorate.

She had no luck the first day. But on the second morning she found deer trails through the trees entering the meadow like streams to a lake. Fresh droppings marked the path. She set the espontoon in the dirt and loaded powder into the Kentucky rifle, dropped the lead ball in and primed the pan. When she set the rifle against the iron stand, it formed a cross. She'd never noticed that before. She waited. A deer came quiet as snow. She pulled the hammer back, squeezed the trigger. The deer buckled. Providence had provided, and the deer had offered up its life. Now she must prepare the meat, the hides, save the hooves and antlers, do women's work.

The next day, after cutting the meat and setting it to smoke, Marie soaked the hide in the river, working the hair loose. She listened for the sounds of Pierre's breathing, loud enough to break the drumming of the rain against the hut. Paul slept, his arm over the dog's neck. They'd named the black dog *"Chien,"* and often he padded with her to the river as she set the willow weir, though she had yet to catch a fish here.

The boys entertained her, and Marie had time to think again, to plan. But her plans were useless unless her husband improved. She wouldn't let herself think of what she'd do if he died. She wouldn't name herself a widow.

Her eyes adjusted to the pale morning light. She'd noticed the few times she'd left Pierre's side to relieve herself that the sky held the same gray cast as the inside of the hut here at this Wollamat place. But the land outside, a green prairie etched with the black charcoal of rich soil, smelled always of good land and light. It soothed her each time she stood, her eyes squinting to bring the distant trees into focus, to identify a yellow-headed bird chirping above her, to spy the squirrel that brushed its tail at her before scrambling up a fir.

Clearings marked the land, dotted with new stumps. Kalapuya people lived here though she had yet to see another brown face. As she worked she wondered how their presence in this place, the hunting, clearing, trapping of this brigade, changed the landscape of such people's lives.

If only her husband improved, this would be a place of great soothing. She worked a hide and dozed, her dreams mingling with rain, old with new. Holy Rainbow appeared in her sleep. "Some things are not of our choosing," the woman told her in the dream. "But we are allowed to pray for what we wish." Her mother-in-law had thumped at the cornmeal she ground, the rhythm of it matching the rain thumping on the hut. "It is how God changes who we are and what we wish for."

"The corn?" Marie asked.

"The prayers," Holy Rainbow said.

Marie started to ask what words would keep her husband living, but the dream drifted into day, her head nodding to her chest and waking her with a start.

Something had changed. Pierre still lay quiet. She crawled to the opposite side. Probably the dog scratched in its sleep. She pulled a robe up over Paul to keep him warm. The air felt colder than before. She opened the tent flap and gasped.

Snow fell. Huge white flakes like those that had fallen on the day they buried her daughter. The snow drifted down, barely touching earth before melting. That was the sound she heard that awoke her: silence, the change of rain to the stillness of snow. She thought to wake Paul, to go out to find Etienne and Baptiste, to show them snow without the pain of loss wrapped in it.

She decided against it. Let Paul sleep. Let Baptiste experience it where he was, staying the evening at the emerging post. Perhaps by day's end snow would accumulate. She pulled the blanket around her shoulders and knelt in the hut opening, watching flakes fall as daylight washed around them.

A snowflake dropped and melted on her knees. Holy Rainbow told her once that each snowflake formed, then fell, then melted all alone. Yet together they made drifts difficult for even horses to plunge through. All single yet powerful when together.

She knew that life and death were part of the cycle of being, of living things formed and then changed. But Holy Rainbow insisted there was more. Her God intended more, even for one such as Marie, Holy Rainbow told her.

More. If that was so, then why did each season of her life carry grieving with it? Why was she asked to give so much with so little to show for her efforts?

She felt a chill. Colder. It was even colder now.

She turned to see if Pierre still lay covered. When she did she saw that his eyes were open.

"I have missed this," she told Pierre while she spooned cornmeal into his mouth. He mumbled something, swallowed, pointed to the loin of venison she'd roasted. "You need fat, too," she said. "Venison is not fat enough for you."

Pierre reached out to her, weakly held her wrist. "You are enough for me," he said. "This is what you miss?" He kissed her, one of his flesh-loose arms pulling her close.

She lifted his arm away, continued to feed him.

"Be terrible to die from something stupid, like being mistook for a bear, eh?" He said the word "terrible" as though it had three parts.

"This is what happened?" Marie asked. He'd been alert now for several hours, his breathing steady.

Pierre nodded. "Old Bellows, I call him." Pierre pushed at the sides of his cheeks to demonstrate the man's rounded face. "I let him use my rifle. Bet him I could get myself a bear before him." He shrugged. "We all make mistakes."

"Does Bellows know that he hits you?"

"Not at first. But he found me. Dressed the wound. Brought Halsey to me, and I guess I was doing all right until I heard the French songs." He looked away, cleared his throat. "No gunshot wound will keep me down, eh?"

"You hurt your leg, too."

"Now that was stupidity, a man falling onto himself."

"Bellows did get a bear in you," she said then, making her voice lighter than she felt. "He wins."

"I win," Pierre told her. "Knowing you were coming made me foolish." He patted her thigh as she knelt.

"You have earrings again," he said.

"A trade gift."

He nodded. "Fine work. You deserve it."

She'd been too quick to believe he might not have changed. She winced at the memory of how she judged him when she'd first seen him.

"We do better when we stay together," she said.

They passed the winter in that prairie place surrounded by clusters of trees. As Pierre gained strength, he returned to hunting, though he limped and dragged his leg. The Kalapuya man whose bullet had struck Pierre gifted him with his presence, carrying Pierre's rifle. Pierre showed

Marie places where otters played, and they waited to trap them. Rain misted, but the high grasses, leafy trees, and dark soil all reminded Marie of her place of beginning along the Des Moines. She had never felt so rested, though she'd rarely worked as hard.

And Bellows's woman came by. She offered a fine basket full of dried berries to Marie and a twist of herbs. She pointed to Pierre's leg to indicate that the herbs were medicinal. She could share no words with her. "These Columbia Indians don't use their hands to speak," Pierre told her as Bellows's wife stood by, solemn. "They use that other language, a trade jargon mixed with French and Indian words. How they traded with the Brits long years before, I'd guess."

Marie knew her gifts spoke healing.

They bantered at Wallace House as they now called the structure on this prairie place. Marie laughed and loved, because for the first time, they placed what mattered higher in the basket of life, balanced it better. Unessential things did not weigh them down. They were there, together and alive.

Marie thought of that as she carried Paul in the small of her back. She worked stripping the beaver of their hides, stretching and drying them in the smoke hut. What mattered was not just what she carried but how she balanced what she placed upon her back.

On New Year's Day, the Wallace House party did not work. The men imbibed and sang and LeClerc, who had become a cook of sorts, fixed a dish with dried berries and cone sugar. The copper kettle hung from the twists of iron forming the trammel, set like tipi poles over the flame. Pierre ate heartily. Once again he did not consume the rum.

And seven days later, when Marie wiped tears from her cheeks, Pierre seemed to understand. He put his arm around her while they stood beside the river, watching as the boats were loaded with bales of dried pelts.

"It is a year now since our baby died. This is why you cry?"

She looked up at him, surprise in her eyes. "I come beside you today then," he said. "Today I come beside you."

By late January, Wallace House stood complete.

"I have been readying ground for planting," Marie told Pierre, a smile on her face.

"Too early for that," he said.

"I walk an area, clear it of high weeds." Marie tapped at her temple. "You should tell Wallace and Halsey that you will stay behind," Marie said. "You can manage this new post. You talk with the Kalapuya, and you have something special now that ties you to them." She nodded toward the healed wound in his chest. "You limp a little, but the crutch works. And I can hunt for us if needed. We'll come to no harm here. It would be a good place to be with our boys."

"Marie…" Pierre said.

"No. Listen," she said, her fingers touching the copper earrings. "There is nothing for us at Astoria. If we go there, you'll hunt and feed the partners and their men, and we'll earn no furry bank notes ourselves. We'll go nowhere, your sons and me."

"I have a debt—"

"I've traded many things, and we've added little to the ledger papers. Here, even less."

"It is too dangerous for us here alone."

"You could ask," Marie said. "Point to your wound. Tell them we're four less to feed in Astoria."

"Maybe they have bigger plans for me," Pierre told her. She field-pressed a bale of pelts, jamming the large log hammer down using both arms and all her weight. Pierre was little help. Annoyed, Marie reminded herself that he still had a healing wound, a fractured leg. He still got dizzy at times with exertion. "Maybe we go back to the States on board the next ship," Pierre said. "To tell Astor back in New York what's been accomplished and what more we need." He pointed to a portion of beaver pelt that hung out from the bale press. She nodded.

"They won't send us on board a ship," Marie told him.

"They have too much trouble going up the Columbia past those dalles."

"You could go that way. You can speak with the Indians without causing a fight like Mackenzie and Stuart did. And if we go back that way, we'll have trade news and contacts for Astor. Valuable information." She took a deep breath. "You would be valued, for convincing the Wallow Wallows and Wascos to trap for Astor, trade with only Astor's men. You could earn Astor's favor for your efforts."

"Unless I go as an interpreter for a partner, they'll not pay a wage," he said.

"See if we can stay here, as freemen. You could trap and have furs ready in the spring. That would pay the debt. Here." She told him. She pointed to the ground. "Let's stay here until then."

Pierre looked at her, reached for her hand, held it in his. The fingertips were white. "You are already as good as a factor's wife," he said.

She pulled her hand out from beneath his. "Where's Paul?"

Pierre turned, pointed to where the boys wrestled on wet leaves, the dog barking and pulling at their shirts' buckskin fringes.

"If they send an expedition back overland," she said, "we go."

He scratched at his chest, a habit formed since the wounding. "Unless McDougall leads it," he said. "I won't go with him as an expedition leader."

"He won't. He's too soft," she told him. "And he's found himself a Clatsop wife, so he's been warm all winter."

"Maybe his mood improves then," Pierre told her.

"You need to be the one to tell this, to help take the news back. This is how Clark gained favor in St. Louis," she said. She slammed the bale press harder, jamming the pelts into the square that would be shipped thousands of miles away to places with names like Sitka and Canton.

"If we cannot choose to stay here where we find good beaver pelts, where the snow comes only a little, where the land promises tall corn with such black soil, then we should go back to the States with whichever partner is smart enough to go that way." She slammed the press again.

"Or we go ourselves, just you, me, and our sons. We know the way." He stayed silent. She slammed it again. "If we do nothing but wait to see what they do…" she complained. "What kind of choice is that?"

When Pierre spoke to him, Wallace agreed. When a new clerk named Alfred Seton arrived to bring back the hides for shipment out of Astoria, the men decided who could stay. Wallace said Pierre—and his family —could remain.

Spring at this prairie place on the Wollamat River was all Marie hoped it might be. Not since she was a young girl poking seeds into the elbows of earth watered by the Des Moines had she smelled rich soil like this. Here she watched the leaves pop out and cover up the lonely look-ing birds' nests that marked branches from the year before. Not since before the time when her family had suffered the pox had she listened to the laughter of children as they explored what the river left behind when the spring rise receded. Tiny skeletons of squirrels and strange new rocks and the scum of old leaves and new bugs entertained the boys for hours as they dug in mud for more.

"We will surprise Papa," Baptiste said, his hands clutching a per-fectly smooth stone he intended for a slingshot.

Marie grinned at him as they fast-walked back through the trees. A thin branch snapped against her face and she winced, grabbed at it so Paul wouldn't be scratched.

Pierre had only kind things to say about her sweetened cornmeal, but he'd scowled when she'd taken the boys with her to work the soil.

"Women's work," he said. "And you could get turned around. Lost." He sharpened his clasp knife. "And sometimes," he added, "my friend Bellows speaks of irritations." He shrugged his shoulders. "The game gets scarce. The Kalapuya notice, even with just the few of us here. They blame us."

"A good place doesn't confuse," Marie told him, pushing down a tingle of fear.

In late May the garden had sprouts and burst with promise, but Wallace returned with orders to leave.

"Those Astorians planned this," Marie said, slamming things into her parfleche. "They let us plant seeds, put those seeds on their ledger books when they knew we wouldn't be here for the harvest." *Engages* loaded pelts that hadn't been taken back to Astoria in March. The letters "PF" for Pacific Fur were painted with tar onto the canvas covering the bales.

"No," Pierre said. "Something has happened. They wouldn't be so foolish to waste the plantings."

"They waste lives. Why would they bother worrying about seeds?"

En route down the fast-moving Wollamat, Marie occasionally heard English words drifting back to her in the wind, words spoken with agitation. Once she heard "Okanogan" and "North West" and "David Thompson." Another time "war." Wallace cursed often beneath his breath.

Pierre didn't notice, or at least he showed no concern. He looked back to check on the small bullboats Marie helped stitch to ferry more items than what the pirogues could hold. They looked like dark ducklings following their mothers downstream.

Ahead of her the canoes pierced through blue water, and they followed behind the V of the break. Except for the *devant* and the *gouvernail*, who stood fore and aft operating the rudders, the men inside those crafts nestled down around leather bales, oaring as needed on the swift stream. She wondered how many of them wanted to return, how many of them knew what the English words of agitation meant. She looked at Pierre. Perhaps he was content to know he could go to the storehouse now for whatever he wanted, even if he never got out of debt.

She adjusted herself in the deep of the boat. Why couldn't she just accept, go where her husband and the partners led her? Why was she always pushing a river that flowed on by itself?

16

Must Push

Sarah Shonowane waved from the shoreline. Parsnip-like plants bloomed white in clusters, making it look like she stood in snow. A round woman whom Marie did not know stood beside her on the Astoria banks. Marie's eyes teared at the sight of her friend. At least this was one good to come of their being tossed around by the partners and clerks like small birds in a wide cage. The women patted each other's cheeks in greeting, and bear grease, used to fool the mosquitoes, rubbed off onto each other. They stood for a moment longer just taking in each other's presence when Sarah turned to the third woman.

"Poi," Sarah told Marie. "She comes on the *Beaver* from the Sandwich Islands. You remember?"

"I heard of you," Marie said.

"Now there are three of us who came from somewhere else. Astoria is a gathering place for women," Sarah said, smiling between the two.

Poi grinned and nodded, the jowls of her fleshy face flapping. "Poi Astorian," she said.

They stepped aside as the *engages* dispatched from the fort came to help unload Wallace's brigade boats. The men bent under their heavy loads grim-faced, determined. Two horse-drawn wagons pulled up beside the canoes. Lean *voyageurs* hurried, speaking little as they worked. No one sang, even with the arrival of a work party long away.

Something was amiss. Marie could sense it. She just couldn't tell what it was.

The women hardly had time to sign and point at the growth of their sons before Pierre signaled Marie to follow him. Sarah, too, started back up to the fort where she'd been when the canoes arrived.

"Femme!" Pierre shouted when Marie paused to look at something Poi pointed to. At his shout, she fast-walked to catch up with him.

Poi sang out, waved vigorously, "As-tor-i-an."

"Not for long," Pierre said under his breath.

"Non?" Marie said.

"The British fired on America." His stride was long, fast.

"Here?" She grabbed at his arm.

He shook his head. "Back East. Last year, while we built our hut at Young's Bay all in silence, these things were going on in the States. We learn only now. The British have sent a warship to take Astoria. Mackenzie discovers this from the North West fur trader David Thompson near Spokane House. The British send a warship to this river," he said. "And no one knows if Astor sends one to help defend Astoria or not."

Her mind raced. "Hunt is here? He says this is so?"

Pierre shook his head. "Hunt's not back yet. Something delays him, too. Dispatches came overland. To David Thompson. A North West man, John George McTavish, brings eighteen men and two canoes, and this news. They camp now at Young's Bay."

"We should return to Wallace House. We'll be safe there."

Pierre grunted. "We're not a part of that decision."

Marie matched his stride, peppered him with questions, walking backward, pebbles pressing into her soft soles. Pierre said no more. Her eyes looked past him, seeking the boys. Paul had followed Sarah. The dog Chien panted up the hill, stopped, sat and scratched at his neck with his back leg, then found the boy and bounded over to him. She couldn't see Baptiste, then noted his thin six-year-old frame bouncing after LeClerc as the latter lifted items from the canoes. The April breeze smelled fresh and cool from the sea. The landscape looked safe and serene. Certainly not the portrait of war.

"Sarah said nothing of it," she said. "She would say if this McTavish is worrisome. She and Ignace know David Thompson."

"You can believe some things I tell you, Marie," he said. "Maybe Ignace and his Sarah are spies. Maybe they come to tear Astoria apart, eh?" Marie gasped, put her fingers over her mouth. Pierre brushed her aside. "What do women know?"

"We'd know that," she said.

She hurried the boys along, lifting Paul by his arm, then hoisting him onto her hip. He still weighed less than a medium-sized salmon; he ate but never seemed to gain weight. She couldn't think of that. Not now. "What should we do?"

Pierre stopped, turned. "You ask me?" He exhaled, scratched at his chest. "We stay," he said. "We fight. If we lose, we become Brits." He shook his head. "English trade goods will be better. Isn't that what you always say?"

They took the boys to the sand dunes, to the drifts of gold pierced by tiny stems of wind-whipped grass. A plant with purple pods hugged the trail south. Marie was pleased to be away from the rumors and tensions at the post.

It felt good to see the children roll in the gold sand, laugh as the dog barked at their dark-skinned bodies tumbling toward the sea. Marie gathered wood for a fire where they would roast the salmon her husband had traded a small deer for. The Clatsop man had been pleased to have the venison. He told Pierre, even he had heard of trouble with the English.

The dunes reminded Marie of snowdrifts, sun, and shadow painted in shades of sandy gray; the boy's laughter of hers and her sister's long year past. Together Marie and her sister had played in the snows, pushed each other on sleds with runners made of leather-covered deer bones. They'd rolled in the ravines above the twisting Des Moines, landing in a heap at the frozen edges of the river. They warmed themselves around fires and listened to stories that moved inside them with the deep tones of their father's and mother's voices heard long after they slept.

The snow time had once been a healing time, a resting of the land and their spirits while they planned for buffalo hunts in the spring and recalled the exploits of family members lost in the chase. They spoke of root digging, planting, and the berry-picking time that would come, the laughter of courting and joining after summer gatherings. All was remembered at the fires while snow-filled winds howled outside. Inside, horses stomped at the end of the long lodge and dogs chased squirrels in their sleep, while Marie and her sister slept.

When the pox came, that all changed. How long ago had that been? 1803, the friars had said. After that, no more stories, no more fires to warm them, no chatter, just the sounds of hollow gasps woven with needles of pain.

Marie's mother had told them to wait for her, that she would return with the friars, the friars would help them, bring them relief.

"Don't follow me," her mother told her with fever-glazed eyes. "Take care of your sister. I'll come back." Then she'd left her children behind and never returned.

Inside the hut, Marie's sister had pushed at her. "We should go, get away from here. I'm older. You listen to me," her sister said.

Marie reached for a wool blanket. She was cold, so cold.

"Don't touch it," her sister hissed. "Something is hidden in the blanket. Bad things. We go to find the priests. Mother tells me to do this."

"I heard her say stay," Marie said. "Not to follow."

"She won't get back. She's too sick. We need to go after her."

But Marie had been cold. She needed warmth. She wouldn't leave what was familiar. Instead she wrapped the wool around her, became hard as bone in her refusal.

"Weak," her sister said finally. "You are weak to need such things."

She'd sighed. "And I am weak too, to let you do this. You make me stay when we should go. I am the older. You should listen to me. We should go."

Pierre Dorion's father had found them the next morning, huddled inside the trader's wool blanket. No center fire burned. The village lay quiet as snow. Her sister lay cold beside her. Of her family, Marie alone still lived.

The priests arrived. Marie remembered them, offering blessings through the fog of her fever, her numb fingers, her frozen toes. The priests said kind things she knew her mother would have wished to hear. But not her. To her, their words felt like sticks of ice, piercing.

Pierre's father had taken Marie to his wife, Holy Rainbow, who had nursed her back to health, saved her fingers from the green wound that could come with too much cold. She had lost all that she held dear.

Within three seasons of snow, one of Holy Rainbow's sons, Pierre, named for his father, took Marie for his wife. And when she wrapped herself in a wool blanket and lay beside him on their marriage night, Marie vowed she'd never be weak again. She'd never stay when she should go.

It took several more weeks before the partners assembled everyone and told them what had happened and how they were expected to respond. Weeks of waiting, assigning hunting duties and tasks as though nothing were afoot, as though the men who worked here were mere spiders on strings being blown by the wind. Blind spiders.

"We have made a trade for the betterment of our lives," McDougall told the assembly standing in the July sunshine around the flagpole. Marie looked for Hunt but knew he wasn't there. No new supplies had come in for Astoria. The only news that came arrived by a canoe that also carried a loud North West man.

"Fair market value for the pelts and stores have been determined after much debate, and the North West Company has purchased them. Us. We will abandon the fort to the Brits. Our efforts to build a fine factory will not have gone for naught. We'll continue on with the trade we have begun in such earnest. We'll just be trapping for the North West Company instead of Pacific Fur. If Astor were here, we feel certain he would concur with this course. It protects the fort, supplies, and international trade.

"No lives need be lost to the British warship when it arrives," McDougall continued. "We will alert them that they have entered British waters." McDougall dabbed at his forehead with a linen handkerchief.

Mackenzie said, "Well then, gentlemen. All that's left is to decide who of you wishes to become known now as North Westers and remain here and who wishes to await the warship and return with it to British ports beyond. Astoria will be known now as Fort George, in honor of the English King."

McDougall cleared his voice. "Or you may be assigned to various work parties in the interior. Similar work, gentlemen. Just under new management." McDougall grinned.

Marie and Pierre stood in the open area, the snap of the flag in the wind like slaps across their faces. Marie looked for Mackenzie, caught his eye. He looked away. They had just celebrated America's Independence Day for the year 1813, and now here they stood, their backs to the flag they said they held dear. Cowards.

Someone blew a bugle, and two *engages* came out to remove the American flag and replace it with one of wide stripes of blue and red. McDougall nodded to McTavish, the North West Fur Company man, and then the assembly was dismissed.

"They will not fight for what they built?" Marie asked Pierre. "They hand it over to those they compete with?"

Pierre shrugged. "Who understands these white men?"

"Non," she said. "Should I wonder if you so easily give up what you say matters to you? Will you wear the British colors after all this time?"

He used his fingers to break open the hard biscuits she'd made. He dipped a section into a red Salal berry spread. Seeds smeared on his fingers and then in his beard. He licked at them. "Just hunt for another," Pierre said. "Become an interpreter for North West. What does it matter who I do it for?" He wiped his face with the back of his palm.

"No!" she said, and she slapped at his hand.

He looked up, surprised.

"You have no loyalty? No one thing you stand for? You did once. You refused to work for Lisa ever. Would you give me up, so easily pass me off in a wrestling challenge?"

"I stand for you, *femme.*" He grinned and tried to kiss her.

She clucked her tongue, slipped away. "This is no time. How do we move in this world where men change who they work for without even sweating? How do we make sense of this for our sons? Where will they go? Who will they be loyal to? No wonder the factors suspect us. We *are* suspect, changing who we fight for."

"They're too young," he said. "The world will change many times before our sons have to decide for themselves. We have a choice. Stay here at Fort George and hunt for the 'new' factors or—"

"They look like the old factors. McDougall. And the old clerks. Reed and Seton and Wallace. They don't honor you. The game will get scarce here, too. And then what?"

"Then at Young's Bay we will plant and eat fish. Do as we have. Trap—"

"No," she said. "Do you wish for nothing more? There's not enough here. Not enough food, not enough beaver or enough wood for fires. Only rules multiply and grow at this Astoria place. That warship may never arrive, or if it does it may fire on us anyway because no one told them we became Brits in an afternoon. There's no guarantee. I'd rather live by what *we* choose."

"You worry too much, woman," he said. He reached to stroke her throat, and she slapped at his hand again. *"Femme,"* he said, his one eyebrow lifted in warning.

She lowered her eyes. *"Pardon,"* she whispered. "You do not understand. It is all we have—what we decide. *They* must not choose how to use us."

In the end Pierre went along with Marie. Later she would remember that she pushed for this. She would run it over and over in the heart of her knowing. She'd chosen what she'd chosen. She would have to live with the blast of that.

"We go back overland then, as a free trapper, neither Astorian nor North Wester. Freeman," Pierre told her. They walked the plain south of Astoria on the way to the salt works Lewis and Clark had built. She thought of it as Astoria, though McDougall insisted it was now Fort George. A thing, like a person, did not change its name so quickly. A wife did not become one by being called by her husband. It was how she chose that made that name's choices over time. The boys fast-walked to keep up with their parents. The dog Chien pointed, then flushed into ferns. Marie carried a pack on her back as did Pierre. They would be out a night, perhaps two, getting to the salt works beside the sea, and then collecting salt enough for their journey, take two days coming back.

"Doing this," Pierre told her, "is not what an interpreter should do. Not what a hunter should do." He puffed slightly, his broken leg still getting stronger. Marie watched for the children. Waves sometimes rolled in farther than expected, and she wanted the boys closer to her. A gull dipped below them. Marie could hear the sea lions barking as they basked on the rocks that tumbled out from the shore.

They all stopped and looked at the ocean. The sight never failed to bring the memory of Sacagawea to her mind, though today the waves wore the pale green of the rainbow. "Worth the journey," her friend had told her and she'd been right. It was indeed a wonder in the world. She felt small here and yet valued. Providence had created it all.

Paul threw a rock. He and Chien chased it toward the waves.

"*Non!*" Marie said. "*Attends!*" She grabbed for her son, lifted him too quickly. "You stay away from the water's edge, or I will bind you up and put you onto my back."

"You hurt me," Paul whined, his eyes large and frightened.

"You're not hurt," Pierre said, his voice holding warning. Paul lowered his eyelids.

Marie thought she saw a smirk on Baptiste's face but couldn't be sure. Then her husband spoke again, "The war will not last forever. People with connections find ways to stick to money like berries to buffalo fat. Astor's American Fur company must still exist. If we win the war, Astor will continue on. Just not with this fort here." He stared out, stopped talking, thinking.

Marie remembered St. Louis and the factors' houses, the finery of small-waisted women. Was that the life she wished for?

"If we do it as I say," she laughed at her McDougall-like words. "If we do this as I think will work," she amended. "We'll go back with our *own* wealth. We'll return to St. Louis in a new way."

Pierre grunted, still not convinced; she knew this though they'd talked of it ever since the flags were changed.

"We'll go as equals to a factor's table. You are equal. You have seen more, done more, been farther than Lisa or even Clark who did not go south on the Wollamat. He stayed here all winter. Even Sacagawea says the winters are too wet for ducks. And you have seen that *boise* place where streams have not yet been trapped. "

"To be a partner…"

"We can take advantage of this war, these many partners and clerks that bring confusion. Good things can come out of a boiling pot."

"If it doesn't get too hot and spill over," Pierre said. "Even I know that."

They set the fire to the salt oven and filled the copper buckets to the brim. It would take several hours for the water to boil and evaporate leaving salt. Meanwhile, the landscape offered tall grass for the boys to explore. The ocean waters lapped gently even at high tide. They stayed several days, settling the plan.

By the time they returned to Young's Bay, Pierre had agreed. Marie promised not to push at him or pick at him about how quickly they moved forward or the troubles they might face along the way. And he promised not to remind her of his "wrestling woman" when things got difficult. "As they will," Pierre told her. "I'm not a betting man, but you can bet what you're intending has trouble written in it."

It meant entering into a winter of risk. And it meant putting themselves once more in the hands of an Astorian partner.

It was the only way, as Marie saw it. And now Pierre saw it her way too.

Marie knew it was already too late in the season for Mackenzie to return overland to the States. It was now well past the time they could cross the Shining Mountains and reach St. Louis before snow fell. The end of July approached.

Mackenzie couldn't go back East, and Marie knew it.

But he could start in that direction and accomplish something else instead. It was just what he planned.

"And we can get ourselves a good stash of horses for the overland journey," Mackenzie told Reed as Marie entered the storehouse. "Four hundred will do it. Enough for any Astor laddies who want to go back."

"It might upset the trade balance with the Cheyenne," Reed cautioned.

"We said we'd be coming back with trade goods," Mackenzie said. "Didn't say what kind." He grinned. "Clerks could lead trapping parties to work through the winter. I'd negotiate for Nez Perce mounts, and come spring we'll meet, trade for canoes to take the Columbia back East. We can pick up the mounts Hunt left with the Shoshone. And uncover the cache of furs we left at Hunt's *boise* place."

"Seems you've always been a North West man," Reed said. "Why not stay on here then? You kept your British citizenship, yes?" Reed noticed Marie, nodded to her and she missed Mackenzie's response.

Mackenzie continued on in English and Marie wasn't certain she understood all of what he said. Something about Astor and an explanation. Then he told Reed, in French, "Aye. We'll gather up bales this winter, make the trade connections needed, and perhaps this war will be over by next year and we'll be able to carry on as started."

Marie became brave. Bold plans required it. "You'll need a hunter," Marie said. "And a free trapper or two."

Both men paused to look at her.

"You'll need help with the hides," she said as though women always talked with partners and clerks inside the fort.

"If you're proposing you and your man go…" Reed said. He looked annoyed, pulled the ledger book open to what Marie assumed was Pierre's page. She'd put many an item against their debt, had been careful about what she added. But she had no clear idea of how much remained.

"You still have quite a debt to be paying. If you add in traps and wintering supplies, as freemen…" Reed did some calculations on a ledger sheet. He turned the book around so she could see it. Marie shook her head. "It'd come to nine hundred dollars, owing," he said.

Marie stared at him. *Nine hundred dollars?* They'd have to trap dozens of beaver pelts to make that up! How had it gotten so high?

She hadn't said it aloud, but her face must have registered the surprise. "Hunt paid the full debt to Lisa," Mackenzie told her.

"I knew this," she said. "I pay against it. All last year."

"Two hundred for the debt. Your stores for the past two years, ammunition, seeds, whatnot. The traps, horses, canoes, all you'll need as free trappers, that's what I'd expect it to run, even at the new North West prices." He ran his finger along the scratching on the line. "Your trading has made some gain against rice and seeds and such."

Mackenzie turned back to Reed as though Marie no longer stood there. The big man hadn't regained all the weight he'd lost, but enough to make his jowls move when he shook his head.

"Imagine he has his Indians there doing that," Reed said.

"*Pardon,*" Marie said. "You need hunters."

Mackenzie nodded. "It's a dangerous place. You remember." He talked now like a parent to a child, but she could see in his eyes his willingness to have them along. He knew her husband could help. Pierre'd been there when Mackenzie hadn't. "Up over the Blues, Carriere disappeared at the hands of those Snakes. Could be Indian trouble, you best be knowing. You and the children might not be safe."

She stared at him.

Reed stepped in. "Not that you aren't trustworthy, Mrs. Dorion," he said. "Certainly *you* are. She…well, there's nothing to worry over her…" Reed frowned at Mackenzie.

"Aye." Mackenzie said. He looked at something beyond Marie's head.

"If you mean to do this," Reed said, " I'll have McDougall make the order—"

"I doubt McDougall will condone Dorion's being a free trapper unless he pays the debt," Mackenzie said.

"My husband needs no permission to—"

"He has a debt yet still on the books before he even adds on wintering supplies."

She squared her shoulders. "It will be paid. If it takes us all our lives."

"You'll have to cross the Blues again," Reed said quietly. "Could be rough."

"Yes," Marie said, turning to him. "We will have to travel over old trails to get to new ones. I have been that way before, to dig a baby's grave."

They left in late July 1813. Four canoes making their way up the Columbia River, east. This time, Marie knew she wouldn't return. She told Sarah they were free trappers now, and they had many pelts to manage to make the passage costs and still have enough furry bank notes for when they reached their destination. "So I will use my teeth more," she said. "Some things are worth a change."

Sarah smiled, patted Marie's hand. "You are so young, so strong," she said.

"I'm not strong," Marie said.

Sarah shook her head. "Someday you'll know. I only hope the lesson doesn't pound you like the ocean at the river's mouth. Two strong forces pushing in opposite directions."

"My husband and me," Marie told her, and the women laughed.

"Then remember this: For a ship to cross from the ocean to the mouth, it needs a guide to follow. A guide can set the course. It can't be changed then, my Marie. Once set to—"

"I know this. I follow my husband's leading when it makes sense. I will never hold back when everything around me says to go. That's why we go now."

"Your guide," Sarah said, capturing a loose strand of Marie's hair, pushing it behind her ear. "I wish your guide to be the beloved of the Lord," she said. "He can make all miracles happen. See, I am named for one who had a baby in her old age. My mother was an old woman when I came as an answer to her need for change. You remember this. And what you say your mother-in-law once told you."

"I'll remember," Marie said, feeling the warmth of the woman's breath on her neck as they hugged. "Tell Poi I miss saying good-bye to her," Marie said.

Sarah laughed. "Poi marries already. Another Sandwich Islander. She travels all this way and marries one who left the same place. She is still an Astorian, she says. It does not matter what the partners call a place."

Marie took one last gaze at the post, this factory, this fort that had once held such promise. "McDougall's wife, Ilchee. She is the madame of Astoria."

"*Non,*" Sarah said. "Such a name belongs to a woman who walks beside her husband, not one who pulls him like a bullboat." Sarah grinned. "Here," she said then. She stuffed a basket made of cedar bark into the hands of her friend. "I learn to do this from Ilchee. I am not too old to learn new things. A gift for you."

Marie wiped the tears on her cheeks and felt at her belt for her knife. "You give so much to me already," she said. She tried to untie the knife sheath from her belt.

"No, no," Sarah said, pushing Marie's hands. "You will need your knife. You are not asked to give away what you need, only that which bubbles over."

The journey up the Columbia took several days. Along the way, Marie traded two pair of the decorated moccasins she'd made for fish and a woven basket. Another pair she put against the debt on Reed's ledger page. She told him she would like to understand the scratchings better, but Reed dismissed her with a brush of his hand. Her face must have shown her disappointment because when they broke camp the next morning Reed said, "I'll teach you the sums if you want, when we get to that *boise* river. Fill up the long winter. If your husband doesn't object."

At the Wallow Wallow River, Mackenzie spent several days negotiating with the Nez Perce, trading for the long-tailed horses that tore at grass near the Blues. Marie suggested that she and the boys and even Pierre might want to walk. "We can save the scratching on the pages," she told Reed. "Not add horses to our debt page."

"Can't be walking now. It'll slow the party too much. We need to build a house and then begin trapping as much as we can," Reed told her.

The Nez Perce granted horses enough for Reed's small trapping party and one each for Mackenzie's group, but no more. They showed no interest in trapping for Mackenzie, to make pelts available to the North West Company for the spring. "We do not trap," their interpreter told them.

"It's not their way," Pierre told Mackenzie. "Come back in the spring. Maybe then they'll accept some goods for the horses."

MacKenzie frowned. That night he went on a rampage, shouting that his packs had been torn into, items stolen. He stomped through the tipis of several Nez Perce, frightening families out of their sleep.

He found the missing items in a distant tipi and, before anyone could anticipate or stop him, Mackenzie pulled his pistol out and shot two of the Nez Perce horses, dead.

He ordered *engages* to prepare the meat, threw some trade goods at the Indians, a fair amount for a living animal, while the Indians spoke to each other in a language Marie could not decipher.

"They've been dishonored," Pierre told him. "The horses are like kin, and the way you did this doesn't look like any justice they recognize."

"I have no care for their thinking," Mackenzie said. "We'll eat the meat. Right here in front of them. Show them times are changing. Best they know that."

"I believe we'll head on out," Reed said. "Leave this to you, Donald."

"No dried meat to take with you? Sure and you'll be wishing you had it come the first snowfall, and you'll remember the best way to deal with these kind of thieves."

But Reed urged Marie and Pierre and the boys and LeClerc the silversmith and some other French-Canadians to mount up and leave Mackenzie. They began retracing their trail into the Blue Mountains.

Reed acted as chief factor of their party. But he relied on Pierre to show them the way back to that *boise* river. They trapped and hunted along the way, intending to winter at the woodsy place.

In early September, the party met the three old hunters Hoback, Reznor, and Robinson, who had remained behind the year before with Crooks. Robinson had taken a wife.

"So you found friendly Indians as you'd hoped," Pierre said.

"We did," Robinson said.

"He could talk a dog off a meat wagon," Hoback told them.

"Almost lost my hair a second time," Robinson told them, rubbing the scar across his forehead. He tied his red kerchief back over his head.

"Some of these tribes aren't so friendly. Got stripped of all our clothes and guns and lived only by the kindness of others not much better off than us," Hoback said. "It's a little hostile in places. 'Course Robinson found an Earth Eater wife to look after him."

"The Shoshone helped Hunt's party," Reed said. "Doubt we'll be troubled if we do nothing foolish."

"As Mackenzie did," Pierre said. He filled the mountain men in.

"We heard another of Astor's men in the Okanogan country hung an Indian for stealing a goblet," Hoback said. "Right in front of his kin. Terrible thing."

The mountain men decided to join Reed for the winter, trapping, planning to be finally back in St. Louis this time next year.

They camped that night in the place where Pierre believed Vivacité was buried. "You won't find her bones, Marie," Pierre told her. "They'll be scattered."

"I know. I only want to see if I can find the stones. Maybe leave something better as a marker."

The men respected her work as she moved a rock here and there, picked at a yellow flower, sniffed at it, then took a step or two, her moccasins firm on the gun-gray rocks. A stream rushed beside the trail. She'd stacked rocks near it over the small lifeless body. Perhaps a piece of cloth would still be there. It had only been a little over a year.

"What're you looking for?" Paul asked her.

"The grave of your sister," she said.

A fleeting look crossed his face. "Don't 'member," he said.

"You were young and hungry and tired," she said. "We all were. Making our way to a new place."

"Why did she die?" Baptiste asked. He carried a slingshot at his belted waist.

Marie considered her answer. "Not enough to eat," she said. "I couldn't make milk for her."

"Maybe we shouldn't have come to a place where you can't make milk. Maybe she would have lived then," Baptiste said.

Marie turned and slapped her son's face.

He didn't cry, just held his cheek, a glare replacing surprise.

"*Pardon, pardon,* Baptiste," she said, regret flooding her eyes. She pulled her son to her and pressed her cheek to cover the red marking his skin. "*Ne pleure pas, je ten prie,*" she whispered into his ear. His frame stiffened, then eased slightly. "Please don't cry," she said. "Forgive me."

He was just a child, saying what he thought. Didn't she want him to speak for himself one day, be a man others would listen to? Why had she struck him? She didn't even have whiskey to blame.

Baptiste leaned away from her but allowed his hand to be taken by hers. "Come," she said. "Let's see if we can find some sign of your sister."

"*Ici,*" Paul called out. He had run in his stiff-legged gait to an area where a few rocks clustered together in an unnatural way. Chien stood on a rock, tail wagging. It was too far from where Marie remembered, but the spring rush of melting snow may have changed the creek's course in the past year. Paul lifted a swatch of cloth. It was a piece of the linen her daughter had died in.

"*Merci,* Paul," she told him. She rolled her hands over his dark hair, pressing his head with her palm. She pulled Baptiste into her side with her other arm, and he allowed it, huddled against her. She clutched the cloth. She had thought finding evidence would bring her completion.

Instead, it filled her with loss.

17

Earth Eater Warning

Wilson Hunt felt sick but less from the wind and waves of the high seas than McDougall's news. He clutched at his queasy stomach. It was bad enough learning at the Sandwich Islands that America had been fired on, that warships sped west. His own troubles in Sitka with damaged ships, recalcitrant captains, and arguments with Astor's Russian fur agents, paled in comparison to the vulnerability of the Astorians. The only good he'd done at all had been getting the cargo transferred to another ship heading for Canton and assuring the passage home of his former camp boys and those Astorians who'd boarded ship with him last August.

Now McDougall told him this fort had been "abandoned to the British." It wasn't even Astoria now, but Fort George. McDougall refused to meet Hunt on board the ship *Pedlar.* Instead he insisted Hunt step foot on British soil at Fort George.

Abandoned. It was how Hunt felt. A few months earlier, and he might have influenced the partners, helped them see another way. Not now. His life was a series of late arrivals.

He'd gathered up what information he could from McDougall, who held his cards to his chest like a crazed poker player. Bit by bit, he'd pulled the figures from the partners, astounded at the losses. Pelts going for six dollars in Canton were transferred to the Brits for two. Mackenzie, McDougall, the rest, had sold the buildings, stock, furs, everything at a pittance. It was a terrible loss, beyond any he could imagine. However would he tell Astor?

Even reading the "Articles of Transfer" the partners had all signed,

seeing in the formal words the despair over limited supplies, the sense
that their only hope of survival came from the North West Company's
protection of them through a peaceful transition, did nothing to relieve
Hunt's profound sense of failure. If only he'd been there to make the
case. *If only.*

Only a skeleton group remained, according to McDougall, though
it was supplemented with McTavish's men of the North West Company.
"The rest trap for the North Westers now and winter where they can."

"But why not attempt a sea passage back, at least?" Hunt had asked.
"We owe these people safe passage back to where they began."

"You just be about that then, Wilson. Figure out how to commission a ship, pay passage, and then get past the English warships headed
this way. With what capital? The stocks aren't ours now. Look how long
it took you to return here by ship. No, those who want to go back will
join Mackenzie in the spring and go overland. We've agreed to provide
horses—if Donald acquires them. What trade goods we have for that are
mere sweepings from the North West table now. Even your loyal guide
Dorion plans to join Donald come spring, and his sturdy wife has
vowed to pay his debt. It's finished here, Wilson. Accept it. We serve
England now. If that's a discomfort for you, then I suggest you depart."

He had. And for the first time he didn't move back and forth wondering what to do next. He'd sped back to the Sandwich Islands with the
prayer he could raise funds to commission an American ship. He'd use
all of his own money to do it. Then he'd return for any Astorians who
wanted sea passage back to the States. It was the least he could do—and
pray that Providence would provide.

Marie looked up to see two grim-faced Indian warriors riding down
hard on spotted horses. Their animals' chests heaved, wore white rings
of sweat. Marie stretched a hide in the late afternoon. The cool evenings
were perfect for keeping the hides sweet even though the September

days brought perspiration to her forearms as she worked. She salted the small lynx hide, allowing herself pleasure from the feel of the reddish tufts her fingers brushed.

"Bannocks," Reznor, the mountain man, said. "Same ones that tore our clothes from us."

Marie scanned for her sons who poked sticks into the water. Chien's ears flopped as he scampered back and forth along the rocky bank of the stream. Marie could always find her sons by the presence of that dog. They'd be safe there with Reed's group between her and the men. But both boys turned at the presence of the intruders. The dog looked up too, barked.

The warriors, scowling and holding the reins tight on their horses so the animals pranced and danced around, scuffing up dust, signed something. Reed turned to Marie, his red eyebrows raised in question. "Their hands work too fast. I don't know what they say."

"Offer them anythin'," Reznor said.

"Food," Marie said. "My husband'll return. He'll know what they want."

The men, four of them, kept shouting, pulling at their ponies. The horses' necks arched, and the animals snorted. One man motioned toward Baptiste and Paul. His flashing gun and grimace made Marie's heart pound. Slaves, some of these tribes took slaves.

One started toward the boys. She threw the pelt down and ran, pushing her children behind her. The dog barked and snapped toward one rider's horse as he galloped, then dismounted.

Paul bolted, but Marie caught his arm. "*Non!* Offer them something," she shouted to Reed.

As Reed reached toward a trade bale, the dismounted warrior grabbed at the dog and, lifting it, slit its throat with a knife. He wiped his knife through the fur to clean it, then tossed the animal to the ground.

Paul screamed and lunged, but Marie held firm. He sobbed as Pierre, the *engages,* and Robinson and his Indian woman rode in.

Robinson's wife stepped forward and said something to the warrior who swung up onto his horse, shook his fist at her. She nodded toward Marie's children, a scold in her voice. Baptiste glared. Paul cried at his mother's shoulder as she knelt. The men spoke back, pointed to the pelt.

"What's she saying?" Reed asked.

"She tells them we don't plan to stay here, that there's enough game for a few pelts to be taken," Pierre said. "And that only the weak look for strength while standing on the backs of women, children, and dead dogs."

"That's my wife," Robinson said, slapping his thigh with his hand. "She's a pistol."

"Are they buying it?" Reed asked.

"What they want is to buy guns," Pierre said.

"Tell them we'll have a fort stocked come next year."

"They know he won't sell them," Robinson said. "They can't defend against their enemies, and we're using up their food. That's how they see it."

"Tell them we will have no ammunition or guns to trade with them _or_ their enemies. We're not here to make war. Tell them."

Pierre used the combination of signs and Chinook trade talk, and Robinson offered a word or two along with his wife. The warriors stared at Paul and Baptiste. The leader barked at the woman, then turned and rode away. The others followed, their faces carrying dissatisfaction.

Robinson sat tall in his saddle, his belly out over his knife belt. He spoke to his wife. She said something back. "I expect we scared 'em with so many of us here," he said. "Or they'd have done their best to lift those boys of yours."

The Earth Eater woman raised her eyes to Marie's, shared a knowing. She may not understand what Robinson said, but Marie could guess: It was not the number of men present that sent the warriors away from her sons, but their shaming by a woman.

"Let's bury the dog," Marie said in French.

"Well, we could eat it," Reznor suggested. "It's already dead and would save us the trouble." He saw Marie's look. "Well, I guess not. Probably not a good idea to take on another angry Indian after we barely skimmed by them others."

Reed's party posted extra guards and moved out quickly at dawn. Scattered groups of Indians crossed their trail as they headed southeast, a few family groups, most looking more haggard than troubling. The presence of women appeared to calm those they encountered, Marie noticed. None of these people looked fearsome, only hungry, though hungry people could be known to do strange things to stay alive.

At last they reached that woodsy area. Wide-leafed trees towered above them with little streams slipping into larger ones that fed the Snake River. High water hadn't taken out the ford there, and they'd be able to trap inland and easily bring pelts to Reed's Fort once it was built. Reed settled on an area for the fort building, set LeClerc and others to chop trees. The women looked for small branches they could bend to form the huts they'd stay in until the more permanent fort was finished.

As they worked, Marie looked at Robinson's wife, struggled to find words. Even with Sacagawea she'd found a way to speak, but this woman's language had sounds unlike any Marie had heard. Marie signed, "Question. You called?" to discover the woman's name, but she looked at her blankly, said nothing.

"What does she call herself?" Marie asked Robinson.

"My wife?" He looked at her and shrugged. "She's just my wife."

Marie wanted to tell her how strong she thought she was to step up to those warriors. The woman looked Marie's age, but she had no children along. She wondered what the woman thought about more people showing up in her country, taking beaver and building huts. She wanted her advice for how to protect her children from threats that might come unexpected at night.

The woman's long, stringy hair hung around her face as she bent over to look at something Paul showed her. She'd looked with gentle eyes at the boys when Marie patted their backs as they grieved the dog's loss.

Robinson and his wife camped a distance from Reed's party. Marie's time with Earth Eater woman was interrupted by the work of scraping and managing pelts. Sometimes Robinson's wife carried her work to sit beside Marie. She did not use her teeth to hold the hides. And her hands seemed clumsy with the effort. Marie motioned to her, showing her how she did the work. The woman merely nodded and kept on doing what she wished. She sat beside Marie not to learn a new way, it seemed, but just to be together.

The men busied themselves with the building. As soon as the three-room Reed House was finished, Pierre and Marie and LeClerc and a few others were to move farther up the Boise River, as they now called the stream, maybe twenty miles or so, to run trap lines. They'd build a shelter and winter there.

It snowed in late October, piling up drifts beneath the trees that the sunshine soon melted. The work of building and trapping proceeded. They finished the first house on Willow Creek, a small stream almost hidden by leggy red willows not far from where that rushing stream entered the Boise.

"Reed is an American?" Marie asked as she and Pierre curled beneath the robe one evening in November. Pierre lay silent. "I think Reed is not yet a true North Wester," Marie said. She lay back onto the robe, crossed her arms over her chest.

"I bet he holds cards in both hands to see how the war turns out," Pierre told her. "Strange things happen during wars, eh? You don't remember when the British—"

"I know the stories." She brushed at his words with her hands. "We Ioways were torn apart too. We had to choose between two groups of white men, neither who saw us as more than digging sticks for what they wanted planted."

"It doesn't have to touch us here. We'll take our pelts back to St.

Louis. Let Reed meet Mackenzie in the spring. By then we'll be halfway back."

Marie lay quiet. "I thought we'd go with Mackenzie's brigade. Turn in the pelts at Okanogan, get paid there, clear the debt. We'd take ourselves and your friendships with the tribes back to St. Louis. Information will sell well."

"We'll make more if we take the pelts."

"Any not needed for the debt," she said.

"There are other pelts back the way we came."

"Across that wide desert again?" Marie said.

"Non," he said. "We'd go by way of Henry's Fort." He whispered low now. "There is still a cache of furs there, *femme.* Lisa's employee left them there. At least fifty packs. They're worth $25,000. We pick up horses there, your Hawk horse maybe. We have the winter to stock up and make pemmican. We'll be all right," he said. "We're free trappers."

Her face felt hot. She listened to the breathing of her boys. Paul whimpered in his sleep, missing the dog, she imagined. "What makes you think you can find the cache?"

"Robinson knows where it is. He and his woman would go with us."

She wouldn't worry over his words now. She had the winter to convince him, that crossing as they had with Hunt would be too dangerous. Her sons needed the safety found in many numbers. They must go back as Lewis and Clark had come out instead of Hunt's twisted trail. Slaves were taken from this place. Sacagawea had been stolen from somewhere in this land. They needed others with them. The faces of those Robber Snakes that killed Chien convinced her of that.

Hoback and Robinson and his wife left early in November to explore another stream west, planning to rejoin Reed's group closer to spring. Hoback arrived back a few days later with a chest wound. He had barely breathed out that the bullet came from a Snake's gun before he slid from his horse and died.

"'Tis unfortunate," Reed said as he ordered the burying. "But we can't let them chase us off." His bushy eyebrows jumped up and down.

"You should trap closer to Reed's Fort," Marie told Pierre when he and LeClerc returned from helping bury Hoback. "We should stay closer together."

"Too many pelts already taken there," he told her. He readied his horse, tightened the cinch on the saddle. "This is how it's done. You know that."

Dog-Rib Soldier Indians rode in a few weeks later as the branches thickened with fresh snow. More than a foot of the heavy white covered the ground now. The warriors threatened, demanded guns and ammunition in exchange for the pelts being taken from their rivers. "Or they'll do to us what they did to Hoback," Pierre translated through hand signs.

"They'll not be intimidatin' us," Reed said. "Tell them we're here to trade and'll treat them fair. Just won't trade 'em guns. 'Tis forbidden. Tell them that."

Pierre sign talked. One of the soldiers pointed at Marie and the boys. Pierre snapped something back and the warrior raised his chin, jerked it toward the other men.

Marie thought to speak up then, her breathing increasing as she sorted out the grim faces, the tone of Pierre's words, the stern hand motions he used. What had the Earth Eater woman said to them to make them go away?

Then, as quickly as they came, the warriors left.

"What'd you tell them?" Reed said.

"Just that my woman has special powers. The boys do too. She survived a long journey and left a daughter near here. We come to honor the daughter and to trap. And we'll leave in the spring."

"We're going to build a second factory," Reed said.

"Now?" LeClerc asked. "Seems like we need to trap, not freeze our fingers cutting timber."

"Farther away from those Dog-Rib Indians would be better," Reed insisted. "If we move, maybe they'll forget we're here."

Reznor decided to trap in closer, and with the *engages,* Pierre and Reed felled trees for the new fort on the south side of the Boise. Trapping slowed again while they assembled Reed's second house. Even Reznor chafed at the delays. He rarely stopped talking of the time he'd been left naked and hungry by the Snakes, yet he never seemed to mention the Earth Eater people who rescued him.

"They don't need it," Pierre said when Marie mentioned that the Earth Eater woman and Robinson ought to come under the protection of their meager fort at night too. "You're just lonely for woman company, even if you can't talk to her."

Before Christmas they finished the building. Reed's fort had a room for storing pelts, a small storage room for additional traps, a few trade goods, and their own food supplies and a larger sleeping room that joined a workspace where pelts were baled.

On Christmas Day, Reed broke out grog that Pierre waved past. They sang songs, and LeClerc recited the Christmas story in French. "We would exchange gifts after midnight mass," he said. "In my Montreal. Here, I have none to give." His eyes twinkling as he reached behind Baptiste's ear and, as though he pulled it from thin air, handed the boy a small leather pouch. He did the same for Paul. "What have we here then?" he said. "Gifts from heaven, eh?"

The boys looked up at Marie for permission. *"Oui,"* she said and smiled.

The pouches held smooth stones and wooden whistles LeClerc had carved himself. Baptiste's was shaped like a horse. Paul had been given a dog.

Marie's eyes watered. "You are so kind."

"Giving to them is my gift to myself," he said. "And what would this day that marks the greatest gift of all be without a few presents?"

Pierre coughed then and handed Marie a piece of cloth. "For me?" she said. He nodded. She wondered if it was another pair of earrings, had a fleeting thought of young Toupin. She unfolded a black ring formed of a horseshoe nail, pounded smooth and round, the perfect size.

"LeClerc makes it," Pierre said when she held it up in her fingers. She cried now, dabbing at her eyes, pushing the ring over her knuckle, holding it to the light. "And I haven't given you a thing," she said to Pierre. "Not one thing."

"Yes, you have," Pierre said.

"I have? What?"

"You're still here," he said. "That's the greatest gift you could give."

They built a wooden fence around Reed's House, kept the horses loose inside the palisade. Daily now, Baptiste with LeClerc or Marie tied on snowshoes, then took the animals out to clearings where they pawed through drifts to tear at grass.

Reed's Fort looked like a real factory, and Marie smiled to herself one afternoon in late December when she led the horses back inside the heavy gates, their feet crunching on the packed snow. She was at a factory that she had helped make. Reed depended on her husband to communicate with neighboring tribes. Perhaps that made her a *bourgeois's* wife after all. Young Toupin always called her madame. She thought of the boy, hoped he'd shared the Christmas with his mother.

She shook her head. Her husband might never be recognized for the skills he had to make peace in a place, to trap and manage the pelts and still live with the people who lived there first. But perhaps her sons would. Baptiste or Paul might lead an expedition like Hunt or Clark's or even Lisa's with scientists to study plants and rocks. Perhaps she'd be the mother of a chief factor someday.

"My wife says we should leave," Robinson told Reed on an early morning in December. "And I'm listening to her."

Reed paced the main room, scratching at his winter-growth beard. "Too much beaver to abandon," he said.

"I'm going to Astoria. Fort George or whatever it's called. This place, she says," he pointed to his Earth Eater wife, "is not safe. For us."

"You're here under the North West's protection," Reed reminded him.

"I'm a free trapper," Robinson bristled.

"Go then," Reed told him. "Turn tail."

"Not cowardly to heed good advice," Robinson said, adjusting his scarf around his head. "And my woman is giving it and sharing it freely. With all of you. Dorion, I'd get on out of here. I've already used up most of my lives. Even a cat wouldn't bet on my chances."

Reed urged Pierre and LeClerc and another *engage* to move upriver twenty or so miles and build a hut there that they could trap from. "That way you won't have to come back the full twenty miles each day," Reed said, "to the fort."

"I'll go with you," Marie said.

Pierre hesitated. "We'll build the hut first. Stay here until then."

Five days later Reznor rode back into Reed's Fort, hard. He jabbered like a crow until finally Reed settled him enough to learn that he'd encountered the Earth Eater woman kneeling in the snow beside her husband's shallow grave. "Couldn't get her to come back with me," Reznor said. "She just sat and stared. I'm getting too old for this. I'll be sixty-seven maybe sixty-eight next year. Can't keep escaping these Indians, no offense, ma'am," he said, nodding toward Marie.

"Might have been accidental," Reed said.

Reznor shook his head. "Signs of struggle. Snake signs. Who cares about the war in the States? I'm going toward the friendly Indians, those Cayuse or Wallow Wallow folks."

"Mackenzie's riled some of those, too," Reed told him. "Besides, crossing the Blues now without a guide? In the winter? Wouldn't make it."

He sent Reznor with Marie and the boys to join LeClerc, another engage, and Pierre at the outlying hut. They loaded an extra pack animal. "Bring hides back when the hut fills up," Reed said as he sent them out on a clear, blue-sky day.

"We crossed here in winter," Marie told Reznor as they rode along.

"So I could make it. We all could."

"He had Shoshone guides."

Reznor chewed on his cheek, saying nothing. Then, "I'm heading back," he announced when he'd delivered Marie and the boys. "See you on the Columbia in the spring."

"So now the one who knows where Henry's cache of furs is buried is dead, and his friend leaves," she said to Pierre as they watched Reznor ride out.

"I can find it," Pierre said. He lifted the boys down from the bony packhorse. "I have luck at such things."

"I will wrestle you for the choice," she told him. "I win, we go back by canoe, then overland. You win, we head for Henry's Fort first."

He laughed. "Agreed," he said.

She looked at her sons, LeClerc, and another *engage* huddled in the hut and said, "We arm wrestle this time. We do it a new way."

"It lacks the skin to skin of a leg wrestle," Pierre said with a grin as the two sat, elbows on a tree stump, their fingers clasped.

"You have an advantage this way," she said. "My hands are so small."

"And my leg has never come back full since the break, so with that wrestle, you'd win, eh? Besides, you press furs and are as strong a woman as I've known." He opened and closed his fingers around hers.

"All in the wrist," LeClerc said. "I have seen this done, and even little men can win over big ones with a strong wrist. We begin, *n'est ce-pas?*" He gave the signal, and the challenge began.

Marie bit her lower lip in concentration. Pierre grunted, his forearm straining. Even in the cool hut with a low fire for heat, they sweated. Pierre's ash-gray eyes narrowed, he licked his lips with his tongue. Her forearm felt tight as a cinch. She could hear the boys cheering behind her. Her wrist ached, her shoulder strained. She'd lose, she knew it.

"*J'en ai assez,*" she finally panted, her forearm quivering.

"Have you?" he asked. "Have you had enough?"

"*Oui,*" she said.

"You heard it, Baptiste. Your mother's given in to me. You remember that." He dropped her arm, released his breath in one burst. The boys pounced on him then, and Pierre rolled them over while Marie watched.

She rubbed her arm and wrist, brushed at the ivory comb in her hair. The sounds of her sons and their father, his deep growls of joy interrupted by young squeals, soothed. Their pleasure together and her comfort in it surprised her. Did she feel excluded by these males rolling now on the floor in a buffalo robe, acting like pups in a puddle?

No. She was a part of their laughter, though different.

She thought of the Earth Eater woman. She hoped she'd returned to her own people, that she had people to go to. It was what one should do in grief, go to family for nurture.

Marie moved to the side of the hut, watching her husband and sons wrestle. She still breathed hard from the exertion, sounded as she did when she danced in celebration.

The image of the Ioway dance grounds rose before her, the colors, smells, and sounds. Women, shoulder to shoulder, their feet moving in rhythm to the drum beat as one, moving around the parade circle, marking out an ancient route. They danced facing outward, the women did, standing straight and tall and looking strong, keeping their eyes on their family. Men performed alone. Crouching, leaping up, faces grimaced as they scanned the landscape with their eyes, replicating wars and hunts, protection and provision. In a time of challenge, sons and fathers built palisades around their wives and sisters and mothers, and women came behind them, sharing strength.

Pierre had won the match. They'd go through Henry's Fort. Whatever he decided would be all right as long as they danced together.

Each time the powdery snow fell that early January, Marie was reminded of cornmeal. The snow here didn't carry the wet and heaviness of her home, but it still built up. Pierre and the others trapped away from the hut, a good two-day's ride from Reed's factory. He left early to check the traps and drown the beaver. The quality of a lynx or wolf pelt was better if the animals were taken quickly, had no time to twist and tear the hide while they tried in vain to free themselves from the steel jaws of the trap. When the men returned, Marie and the boys worked the hides in the hut while Pierre warmed his cold hands at the fire.

Marie and the boys spent their days in the warmth of the hut, as the snow fell steady, desperate to make itself known. The fir trees thickened with it. Then the air turned cold. It reminded Marie of the winter when they'd come through here with Hunt and nearly starved but for the band of kind Shoshones who later gave them three guides to move across the Blues.

Marie didn't worry about starving now. They had corn and dried venison and vinegar. She fixed the meals for Pierre, LeClerc, and her sons, carefully rationing the food they supplemented with fresh game. A wild turkey proved tasty. They speared a salmon they roasted and ate fresh. Fur pelts piled up.

The trappers had been out since early morning. Marie and her sons were alone.

It was the anniversary of her daughter's death. A familiar melancholy settled on her as she went about her chores.

Hearing the sound of a horse and the pounding on the puncheon door, Marie pushed open the heavy half-logs. The Earth Eater woman stood there, wrapped in a blanket, her brown eyes wide in fright, her stringy hair dotted with white snowflakes. It was midmorning and wind blew so the snow looked to be almost coming at her sideways as it fell.

With her hands, she made the motion of a throat being cut and a sign for dog.

"Dog?" Marie said, making that sign. The woman shook her head, pointed to Marie's heart. She made a sign for white men and repeated the knife across the throat.

She struggled, her lips moving without a sound then shouted, "Go! Now!" She picked up rabbit-fur mittens that dried by the fire, shoved them at Marie, then pointed to the boys, threw her hands to her face, sang a screaming song that sent chills down Marie's back.

Marie grabbed at Paul, shouted to Baptiste to put on his robe coat, his leggings. She turned to see if the woman knew which direction to go, but the woman was gone.

"Catch up the horses. Quick. We go tell Papa. Something bad has happened."

She clutched at her belt, the knife. She reached for Paul, threw a blanket around him, carried him, running out to where the horse was corralled. *Smoke? Was that smoke?* She sniffed, not sure what direction it came from.

She loaded the boys onto the horse, an old horse, steady but slow. She yanked at the reins to pull it away from the hut. She'd lead them.

Which way? Which way had the men gone that morning? Away from Reed's fort or back toward it? Snow covered any tracks. She thought she heard war screams in the distance. From Reed's Fort? No, that was too far away. The shouts were closer than that. She felt rather than heard running horses.

They were coming her way.

18

Her Next Step

Wind and snow confused her thinking. Her heart pounded as though she'd been dancing for days. She gasped as she pulled at the horse, scanning the landscape, seeking refuge and her husband.

She'd thought she saw a trail marked with hatchet chops onto the sides of a wormwood tree. She'd followed it, not certain for how long, when the sounds of many horses came closer. She'd have to find a ravine, hope the Indians would pass by them. That she and the boys would be hidden by winter and wind.

Thick snow blanketed the hide coat at her shoulders when she bent beneath branches. *Find a place, find a place.* What she needed was a cleft, a cave off from the trail.

She pulled the horse in the opposite direction, led him around fallen logs, his legs stumbling through drifts, breaking through thick shrubs and into a swale. She could hear a stream. She tied the horse, yanked the boys off, and pushed them beneath the branches of a hackberry tree, brown leaves still clinging. She thrust the blanket around them, her children huddled in her arms. *Mon Dieu, bon Dieu, please, oh please, save these children. Keep the horse silent. Make us invisible. Make us one with gray snow.*

Paul started to cry. *"Non!"* She silenced him with her hand, gentle across his mouth. Her heart pounded, she tried to calm her breathing. Baptiste pointed then, as twenty warriors like shadows rode by them, so close she could smell the sweat of the mounts, see the grimace on the riders' faces.

She put one hand over her own mouth to stifle the scream of disbelief. *This couldn't be happening, it couldn't be!* In the distance, she heard whoops, songs of revenge.

They shivered in the ravine long enough that the snow stopped and shadows shifted. Hunger ached in her stomach, and she knew it must be so for her children as they huddled. They didn't complain. She should have grabbed food. A good mother would have remembered to bring food. She whispered stories to them, kept them tucked beneath her arms.

She laid the robe down and motioned to the boys. They crawled stiffly. In the palms of her hands she melted snow and they drank it. It was too dangerous to build a fire. In the distance, she thought she heard war whoops.

She held her sons close to her. She felt Paul's slender body shiver. Perhaps she'd made a mistake. Perhaps they should have waited for Pierre to come for them at the hut or headed away from Reed's Fort instead of toward it. But waiting was not what she did, was not who she was.

By late afternoon she felt braver. She had the boys lie on their bellies and drink from the icy hole she cracked in the stream. Snow sparkled like stars beneath a brilliant blue. She put the boys on the horse. She'd use her body to break the trail, opening the drifts for the horse. Without snowshoes, she sank into drifts, her thighs aching from the strain. She'd go away from their hut, follow the tree marks, maybe meet Pierre coming back.

By midafternoon she noticed tracks, then nearly cried when she recognized them as her own, made earlier in the day. She had to concentrate on the trees, on signs that someone had been that way before.

It was nearly dark when she spied what looked like a lean-to, something the men made for temporary shelter when checking the trap lines. The top of a steel trap stuck up through the drift. They were close then.

"Look, Mama!" Baptiste whispered. He pointed toward the snowy mound off to the side. Something lay there, covered.

Cold. She felt so cold, so stiff with the knowing, so afraid to go close.

Then the form moved, tried to sit up, snow falling from his back.

"I help Papa," Baptiste said, sliding from the horse.

"That's not Papa," Marie said. She could tell by the bulk. It was LeClerc, the silversmith, the man who had made whistles for gifts. With high steps through the snow, Marie bent to him.

"LeClerc?" she said. Blood covered his head, his shirt, his pants. He had a dozen tears in his leather clothes. All of them oozed blood.

"Pierre," she said. "Is he in the shelter?" She rubbed blood from his face, his eyes. LeClerc stared into the distance, his face nearly blue as first milk. "Where's Pierre?"

"Non, non," he said groggily.

Marie kept one fur-covered hand on his shoulder, scanned again, her eyes squinting.

"All dead. All dead. Dorion. First." LeClerc pointed, barely able to lift his arm, letting it drop like a stone. Marie stared, couldn't see anything. "I find him. Dead." LeClerc's fingers lifted in a jerky wave that took in the emptiness before him. Lance marks punctured his body. His throat rattled when he breathed.

"Baptiste. Bring the horse," Marie told her son.

"Sh-h-h," LeClerc said, looking up at her. "Still here. Dog-Rib Soldiers, those Indians, here. Sh-h-h."

Marie looked about. Snow-filled tracks and signs of horses trampling the ground were everywhere crisscrossed by bloody trails at least several hours old. How had LeClerc survived so many wounds?

She took the lead rope from Baptiste. The horse pulled back, ears twitching at the scent of death. Marie turned. Another snow-covered mound. Pierre? No, too small. It would be one of the others.

LeClerc's head dropped to his bloody chest. "Dog-Rib Soldiers," he coughed. "Before Dorion could even say or sign they—"

"Are you sure?" Perhaps LeClerc was wrong, had gotten it wrong. If he'd seen Pierre struck down, it had to have happened close. LeClerc was so wounded but he lived. Maybe Pierre lived too.

"Sh-h-h," LeClerc whispered. "Still here…"

She looked around. Should she build a fire? She had to look for Pierre. Try to bandage LeClerc. Her sons would be safer at Reed's Fort.

Paul screamed then. He'd eased off the old horse. "Papa! Papa!"

"You've found him?" She patted LeClerc's shoulder. "I'll be right back," she said. She high-stepped through the snow to where Paul knelt on his hands and knees staring into the lean-to.

She knelt down too, reaching for her son.

Just inside the shelter of hide-covered brush lay her husband, his bad leg twisted beneath him, a hatchet in his head.

She put her hand over her mouth and began keening, a wail joining Paul's frightened sobs. He shook beside her, and she reached for him, knelt so his face pressed against her chest, his fear breaking into her grief. "So, so," she crooned. "We go. Help LeClerc now."

She would never get the image from her mind, not ever. That hatchet, her husband's face covered with blood. She turned back once, lifted Paul to her breast, crossed herself over the back of her son, then touched Pierre's moccasins with her fingertips. A prayer she half remembered came to her, about God being with her at the "hour of our deaths." Then she whispered, *"Adieu."*

"Is that Papa?" Baptiste asked from behind her.

"Oui." She turned him away from the hut.

Baptiste stared at her, his eyes glassy.

Marie said, "Take your brother back to LeClerc. Go now. As I say."

Baptiste's hands formed fists at his side. "A closed fist receives nothing," she said gently. She reached out Paul's hand, placed it into Baptiste's.

"Eh?" Baptiste said. Marie blinked at his use of Pierre's word.

"Go," she said. She waited until he led his brother back through the tracks she'd made. She went to the other snow-covered form. It was the other engagé. She crossed herself again and spoke a parting prayer for him, for all of them.

With Baptiste's help, she stood LeClerc against the horse, put a wad of mane in the man's weak fist, then she ducked under the animal's neck. Across from him, she reached to pull LeClerc onto the horse's back. He lay like a drying filet over a slender pole. She lifted Paul and set him in front of the wounded man, put Baptiste behind.

"We can't go back to the hut," she said. "The Dog-Ribs rode that way." He wouldn't live. She could see that. "Get food and dressings," she said mostly to herself.

"We'll go to Reed's Fort. We'll be safe there." She had to make them feel safe.

The horse trudged out into the snow-filled trail.

LeClerc fell off, knocking her sons with him. She got him back, pulling him over as he moaned. The second time the horse's jarring slid him off, she thought she heard distant hooves. Her animal's ears twitched and he pranced. Men were coming in the distance.

She held the horse's soft nose with her hands, signaled silence to the boys. LeClerc lay in a heap nearly under the horse. She heard the clatter of men riding beyond the thicket. Her heart pounded, and she begged silence with her eyes.

She spoke then, out loud, to the friars' God, Holy Rainbow's, too. Sarah's guide, her Jesus. He would come with just her asking, Sarah had said. *Let them pass. Let them pass. Make us like gray snow.*

Stillness wrapped them. A small bird flitted from one branch to another. A clump of snow no larger than her thumb dropped off, sinking into the drift below it. No other sounds. Only the smells of a wet horse, human fear.

She tried desperately to lift LeClerc from his heap at her feet, but the heaviness of him, his delirium now, pierced by strange, soft moanings, and the constant fresh smell of blood agitated the horse. The animal wouldn't allow the man to lean on him so Marie could pull LeClerc up and on. She was weak, so weak.

She looked for a log she might drag closer to him, so he could try to stand on it. It was nearly dark. She spied an overhang of rocks and dragged LeClerc to it, then huddled again with her boys in her arms. Should she strike a flint, attempt a fire? She didn't dare. They were seeking them, those Dog-Rib Soldiers. The scent of smoke would bring them.

Instead, she laid the buffalo robe around them all, and there they spent the night, she and her sons, shivering together, holding a dying man.

LeClerc lay stiff in death by morning.

She covered LeClerc's body with snow-drifted branches, her fingers icy cold inside her mittens. *To Reed's. Go to Reed's.* Find food for her sons. Find safety at Reed's.

Snow still covered the trail, but she recognized this place, the chopped trees that pocked the outlying areas from the fort. The sky was clear blue now. The snow sparkled like cut-glass beads.

They walked slowly, the horse as hungry as her sons. She still broke the way for him, her thighs wet with the effort of pushing the drifts. He whinnied once, and she halted, her heart pounding, but she heard no sounds of other horses. Only stillness broken by the clanking of the horse's iron bit.

At Reed's House the gate stood open.

"You stay here," she told Baptiste.

"I come with you," he said.

"I'm hungry," Paul whined.

"Sh, sh, now. I know," she said. "I'll go." She couldn't let them follow her, couldn't risk what other horrors waited. "You stay."

"Papa would want me to go," Baptiste said.

"No! Lie down." She heard the pleading in her own voice, changed it, "Now!"

Paul hiccuped. "Cold," he said.

She wrapped the robe around both boys, gentled the buffalo curls close to their necks. "You stay," she said. "I go to see about food."

Under cover of dusk, she made her way through the open gate. Inside, an eerie stillness covered the remains of chaos. Nothing moved. No fires burned. Doors to the storeroom stood open. Marie swallowed.

When she stumbled over a body, she gasped. *Reznor!* He hadn't gone on to Fort George! He'd come back, one more time. She shook, her hand tight over her mouth to keep from screaming. She backed away. *Reed.* He leaned against the wall of the main house, both arms severed by a hatchet chop.

She backed out, bumped into something, turned, her hand already at her waist, reaching for her knife.

"Baptiste! I told you, no! You go. Now!"

He stared at the carnage before him. It was bad enough Paul had seen his father lanced and pooled in blood, now Baptiste would witness here six or seven brutal deaths.

She grabbed at her son, pressed his head into her breast. She stumbled over another body, two, three. So many French-Canadians who came so far to end like this. High, piercing sounds ripped through her head like lightning formed of screams. Was that her or Baptiste? She ran out into the courtyard, dragging Baptiste. Her eyes caught at limbs separated from their bodies. Her stomach reeled at the stench and stiffness of the dead.

Outside, she looked for Paul. He was gone! She retched then, her palms shaking as she wiped her mouth of the horror.

She pulled Baptiste along, risked calling Paul's name. Beyond the horse, she saw movement. Paul! She left Baptiste by the horse and made her way to the drift Paul had fallen into. She pulled him out. So cold. Both her sons looked so cold. She must risk a fire or lose them.

Keep them alive. Feed her children. That was her goal now.

It looked like they'd taken every bale at the fort, all the trade goods, traps, kettles, blankets. "We'll snare a rabbit tomorrow," she told them.

Her own hunger mixed with that of her sons' drove her now. She tied the boys in the buffalo robe, the reins acting as the binding knots.

"I won't follow. I won't," Baptiste begged.

"I can't have you in there. Maybe Paul runs off again. Then what?"

Back in the fort, she eased past the bodies, past the terror, moving to Reed's storehouse. Empty. They'd taken everything. Every bale of furs, every coopered barrel LeClerc had crudely formed lay smashed. Before she slipped out, despair nipping at her stomach, her eye caught a glimpse of a parfleche beneath the tumbled chairs and table. *"Merci,"* she whispered when she opened it.

The boys tore at the fish and dried meat.

"Where do we go, Mama?" Baptiste said, wiping his mouth.

"I don't know," Marie said.

"Stay here?" Paul said. He chewed with his mouth open.

Could they? She didn't see how. Their hut held no safety—if it still stood. Seeking Robinson's wife would only bring danger to her. No. There was only one thing to do.

That night, she built another small fire and the boys slept. She rolled up with them into the curly-haired robe. Marie shivered, pulled her boys closer. She'd been here before, kept herself and her children alive, as they'd followed Hunt and her husband. They had kept on then. Pierre had been with them. This time they traveled alone.

Stars prickled through the trees like tiny candles decorating a St. Louis Christmas tree. There were no gifts beneath these boughs. Only an empty hollow and memories. She wanted to disappear, let her heart, so pierced with emptiness, pour out its grieving onto this cold ground and simply melt away. But she had two sons, alive beneath these trees. Her sons were gifts enough.

Aching from the cold in the darkest hour, she thought of Pierre, of how they'd gotten here in the first place, of her pushing and pulling. They might all be working beside Sarah at Young's Bay or walking to the salt works near Astoria, watching the big fish called whales move down the shore. Maybe Hunt would come back and reverse the partners' decision to become Brits. No. She was here, responsible for her sons. There was no one to argue with about coming or going. Pierre was dead. She could not even witness his dying without risking his sons.

But what to do? What was not foolish? She only wished to sleep. To lie down and sleep.

"Woman, strong you may be, but you have not wagered well with this choice." She woke up, the words remembered from a dream, no, spoken before they'd left St. Louis on the Hunt expedition. She'd insisted, in fact. And even that one time when she had changed her mind, back at the Osage camp, and Pierre had struck her without whiskey for excuse, struck her while the Astorians stood and watched, she had said it was her choice. To go or stay. She had done both. She'd stayed with him. But after their daughter died, she'd left herself for a time. She must not grieve in those ways now.

She thought of her own mother, of her sister. Help had not come in time. Holy Rainbow would have disagreed, she thought. For Pierre's father did come to rescue her. And even with the Hunt expedition, with all its bitter blasts of wind and hail, people had survived. Shoshone guides had appeared, brought them to safety. They'd had enough to trade for, enough to make the journey, reached their destination at the sea.

"You do not recognize when God looks down on you," Holy Rainbow had once told her.

"But I have not been baptized, remember?"

"Ah, our souls all seek him out," Holy Rainbow told her. "It's a part of who we are. He knows your voice, your name. You could just stay in one place, and he'd find you there."

"He'll find me faster if I'm moving," Marie had said.

Holy Rainbow laughed. "So that's why you keep busy, going from here to there," she said. Marie felt her face grow hot. "It's not a sign of weakness but of strength, wanting to be found. However you choose to do it," the older woman told her then.

The memory of Holy Rainbow's words comforted. If not for herself, then for her sons. "If you are there, " Marie prayed aloud. "tell me what to do now."

She waited in the dawn.

"Mama?" Baptiste said. She looked at him, returned to the present. She stroked the side of Paul's chapped cheek

"The horse is tired," Baptiste said. "We need a new horse. Like ones the Cayuse ride."

Calmness fell onto her shoulders. They needed a new horse. Yes. The sight of the Cayuse woman, Calming Water, who had brought healing to her after her child died, the friendly people who greeted them on the other side of the Blue Mountains near the Umatilla River, that was where she should head now. To them. She tried to remember how long it had taken the guides to come from this woodsy place, up over the route where her daughter had been born and then died, how many days before they arrived at the Umatilla River? That was the direction she must go. She could not stay here.

She looked at her son. Was this how prayers were answered? By a son's words spoken while they sat, seeking warmth? *Seek the horses. Oui. Le bon Dieu. You are a good God.*

It had been nearly the same time of the year when they'd crossed those mountains and they'd been hungry then, too, starving. The three Shoshone guides had led them. She remembered hills and rocks and a grand river and valley. She recalled the things of landscapes like Hunt remembered scratchings in his book. He could "read," he said. So. She could too.

She would make herself remember so they could go forward. She would make herself go forward in order to remember.

She made one last foray into the storehouse, found only three strings of rawhide tossed to the floor. No rifles, no powder. She felt for her knife. Her boys had their pouches with stones for their slingshots. They set off, leading the horse.

She scraped at snow-covered grass for the horse, patted the rump of the spotted pony. "I would send you to the camp of the Earth Eater woman," she said, "but we have need of you a little while longer."

The horse whinnied, and Marie set off to save her sons.

The pattern of their days became the same. She gave the boys small amounts of dried fish each morning, drank water to fill. Then Marie broke snow for the horse, allowing him to eat before the boys mounted and they left. After crossing the Boise and the Snake River at that ford, they followed a remembered trail beside the meandering river. Marie used the sun and the stars. At a place where she recognized a deep and swooping river bend, she headed away, northeast into a valley. It was how the Shoshones had gone. It was near here her child had been born. Yes, she knew this place! A wide, gentle valley with tree-covered snow-capped mountains all around.

"We can stay here?" Baptiste asked.

She shook her head. There were no areas marked by tipi rings, no firepits left behind, signs of this being a wintering place. "We don't have enough food," she said.

Still the valley nurtured. Here, her husband had thought to save her from the pain of disappointment, yet had reminded her of the choices she'd made that put her infant child at risk. Here the *engages* and Hunt had celebrated the New Year. The grass was not so deep below the snow. The wind stilled and the horse could eat.

"We stay a day. See if we can snare a rabbit," she said. "That looks like a rabbit run."

Baptiste found a large, flat stone. They set the trap with the stick in a loop where a rabbit would trip it as it moved from here to there. It did. Marie built a fire, skinned the rabbit, and they ate.

They walked the length of the valley, rose up through a cut in it, and Marie surprised herself with the lightness she felt when she recognized a high, treed ridge and knew that just beyond, there was an opening sliced by a slender stream. They'd follow that stream and rest soon where Vivacité remained.

But when she got there, she wasn't at Vivacité's stream. She wasn't where she thought she was. Snow had begun to fall, and they were in a narrow place with high gray rocky ridges tumbling out like hog cracklings on either side. Somehow she'd taken a different deer trail out of the valley. She believed they were in the Blue Mountains, but she wasn't sure where. She portioned out the dried fish until none remained. The rabbit was gone.

She struck a flint that evening to start a small fire, then wrapped her sons inside the buffalo robe beside her, using her own body to offer added warmth. Her hips ached with the cold, her fingers looked white as bone. It did not frighten her; it reminded her: She had walked this way before and could do it once again.

But the silent time when the children slept, their breathing fast yet even, brought pictures to her mind. Of a husband, gone. Of words not spoken when she might have. Of emptiness and sorrow. Maybe someday she'd return to mark the place where he had died. Or perhaps she'd raise her sons to do that, to remember a man who had made a change for them, for her.

She sat up. She still had his debt to repay, the money they owed to Hunt. That would be how she'd honor his living and his dying. He'd be remembered then as the Astorian guide who led them safely west, not as just another mixed-blood always tangling with disaster. And if no one else knew of the hidden furs at Henry's Fort...after this was over, after her children were safe, she'd think more about that cache. Henry's Fort was so far away—and could she find the cache? Maybe Lisa already had! First, she'd repay the debt. So no partner could ever claim her husband took advantage, used the Astorians as a tool for his own gain.

The thought gave her direction, another step.

The day found her exhausted from stepping through the deep snow, her arms tired from leading the horse, pushing through drifts. They'd have to remain in this place until spring. It took too much energy now to make the miles. She couldn't carry the boys very far. Paul, perhaps. But she had no more fat stored on her body. She knew horse meat would be their only hope.

They were nearly at the tree line, but the area had rabbit signs, limbs to hang the meat from to keep it from wolves that howled in the night. The horse had become so gaunt, Marie knew if she didn't kill it soon it would have nothing but bone to spare. The wolves would take it anyway, feel the desperation of these travelers and, perhaps, attack. The snows drifted deep. She calculated it was late January. Paul had just turned four. The boys had become silent, their cheeks hollow. Their dark eyes dull. She could see the outline of their faces as though a thin web of skin covered a skeleton. They would surely die if they didn't eat the horse. She'd be burying all her children here.

So. They would have food, preserve their strength, wait until the snows thawed, and then walk on to the Cayuse. They needed meat now, not transportation.

She built a frame with brush, everything taking longer, her mind sometimes getting distracted. She cut long slender branches with Sacagawea's knife and nestled a hut in the shadows of an overhanging rock. A stream ran not far from them. Frozen, but the ice was thin enough to crack. She told the boys to gather sticks for a fire. "Not too far out," she said. "Not too far now. Here we'll stay for a time. Until the snow is not so deep."

And while their little backs were bent to work, she carried the parfleche, laid it open near the horse. She lifted his leg and using Sacagawea's knife, she scraped ice from inside his hoof. He leaned into her, nickered low, pushed his nose against her. She put his food down and pressed her face against his neck, her fingers stroking the velvet of his nose. His head dropped. "I'm sorry," she whispered to him. "You have been a good friend, and I thank God for you. But I choose life for my sons."

Then with all the strength she had left, she slit the horse's throat and stepped away so he wouldn't fall on her, his body a thud against the earth.

She quickly moved the parfleche, to catch the animal's blood. She'd heat rocks, put them inside the bag and warm the soup. First, she had to remove all he had to give them from his stomach and his skin, being thankful as she worked.

Her only tool was Sacagawea's knife. Holding it made her think of the Shoshone woman. Marie wondered if she'd borne a healthy infant, delivered a girl or boy. Had her husband helped her? Would that child be raised by Clark too? Would Sacagawea get to choose?

Her face flashed hot. Marie would raise her sons. She would keep them from too much influence of the Hunts and McDougalls and Clarks who carved their way into new places. She could carve too, and would. She was stronger than she'd thought. Wasn't her being here proof of that? If she kept her sons alive, wouldn't that be proof?

She'd saved even what remained in the horse's belly, cooking the greens there to survive. She sliced lean meat off the thighbone, stuck it on sticks to roast at the fire. She quartered the rest of the animal, and with the reins from the bridle hoisted the meat up into the trees. No need to smoke it in the cold.

When they'd eaten, she scraped the shoulder blade to make a plate of sorts, something to put food into, a tool to drink water from its shallow hollow. When she'd removed the meat from the skull, it would make a carrying bowl.

Baptiste asked to use her knife, and with it he sharpened a section of leg bone. "If something comes, a bear, a cougar, I'll protect us," he said. She smiled before he added, "It is my job now that Papa is gone. Nothing for a woman to do."

Through that night Marie scraped at the horse's hide, stretching it as she could to cover the branches of their rounded hut to keep cold out, warmth in.

The days that followed varied from cold to colder, from hours of soft snow falling to whole afternoons of sun. They snared a rabbit or two. Baptiste felled pine jays with his pouched slingshot. Watching him reminded Marie of a story Sarah told them, about a man named David and a giant called Goliath.

Sometimes they heard large animals, no doubt elk, as they crashed through branches in the distance. Scratching sounds proved to be porcupines climbing slender trees. Wolves howled, and Marie tied her knife to a long stick as a lance should they choose to attack. Baptist's bone knife was readied the same. But the fire must have kept them at bay.

All they'd needed had been provided.

"We should sing a soft song for your sister," she told the boys.

"Does she hear us?" Baptiste asked.

"Maybe," Marie said. "Maybe."

They heard sounds in the night. Owls screeched. Wolves howled with triumph of a kill. In the morning they stewed a rabbit Marie snared. She wondered if she had killed the horse too soon. Perhaps if they had waited, they could have lived on rabbits, saved the horse for later. But no, there was no value in looking back. What next, that was the question she had to answer. What next and what had she learned from the past?

She handed out the food in small amounts, her eyes trying not to see the hollows of her sons' cheeks, the thinness of their fingers. To pass the time, she told the boys stories of her people, of life back in her river home, of her father's people, too. Time, she told them, was only that journey between experiences tied together with a story.

She made the boys move each day to keep their muscles working, gathering little sticks they dried beside the low fire to burn. Her own legs quivered in weakness. Paul's large smile sank into his narrow face. Both boys gazed out for long periods as though visiting someplace far away.

As the weather warmed more each day, Marie knew they'd have to smoke what was left of the horse. They could take the meat with them, pound up the coarser parts, maybe find dried berries to add, make a pemmican, if she had the energy to try. They needed fat, but the horse had no fat, almost as starved as they were by the time it gave its life. Marie had to calculate carefully. When she caught another rabbit, she would smoke it, save it. When the weather was right, they would leave. She just didn't know when.

She marked the days on a green branch, remembering Reed's beginning to teach her numbers. She had hoped to count hides, not days that she lived, not days since her husband's death, not weeks since her last full belly. But this was what she counted now. Five rows of ten days since Pierre's death, since she had chosen to leave him behind, save her children.

Her flow started one morning at the confidential place she'd made for herself. She worried that the scent would bring animals, trouble. But it was small, lasting only a day. Even her body resisted the natural way of things now.

"Mama, look," Paul said. She woke with a start to his words, saw a strange, pinkish light when he pointed toward the northern sky.

She crawled out of the hut to stare. It was like the night Pierre had awakened her to see stars dotting an obsidian sky. But this time the night was swept with the colors of wild rose, deep and shimmering pink. "Woman's work," she thought, remembering her mother's words. "Sweeping the hearth, seeking what's lost." Pierre had said that brilliant stars in a night sky were like the baptism of the Lord, water against the world. Here she had both. Work to do and the Beloved to see her through.

For so long she had carried the weight of her mother's death on her shoulders. Maybe even anger that her mother had left to find help, then deserted her to death. But she was doing her "mother's work" when she sought the friars. Her mother's palms had been open to receive, and while God had not saved her mother's life, he had saved Marie's.

Marie had been a mere child, making child choices then. Now she was grown and must choose something new. Perhaps she lived then to keep her sons alive now? Perhaps she kept the Lord at bay because she could not believe he swept the hearth to find her.

The next morning, she decided. She roused the boys. She knew that the seed-planting month of April must be many days away, and yet the air felt warm for the third day in a row. The stream rushed again, pushing through ice as thin as an old woman's skin. Spots of muddy green grew wider around the tree wells as the snow receded into melt.

Marie imagined the bare hill beyond this ridge of trees, the deep valley below where they had once met up with kind faces and food. The Cayuse did not eat horses or dogs. She remembered that. But perhaps they had never been in the snow mountains alone with two children. People never knew just what they might do when they were broken.

They'd gone four days with no signs of rabbit, nothing new for their larder. The meat of the horse was all but consumed. They had only a few days' nurture left.

"We will have the comfort of the fire one more night," she told the boys. In the morning, she filled the bladder of the horse with stream water and tied it with a strip of rabbit hide, and hung it around her neck. The buffalo robe that had warmed them all, she wrapped inside the horsehide, rolled it, and she carried this on her back.

"You can walk?" she asked the boys. They nodded yes. "You're strong. I'm proud of you."

Both boys beamed, and Marie wondered how long it had been since she had spoken praises to her sons.

She turned back once to look at the rock ledge that had harbored them these weeks. "You gave a comfort," she said to the hillside. Who would have thought a rock could give comfort, something so heavy and gray.

The first night away from their mountain camp, they huddled in a ravine. She clawed brush aside, laid the horsehide down followed by the robe. They drank water, ate the portion of meat. Baptiste grabbed for more, consumed it before she could stop him. "I'm hungry," he said.

She nodded. The meat she ate didn't fill up as she thought it would. They were exerting more now. She hadn't considered that. She'd waited too long to move.

They slept to the noise of their stomachs.

The second evening out, when Marie handed them pieces of dried horse meat, she realized that what she gave them was all there was. She looked at Baptiste. Her son ripped at the food, worked hard to chew. Had he somehow eaten more during the day when she hadn't noticed? Maybe when she went to relieve herself? How could he? He had carried the water, not the food. Or had Paul? Or maybe she just hadn't kept track well.

Wet snow woke her in the morning. Wind whipped around them in the crevice she'd picked to sleep in. A gray rock with a rounded top stuck out of the snow above her. She shook the white off. It was heavy snow, wet. Something in the weight of it as she brushed it from the robe told her the boys would not be able to move through it. She could not carry them and carry herself. They had no food to sustain them. Only water. They lay sleeping, barely twitching.

They were going to die. She knew it then. Just as Pierre must have known that Vivacité would die, was too fragile to live. He had meant his offer as a way of saving his daughter from the torture of starvation, saving the child's mother from watching her daughter drift away, unable to stop it.

She looked at her sons. They had suffered enough.

She turned on her side, pushed herself away. She felt the knife at her hip. What choices a mother had to make. How to know what was best for her sons? Who was she to judge another? If a mother like Sacagawea chose to let another raise him, to leave her son behind, then it needed honoring. Sometimes, a mother was too tired to decide and yet she always did. Even not deciding proved a choice.

Paul snuggled up against her. She brushed the snow from the robe again. That robe, which had come all the way from St. Louis. Those boys, too, had come all the way from St. Louis. To die like this? Starving?

She knew her next step.

19

Dancing with Stars

"No, Mama! No!" Baptiste cried. He fought her as she rolled him next to his brother inside the buffalo robe, used the rawhide thongs to tighten them. "Mama. No!"

"I have to," she said. "Oh, please understand. Please." She was crying, sobbing.

Paul screamed, spit at his brother lying tight beside him, the boys face to face on the ground. "Listen, listen," she said. "Please, listen. It is the only way."

Baptiste struggled again against the cocoon of buffalo robe his mother had made. For a moment he allowed her to stroke his hair. She touched the face of Paul who quieted, his eyes like dark huckleberries set into snow. Baptiste struggled again. She brushed wetness from her own eyes, her whitish fingertip pressing tears from Baptiste's face.

"I can't carry you. There's no more food. I can't let you follow me and you will try, I know you will. It's the only way. I will put branches over you to protect you, so you are unseen," she said. "I leave the water dripping slowly. We'll all have a better chance if I go alone. I have to tie you tight here," she said. "I have to."

"I won't follow. I'd stay with Paul."

She shook her head. "You'd wander, and I'd never find you."

"You leave us," he cried, disbelieving.

357

"Could I forget my own sons? Never," she said. A saying of her mother's came to her. *Can a woman forget her sucking child?* She made the sign for the word *remember* as heart knowing. "I'll remember you. But you must be here when I bring help. You stay here. Bound. You think of horses. You tell Paul about horses." She swallowed.

He glared at her. She couldn't make him understand. What she couldn't tell him, wasn't sure made sense herself, was that knowing her sons were bound tight inside that robe, needing her to bring back help, gave her strength. It was another step, like keeping Hunt from slaughtering her horse back on the expedition. As long as they had hope, they could all make it.

And she'd already killed their horse.

"Tell him of the Cayuse mounts," she told Baptiste as she tied the knot, her voice stumbling over tears. "Tell him of the handsome animals." She imagined them running wild. Spotted horses, surging through grasses, their tails separated by the wind. "Remind him of Hawk and the whistle in his mane. Tell him of young colts roaring up through the herd, safe in the numbers, pushing past their elders, kicking, playing, pretending to lead." Her sons would move through life just like that, she realized.

One day they arrived from her body. The next day, they raced past while she stepped aside and just watched. They were of her, but not hers. So long as she kept them alive. "Think of the horses," she said. "Imagine them coming to greet you."

In places, the snow rose to her knees. Each step weighed as heavy as stone. But this was not the difficulty. She would keep taking the next step. It was the swirling white, the blazing ivory glare that blinded her when the sun came out. It burned against the snow without heat, burned her eyes. She squinted. Was it still snowing? She put her hand out to catch a flake. She could see nothing, not even her fingers.

The mother lay facedown on the crust of snow. She spread her arms out, held the earth, though she imagined herself sinking through the drifts of white. Marie's mind filled with the image of her children rolled into a buffalo robe. How far had she traveled from her sons before she realized the world was white? She tried to imagine where she was, what she had seen before her eyes betrayed her. Trees to her left, she thought. A rock outcropping on her right. Perhaps she could make her way toward those rocks, sit for a time. Cover her eyes with her hands. Snow blindness came and went, didn't it? It took time to heal, that was all.

She didn't have time.

She felt her heart race then slow. Hunger. Weakness.

Perhaps she should have tried to carry her sons. Maybe they would have listened to her and stayed in one place without her binding them. Maybe she should have stayed with them. Her sister had wanted to keep going, to follow. And yet her mother had said stay, maybe for the same reasons she'd given Baptiste. So no more harm would come to them, so they could be found when her mother returned with the priests.

She'd wanted to please her mother. She'd paid attention to her mother's words. It was her sister who had died.

Could her sons forgive her for what she did, bringing them here, pushing their father?

The wet ground cooled her face.

She pushed herself up. Felt a breeze. It came against her left cheek. If she moved slowly, kept the breeze on that side, she could keep going. The sun would surely warm soon. She put her hand out. She couldn't see it, but no snow drifted onto it. It had stopped snowing. She wouldn't feel the iciness of her fingers all day. Surely, the sun would warm. She shivered, took the next step.

She must have dozed. When she awoke, the breeze had stopped and what little warmth had been offered by the sun was gone. She heard an owl hoot. It was likely night. Her eyes burned so. She would crawl, not try to stand to walk. Just reach for the ground in front of her. She clutched at snow, ate it. Sounds of animals scampering loomed loud. The frozen earth crackled close to her ear. The pain of her earrings pressed by the ground told her she lived. Pain told her she lived. Her body shook now, and her teeth chattered. She felt so cold, so very cold. Tired.

So this is dying. This quiet laying down to sleep is all there is then. She wasn't frightened. Felt a calmness pierced by longing, a sweet sadness that she would not see her sons again, had not been strong enough to save them. Such a rich life she'd had, yet not enough. She hadn't held her sons long enough to ensure their place inside this world.

Now who would look after them? Perhaps no one. Perhaps they, too, took on the sleep of resignation.

She had regrets. So many. For her children, for their futures lost. And for Pierre. Perhaps if they had had the marriage blessed. Perhaps if she had lived up to her name, Her to Be Baptized, this would not have happened, this dying of them, all on the west side of the mountains.

"He provides all we need, every helper, every hide to bind us tenderly to the ones we love. We need only ask," Sarah said once.

Her knees shook, couldn't hold her. She laid her head down to rest.

She dreamed of her sons rolled into a buffalo hide. They smiled, laughed. Pierre sat beside them, then wrestled with his sons as he untied the rawhide and pulled them out into life.

In her dream, the sun glinted off a bone-handled knife lying beside them.

When Marie opened her eyes she stared at a human silhouette. It reminded her of the morning she'd met Sarah, after the night she'd decided to be honest with herself and tell Pierre he could not hurt her ever again or she would leave. The night she bound him up in skins. That was the day she and Pierre both knew she'd been strong enough to do it.

Why was Sarah standing in front of her? Had Marie lost herself then and passed into another world? Perhaps it was her mother.

Marie reached her hand out and the silhouette touched it. Flesh against flesh.

Sun warmed her face. A horse stomped and she smelled its earthy scent. She wiped her hand across her face and tasted muddy snow. The person who shadowed the sun now bent to her, lifted her head gently and held a cup to her lips. Water dribbled in, followed by a piece of dried fish. The woman smelled of fish. It wasn't Sarah.

"My children," Marie said, her voice hoarse. She made the sign for male, lowering her finger to the height of her sons then trying to rock her arms as though she held a baby.

The silhouette spoke.

Marie couldn't understand the words.

The woman said something to someone else, and Marie repeated, "My children. Find my children."

Marie tried to rouse herself then, to stand and point. She was too weak. She heard voices, men, off to the side. *Not Dog-Soldiers, please, not them.*

She saw horses now. She told the woman, "two babies," and made a sign as though cradling them. "I bound them," she said. "To keep them safe. Only to keep them safe."

She pointed and described as best she could the rock, the soft place in the ground where she'd covered them with branches. How far had she traveled from her sons? How long had she been gone? The snow melted in patches. Had she left marks in the mud? She pointed in the direction she believed she'd come from. She felt tears form, hated her weakness, hated not knowing their words. "A gray rock," she told them. "It leans over, rounded at the top." She made the shape and remembered then that the rock reminded her of a friar with his habit close around his face, leaning forward. She didn't describe it well, she knew that. But hitting her palm with her fist for "hard rock" must have been enough, for the two men rode off in the direction she was sure she'd come from.

They rode good horses, but they were not the Cayuse. Something was different about them. She did not know who they were, but they had arrived when she needed. Help when she needed, for her sons.

She felt separated, as though who she was walked just above the ground, leaving no tracks. If she lived and her sons died, what was she then? Her stomach ached with the fish she'd been given. How long had it been since she'd eaten, since the boys had eaten? How long had the snow kept her blinded?

The woman motioned for her to take another drink, slow. Marie's eyes squinted into the distance. She waited, a feeling of dread rising as though sinking in water up to her chest, her neck, her throat. She could live with Pierre's death if her children still breathed. Otherwise, who was she? No longer a *femme,* a sister, a mother. What name could she take?

A knife of ice pierced her spirit.

The woman signed, "Question. You called?" And when Marie told her, she gave her own that sounded like "Josette."

"I'm strong enough now," Marie said. Josette smiled, but by her blank expression Marie knew she didn't understand. Marie pointed with her fingertips, indicating her desire to follow the direction the men went.

The woman looked puzzled, gave her more water, and then helped Marie up onto her horse, a tall animal with tiny white specks like stars all across his rump. Josette swung up behind her. Her arms felt muscled and firm wrapped around Marie. She wore a skin robe, the deer fur turned inward. Kneeing the horse gently, Josette headed them in the direction of Marie's sons.

They met the men coming back.

Marie had known reunions. The time she'd given birth to Baptiste, for one. Pierre had not been present when Holy Rainbow delivered Marie's first child. When her husband returned, she had the joy of seeing his eyes spill over with pride. A son, she'd given him, their first son.

When Pierre had been lost on the overland journey, when she'd seen what it would be like to be without him going to that new place, she had rejoiced in his arms, vowed to never wish him out of her sight again.

She had, of course, wished him out of her sight again. But that did not diminish the joy of the embraces. Nothing stayed the same. All things changed. Even choices once made had to be remade again and again.

She was a mother. Would always be a mother. As she gave birth to them, helped create them, they created her too.

Did the men ride alone? Was no one behind them?

"Mama! Mama!" It was Baptiste's voice, a croaked whisper, his arm flapping loosely. She narrowed her eyes to see if Paul, too, rode. A small hand lifted in the air behind the second man. Paul. Marie waved back.

She had known many reunions, but none so grand as this.

Marie could hardly stop holding her sons. She cried and wailed an old Ioway greeting song, drawing on the ceremony of a former time. "I'm so sorry, so sorry I had to leave you." Baptiste's arm felt like a rabbit's bone. He was silent, but he put his arms around her neck and held her close. "We'll never be parted now," she said. "I'll never ask such a thing of you again."

"Paul was scared," Baptiste said.

"I was scared too," she told him. Just talking took energy from her, a strength she didn't have. "There's nothing wrong," she said, "with being scared. It's what you do anyway that matters. You kept your brother safe. This was a good thing."

"He bit me," Baptiste said. He showed her the bite marks on his cheek, red and sore.

"He was scared, remember?" Marie touched the spot tenderly, bent to kiss it.

Baptiste grunted, and Marie felt her breath escape as though she'd been propelled to another time. His father had had that grunt. It always told her he heard but disagreed with her words. So it would be like this then. She felt a pierce of grief below the heart so unexpected. A nod, a smell, a touch would propel her back in time as though it was a story begging to be told.

One of the horsemen handed Paul down to her as she crouched beside Baptiste. Paul wide-walked to her side, bowlegged as though he'd been riding all his days. "My baby," she said and buried her face in his matted hair.

She loosened Baptiste's arms from her neck. "I must clean you both," she said, looking around. She had nothing. She wondered how to take care of this simple basic need of her sons.

Josette handed Marie moss wrapped inside a cloth. She motioned with it, and Marie saw that it was a portion of the woman's scarf that had filled the inside of her bodice. Josette motioned again, but she gave the moss to Paul. The boy took it. She saw Baptiste use snow to clean himself. Paul watched then did the same. Marie nodded.

All I need will be provided. It will be enough.

20

The Factor's Wife

A great gathering of horsemen and horsewomen clustered in the valley below them. At first, Marie thought it was the same valley she and Hunt and Pierre had come to, but it was not. Walla Walla Indians tended this valley, not the Cayuse. These people, too, were tall as Marie was, handsome with high foreheads and slender frames, with faces that easily smiled. Marie thought they might be of the band that Mackenzie had tried to trade horses with, the ones whose horses he'd shot.

For a moment Marie wondered if she was safe here. Had they heard? Did they know she once traveled with Mackenzie?

But they had done nothing but show kindness to her as they did now, taking Marie and her boys to their village at the confluence of the Wallow Wallow River and the Columbia.

"Cayuse?" Marie asked and they signed that those people were farther west. So they had come close to where she intended to arrive, close to what she planned.

They approached the dozens, no hundreds, of horses and camps pitched in clusters like mushrooms in spring forests. These were the people Mackenzie had dishonored. Nez Perce people along the River Wallow Wallow.

Mackenzie would come through here in the spring, if he did as planned. Travel by canoe up the Columbia, the Snake, make the mountain portage with the Shoshone horses they'd left behind, then head back to St. Louis.

Did Mackenzie know about the fifty-pack cache of furs?

Back East. Was that where she should go? Had Fort George been fired upon? She wished she could speak the language here so she could ask, could know these things. Words. She had to learn words if she would keep her children safe in this place.

The boys ate dried berries and fish and shared in the elk brought by Josette's uncles and her husband. Within a few weeks Baptiste and Paul were running, chasing after dogs and moving in and out of tipis of strangers soon made into friends.

And when the boys asked about their father, why God had let him die, Marie tried to answer, "Not everything comes when you need it. Not all the answers come at once."

The tipi of their hostess also held room for Josette's family, including three children, her husband, as well as a mother-in-law and two sisters. They permitted Marie to help as she could but made no demands on her. The wounds on her hands and her knees from crawling had begun to heal. Their care for her helped stop the drain of the hope she stored in her heart. She had no way to tell them of her losses. She was a widow now. Alone. With no one to come beside her.

The tribal gathering announced spring, the time of root planting and new beginnings. Dancing had been going on for several days. Trades and exchanges occurred daily, including betrothals and marriages.

Sometimes Marie walked out in the warming night to listen to the drumming and the laughter. She could see faces flashing in the firelight and her heart knew this ancient ritual of meeting new people, dancing, taking mates, making trades. She had come often to such events as the wife of a trader, fewer times as a mother, but frequently as a young child.

With all these people mingling at the gathering, Marie wondered if she might overlook Mackenzie's party if he came through here, heading east. She had to tell him about Reed, her husband, the others. It was her duty, to let him know. And she'd wanted to tell him that she would repay the debt someday, so he could let Astor and anyone else know who might otherwise remember her husband poorly.

She felt at home, listening to the music with no pressure to move on. "My mother's brother," Josette told her in signs, "dances alone." Both women stood outside the tipi, blankets crossed over one shoulder, under the opposite arm. "He comes to see you later. I ask him to do this."

She knew her new friend was being kind, knew she soon had to decide what to do next, where to start over. She touched Josette's arm, smiled. "He has many horses?"

Josette lifted her chin in that way she had, gave her a half-grin. "Women here own the horses," she said. "As much as the men. We will ride together when you're well."

Mackenzie bargained with the wrong people, here, Marie thought. *He should have been dealing with the women.*

"This place of belonging is mine too," Josette said, turning to look at the tipi. "I decide who comes in and who goes."

"It is too soon," Marie signed. "Too soon to think of new feet tangled under a blanket or even in a dance."

She wasn't sure she could ever take another to her bed. She didn't tell Josette that. She had two sons to raise alone. But if she did not marry, then what would happen to them? How would they live? Who would she be if not someone's *femme?*

Women own the horses.

It would take years for her to have such wealth. And she wasn't sure that horses were what she longed for. The wealth she wanted was respect for her sons. They needed to learn the languages. She needed to learn them too. The words of *this* place, of more people than just the Ioways and Sioux. Then her sons could become full partners in a company someday. These skills would give them value, allow them to shape their lives instead of letting others carve them like a bone.

Marie watched her sons play with these handsome people. Cayuse and more Nez Perce rode in now and people from the area near the Spokane House, that place of David Thompson's. Her children slipped in and out among their children as though they'd never left the villages of their father or her own Ioway people. How quickly they forgot their lives in the fort of Astoria.

Yet the peeled-log houses of the fur trade would be their future. They would become fine men, capable men, educated men who could negotiate. Men, working for others, helping themselves, using words.

She'd help her sons get where they needed to be. But not push them as she had Pierre. She would put a bridle on her ambition. Yes, that word the white men used. Ambition. Astor had ambition. Hunt and Mackenzie. Her husband, too. They did not use the word to describe women's work. But it could be there. A mother knew: Ambition tempered by compassion marked the beginning of great things.

"You looked for the big man with red hair?" Josette asked Marie one morning a few days after the celebrations ceased. Many with horses still gathered. A fog that promised to burn off with the sun rose from the river. Several women sat in a circle and rubbed dark husks from roots, placing them in a pile, their fingers stained black. So were Marie's. "You're looking for this man?"

"You've seen Mackenzie?"

"A brigade passes through. No horses are traded."

Marie stood, catching a handful of roots that fell from her lap as she did. She squinted upriver.

"My uncle will take you," Josette said. She grinned when Marie hesitated. "He expects nothing in return. It is a favor."

Marie called for the boys, and Josette's uncle motioned them to join him in a dugout canoe. "We go to find Mackenzie," she told Paul, who flapped his hands in excitement. "Tell him what has happened to the Boise expedition led by Reed."

Marie picked up the oar and in the same rhythm as the man, dug deep into the water. The boys chattered in French as they moved upstream. Marie remembered the journey when Lisa chased them up the Missouri. Had it only been three years before? She'd met Sacagawea then. So much had changed.

"*Attends un moment!*" Baptiste shouted, standing now. "See, Mama? There they are."

Marie spied the canoe brigade ahead. She shouted too, and the big pirogues of Mackenzie slowed, an *engagé* turned around. Six or seven men sat in the boat. One woman did too. The *engagés* waved as they saw the boys standing, then pulled onto the shore.

"Dorion's wife," Mackenzie said as she stepped out. "I figured Reed would get here eventually, but we had to push on." He looked beyond her. "Where is Reed?" He looked around. "Did he send you, then? Do you have pelts?" Confusion and interest marked his jowls. He'd been eating well for a time, that was clear.

"We are all that's left," she told him. "Me and my sons."

"What?" Mackenzie said. He pulled at his red beard, hung his thumbs into the strap of his powder horn spread across his ample chest. The clerk named Alexander Ross stared at her. She remembered him from Wallace House at Wollamat Falls. He'd been sent to the Okanogan country when she and Pierre joined Wallace and Halsey, that fine winter of warmth.

"Well what happened to them?" Mackenzie said.

Marie told her story. A slender woman with a single long braid pulled around her shoulder sat behind Ross. She had deep-set eyes that showed interest. She seemed to understand French. As Marie spoke, Ross pulled out ink and a quill pen from a writing desk at his feet. The woman leaned over, pointed to something on the page, and Ross nodded, drew a line and rewrote.

She could read, Marie thought. Here was an Indian woman who could read!

Josette's uncle stood waiting. Once or twice Marie saw him go to the boys and bring them back into a place of safety. He was a good man. Marie could see that. But now was not the time.

"My good woman…my good woman," Mackenzie kept repeating as she finished her story. "I…how did you endure it? Mere men would have succumbed in the effort." He gazed up at the Blue Mountains still dusted with snow, though it was now nearly May. "A fitting ending to Astor's journey of disaster."

"All was provided," she said, her eyes averted. "Your fort, Reed's Fort is lost."

"They didn't burn it though?"

She shrugged. "Not while we were there. But the first was burned. There may be some pelts they missed in caches. Heavy pelts come from there. The streams are rich." It felt good to speak in French, good to talk about the streams, about what she knew.

Mackenzie stood silent for a time. "Sixty," he said. "We have lost sixty men counting the *Tonquin* deaths, our own journey overland, the disasters on the expeditions. Now this. Nine more men lost. And here you stand, you and your two sons, and you talk of trade routes and pelts. Spoken like a factor's wife."

She had nothing more to say.

"What do you propose now? Go back with us to St. Louis and tell this tale, return to your people? Head back to Fort George and…"

She'd known these questions would come.

"I pay Pierre's debt."

"That's not needed, lass," Mackenzie said. "Pierre's pittance is nothing compared to your losses, all because of Astor's poor management."

"This Okanogan place," she said, nodding to Ross with her chin. The clerk looked up, startled. "This is a place for a woman and her children?"

"Well…I…"

"Ross's woman there," Mackenzie said, "she's an Okanogan chief's daughter. Sally's her name. She could tell you. Don't know exactly how you'd do there—"

"We'll be no burden. I'll trade for what we need." She took the knife Sacagawea had given her from her belt, the one she'd cut the branches with, killed the horse with. She handed it to Mackenzie.

"Just a trade knife. Not worth much." He turned it over in his hand. "Good antler handle, I'll say that." He returned it. "You keep it."

"Captain Lewis gave the knife to the wife of his interpreter. To Sacagawea," she said. "The Shoshone guide."

Mackenzie raised his eyebrows. Marie had read him well. He was a man who understood the stories and the power in a sign.

"She gives it to me, a woman on a journey across the mountains. Like her, the wife of an interpreter, a *metis* husband. Like her, a mother worrying over her children. I trade it now for something more precious than a reminder of what happened, what we survived. I trade it for a beginning. For seed beads from the store. For hides from Astor...no, from the North West stores now." She thought she saw Mackenzie nod. "So. I'll take my sons to the Okanogan, to that river. It is a new place. A safe place?"

"Relatively," Mackenzie said.

"I'll make moccasins," Marie said.

"I remember Reed saying that you had a nice hand at beadwork," Mackenzie said. "He doubled the value in trade."

Marie thought of Sacagawea's blue-beaded belt traded for the sea otter robe Clark said he had to have. She'd given much and claimed the right to vote because of it. Her voice had been heard because of her willingness to give what was only hers to give.

Marie's voice would be heard too, but in a new way.

"We'll be no burden," Marie insisted. "Even passage to Okanogan I will pay. Add it to the ledger page owed by my husband."

"What do you think, Ross?" Mackenzie said. "She fit in there?" He turned back to her. "Winters are pretty rough, not like at Astoria or the Wollamat," he said. "Think you can handle all that snow?" She stared at him, and his face colored as if he'd realized what he'd said. "Aye, and you could, coming through what you have. Well, Ross, maybe your fiancée needs a helper. She'd be under your tutelage—" He looked back at Marie.

"A free woman," Marie said. "I'd be a free trader. My own work. My own name."

Sally stared at her, but Marie thought she saw the slightest lifting of the corners of her mouth.

Ross touched his fiancée's hand. She raised an eyebrow at him, nodded once so slightly it could have been a blink. Something passed between these two. Love lived there, Marie decided. And when it did, many a bitter blast of life could well be born. She was proof of that.

"A mother does what she must," Sally said in perfect French. "It's all in her choices. This woman chose well. She will find good things in Okanogan."

21

Beginning

Marie kissed both cheeks of her Walla Walla friend, Josette, telling her good-bye. She signed as best she could what she intended and told her that in the spring, next year, she would come back during the seasonal round. "I will dance with your uncle," Marie said. "We will see then what we will see."

Josette nodded, no judgment crossing her doe-like eyes. She brushed a strand of dark hair from Marie's center part, tucked it back behind her ears.

Marie wished she had something to give her for the kindness she had shown. Marie had little left; she'd traded her earrings already. She'd offered her the knife, but Josette refused.

"You'll need that," she said. "I visit sometime. You feed me."

She had nothing else but the ring Pierre had given her, and she wasn't ready to part with that yet.

Marie put her hand back to tighten the knot of hair at her neck and felt the ivory comb. "Take this," Marie said, handing it to her. "And I will still feed you when you come." Josette gazed down at it and delicately placed it in her own dark hair.

There was nothing left to do now except press her cheek to her friend and whisper words of thanks.

"I'll make you moccasins," Marie told her, "with a design as you have never seen."

"In spring," Josette said, making the sign for "little grasses."

And so Marie and her two boys stepped once more into a pirogue. This time, they rode with Alexander Ross and his fiancée, *engages* and laborers, a blacksmith, a Sandwich Islander, another hunter, and other former Astorians bound for the Okanogan fort. Many would continue on with Mackenzie all the way to St. Louis. He'd be back, he said. She'd know then if he found Henry's cache or if she should seek to find those pelts and so make one last way that Pierre could help his sons.

She'd had her journeys on this Columbia River before, though farther west. The wide stream ran north here, into dry, treeless country where horses roamed and arched their necks as they snorted and galloped.

Rocky islands, white water, and sand bars challenged them. But Marie felt at home in this boat on the river. She was doing what she knew first under the comfort of sky as the canoe split the waves. It felt familiar though she'd never been this way before.

Game bounded, startled from the shade of willows. They camped to the serenades of coyotes and wolves. She wondered if Ignace and Sarah still stayed at the ocean or if they'd gone back to visit their old employer David Thompson.

As the *engages* paddled the canoes, Marie could see that the landscape lacked the thick foliage of the Des Moines, the Wisconsin, or Mississippi. This place had wider vistas. Hot sun beat down in this month of planting. It shone without the demand that their bodies give up sweat. The climate put its arms around her as she needed it, let loose at night for cooling sleep.

In the morning, gray fog folded over the river like a cocoon. If she hadn't seen the river with her own eyes, she would not have known of its presence. The boys slept. A gentle breeze snapped at one of the unrolled sails. She walked farther up the bank, finding a place in the grass to sit and watch the fog rise. She wrapped her arms around her knees.

She missed her husband's strong embrace, the smell of his beard, the sound of his voice. She lowered her head and wept.

In time, she looked up, wiped her eyes. She clasped her hands, noticed the whiteness of her fingers. The cold in the mountains would stay with her now, a reminder carried in her bones.

The fog began its slow lifting, urged on by the warming morning and the breeze. Suddenly Marie was shrouded in the gray mist. She couldn't see anything around her. For a moment, she felt her heart race with the great unknowing, not seeing anything but smoky swirls of cloud. She took a deep breath. It would lift, this fog. Everything was still there, the river, the boats, her sons. She wasn't alone. She was in the middle of it, but it would lift and they would move on. The fog could not hurt her. It could only leave her disoriented for a time, but it would change. It would drift away if she just waited.

So would her pain.

Ross's fiancée walked up through the mist that swirled and lifted. She pointed. Marie looked up behind her, watching the cloud separate and drift, clearing so she could see the bare hills with tiny clusters of trees in the dimples. Hawks soared above them. White clouds like sea foam dotted the blue.

She signaled for Marie to return. They loaded up. As the boats moved upriver between the round, treeless ridges, the wind pushed the clouds. Marie watched the changing shadows against the hillsides. They moved like a blanket softly unfurling down the rounded ridges, settling gently at the bottom. She was settling gently too.

The air felt dry, not like Astoria or even the fall weather at the woodsy place. It had taken them five days to get here. It was late spring, and the soil promised a good place for seeds. Marie had a next step to take.

Her earring trade had been made with Ross for a small dent on the debt before she left Walla Walla. He promised her a little credit so she could purchase beads and seeds. "Good quality copper earrings," Ross had said. "Looks like LeClerc's work. Is it?"

Marie nodded.

"They'll trade well," he'd said.

So would she. At harvest, she'd trade the pumpkins and corn for more seeds, maybe even a fruit-bearing tree. She'd exchange work for more beads, and she'd get hides to make beaded bags and clothes and moccasins for her boys. Then she'd exchange some of the hides for a horse. She knew how to trap. She knew how to track and shoot a deer. She would learn how to bring down an elk, maybe even a moose. She had watched her father hunt buffalo, her mother keep away the wolves. She could do this too, with practice she could.

And she would teach her sons. Perhaps they'd learn how to read like Ross's woman. She would do what was right for her sons. And she had the knife. She would keep it so she always had a next step.

Mackenzie left them then. Marie stood at the mouth of the Okanogan River in front of the North West Company's factory. He tipped his fingers to the boys in salute, then nodded good-bye and set off.

Marie turned to her sons. "We've a rounded hut to make," she said. "And ground to clear for a garden."

"If you'd prefer, you're welcome to expand the garden plot just outside the fort," Ross said. "Snakes are a bit troublesome, but the fences will keep the hogs out. Or should."

"My boys will chase the pigs. For a price." Ross opened his mouth to protest, and she grinned. "*Je taquine,* I tease. Some things are gifts."

He nodded, and Marie followed him inside the factory storehouse. She held the paper with its marks that indicated the worth of the earrings she had traded to him earlier.

Here she'd begin anew through the gift of a friend.

She sorted through the beads Ross showed her. She named the things she wanted. A copper pot. "British," she said. He nodded. She wagered back and forth, Pierre's words about her "being a strong woman" who didn't always "wager well" coming to her. She would do her best, make him proud.

But inside her heart already sang. Not for the abundance piling up before her but from Mackenzie's words spoken just before he left.

"Good fortune be to you, then, Madame Dorion." She'd blushed. "And so you are," he said. "As good as any factor's wife, any *bourgeois's* wife. It's been my pleasure to make your acquaintance." He'd bowed at his waist, then left.

Madame Dorion. The name of a *bourgeois's* wife, a chief factor's woman. She smiled. Mackenzie was wrong. This strong l'Ayvoise, Ioway, Indian mother, former *femme,* widow, sister, friend, prayed-for daughter, daughter-in-law, Her to Be Baptized woman, did not need that *bourgeois* title.

She already had a name of her own.

Author's Notes

A Name of Her Own is a true story imagined.* Marie Dorion lived and breathed and made choices as part of the fur-trapping society of early America. Until 1835, few knew of her except those Americans and French-Canadians who were part of Wilson Price Hunt's 1810–12 Astor Expedition, the first cross-continental journey of what would become the Northwest States following the Lewis and Clark Corps of Discovery.

There is credible evidence that Marie Dorion and the Shoshone woman known as Sacagawea did indeed meet at the Arikara village in 1811. H. M. Brackenridge, a writer traveling with Spanish trader Manuel Lisa, records who joined them, including "Charbonneau, with his wife, an Indian woman of the Snake nation, both of whom had accompanied Lewis and Clark to the Pacific, and were of great service. The woman, a good creature, of a mild and gentle disposition, greatly attached to the whites, whose manners and dress she tries to imitate, but she had become sickly, and longed to revisit her native country."

Oral histories of the Shoshone question which wife came along, as Charbonneau was known to have more than one. Brackenridge's identification that it was the wife who went with Lewis and Clark to the Pacific would make this woman Sacagawea.

I was intrigued with the story of these two Indian women sharing time for a few weeks in the summer of 1811. Both were mothers, though Sacagawea did not have her children with her. Both were likely pregnant. (There is a report that Sacagawea had an infant daughter in late 1811 or early 1812.) And both women were affiliated with expeditions of white men while being married to mixed-blood French/Indian interpreter husbands. Sacagawea was returning to her people. Marie was just beginning her journey west. They were within a few years of each other in age. They were Indian women living in a white man's world. Names would have mattered to them both. (In his journals, William Clark did refer to Sacagawea as "Janey.") These women would have had much to share.

Marie's remarkable story became known to the world when Washington Irving published *Astoria* in 1836. He used the notes of John Jacob Astor, financier of the expedition, of Hunt and other partners, and of fur-trapper clerks who were, in the hierarchy of fur-trapping society, just below the status of partners. Within weeks of its occurrence, one clerk, named Alexander Ross, wrote down the story of Marie's survival in the mountains with her children. Ross and another clerk, Franchere, both transcribed accounts in French, one of which was published in Europe prior to Irving's book.

Throughout Irving's nearly 500-page English edition—and the other accounts—Marie is known only by her affiliation with others: Dorion's wife or woman; a mother of two; an Ioway Indian woman, a *sauvaguesse de l'Ayvoise.* Never as a woman with her own name.

The Yankton Sioux do record a name for the wife of Pierre Dorion as Wihmunke-Wakan. No translation of the name could be found. The French-Canadian records note that Marie's mother-in-law's name was Holy Rainbow. The cut beef station records (accounts of families eligible to receive meat under treaty agreements) of the Sioux people verify this name. The Iowa language and Sioux language are sister languages and, being married to a Yankton Sioux/French-Canadian man, Marie may well have had a Sioux name. The name, Her to Be Baptized, is fictional, though it was included as a family name in a later genealogy completed about Paul Dorion, Marie's son. Its meaning fit for this story.

The meaning of the name given to the Ioway people, Bah-Khi-Je meaning "gray snow," which also referenced "bone marrow," was provided by the Iowa people and from the book *The Ioway Indians* by Martha Royce Blaine. While Marie's people are now known as "Iowas" I chose to use the "Ioway" spelling as an older usage of the tribal name.

We do not know for sure where Marie was born or when, except in the "St. Louis Territory" which covered much of the land from present day Dakotas to Louisiana. Along the Des Moines River, a small fort named St. Louis was built, and Pierre Dorion was known to be clerking for the man who ran that fort. Marie might have been born at that

St. Louis or met Pierre there. Some say she was born along the Arkansas River. The Iowa people today believe she would have come from the upper Des Moines River area, though the Ioways first lived near La Crosse, Wisconsin, long years before. The Iowa people had affiliations with Winnebagoes and Otoe, with the French and English. La Crosse and Prairie du Chien are credible places for her family of origin. In this story, I've placed her beginnings along the upper Des Moines River. Marie's remains are in St. Louis, Oregon, but that's the rest of the story.

The pronunciation of Dorion, Marie's husband name, also has a story. The Iowa Tribal Historian, Marianne Long, believes that Dorion would be pronounced as DeRoin. And an early land adjudication record from 1799 referencing the Dorion family supports this pronunciation with the spelling of "Derouin." Even William Clark's phonetic spelling in his journals challenges the typical pronunciation when he writes "Durion" with reference to Marie's husband, Pierre, and her father-in-law of the same name. I maintained the common spelling for ease of reading, though I found myself thinking of her as "Marie DeRoin."

Upon her baptism, an event of merit to be told in the second book of the series, the Catholic church records translate her name as sometimes Marguerite and sometimes Marie. Both are considered "mother names," which were frequently given at baptism. For many years, the connection to the Marie Dorion of the Astor expedition remained lost to researchers since she was sometimes listed as "Marie Aoie" and "Marie L'Ayvoise" (the French for Ioway) and sometimes as *"sauvaguesse de le nation de Ayvoise,"* meaning "female of the wilderness, of the Iowa tribe." Indian women were often given a Christian name and the last name created from their tribal affiliation. Thus someone named Marguerite Cayuse would be Margaret of the Cayuse tribe.

Marie did have three children with Pierre Dorion, at least two boys. One account reports the eldest child's name was "Paul." All others recorded Jean Baptiste as older, which is the name I've used. The name or sex of the third child is not documented. The infant's birthplace near North Powder, Oregon, is commemorated with a plaque.

The cast of characters that begins this book denotes who was real and who wasn't.

William Clark, Reuben Lewis (brother to Meriwether), and Manuel Lisa were partners in the Missouri Fur Company. Fort Clatsop where the Corps of Discovery wintered in 1805–06 was known to the early Astorians who secured their salt from the same salt works near present day Seaside, Oregon. Camp boys Jean Toupin and George Gay were real people.

In Astoria in 1812, there were indeed two Indian families living on Young's Bay with two children each, facts we know from the records kept by the clerks at the fur-trapping post. Ignace Shonowane came across Canada into Oregon Territory with his wife and sons with David Thompson; there is credible evidence of his Christian faith as portrayed, lending credence to the view that the first missionaries to the Indians were in fact other Indian people. A Sandwich Island woman came with the Astor supply ship, and many Clatsop and Chinook women, including Ilchee, the daughter of a Chinook chief who became McDougall's wife, would have had tender ties to Marie.

Hawaiians known as Sandwich Islanders or Kanakans or Owyhee people first arrived in Oregon as part of the Astor adventure. They lived in what later became Oregon along with French-Canadians, Indian people from eastern tribes and the very trade-savvy Clatsops, Wishrams, Chinook, Wappatos, and others. Native peoples offered a diverse and complicated society into which Marie Dorion, her husband, and two children arrived. Community life in Astoria began long before the emigrant migration from wagon trains populated the west.

The volatile aspect of the relationship between the Dorions is verified in the historical record. Sometime along the expedition route, however, the reports of Pierre's violence subside. While at Astoria, with the clerks recording everything, it seems, from unusual treatments for syphilis to the pitiful state of men's laundry, there is no further reference to Pierre's treatment of his wife or the liquor consumption that resulted in the Missouri River race retold here. Instead, we learn of Pierre going on special brigades as an apparently trusted member of the party, with his wife and children along. The issues related to Manuel Lisa, the debt, the race, the duel, the cache at Henry's Fort, and Pierre's nine-hundred-dollar debt in Astoria at the time of abandonment, are all based on fact.

The abandonment of Astoria, the role of the North West Company, the Missouri Fur Company, the expedition, and the events at that *boise* place are based on fact. Because there were many partners and many French-Canadian engages as part of the Hunt expedition, some activities and personages were combined for readability. For example, mountain men Robinson, Reznor, and Hoback did work for Lisa once and died at the Boise River along with many others, but it was a man named DeLauney who left an Earth Eater woman a widow, not Robinson, and a Canadian named Landry, not Reznor, who grieved his colleague's passing.

As much as possible, the affiliation with and uniqueness of Indian tribes is accurate, and the behavior of men like Mackenzie toward them is documented.

Marie Dorion, like other Indian women of her time, did have choices even in a world of men. Her life, the protection of her children, and her ability to endure, all support her as a strong woman, sustaining mother, and supportive wife who pursued goals and faced barriers not unlike women today. Was she powerless, self-centered, or ambitious? Or did she have the courage to seek her heart's desire? Therein lies the story.

We are bound by our vulnerability, I believe, and by our eternal search for meaning as spiritual beings. Marie's story—whether I've retold it well or not—ties us tenderly to the richness of the past and what it has to tell us for today.

At the time of her death, Marie was known as Madame Dorion. The wife of a chief factor or *bourgeois* was often known as "madame." Whether this was how Marie acquired the title isn't known, but it serves as speculation for more of this true story, imagined. I hope you'll return for it.

---

* Thanks to author Linda Crew for the characterization of "a true story imagined."

Acknowledgments

The list of people involved in the research of this Tender Ties series is laudable. The authenticity and enthusiasm grew from many; any errors belong to me. Thank you is incomplete but heartfelt, and several deserve special notation.

To Roger and Brenda Howard, who opened their St. Louis, Oregon, home to a stranger on a cold rainy day and shared materials enough to begin this series, my deepest thanks. Their care of Marie's story, their sharing of the John Clymer paintings commemorating Marie, their tending of the St. Louis Catholic Church where she's buried, and their confidence in me brought this story to life.

Gratitude goes to the people of the Iowa Nation, Iowa Tribal Chairman Lawrence Murray who supported the telling of this remarkable Iowa woman's story; and to Victor Robidoux and Marianne Long, Iowa Tribal Historians in Oklahoma, for being present on a day not expected and for talking with me about names, and about this woman in particular, and for reviewing a copy of the manuscript to make it real. The author and publisher appreciate the Museum at Warm Springs' staff and board for use of the floral pattern on the cover, which is from a beaded bag in their permanent exhibit gallery. To our cousins, Bill and Cleta Kirkpatrick of Ponca City, Oklahoma, who lived down the road from the Iowa Tribal offices, thanks for willingly going with us on this journey to the past.

To Erhard Gross of Astoria for his passion for the fur-trapping period, for Astoria the coastal city, and for Lewis and Clark and their connection to this story, a special thanks. He first noted for me the historic meeting between Sacagawea and Marie Dorion and suggested Marie Dorion as a remarkable woman of the West whose story is little known. I thank him for directing me to the Astor collection at the Astor Library of Astoria, the Clatsop County Historical Society and for introducing me to the staff at Fort Clatsop National Memorial and the people there also passionate about Marie Dorion: Ranger Sally Freeman and Superintendent Don Striker. Erhard's willingness to answer questions about knives (he is the person who identified the only remaining knife of the Lewis and Clark expedition, which, incidentally, is the knife given to Marie Dorion by Sacagawea in this novel) and trade, and his reading of the unedited manuscript is deeply appreciated. The hospitality shown my husband and me by Erhard and his wife, Elfi, made this journey to the past rich with pleasant memories.

To Bob Moore, historian, Jefferson National Expansion Memorial in St. Louis, profound admiration and appreciation for accessibility and responsiveness to details about Lewis and Clark, Sacagawea, languages, trade goods, the Dorions, baptismal records, and for speculations about comments made of Indian women written down by European and American men.

To the Hudson's Bay Company archivists in Winnipeg, Manitoba, Canada, especially Carey Isaak, research assistant, for sorting out work records of Marie's fur-trapping acquaintances; and to Nancy and Bob Noble of Salem for their enthusiasm and for discovering details at the Oregon State Archives including the copy of a map of the tragic Boise site that David Thompson is said to have drawn; and for locating a reference that gave me a plausible way for Marie to have met a young *voyageur* who touched her life years later, my deep appreciation.

To author and researcher John Henley of the Great Northwest Book Company for copies of old journals and books; librarians at Oregon State Historical Society; Rick Laughlin, visitor use assistant at the Whitman Mission National Historical Site; Diane Biggs, director of the Frazier Farmstead Museum in Milton-Freewater, Oregon; rangers at the Champoeg State Park; readers and lovers of history in Boise, Idaho, and Okanogan, Washington, and accompanying genealogy societies; and researchers in St. Paul, Oregon, who contributed to the second book in the series as well, I extend my great thanks for enthusiasm and a love of history and story.

Thanks go as well to Swiss-born Madeleine Ladd for her review and correction of my use of French and for her unmitigated enthusiasm for my stories.

A suggested reading list that follows displays the many people whose love of history gave context to my research and this story. The unpublished work of Roger Riolo about early trade routes and materials answered important questions I found nowhere else. I thank him for sharing his work with me. Award-winning fiber historian and basket maker Pat Courtney Gold, Wasco/Wish-ram tribal member, lent her expertise on basketry and Okanogan connections, both fodder for the continuing story. Author John C. Jackson *(Children of the Fur Trade)* loaned me notes on early Montana fur trappers and offered critical comments on the manuscript; and author Laurie Winn Carlson *(Sidesaddles to Heaven)* offered a different way to view events at Boise through her observation of Mackenzie.

As before, I am indebted to my editors Erin Healy, Lisa Bergren, and Traci DePree; my Web site manager and niece, Michelle Hurtley; agents Joyce Hart of Hartline Literary Services in Pittsburgh; and to the team of professionals at WaterBrook Press, a division of Random House, for their commitment to and appreciation of the power of stories in our lives.

The support of friends in Oregon, Wisconsin, the Warm Springs Indian Reservation, Canada, Pennsylvania, and beyond can never be sufficiently acknowledged. But to my friend Blair Fredstrom who has shared her children with me for twenty-five years, who perused the Internet to locate information for me, who tells total strangers about my books and who never calls when I'm on a deadline, I express my deepest appreciation and admiration. She is a strong mother like Marie, and this book is dedicated to her and the Iowa Nation from whom Marie descends.

To all readers and bookstore owners and others who toil in the bookselling trade: Learning about the furry notes of the early 1800s has brought new appreciation for commerce, markets, and the politics and prayers that make it happen. Thank you.

To my immediate family and to the families I have known and worked with through the years, my thanks for sharing stories with me about parenting—both on the days you were pleased by your choice and the days that you weren't and still showed up to do your best. You have my deepest admiration. You've all found a name of your own.

To my husband, Jerry: for the map drawing, the late-night listening, unconditional support and encouragement, research assistance, and occasional dialogue inspiration, my love and appreciation. Thank you for still being here.

And finally, to you readers: Thank you for co-creating with me by entering and living inside this story.

Sincerely,
Jane Kirkpatrick
www.jkbooks.com

Suggested Additional Reading

Bagley, C. B. *Early Catholic Missions in Oregon.* Seattle: Lowman and Hanford, 1832.

Bancroft, Hubert Howard. *Bancroft's Works,* vol. XXVII, *History of Northwest Coast, 1800–1871.* San Francisco: A. L. Bancroft and Co., 1884.

Barry, Neilson. "Madame Dorion of the Astorians." *Oregon Historical Quarterly.* Portland: Oregon Historical Society, September 1929. Numerous additional articles from the *Oregon Historical Quarterly.*

Betts, Robert B. *In Search of York: The Slave Who Went to the Pacific with Lewis and Clark.* University Press of Colorado and the Lewis and Clark Trail Heritage Foundation, 2000.

Blaine, Martha Royce. *The Ioway Indians.* Norman: University of Oklahoma Press, 1995.

Carlson, Laurie Winn. *Sidesaddles to Heaven.* Caldwell, Idaho: Caxton Press, 1998.

Hafen, LeRoy R. *Mountain Men and the Fur Trade of the Far West.* vols. I, II, VI, VII, VIII, and IX. Glendale, Calif.: Arthur H. Clark, 1971.

Howard, Harold P. *Sacagawea.* Norman: University of Oklahoma Press, 1971.

Hunsaker, Joyce Badgley. *Sacagawea Speaks: Beyond the Shining Mountains with Lewis and Clark.* Guilford, Conn.: Twodot Press, 2001.

Irving, Washington. *Astoria.* Clatsop edition, 1836, Portland: Binfort and Mort, 1967.

Jackson, John C. *Children of the Fur Trade: Forgotten Metis of the Pacific Northwest.* Missoula, Mont.: Mountain Press, 1995.

Jones, Robert F., ed. *Annals of Astoria, 1811–1813.* New York: Fordham University Press, 1999.

———. *Astoria Adventure: The Journal of Alfred Seton, 1811–1815.* New York: Fordham University Press, 1993.

Klein, Laura, and Ackerman, Lillian, eds. *Women and Power in Native North America.* Norman: University of Oklahoma Press, 1995

Moulton, Gary, ed. *The Journals of the Lewis and Clark Expedition.* Lincoln: University of Nebraska Press, 1986–2001.

Munnick, Harriet Duncan, comp. *Catholic Church Records of the Pacific Northwest,* St. Louis, 1982, vol. I (1845–1868) and *Catholic Church Records of the Pacific Northwest,* St. Paul, 1979, vols. I, II, and III (1839–1898). Portland: Binford and Mort.

Nisbet, Jack. *Sources of the Rivers: Tracking David Thompson Across Western North America.* Seattle: Sasquatch Books, 1994.

O'Meara, Walter. *Daughters of the Country: The Women of the Fur Traders and Mountain Men.* New York: Harcourt Brace, 1968.

Peltier, James. *Madame Dorion.* Fairfield, Wash.: Ye Galleon Press, 1980.

Robertson, R. G. *Competitive Struggle: America's Western Fur Trading Posts 1764–1865.* Boise, Idaho: Tamarack Books, 1999.

Ronda, James P. *Astoria and Empire.* Lincoln: University of Nebraska Press, 1990.

Ross, Alexander. *Adventures of the First Settlers on the Oregon or Columbia River, 1810–1813.* Corvallis, Oreg.: Northwest Reprints, Oregon State University Press, 2000.

Russell, Carl P. *Firearms, Traps, and Tools of the Mountain Men.* Albuquerque: University of New Mexico Press, 1998.

Schmerber, Ruth. *Only the Earth: The Story of Marie Dorion* (fiction). Woodburn, Oreg.: Pacific Printers, 1990.

Shirley, Gayle C. *More Than Petticoats: Remarkable Oregon Women.* Boise, Idaho: Twodot Press, 1998.

Thwaites, Reuben G., Brackenridge, H. M., ed. *Journal of a Voyage up River Missouri, Performed in 1811.* Cleveland: Arthur C. Clark, 1904.

Van Kirk, Sylvia. *Many Tender Ties: Women in Fur-Trade Society, 1670–1870.* Norman: University of Oklahoma Press, 1980.